'They make you one of them.'
Jay squeezes her hand so hard the bones grind.
'They drive you mad, they torture you,
and make you one of them.'

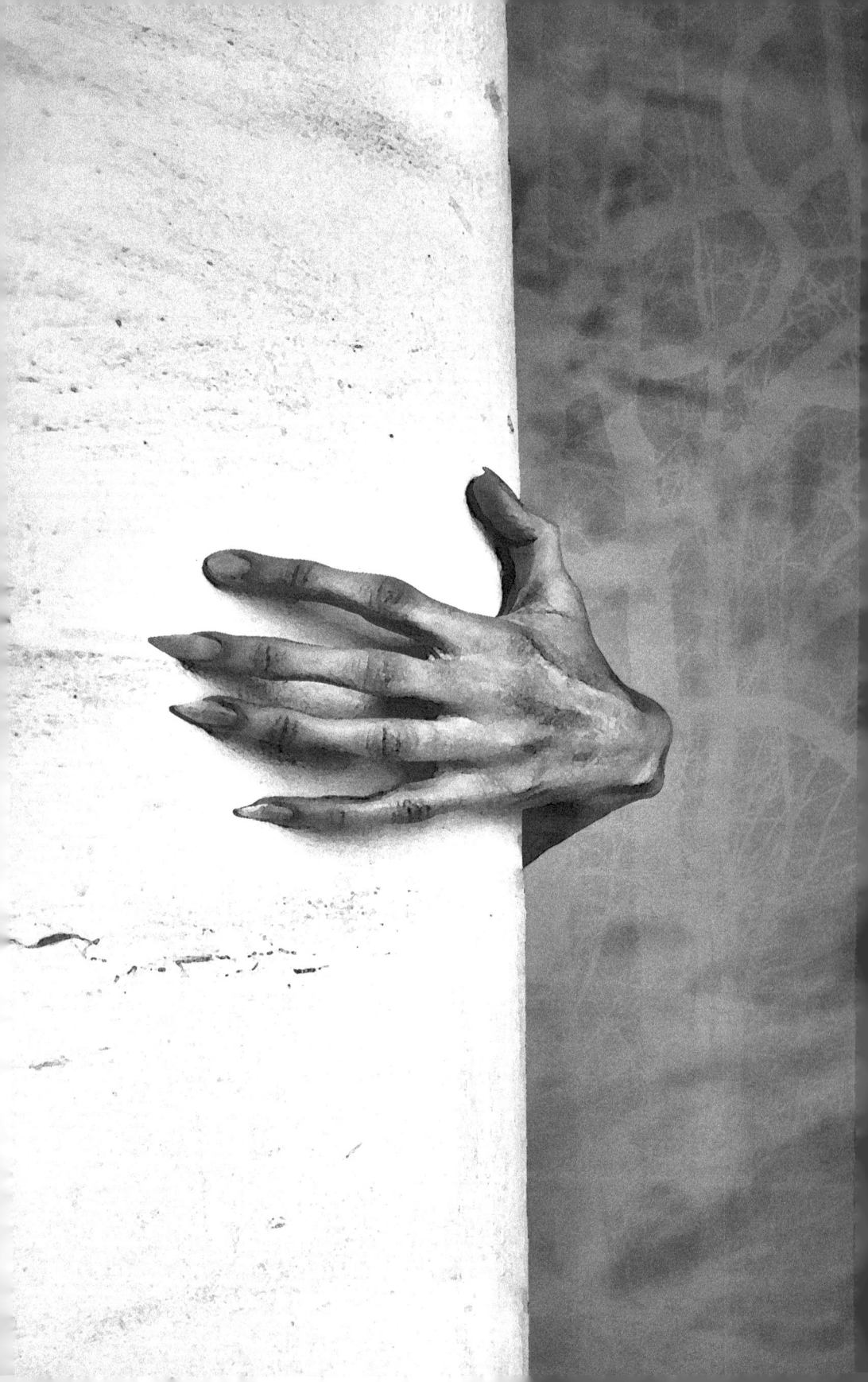

ROSIE CRANIE-HIGGS
KARLIQUAI

Livonia, Michigan

Also by Rosie Cranie-Higgs
Whiteland

Editor: Jamie Rich
Proofreader: Tori Ladd

Lyrics to "Ragnarök" written by Rosie Cranie-Higgs. Reprinted by permission of Rosie Cranie-Higgs. All rights reserved.

KARLIQUAI
Copyright © 2021 Rosie Cranie-Higgs

All rights reserved. No part of this publication may be reproduced, distributed, or transmitted in any form or by any means, including photocopying, recording, or other electronic or mechanical methods, without the prior written permission of the publisher, except in the case of brief quotations embodied in critical reviews and certain other noncommercial uses permitted by copyright law. For permission requests, please write to the publisher.

This book is a work of fiction. The characters, incidents, and dialogue are drawn from the author's imagination and are not to be construed as real. Any resemblance to actual events or persons, living or dead, is entirely coincidental.

Published by BHC Press

Library of Congress Control Number: 2020937792

ISBN: 978-1-64397-233-6 (Hardcover)
ISBN: 978-1-64397-234-3 (Softcover)
ISBN: 978-1-64397-235-0 (Ebook)

For information, write:
BHC Press
885 Penniman #5505
Plymouth, MI 48170

Visit the publisher:
www.bhcpress.com

For Hugo, forever the best.

'By the pricking of my thumbs,
Something wicked this way comes.'

Act 4, Scene 1, *Macbeth*,
William Shakespeare

Prologue

The forest is dark; this is the first thing. The second is the knowledge that she can't make it light.

Freya blinks. Nothing changes; nothing but herself. It melts into her skin, creeping through her being and knocking rudely on her bones. It doesn't wait for an invitation, and soon she's awash with it. Soon, she's shivering. Soon, she's new.

She turns, but the forest is endless. Row after row of trees, a stretch of marching black. No sign of where she came from. No indication that, even if she wanted to, she could get back. Taika's fires, the wailing wife, the echoes and the dead. They've faded into nothing.

She turns back and mild bewilderment jolts. Where the night was impenetrable, now there's a road, quiet and glinting with snow. The edge sweeps past her bare toes. The middle is churned and choppy, deep, trampled by many feet. It's as if she's been stood here for years.

Move. Like a whisper through the trees, the word curls around her. *You've been taking too much time.*

Swatting at the voice, Freya shakes her head. Soon the women will be strong, and not easily dislodged, but now…she can't help staring at her feet, at the ground. Covered with the pine needles scattering the snow, they're as speckled as river-bird eggs.

As speckled as river-bird eggs? Freya frowns. Never in her life has she thought such a thing. Ørenna only knows why she thinks it now. Maybe the change stopped her knowing anything; maybe she'll never know anything again. Maybe this is how Anneliese became who she was—how she was—*what* she was—in the end.

A person, plagued by things she can't explain? Human? Freya twists her nails into her temples. The sharp, cold pain makes her focus. She's not losing herself; she's adjusting. She wouldn't be here if it would make her lose her mind. From the way the women talk, by the end of Anneliese's ice plains pilgrimage, she was as disappointingly normal as anyone.

Looking up from her feet, Freya steps from the snowbank, and sets off down the road. Her legs, her back, her fingertips; even her insides shudder and tingle. Thinning her lips, she looks around.

The road is all there is. Fringed with the unbroken, battle-ready tree lines, there's no end, either forward or back. A long, straight hill, a moonless night, and a crisp, lifeless silence; this is her eerie welcome to the outside. This is the witching hour, and she is having fun.

Hopefully minus the witches. She may be a monster, but magic scrapes her skin.

Oh, but none of this *matters*. A breeze blows through her, and suddenly she's light, the breathy air itself. Her insides thump and settle. A curtain lifts, like the end of a sickness. Freya speeds up. She's complete.

Almost skipping, almost running, the balls of her feet barely brush the snow. Her toes scrape the crust, flicking powder at her legs. It's sharp. It's refreshing. Freedom is a tang; winter ghosts on her skin. The cold hisses *oh, how alive.*

Alive, and horrifically cold. It hits her like the entrance to Taika's cave, that icy, smothering suffocation before it lets you in. Freya grimaces. She'd never miss that nefarious dress, but it's the coldest she's ever been. Every inch of her is bare. The frosted road needles her feet. Her fingertips throb and freeze, the pain burning, biting, blistering. If she doesn't move faster, she'll drop. Fold, collapse, frost over. Numb. As light as the change has made her, her body's starting to stiffen.

Freya's heavy lips curl. Her new form is blasphemy. Her old skin was better. Regret twinges through her, and flees as quick. Before, she was so much more suited to the cold. Her skin was coarser. Now, it's smooth. From what they showed her in the pool, it's the only change she'll miss. Her eyes have lightened from violet to glaciers, but that'll make her blend in. Her tail crept back inside her with the change, and that'll make her blend in. Her hair is the same. Her shape is the same. Her old skin, though, she could do with, its thickness, shield, warmth. No one would be able to tell.

They would. The voice sighs inside her head, less a whisper, more concrete. Freya ignores it. What bothers her more, snaking in like seduction, is something she hadn't expected: weakness. Weakness that goes beyond physical strength. Her mind feels dulled and tame. Her hearing is rounded and contained, and her sense of smell, before so wickedly voracious, now hovers close to her head. It leaves her vulnerable. It leaves her *weak*.

She's always despised feeling weak.

But that's it. Rattled by a violent shiver, Freya dredges her mind into focus. She's going to be vulnerable; she's going to be weak. She's going to be human. She *is*.

Urgency judders through her legs. She pushes them faster, faster. The aching air throws her hair back from her face, rushing, throbbing, electric. A heart-shaped face, a pale face, born of twenty-five years in the forest. A more human face, ever so slightly; the pool showed her that, too. Less unsettling.

A little more tame.

Freya swats this away. If she even contemplates griping, the time in which she has to leave will leave her in time. Being abandoned here, running down a hill that would never truly end, would be worse than never having left. Mathew would pass by and continue to the outside. She'd watch him go, and be stuck. Forever.

She grits her teeth and pushes on. Her chest pounds. She's abnormally breathless, but she has to keep going, and going, until—

Until the road blurs and evens out. Ending in an unforeseen blaze of light, drenching her limbs and through to her bones, it brings her to a jerky stop. Her feet skid and scratch. Throwing up a hand, Freya shields her eyes. It's everything she's never seen.

The moon, wearing an expression as surprised as hers. The stars, behind a dusting of cloud. A strange lamp hanging from the eaves of a cabin, skulking across a grey stretch of ground…and the vivid, unnatural torches of four startled men.

Perfect. Allowing herself the shortest of smirks, Freya stops to wait for Mathew. The men's mouths are open, their eyes all white. She sleekly recovers her poise and guile. They couldn't be more perfect…until they're dead.

In the whispering cold, Freya still waits. The men are silent. Irony twitches inside her; now that all language is different, she can't make so much as a sound. Not until someone speaks to her, when her lingering otherness is meant to kick in, but when no one says anything at all…

Ah. Peering through the onslaught of light, her bemusement leaps into scorn. They're men; of course they're quiet. As the silent seconds pass, their eyes rove her body, two mouths parting and the other faces gormless. She fights to keep her face innocent. She can't blame them; she appeared in the night like a spectre, powering down the road with not a stitch to wear. White-haired in the moonlight, with her naked curves opaque, their thoughts would be far from conversation.

Good. They regard her as though she's a tropical creature, a grasslands dancer, a wonder, a gift of the darkness and a far-distant world. It makes everything so straightforward.

Footsteps crunch behind her. Conveniently trembling in the breath of the breeze, Freya flinches. Oh, it's perfect.

'Help.' She mouths the word, taking a quick, halting step. One man jolts. Freya glances back at Mathew. Tall and shadowed, he's almost here. 'Please.'

Spinning, slipping, shivering, she widens her face into vulnerability. Considering the bitter night, numbing her feet and hollowing her limbs, it could be a lot more difficult. *'Please.'* Another halting step forward, another panicked glance at Mathew. Hands in his pockets, he looms behind her, and skittering forward, she hugs herself tight. 'He'll hurt me.' She strangles a sob. 'I need help.'

They won't understand what's happening—even less what's going to happen—and that's perfect. They don't need to. All they need to do is be charmed.

They are. Eyes flitting to Mathew and back, the men shift from astonishment to concern, and as her dim eyes continue to adjust to the light, she's starting to tell them apart. No longer simply one awestruck mass, they are two tall, one short, two with beards, one with grizzled stubble, one without anything at all. One with a thick, furred hat, one still dreamily smiling. One pushing auburn hair away from his forehead, one with a frown as he works to summon words. And all of them defenceless.

Drawing closer, Freya fills her face with anguish and meets the dreamer's eyes. One, two seconds. Switch. The second man, third, fourth. They don't see it coming, and before they can react, they're frozen. Useless. Stone.

Their eyes can't leave her. Their legs can't move. Consternation, confusion, and panic map their faces, but as their minds swiftly falter, it all smooths away. Freya drops her act with a wicked smile. Sliding close enough to the dreamer to hear his brittle gasp, she feels the heat rise to his face, and sees the whites of his eyes take over as she closes her hands around his throat.

The breeze whips her ankles. The men smell strange, of an ugly smoke and something far too sweet. Turning, slowly and carefully, she takes them, one by one. Long fingers, red marks. The rattle of losing breath. One by one, they crumple. One by one, they die.

Pathetic. Freya regards them. Now all their lives have gone, they're pathetic, indistinct. Kneeling by the smallest body, the wicked smile returns. She's neither; she's remorseless. The ability to charm, hypnotise, paralyse should be waning, yet she's never killed this many at once. Never. Her coldness should thaw into caring, yet her humanity doesn't squeak. It's exhilarating. More than that, it's a comfort.

It will be neither if you freeze. The words hiss into her thoughts. Freya tries to swat them away, but they linger, like the echo of a raven in the forest. They're getting stronger.

Well, she knew they would. She glances back at Mathew. He's as mute as the men, but slightly less dead. *Can you not make him speak?*

The women seem to hum. *Not yet,* they whisper. Freya frowns, but lets it go. Someone, somewhere, will say something, and give her back her tongue.

Not if she freezes. She tunes her muddy human eyes to the body at her feet. Its clothes will do; they're fairly atrocious, but they'll more or less fit, and until she can change them, that's more or less enough. Beneath the garish winter coat sags a vest, sea-blue and dragged to the knees of a skinny pair of trousers. Oh, the joys of the outside. Shorn hair and too many colours; his companions are even worse.

Clothing herself, Freya appraises them. Them. Mathew. Them. Mathew. If she thinks at him, will he understand?

That one, she tries, because she might as well. The silence reminds her too much of the forest, of shadows and hiding and no way out. Too watchful. Too still. Waving for Mathew's attention, she waves at the smoky redhead's clothes, raids as many pockets as she can find, and straightens. Enough of Atikur; enough of Whiteland. She's outside, and already, she's so much more *herself*. She's kept a part she expected to lose, and it kicks up dirt at the rest.

The outside's daunting promise. The lack of focus in her vision. The dullness of her mind. None of it feels as bad as it did, and harnessing her drifting senses, she turns from the glinting track. By the forest's edge, the snowy field sweeps off. Somewhere in its heights sits Karliquai, the old chalet, waiting alone.

Not for long. With sly satisfaction, Freya turns from this, too, to the wide grey curve around the trees. Time to leave.

Fastening her ugly coat, she lifts the ugly hood. At least she's warm, if smelling unwashed. 'Ready?' She mouths the word, waving at Mathew. Extending his newly gloved hands over the four dead men, he nods. The bodies flicker, glittering slightly, and in a blink, they're nothing but air.

From family father to the Kyo's plaything, Mathew is their witless marionette. Freya smiles. If she cared, she might pity him, watching him straighten up again with no mind to call his own. As it is, though, she doesn't.

What matters is that they're ready.

Slipping into the moon-cast shadows, she begins her path down the mountain. It still smells of pine, of the glass-sharp winter, but she's out. Every step takes her farther from the cold reach of Whiteland; every step and every second, it recedes. It's a raging, frozen fire, and it's losing its flames.

Inside her, the Kyo's voices cackle. Soon, they'll grow as strong as they are within Mathew. Freya doesn't fight. They watch, they spy, they sigh directions; without their voices , she'd be nothing.

Their message is clear as she slips through the night, down the road to the world and away.

Time to make them scream. Time to make them run. Time to make them try to hide, in the hellish veins of nowhere.

It's time to find the sisters.

1

The past

Papillon of winter light. Are we dead when we have died?

Romy probably meant it as a comfort. In a strange, morbid way, it is. Icons of snow, a star, the moon; it's a ghostly, ghastly, cold reminder. On this day a year ago, their parents died.

Kira rarely thinks about it. She rarely lets herself. It's too liable to drag her down, like fingers from the grave that crave her. When they scrabble through the soil, she silences them. Stamps them out, studies, listens to enough Romy-style metal to feel better, or at least numb. Usually, it works. Today, though…

Today's different. Kira sets the phone down, Romy's message on-screen. *Papillon of winter light. Are we dead when we have died?*

Are they? Maybe not. Hopefully not. Nestled knees-up in the window seat, with fat, lamplit snowflakes floating outside, Kira's thoughts drift back, back, back. Back a year. Back to horror.

Back to Whiteland.

The wolf took her and Romy to the far side of the plains. Hour after hour of riding, until she saw glittering white wherever she looked and her mind drifted off to nothing. Another distant polar bear crossed their path. Towering crags of ice threw shadows, and the plains traversed a minefield of water holes, but she didn't see; not really. After what had happened, she couldn't bear to see, and certainly couldn't bear to feel. She'd survived Whiteland, and for what?

If she hadn't come, nothing would have changed. Anna would have given her life for Romy, and in the process, Matt would have died. Kira's valiance meant nothing. *Nothing*.

Bumping on the wolf's back, the word hung in the air. It was in Romy's sagging head, in her bluish, bony neck. It numbed the nausea that hugging Romy curdled, the knowledge that she killed their father. Nothing. This ruin meant *nothing*.

If only she'd been faster. If only the wolf had been faster. If only she'd spent less time on the island. A stream of *if onlys* paraded through her mind, even though they were useless. None of it mattered. She hadn't been faster, and she hadn't yanked Romy away in time. Maybe Anna could have done more. Maybe Romy could have fought the Kyo, or Matt could have fought her. Either way, the only thing to come of this was death.

Nothing was bitter and yellow, but *death* was black and cold. Decaying, putrid, chaotic, a chasm. Her dad's death. Her mum's death. Callum's death.

Callum. All hope of finding him disappeared when the wolf took off, across the ice, to spirit her away. Abrupt and final, it was over. She closed in on herself, like a flower at night, and stayed there. It didn't matter; Romy didn't wake. After her moment of crowning glory, Romy did nothing at all.

Kira drifted back to her mind when the wolf slowed to a trot. The ice was becoming powder, tailing into snow-covered woods. Ash and oak and wide-spaced trunks, hints of green through the white. A squirrel scarpered up brittle bark. Kira slipped from the wolf's back in a haze. How ordinary. How tame, compared to the forest beyond the river. The trees seemed to breathe with life. Normally, it would have been nice.

Normally, her parents would be—

Kira bludgeoned the thought before it formed. With her insides slumping back to dull, she helped her sister to the ground. Romy's eyelashes were fluttering. Her fingers were starting to flex, and her throat let out a small hum as Kira eased her toward the trees. If she woke up and saw this…

'Thank you.' Sparked with heavy urgency, Kira turned back to the wolf.

It was gone. The ice plains were gone; all around them were the woods, as if there'd never been anything else. Kira's chest panged faintly. There were snow-drifts, and delicate thorns. There were branches bowing low to the snow. Tightening her arm around Romy's waist, she carried on into the trees.

Small, soft, and sighing, flakes of snow began to fall. Kira let them settle on her hair, on her cheeks. She was tired; so tired.

And then she caught the noise. Her chest panged again, with hope. Somewhere, floating on the air, was music. Somewhere, there was a crowd, laughter, echoing shouts, and static. They must have left Whiteland.

Swept with a bitter relief, she nearly cried. The trees felt like Christmas Day. The air was warming up. Cosy, coddled, comforting, it was atmosphere and life and *home*. She could have stopped there. She could have sunk to her knees, and surrendered. The strong, aching, whimsical magic was wistfully all-consuming, but following it like a trail of breadcrumbs, Kira dragged herself on.

On, though her feet were white-hot blocks. On, though her arms were tensed and shaking. On, though her eyes were swollen, and her head throbbed, and her mind keened. Heaving Romy through a clump of bushes, beneath branches of feathery snow, Kira dragged herself into a park.

It hit her in a sound wave. Children. Adults. Hook-a-duck stands. The spices of mulled wine, the smell when funfair food combines. Candy floss and popcorn, hot dogs and churros. People everywhere, milling around, waiting for something to happen. A barrier and open space. Music playing, loud bass. Synthesisers. Distortion. Lights sparked in Kira's eyes, brilliant and blinding. An invisible ride rattled and clanked. Buildings lurked in the dark, far across the white-brushed grass: offices, apartments, restaurants, banks. Cars. Buses. *Noise*.

It was cacophonous. It was unbearable. Kira's head swooned hot, and her knees gave out.

Romy cried out as they tumbled down. Kira clapped her giddy hands to her ears. Her hips jarred on the winter ground. The snow soaked her jeans, and she crawled onto her knees, squeezing her eyes tight shut. Too bright. Too loud. A deafening, crackling microphone squawked, announcing the city's fireworks. Kira heaved her head up. A British woman, loud and brash: were they home?

Ten, nine, eight, the cockney woman crowed. *Seven, six, five, four.* The illuminated people cheered. *Three, two, one,* they whooped. *Happy New Year.*

Fingers gripped Kira's arm. Black swarmed in butterflies, and Kira jerked around. Romy was propped on one frail elbow, thinning her eyes to focus. Her eyes were bruised with exhaustion. Her peeling lips opened and closed.

Where are we? she asked. The words were dry and small.

Kira shook her head. *I don't know.*

The butterflies gathered, whipping up a storm. Romy bobbed in a drunken blur. Did she speak? Did either of them? Kira lowered her forehead to the snow, arms trembling. The noise, the people, the whole of Whiteland…they cracked her skull like a tumble of bricks. Her face burned. Her body was lumpy, dark and untamed.

And people were starting to stare.

Her peripheral vision caught them. Two men, coming toward her. A group of women, red-cheeked, exchanging baffled looks. Panic drove its hands through her chest, squeezing the life from her lungs. This was wrong. So wrong. They shouldn't be here. Not alone. Not like this. They should—

In a fiery riot, the fireworks burst. Kira flinched away, from the whine and the bang and the crackle and the cheer. Screwing up her face, Romy curled toward her. *Kira,* she moaned. *What's happening?*

One of the women crouched down. Kira twisted away. *Don't tell them anything,* she urged Romy feebly. *They won't believe you if you tell them what happened. Just say you don't remember.*

Nose to nose, Romy blinked at her. *What am I meant to remember?*

On the window seat next to her, Kira's phone buzzes. It rips her from the park, from the band around her chest, from the moment when, in viscous thumps, her heart fell away. She was the only one who remembered. She was the only one who knew.

Squinting at her phone, Kira swallows the memory, the hopelessness threatening to rise. *Did you ever think we'd be lost among this?*

Romy. Perfect, bitter timing with the perfect, bitter song. Kira locks the phone. Breathe. Looking back to the window, she fixes on the snow, on the blue-white glow from the moon. Her eyes flicker with afterglow, imprinting the lyric on her eyes. Around her, the room has settled into night.

Romy. Kira thunks her head against the frosted glass. For a while last year, Romy asked what happened. She assumed Kira knew, because she herself didn't, and although she was right, Kira never let on. All her sister remembered was stumbling off to the woods; as a result, she formed a truncated truth. Romy never returned from the forest. After a couple of days, first Anna, then Matt, then Kira herself went looking…and after that, the story's a blank.

It's the tallest of tales, and Romy never seemed convinced. But other than Kira's niggling guilt, what does it matter? No one in the village ever spoke a word, and everyone else is dead.

Fingers from the grave that crave her. She wasn't wrong; she's sinking. Wrapping her arms around her knees, Kira shuts her eyes. She sometimes envies Romy, when they FaceTime. Wouldn't it be bliss to be oblivious? Her life trudged back to how it was before, and if it was more miserably mysterious, okay. Misery was always her, and she was always misery. All she had to deal with was loss.

All. Kira curls her bare toes in the tasselled cushions. It sounds so callous, so dismissive. It may well be *worse* for Romy. To have no idea of how her parents disappeared? To not understand how she ended up in England, in the state they were in, alone? Romy bottles it up, but it must be impossible.

Downstairs, a bottle pops open. Eva's hyena laughter shrieks. Kira keeps her eyes shut, and breathes in the candle, the nutmeg she lit to keep herself calm. Knowledge is both a blessing and a curse. It could help Romy, or it could shred her; either way, it's not a chance worth taking. The emotions would be as wretched a mess as the worlds.

Hers are enough of a mess as it is. Although she hates it to a raging, blackened bruise, she can't shake a melancholy ache for Whiteland. It was clear. It was beautiful. It harboured dangers beyond belief, but also so much meaning; so much more than the outside world. It's more vibrant, more gritty, more acutely alive.

More willing to play with lives. However it tugs at her sometimes, she'll never forgive what it did to her family, and what she lost when she left.

Her mother. Her father. Her friend. Herself. The stairs creak, and Kira drags herself back, before the huldra-sized rabbit hole yawns. She'll never understand how her mum was a monster. She'll never understand why the Whispers, set on vengeance, had to play the whole charade. She'll never understand why Anna went back. She must have known what would happen.

Did she? Did she not? Or did she not care?

A knock taps the door. 'Kira?'

Time's up. Unbending her legs from the window seat, Kira tugs her dress down, moves to the wardrobe, and tries to look like she was rummaging. 'Hmm?'

The door huffs over the carpet. Heels in hand, she turns.

'Oh, *yes*!' Glowing in the hall light, Macy steps in. The step becomes an instant bounce, her teal dress shimmying up her thighs. She claps her hands. 'Oh, god, you look amazing. We all look amazing. Are you ready?'

Kira lifts the shoes. 'Just about.'

'About time!' Macy claps her hands again, her beaming cheeks as red as her hair. 'I'm so ready for this. You have no idea.'

She bounds away. Kira's eyes drift back to the glass, and she lets her arm droop. She had sat for close to an hour, watching the stars lift over the city. The fallen snow lies picturesque. On the peeking cobbles, the lamps pool amber. The introverted night is calm.

She'd rather stay in and watch it, but she promised she'd go out. Not just to her housemates, but herself; she'd grieve, and then she'd stand up tall, and start the new year strong.

At the very least, she'll be tall. Wobbling into the mad black heels, she pulls the band from her hair. She's never been so tall. She's never been so…tidy. She combs her fingers through her tangles. As an act of goodwill toward Macy, she re-dyed the fading brown, trimmed the ends to bra-level, and put on a skater dress. That was enough. She drew the line at curling her hair, and going out braless.

'Kira!' Veronica shouts up the stairs. Grabbing her bag, Kira hesitates. It's too small to shove a shirt in, but…

'Kira!' Eva adds to the chorus. 'You're missing all the gin!'

Briefly, Kira closes her eyes. It's fine. She'll be fine. Lifting a red-checked shirt from the mirror, she ties it around her waist. Now, she's more herself.

The tattoo stands out stark on her wrist. She rigs a smile, and breathes. Blowing out the nutmeg candle, she navigates the stairs, surrenders to sarcastic applause, and accepts a mug of gin. Time to be tall. Time to stand strong.

This year can't be worse than the last.

2

Unravel

The bar is a circus. Music booms like cannon fire, thudding against the walls. Linking hands with Veronica and Macy, Kira follows the weaving Eva.

'Marco!' Eva yells into her phone, covering her other ear. 'No, don't just say "Polo." Tell me where you are!'

She veers toward a gap to the right, through a knotted group of guys. Rolling her eyes, Vero waggles the sweet pack. Macy nods. Kira mouths *please*, and a tequila-drenched gummy bear finds its way to her mouth. It's gross, but potent. That's all that matters.

'Marco!' Eva shouts again. Lit by throbbing neon lights, she guns for a table at the back. It's chattering and crowded, tucked in a corner. She throws up her hands. 'Finally! Polo!'

'Ladies!' Seb cries, as Kira squeezes onto the bench. Flopping a large arm around her shoulders, he slots a drink in her hand. 'It's called a Green Lantern. If you'd been much longer, I'd have drunk it myself.'

'Please.' Kira clinks her dainty glass against his. 'Feel free.' Tilting it to the side, she frowns at its murky contents. It smells of disinfectant and tastes like kiwi. 'It looks like it came from a swamp.'

Chastising her with a pointed look, he drains his own glass dry. 'How rude.' He plants an alcoholic kiss on her cheek, loud and wet and smacking. 'Did you never learn about gift horses?'

Kira screws up her face. 'No. No, I didn't.' She plucks the sweets from the sticky wood table. 'Here. Have a gummy bear.'

Inch by inch, the night takes over. Inch by inch, as Seb spies on this fine face, that dapper shirt, or this outrageous beard, Kira floats into calm. Inch by inch, as Seb acquires blue drinks, Whiteland starts to fade.

'Shots!' Bespectacled, bearded Ron appears, enthusiastically brandishing a tray of drinks. It lands on the table with a clatter and a slosh, and he leans down to kiss Macy as the thirsty parties pounce. Kira takes a glass, calls her thanks, and drinks; again, a while later, and again, and again, until Seb hisses for her help and leads her out to dance.

'I hope you don't mind,' he shouts over the music. A playful smile quirks his lips. He knows she never minds. 'I want to see if he likes me.' He nods vaguely through the crowd. 'You know. Red-trouser-guy. I'm hoping he'll see me with you, realise what he's missing, and whisk me away for a lifetime of passion. The usual.'

Laughing, Kira lets him spin her, around and around and around. Many nights have seen these plots, and many nights, they've failed. This one has failed already, but she won't be the one to tell him. It failed before they left the table, with red-trouser-guy locked by the lips to a short-haired girl in gold, but if Seb didn't see, she won't disappoint. When he's enjoying himself, so is she.

Especially now she's swirling around. Caught by sweaty bodies, she forgets. The bar is a maelstrom of cloudlike light, of bass that thumps behind her ribs. The air is hot and sweet and stale, and she's one of many, just a—

'Damn!' The spinning stops abruptly. Kira staggers. Above her, Seb's round face falls. 'Damn, and blast, and…*damn*.'

Kira turns. Ah. Red trousers and gold dress are spiritedly dancing, whirling up what looks like a practiced storm. She turns back to Seb. 'That's…unhelpful.' She squeezes his slouching arm. 'Never mind?'

With a scowl, a pout, and a sigh, Seb shrugs. 'Never mind,' he agrees, as the bassline changes, doubling speed to a jitter. It feels like a heart attack. 'Dutch courage, my lady?'

Cheerily, Seb recovers his smile. Kira nods, and returns it. This routine is well-rehearsed. 'Excellent!' Seb takes her hand, gallantly leading the way to the bar like a bull through bowling pins. 'And do you know'—he leans on the juddering wood, tapping his shiny nose—'why I'm going to indulge in Dutch courage?'

Avoiding the beer stains, Kira clicks her fingers. 'Because you're Dutch, and we're in Holland.'

'Perfect!' Seb throws up his hands. His blond mane flies. 'Barman!' He waves to the eyebrow-arching woman. 'Two absinthes, please.' He lifts a thoughtful finger. '*Actually*, barman, two absinthes and two amarettos. We need it.'

'Seb!' Kira exclaims. The shots line up before her, even more eclectic than normal. 'That's beyond disgusting.'

He throws her a wink, and hands her the drinks. She sighs, with the gusto of a melodrama, but takes them. To be fair, he's not wrong.

'One for each hand.' Seb winks again. With a clink and a cheers, they take a breath, and swallow the shots in a chain.

It burns. The pungent flavours are chaos. Warm and bitter and spicy at once, they barrel down Kira's throat. 'Aagh.' She coughs, looks up at Seb, and laughs. His face is a flushed, bug-eyed wonder. 'Wow, that never gets old.'

'I think you mean…' Seb wheezes. Blinking hard, he wags a finger, and clears his croaky throat. 'I think you mean never again.'

'No.' She kisses his contorted cheek. 'You were born for the stage, Seb. Back to the table?'

She offers her hand. With an unsteady nod, Seb takes it. This routine is well-rehearsed.

'We've got friends!' Macy proclaims as they retake their seats, having taken a clumsy age in the flashing, smoky air. She flips her hands, one at a thickset man near Ron and the other at his friend. Deep in conversation, only his mess of brown hair is visible. 'They're Ron's friends from Spain. Madrid.' She glances at Ron. 'I think?'

With a vague, merry nod, Ron taps the thickset man's arm and heads away to the bar. 'Dance?' Macy claps her hands, looking around the table. 'Eva? Kira? Vero, you will.'

So many blurry faces. Kira blinks. The words, the lights, the noise fade in and out and round. So many blurry bodies, getting up to dance. Their forms swim through water. Are there dozens of chairs, or has she started seeing double?

Both. So many people. Inelegantly, Kira stands, laughing, clutching Eva. The chairs are playing tricks. The table's growing edges, crowing like a witch.

'Whoa.' Eva stumbles on an outstretched boot. Grabbing on to Kira, she rights herself and wobbles off.

Kira sways. 'Thanks, Eva,' she mutters thickly, reaching out a steadying hand. It hits a shoulder. 'Sorry.' She flaps her other hand at the owner. 'Don't mind me. I'm just…'

Sparing the shoulder an unbalanced glance, she totters after Eva. These *shoes*. Damn Macy. This is why she doesn't go clubbing.

The drunken weight lifts off his shoulder. Arching an eyebrow, he nudges her upright, or as right as she'll manage to be. Her laughing puff of breath drifts off, hot and oversweetened. He huffs. These drinks are awful. This place is awful. Give him a beer and a plate of chips, and—

Watching her go, he stills. No.

Even if she hadn't caught his stare, it sears two holes in her back. Faintly irritated, Kira ignores it, tightening the shirt at her waist. If he thinks for even a *second* of approaching her, of doing more than stare…she may be drunk, but she won't be seduced. She didn't really look at him, admittedly, so he might be an Aquaman rock star, but alcohol only makes men annoy her. He doesn't want to try it. Not tonight.

Not on the anniversary of—

Kira stamps her heel on the wayward thought. She promised herself she wouldn't think about that. Squinting around for Macy and Eva, she squeezes past a grinding couple, winces at an elbow to the arm, and stops. Yes; not only will she not think about it, but she'll drown it. Death is the best revenge.

The bar. Where?

There. Kira turns, pushing back past the couple.

A hand on her arm spins her around. Her head swoops, and steadies. It's Ron's goddamn brown-haired friend, who doesn't know when to stop staring. Fire flares fierce inside her. He approached her. He's in the way, and she needs a drink, and not thinking about it isn't going so—

Wait. Kira stops. Her mind goes tabula rasa, and she blinks. The brown-haired friend isn't saying anything. Not speaking, not trying to dance, not forcing a drink in her hand. He's just staring. Wide brown eyes, a shock of brown hair, the faintest shadow of stubble—

'Sorry.' He lets her go, and her focus is broken. 'You look like someone I used to know.'

He turns to head back to the table. Kira looks after him, squinting to sharpen her wavering vision; she can't catch in his face, can't snatch in his voice, what she somehow thinks she should. A lilt. An image. A memory. A name.

From a corner deep inside her, something starts to scream.

It's not.

It can't be.

What if it is?

He glances back. She's watching him, and he stops and turns. That checked shirt. That pale skin. The way she pouts when she frowns. It's not. It can't be.

What if it is?

'What's your name?' he shouts.

Kira's thoughts float away. She blinks. 'Um.' The raucous club is a pulsing bubble, smoky-pink and blue. Isn't she meant to be dancing? 'Kira.' Her voice doesn't feel like hers. 'I'm Kira.'

In the middle of the crowd, Ron's friend stiffens. 'What?' he mouths, rather than calls. He looks like he's seen the Wild Hunt, or apocalyptic horsemen. 'What did you say?'

Jerking forward, he elbows his way toward her. Kira snorts as he grabs her shoulders, looking hard into her face. If he wants to be weird, and freak out, then let him; her shots are working magic, and she no longer cares. Cloudy down the rabbit hole, she's off to Wonderland.

'I said…' She smiles dreamily, swaying to the music. This, now this is fun. The smile bubbles into a giggle. The lights, the music, the warmth in her brain. His strong hands on her shoulders. Perfect.

The friend doesn't seem to think so. His forehead tightens, like the Wild Hunt have caught him and stuck him with their spears. Kira squints to read his lips. He's mouthing something, squeezing her shoulders.

'What?' she shouts. As lulling as the bass is, it's far too loud. She waves a sloppy hand. 'I can't hear.'

Gripping her tighter, the friend bends down, putting his mouth to her ear. Cologne that triggers something, the dim smell of beer. 'How old are you?' he asks.

Kira snorts. 'Are you a pimp?'

He straightens up, but says nothing. Perhaps the words aren't clear. Nothing's clear. She gives him a dutiful nod. 'Nineteen.' She salutes, as if to a colonel. 'Sir. Anything else you—you—'

She slows. Something inside her clicks.

The cloudy warmth recedes. The scream cranks into life, in her chest, in her mind. Something in his accent, strained above the music. Something in his wide eyes, his scruffy heathen hair. He said he thought he knew her. Oh, god. Kira screws her eyes shut, and drags them open. The scream is filling her head with darkness. Why is she so *drunk*?

'Kira, who's nineteen.' The friend leans in again. He looks her up, down, up, down. 'Kira, who's nineteen, looks like a pixie, and brings a checked shirt to a club.' He lets her go, rubbing his eyes. 'Jesus. Is it not you?'

Kira's gaze wanders away. Her chugging mind is whirling. Club lights glinting off bottles at the bar, scarlet, jade, gold, blue. Red trousers and gold dress, dancing up their storm. It can't be.

Or she's not letting it be. She locked it all away, but now…

'Kira.' The friend grabs her wrist so hard it hurts. She looks back, woozy, her chest swelling, but he's letting her go and walking away. *Tattoo, tattoo, tattoo,* she hears, but did he say it? She staggers. He's barging through the crowd, and with the swelling barrelling up her throat, hot and bulbous, she knows for sure. He walked away like this after the first day in the forest. He bandaged her skin when the mist attacked; he followed her to Whiteland. He was there when she fell asleep in the boat, and then he disappeared.

Just as he's doing now.

No. Kira squints through the crowd, but the flashes of memory, sparking and vivid as they shoot through her irises, made her lose sight of him. Where did he *go*?

Two girls shoulder past. 'Sorry!' one calls back. Kira teeters, catches herself, sways. Her brain keels, as off-kilter as a one-wheeled wagon. The club blurs, sound and smoke, people shouting, singing, drunk. Her body vibrates with the music. She spins unsteadily. Where did he *go*?

Sparking. Vivid. Lurching out of the mist with Romy, smirking at her, catching fish. Her senses return with a pointed wallop, and Kira staggers into the fray. He's not at the bar, not by the window seats; she scans the dance floor, but he's not there either, and she wouldn't expect him to be.

If it's him. Kira digs her nails into her scalp, fixing her brain in place. Again. Fading in, fading out, she's not here, not aware.

Suddenly, she's outside.

Kira blinks. The blackout clears, and she looks around. Oh, no. No, no. Too drunk. Please, no. The snow patters cold on her head. The winter needles her face and arms. Did she get thrown out? Did she leave on her own?

Behind her, the music thumps. Cigarette smoke puffs in the air, curling around like ghosts. People are queueing around the corner. How British. Kira rubs her arms. Nothing's real. What is she *doing*?

'Oops-a-daisy, you'll catch your death.' A reedy man, all drooping spliff and upturned collar, slinks an arm around her waist. His attempt at seduction quirks a smile and hoods his bloodshot eyes. 'It's freezing out here. D'you fancy a drink?'

'Get off,' Kira mumbles, as he reels her in. His smirk murmurs more than good deeds. 'Get *off*.'

He does not get off. 'Why don't you smile?' He croons around the spliff. Moving one hand from her waist to her rear, he tips her mouth to his.

'No.' Wrenching her head to the side, Kira stumbles. The air shoots slivers of sobering ice, but the pavement is frozen, curse these *heels*—

'Oops-a-*daisy*!' The man scoops her up, pressing her into the wall. With a flick, the joint is consigned to the floor. His groin pins her tight, and he leans in close. 'You really should be careful.'

'No.' Scraping her back against the stone, Kira fumbles for her self-defence. This is why she took those classes. Exactly why. 'I told you—'

In a rush of frozen air, he's yanked back. Kira staggers, but before she can fall, someone catches her. He doesn't leer. He doesn't say *oops-a-daisy*. He's beer and cold and faint cologne, a scarred hand.

Callum.

'Are you okay?' Callum asks. Gripping her numbing shoulders, he rights her.

'After the same thing I am.' The joint-less man spits at the ice. 'Betcha.'

Callum angles his head sharply. 'Fuck off.' He turns back, peering into her face. 'Did he do anything? Because I *will* hit him.'

Cursing, the man stumbles off. Kira shakes her head. 'No.' She shakes it again. Callum. Callum, Callum, Callum, *Callum*. Slowly, she looks up at him. The word taking shape is as light as lies. 'Callum.'

Callum's eyes crinkle. His body seems to sag. 'Kira.' He brushes her wrist, the tattoo. 'This is—I—'

'Oh, my god, Callum.' Kira throws her arms around him, burying her face in the hair at his neck. Her alcoholic fog sweeps up, lifted like a curtain. Callum. *Callum.* 'How are you *here*?'

Tears rise hot in her throat, cracking at her words. Hugging her hard, Callum only shakes his head.

It's a long while before Kira lets him go. Slowly disentangling herself, she wipes her eyes with the back of her hand, half convinced that he might have disappeared, that the man she was hugging is a stranger.

But, 'Where do you live?' Callum asks. It's him, wild hair and a face so open, so lost, broken, stunned. Unsteady, he steeples his fingers on the wall and raises his voice above the bass. 'Did you bring a coat?'

He glances at the entrance to the bar. The throng still snakes along the length of the building, and he pulls a face. Too many man buns, short skirts, sticky chemical drinks in bottles that spill sweet stains on the floor. 'Sorry. I went back for mine, but didn't think about yours.'

Kira's expression twists in tandem. 'I'm not waiting in that. I'll be fine. Let's go.'

Motioning down the road, she walks off, cautious and covered in snow. Callum carefully pushes himself upright. She never did hang around. 'Are you sure?'

'Yes.' Fumbling with her shirt, she taps her pocket-sized bag. 'I only live ten minutes away, and I have this. If one of my friends doesn't bring my coat, I'll go back tomorr—oh!'

She flings out her arms, skidding to the side on a patch of black ice. It glints beneath her ridiculous heels, and she rights herself on the wall. 'Wow.'

Sheepish and bright-eyed, she looks back at him, and in that moment, he could frame her. Kira, alive in the winter night. Kira, lit up by streetlamps and clumsy on the cobbles. Kira, tottering, half-smiling, pushing back her untidy hair. His chest aches, a longing deeper than the cold, and it becomes a rueful smile. She's *alive*.

He catches her up at the mouth of a side street, where the bar's thumping finally fades. Along a black, L-shaped alley, a frigid little wind tunnel. Out onto a road hung with star-shaped lights, where a small, bundled-up crowd watches a burly fire-eater. It seems as if they're home in seconds.

Thank God. Wincing in her pinching shoes, how she managed it is an enigma. She had a few moments of clarity, but with movement, the alcohol swept right back. Muddling with the key, Kira shivers. Her shirt's soaked. This isn't right. She shouldn't be seeing him again this drunk; she shouldn't have drowned the memories. Not tonight. She shouldn't have gone out, when she knew she was stuck in the past. She should have clung on to her wits, her sense, her mind. Her dignity.

But she wasn't to know she'd run into Callum. She thought he was dead, yet here he is: following her through the squat, cherry door, into her squat, quaint house. He's far more real than she feels, shaking his snowy coat from his body and kicking off his Vans; is it definitely him?

Yes. She might be drunk, but she's not crazy; just an idiot.

'Where to?' Callum spreads his hands. Even in the gloom, it's him. 'Where's the warmest place in this house?'

'There.' Slapping on the light, Kira gestures to the living room, stumbling down the hall. A mess of blankets swallows the couch, colourful, patchwork cloth. Normally, she and Macy would be huddled within them, drinking something experimental and watching dippy films.

'Oh, *beautiful*.' Callum throws himself down, with a great whoosh of a sigh. 'Down you come.' He grabs her arm. Her head swoops, and she collapses beside him with a squeak. 'You're freezing, I'm freezing. Let's not die. Again.' He yanks a blanket or three from the rest, spreading them out and tucking them in. Checks, snowflakes, monochrome stripes. 'Good?'

Kira hesitates, but she's oh, so tired. Resting her cheek on his shoulder, she nods. 'Astonishing.'

Callum works his arms around her. 'That pretty much sums it up.' He sighs. 'Jesus. I don't even know what to think. I spent ages trying to find you, after I got out, but social media failed abysmally. Plenty of Kiras, none of them you.'

Kira huffs. 'I don't use social media.'

'Well, that would explain it.' He lifts his head to look at her, his practised eyebrow arched. 'You're one of those.'

Kira smiles up at his light-sparkled face. Everything is softly blurred, cosy, tranquil, warm. Heavy eyes. Heavy head. Spinning like a carousel. 'Mmm.'

'Of course you are.' Callum tips his head back, shaking it dryly at the ceiling. 'Of course you are.' He stills, his arms tightening. 'It killed me, though.'

It killed me. It killed me. The words loop through Kira's head. They're the turtle, the porpoise, the whiting, dancing the lobster quadrille. *It killed me. It killed me.*

She hugs his chest in silence, and then there's only sleep.

3

The present

Kira squints awake to morning through the frosted window. So much light. Too much light. Pain in the faint throb of her head. This is why she has blackout blinds; perfect, indestructible blackout blinds. She screws her eyes shut again, digging in her knuckles. This is abominable. Her brain chugs like an old-time steam train. Her neck's cricked. Three of her toes are starting to cramp. If she's not in her bedroom, with her blackout blinds, then where on earth did she—

The steam train whistles, pulls in, and stops. Her grogginess departs like a violent sleep twitch. The living room. The sofa. Callum.

Tangled like an inverted princess and the pea, Kira uncoils her stiff limbs and wriggles around. Her shirt smells damp. Her hair is in snarls. The blankets are knotted around them.

Them. Her chest cools and sparks and jumps at once. Last night was real. It can't have been, but somehow, it is. Callum is here, on the sofa, with his head on his arm and his mouth half-open. He's got a freckle underneath his jaw. She never noticed.

'Mmm.' Slowly, Callum lifts his head. 'Creepy to watch people while they sleep.'

This is too unreal for embarrassment. 'I wasn't.'

'You were.' Yawning, he rubs his face. 'And you missed the New Year.' He scrapes a bleary hand through his hair. 'I wasn't far behind you, but at least I heard the bells.' He smirks, lazy and tired. 'You've got a thing for suddenly falling asleep.'

Levelly, Kira meets his eyes. 'You've got a thing for letting me.'

Callum holds her gaze, and snorts. 'Nice to know you haven't much changed. Your hair's different, but the rest of you…' He considers her, mostly covered by the blankets. 'I guess I'd be more sure if I saw you in jeans. Jeans and boots and a little black coat.' He tilts his head. 'Or naked.'

Okay, so embarrassment still has its place. Heat becomes a sauna in its rush to Kira's cheeks. 'You beast!' She slaps his chest. 'You're such a pig. Such a *man*.'

'Hey!' Callum laughs, as she slaps him again, the action half-hearted but her chagrin fully blown. She'd thought the pool was dark. 'It was only once, and underwater at that! You really haven't changed.'

'Neither have you.' Kira shoots him a glare as half-hearted as her slap. She should stand up against objectification, or chauvinism, or something, but she can't help it; her face is on fire, but his teasing is comforting. It's familiar, even after a year.

And it holds what they need to say at bay.

'When I left England, I needed a change.' Kira flicks her hair, stalling with lightness. Inside, the questions are starting to churn, up to boiling, up to burn. 'Place, people, clothes, hair. It used to be a lot darker, and for a while I wore hipster dresses and Docs.' She grimaces. 'I hate hipster dresses and Docs.'

She glances at Callum, and her lightness sinks. He's watching her with a deep kind of quiet, such a drop from his laughter that the questions roil. After all this time, he's here. *Alive.*

'How are you okay?' It bursts from her lips, with so much force that he flinches. 'Sorry.' Kira drops her eyes. Heat floods back to her cheeks in waves. 'I mean…when we were in the boat, I woke up, and you were falling over the edge. All I could see was this woman, laughing and dragging you down. I tried to stop her, but…' She pushes back the blankets, sitting up cross-legged to face him. Her whole body is heating now, threatening tears at the memory. She clenches her jaw. She cried enough at the bottom of the boat, and besides, he's *alive*. 'I thought she'd killed you.'

Pulling the corners of his mouth taut, Callum looks away.

Guilt surges up. 'I'm sorry.' Kira dips her chin, letting her hair fall in front of her face. 'I should have waited. I know I should have waited, but it just… slipped out.'

Shaking his head, Callum sighs. 'Ah.' He runs a hand through his sleep-mussed hair, dragging it down his face. 'It's the elephant in the room. Do you like elephants?'

Kira lifts her eyes. 'Um?'

'I don't.' Callum taps her arm, one, two, three. 'So it's fine. Word of advice, though.' His tone turns dry. 'Listen to ghosts who warn you off sirens. It's not the most fun I've ever had.'

He drops his scarred hand to the blankets. Kira twists her mouth. If she was more assertive, she'd take it, but before she can decide, it's rubbing his jaw.

'What happened?' she asks, entwining her fingers. Maybe he'll take hers.

Callum huffs. 'Oh, it was great. A little while after you fell asleep, someone started singing. I knew I shouldn't be curious—I *knew*—but I was. I looked over the edge of the boat, to see if it was coming from the water, and then...' He frowns, moving his fingers to trace her tattoo. Her skin prickles with a shiver. 'Then I was so far underwater that I couldn't see the surface. I don't remember leaving the boat, and I certainly don't remember you trying to help. A woman was holding my arms, though, and yeah, she was dragging me down. But what she wasn't doing was watching me.' His eyes flick up to hers. A shadow of a smirk dimples his cheek. 'So I kicked her, and when she let go, I punched her in the face.'

A surprised 'ha!' splits from Kira's lips. 'You punched her in the face?' she exclaims. Catching herself, she holds up her hands. 'Okay; I'm sorry. Go on.' She bites her lip hard. 'I just...you punched her in the *face?*'

Callum nods. Trying not to grin, Kira turns down her lips, a rolling nod of approval. 'Wow.'

'I thought you'd like that.' Callum's smirk only grows, doing nothing to help her amusement. 'It'd make a great party story, if anyone would believe it. Anyway...' Teasingly, he meets her eye, setting off another tiny shiver through her skin. 'After she let go, I started swimming and didn't look down. I didn't see where she was taking me, but I guess I wasn't meant to wake up so soon.'

Kira fights her face straight. 'Damn light sleepers.'

'I know.' Dramatically, Callum sighs. 'Always foiling succubae's plans. Who knows what was going to happen. Maybe, once we got wherever we were going, there'd be something to stop me from ever waking up. Maybe she was going to kill me, maybe steal my soul. Maybe'—he wags a finger—'and this is my personal favourite, she was going to seduce me, make sure I'd never want to leave, and name me king of the merpeople.'

Kira cocks her head. 'Like Aquaman?'

Callum winks. 'Wouldn't that be great. Either way, she didn't follow me.' He pulls down the corners of his mouth: *search me*. 'I've often wondered why.'

'Probably because you punched her in the face.' Kira's smile wins out; again, she can't help it. This is so impeccably *them*. 'She was a siren. A wrinkled, ugly one, but she won't have enjoyed an abusive seductee. It doesn't make sexy folklore.'

'Sexy folklore?'

'Hang on.' An image pops up like a flash card. Pushing out her lips, Kira frowns. 'If you got away, why didn't you reappear? I was watching the river for a long time, but I never saw you come back up.'

Callum shrugs. 'Whiteland worked its magic? I barely reached the surface before I ran out of breath.' His face tightens briefly, the quick flick of pain. 'I was halfway to fainting, and it took me a bit to realise that I wasn't *in* Whiteland. I was, I don't know, fifty metres off a beach, and the waves were pushing me toward it. Just picture the faces.' He smiles, small, subdued. 'A man appears out of the sea, wearing jeans and a T-shirt that says *Am I Alive?* I felt like a rare type of fish. Or a dragon.'

Kira flashes her eyebrows, picturing away. The image is perfect: an exhausted Callum, crawling from the shallows, giving a weak yet jaunty wave before wandering away. The incredulity of the onlookers, the silence left in his wake. The sodden, sluglike trail of water that he would have traipsed around, the wide-eyed, confused attempts to determine where he was. However the scene played out, it'll have been far funnier than hers.

'So where were you, if not Whiteland?' she asks, focusing back on Callum. He's toying with a tassel on a fox-patterned cushion, looking around the cluttered room. Sunlight glints off the television, rainbow colours spinning off the crystal in the window. 'Me and Romy landed in London. New Year's Eve, lots of fireworks, lots of people.'

Callum huffs a laugh. 'Subtle.' The laugh becomes a yawn, and he stretches. 'Ah, I don't envy you that. And I didn't think there were other ways out of Whiteland, but there you were, and there I was. In a tiny town in Croatia. Near where they filmed *Game of Thrones*.'

Kira blinks at him.

He tips his hands. 'Fair enough, not a fan. Anyway, it was freezing, and the water felt like death.' He shudders once. 'I couldn't believe there were people on the beach. I sat on the sand for a bit, trying to ignore them while I recovered, and just as I was psyching myself up to leave, a woman came along. Tapped me on the shoulder, asked me if I was all right. She tried three different languages before hitting English, and when I said no, not really, she asked why. I asked where I was, she gave me some unpronounceable name, and when I asked where *that* was, she said Croatia.'

He stretches wider, screwing his eyes up for another colossal yawn. 'That's when I realised I was well and truly fucked.'

Kira slots her hands under her head, resting them on the sofa. 'At least you were somewhere pretty.'

'Yeah.' Tilting his head side to side, Callum nods. 'Yeah, that's true. I could have landed in Glasgow.'

'Or the middle of the outback.'

'Okay, I got lucky.' Callum rolls his head along the couch-back toward her. 'Anyway, I thanked the woman, asked her where the nearest airport was—she was very confused at the question, mind, but told me anyway—and after more or less convincing her I was going to be fine, I saluted the sunbathers and set off to find a phone.'

Kira sits up again. 'To call who?'

'Ah.' Callum flashes his eyebrows. 'This is where it gets interesting. I called my mother.' He looks up at her. 'And she wasn't surprised.'

Kira frowns. 'What?'

Thoughtfully, he resumes his tracing, up and down her tattoo. 'My mother knows about Whiteland.'

'She *what?*'

'She explained when she flew over with my passport. Turns out, she's always known.' Callum lifts his hands, and drops them down. 'Typical. The village is one of the gateways, and wherever there's a gateway, there are "watchers." People who know, and people who have contact with someone inside.'

Slowly, Kira nods. It's pretty much as she thought: everyone watching her family, from the moment they arrived. 'So your mother's a watcher. What does that mean?'

'It means she can do things.' Callum makes air quotes on the word "things." 'Which I'll tell you about another time. They sound fun, but they're bloody irritating.' He lifts a tangle of her hair. 'And that, as they say, was that. I went home, hit a dead end trying to find you, and went back to university. I tried to carry on from there, but obviously never managed. Without social media, a last name, or a hometown, I was a modern day rock-pushing Sisyphus.'

Kira watches his fingers curl her hair. 'And the village never spoke.'

'Nope.' Callum shakes his head wryly. 'Nobody I talked to would admit to knowing a thing. All of you had been wiped from the hotel—records of your arrival, credit cards, the lot. All your things had gone, too, although Hazal claimed you took them when you left. I pointed out that I was with you when you left, but she wouldn't budge. Nobody would. It was as if none of it ever happened.' His lungs empty in a gusting sigh. 'But there you go. Whiteland was exasperating. Your turn.'

Nearly. She went through it all herself last night. 'You never told me you were at university.' Geography. Sociology. She'd bet her life on something vague. 'What do you study?'

Callum grins, almost cunning. 'Philosophy.'

For a moment, his smugness strikes her as odd. He winks, and suddenly, Kira remembers: the conversation in the boat. 'Oh, you're unbel*ievable*.'

'I'm doing a master's now.' Callum's smug grin broadens. Clearly he's remembering too. 'Thought about leaving after the bachelor's, but I couldn't stay away. I love Madrid. It's where I met Ron, before he dropped out. A book-worthy coincidence, really. I never thought the world was so small.'

Above them, the ceiling groans. Callum glances up. Someone, Kira thinks with a pang, is waking up. Their time alone is fraying. 'Well, that explains the shirt.'

'Precisely.' Callum nods once. 'What about you, milady?'

Banishing the pang, Kira tries for a smile. 'I'm trying everything, with a major in English.'

Callum's eyes drift down. 'Including art?' He taps her wrist. 'You got a tattoo. It made me sure last night it was you.'

So he did notice what he was tracing. It would be kind of hard not to, but still. He might not remember the significance. 'I felt like I should.' Kira spares it the briefest of glances. A sketch of a tree trunk, four branches, a line. 'I don't like thinking about what happened, but I wanted a reminder.' She waves a hand, a gesture of grandeur. 'A mark of the world that consumed my life, or something equally pretentious. Of how small we are. You know.' She averts her eyes. 'How easily we can be washed away.'

Callum taps her arm, one, two, three. 'Memento mori.'

Kira shrugs. 'I guess.' She turns her arm over. It needs to be there, but she doesn't like to see it. It hisses of every unanswered question, and everything she's lost. 'We saw the symbol so many times, and I saw it even after I lost you, so it seemed to sort of fit. Even if it is masochistic, or macabre, or whatever. I wish I'd asked someone what it meant.' She frowns. 'Every time I thought of it, it seemed to run away.'

Staring at the place where the ink had been, Callum opens his mouth. Closes it. Opens it again. 'Just another part of Whiteland, thinking on its own.' Lips apart, he shakes his head. 'It's actually been hanging in the kitchen for years. A sketch on the wall. Like you, I never thought to ask what it was.'

Kira's eyebrows fly. 'Really?'

'Yep.' Dryly, he meets her widening eyes. 'I know. I barely noticed it until I got home. Mum doesn't know what it means, but she assumed it didn't matter who saw it. You either know about Whiteland or you don't.' He lowers his gaze to Kira's arm. 'I couldn't understand why she wanted it there, but now that you…' He looks up again. His eyes narrow, then flick away. His struggle for words is obvious, for a question that doesn't stumble down a pit he shouldn't fall into. 'What made you…'

Wriggling out of her stale shirt, Kira draws the blankets up to her chin. 'I wasn't as lucky as you,' she murmurs. Hesitating, deliberating, she rests her head on his shoulder. He works his arm around her, and she bites at her cheek. Reliving this, she's going to need the comfort.

The aftermath of his disappearance. The peculiar bishop-fish, and his promises of help—which must have been brutal, barefaced lies. Being rescued by Klaus, the man from the grasslands. Spending the night in a village of tents, nestled in a grove of trees.

Outside, doors slam. Cocooned in the blankets, Kira burrows down. Traffic trundles past. It roots her. She's safe. She's on the outside. It's New Year's Day, and it snowed last night, and through the windows, the world is white. Vero's air humidifier hums. She's safe.

Kira sighs, and carries on. Taking a horse through Monte Yuno, with the devils and the demons and the dead. Bursting out onto the ice plains, following the wolves. The tremendous frozen corridor. The horse failing, and the wolf in its place.

Callum's eyebrows soar, but Kira shrugs. Just another part of Whiteland, thinking on its own.

Then comes the worst. The pain that feels so hollow, but at the same time, so *full*. The wolf flying across the ice. Running toward her mum and Romy, their dark standoff stark. Arriving too late to save her dad.

Watching her mum fade out.

Kira's voice cracks and stalls. She whispers the words about the wolf, and quiets. God, how Whiteland screwed them all.

The ceiling creaks again, and again. Kira leans into Callum's shoulder. The morning has worn on, the sun bright enough to banish the window-frost, and this moment—this necessary moment, after so much nothing, of peace, of quiet, of their otherworld life—will soon be snatched away.

'I'm sorry,' Callum murmurs into her hair. 'I really—'

'It's fine.' Kira cuts him off. Turning her head, she softens the words with the tiniest of smiles. 'I don't want to sound strange, or uncaring, but I've had a year of sympathy. You don't have to give me any more.' And it'd be really great if you didn't. 'Just let me finish.' She pokes his arm. 'I need to get it out.'

Callum's mouth crooks up to the side. 'Okay.'

After the worst comes England. London, after she and Romy emerged from the woods like dogs among the deer. Hospitals. Doctors. Police. It passed in a dark, murky blur: *Who are you? What happened? Where are your parents? How did you get here? Where do you live?*

Devon. Gran and Gramps, taking them home. More questions. More police. The beginning of an endless, circular attempt to find Anna and Mathew McFadden.

'Did they get anywhere?' Callum asks.

'No.' Kira rubs her tired eyes. 'I could have told them that at the start, but it would have made everything worse.'

Callum huffs. 'I can imagine. Lally clammed up. Whiteland's got it like—' He mimes something crushed in a fist.

'I figured.'

As alive as Whiteland is, it couldn't risk discovery. She realised this early on, when she heard the hotel were claiming they vanished, and the village had nothing to say. Not a mention of the man who vanished with them, or the woman who never came home. She supposed the village would never speak.

And neither would the world.

'I'm surprised you didn't make the news.' Callum scratches the back of his head. 'Causing a scene in the middle of London, wrapped in furs and looking like death. You should have been riddles for years, but no.'

Kira tilts her head toward him. 'Does that really seem strange?' She shrugs. Upstairs, Macy's coffee machine growls. Her breath hitches. They're running out of time. 'Whiteland silenced a village. Why not a city? I don't know how it works, but it did, and I'm glad.'

It meant she could go back to sixth form. It meant that she could *leave*. Romy slipped back to her caustic mind, facing off the world with mood swings and music, but Kira couldn't be so graceful. She couldn't wait to get away. This life…it no longer felt important. The friends, the parties, the beach, her job. How could she spend weekends selling paint, when everything was desolate, and she'd survived another world? How could she constantly dodge the questions, slipped softly in by her grandparents at every opening? How could she constantly fend off the looks, from the neighbourhood who thought they knew the worst, and understood?

The worst was not her missing parents. The worst was all of it.

She couldn't take it. She couldn't stay there, in her childhood town, with the memories and the ghost of herself. Here was where she crashed her bike, when Anna taught her to ride. Here was where she'd paint on good days. Here was where she'd paint on bad days. Here was where she caught Romy and a boy, where their batty cousins fell off the pier, where Mathew liked to go for a beer, where they went on her eighteenth birthday.

Too much. She couldn't do it, living two miles from home, knowing what she knew. She couldn't keep pretending, as much as she tried, that she hoped her parents would be found. Whiteland was the catalyst, for change, metamorphosis, ruin. From that, there was no going back.

'So I left.' Kira's voice shrivels to a breath. Soon, it'll be over. Soon, she'll be done. 'I guess me and Romy got closer, but she didn't need me to stay. She never needs anyone. I left to be a stranger.' She sighs. 'In a morbid way, it was perfect.'

For a moment, Callum is quiet. The Nespresso machine growls again, juddering the ceiling. A brave wood pigeon hoots in the cold. The smell of coffee curdles her fairly fragile stomach. She could do with an omelette, or a very large gin.

'Christ,' Callum murmurs eventually, shaking his head against hers. 'That's…'

Kira tilts her head to look at him. 'I know.'

'It's not perfect.' His throat works, and his jaw hardens. 'None of it even comes close. That place screwed us over. We're alive, sure, but we're not the same.'

He meets her eyes. Kira's breath skips. They're close, so close. She can smell his skin. In a book she read not long ago, the girl, caught by surprise, realised why it's called eye "contact." Now, she understands. Callum's eyes seem to darken, the brown growing deeper. Too loud, Kira swallows. She's never been so aware of her lips, of the inside of her mouth. Did his arm just tighten?

Yes. Callum's fingers brush her cheek, all trace of humour gone. He's watching her, deepening—

A rude vibration makes them jump.

'For the love of…' Callum shuts his eyes, tipping back his head. 'I hate my phone. I'm sorry.'

Kira looks away. The quacking isn't exactly dulcet, and as Callum digs around the sofa, she buries her mouth in the blankets. Her heart is chattering, birdlike. Their miniscule moment has passed.

Shooting her an unreadable look, Callum puts the phone to his ear. 'Andre?'

A barrage opens fire. A rampage of words, a flurry of oaths. Callum winces. 'Yes, I know. I've caused you to panic, I've ruined your life. You could have rung me earlier, you know. You had that power.' He listens to a second, quieter barrage, more of a scuffle than the Battle of the Somme. 'Yes, Andre. Ten minutes. Twenty, if I get lost. Yes, you can trust me this time.' He scrapes a hand down his face. 'Yes, Andre. Bye, Andre.'

Ten minutes. Twenty, if he gets lost. Horror, desperation, sadness, dread, riding storm-battered waves through her chest. Kira makes herself breathe. He's leaving already.

'That was Andre.' Callum looks up at her, awkwardly shoving his phone in his jeans. His expression is a blend: the universal face for *typical*, combined with *what can you do?* 'The other guy from last night. We have a flight to catch, and he's worried I'm going to make us miss it.' He attempts a smile, but it doesn't work. He gives it up at once. 'I'm sorry.'

Kira bites down hard on her cheek. Breathe. She won't make a fuss; she won't make it harder than it has to be. She was a naive teen in Switzerland. Whiteland made her an adult.

'I know.' Composing herself, she forces a smile. 'At least we know what happened, at least we know we're alive, and at least'—the smile becomes genuine, wry—'I know I didn't imagine it all.' She puts her arms around his neck, hugging him tight and pulling away before the storm can return. At least Whiteland didn't take everything.

But god, if he could stay.

'Don't you dare disappear.' Callum battles with the blankets. The war is won far too quickly, and stiffly, he clambers to his feet. 'We're so not done here. Where's your phone?'

Reluctant to leave her nest, Kira takes his proffered hand. It's warm, and makes her ache, and she quickly lets it go. 'What's your full name?' she asks. Her bag lies skewed in the hallway, and she crouches for a rummage. Many missed calls. Wonderful. She hands her starry phone to Callum. 'The bishop-fish shrieked something, but I couldn't remember what. Something like Lee?'

Callum fiddles with her contacts. 'Close enough.' Returning the phone, he sticks out his hand. 'Callum Reeve. Pleased to meet you.'

His other hand is calloused, hard and smooth. It burned in the fire in Erik's home, before she was chased out of town. 'About time we got acquainted.' Nodding curtly, Kira shakes. 'In the usual way, I mean. Kira McFadden.' A smile breaks, and as sad as she is, she dips a curtsey and lets it. 'I do hope we stay in touch.'

'You can count on it, milady.' Releasing her hand, Callum bows his head, and doffs an invisible hat. 'If you so desire, do visit me in Madrid. Preferably before our semesters begin. For now'—he moves to the door, his reluctance almost jauntily masked—'I fear I must take my leave. Will you see me out?'

Reluctance masked by jauntiness. Kira's heart is too hot, beating too fast, but she's not a little girl anymore. 'I will.' She dips into a second curtsey, sweeping his discarded coat neatly off the floor. 'On one condition: reassure me every so often that the crazier parts were real.'

Callum shrugs into his coat. 'No problem.' He meets her eyes, and stops. 'Hey.'

He opens his hands a little. Kira takes them in, and smiles. 'Of course.' Closing the gap between them, she wraps her arms around his waist. He enfolds her, resting his forehead on her parting. Breathing in, she shuts her eyes, contorting her face into a coil. He's leaving. Breathe. He's alive. *Breathe.*

Warmth. His chest moving. The last of him.

Smoothing her face, Kira pulls away. 'Don't you dare disappear,' she says.

Callum laughs. 'I wouldn't dream of it.' Opening the door, he steps outside. Pulls up his collar, peers at the sun. 'I'll see you soon, Kira.' Squinting through the glare, he offers her a last, Callum-ish grin. 'I meant it about visiting. Either that, or I'll wind up at your door and wreak havoc.'

'Deal.' Kira leans against the wall. 'We're good at havoc.'

Callum doffs his hat again. 'That we are.'

One hand raised in a wave, he turns to trudge through the slush. A few paces and he turns the corner; a last look, and he's gone.

Sun glitters on the cobbles. The bright snow is melting. With a sigh, Kira shuts the door.

'Who was that?' Macy ambles past, making a careful beeline for the kitchen. 'Ow.' She puts a ginger hand to her head. 'Too loud. Coffee hasn't worked. Is it the guy from the couch? Did he leave?'

The fridge door opens. 'Just…' Kira shrugs uselessly. Just what? There's no "just" about any of this, and all at once, she's exhausted. 'Someone I used to know.'

Macy emits a vague 'hmm.' Kira stays where she is, watching the door. Is it likely? No. The sounds of scavenging clatter on, and she digs her nails into her palms. Would she love it to be? More than anything.

Callum doesn't come back. She didn't expect him to; she hardly let herself hope. It's something from a film, or a book, or a song. The real world isn't that fair.

With her throat aching, she turns away.

4

The travel

If anyone were to see him, they'd think nothing. Nothing but another traveller, waiting for the first shuttle out. Drawn and tired, as you would be this late, fuelling up on BLTs and vanilla-sprinkled coffee. They're preferences the voices don't know, but when he's so willingly, if unwittingly, given up body and mind, why not treat him well? Were it not for his pliable knowledge of the outside, a great deal of this would be impossible.

Places, transport, roads. Customs, language, money, food. Even the skill of compulsion; if Freya had launched into the fray with neither Mathew's stolen aid nor magic, it would have been a shambles. As it is, it flies as smooth as the Zaino, as bright as the night-birds of the forest, and as far as they can be, they're grateful.

Strips of fake light blind from above. Curling him up on the hard blue seats, the voices let him sleep.

5

The king of Hallowe'en

0:07.

She feels like Little Red Riding Hood. Laughing her way to the main house, a basket on her arm.

No; a *hamper*. Romy corrects herself with a marked eye roll. Harvey's parents are the type of people to leave a hamper in the guesthouse, for the convenience of their picnicking guests. Top-notch. Upper-crust. If she remembers correctly, they also own a dog called Colin.

'Oh, darling, do bring some cucumber sarnies,' Harvey shouted after her, to which she responded with a clump of mud. There were several peals of laughter, then, more sombrely, 'And a washcloth.'

'Sausage rolls, pumpkin,' Hamza had added, in an odd, half-drunk falsetto. Marnie screeched her witching laugh, and was requesting elderflower water, in a thin glass bottle, when two more clumps of mud hit home.

The outrage squealed. Romy grinned, and skipped away. Unscrewing her hip flask, she washed her pill down with vodka, unappetising and warm. Now, she takes a sip, pushes it into her pocket, and strides through the clipped gardens. The night is frozen, but the moon is full, so at least she can find her way; the guesthouse cowers so close to the river, and at such a winding distance from the mansion, that it would seem, despite the picnic basket, as if the Blakes hated guests.

They do, Harvey snorted, into his glass of appropriated vintage wine, when she asked this earlier. *I'm their perfect visitor, which is why I keep coming to stay. I keep myself to myself, make no noise, and pretend I don't exist.* He chuckled at his cleverness. *Even better, if anyone asks to stay, they can reject them on the grounds that their son needs the solace. I'm oh-so-troubled, you know.*

Now, as then, Romy flips them off. What a luxury; what a life. Rubbing her arms with vigorous friction, she speeds up through a moonlit glade, across the last snippet of grass. The house puffs out its chest above her. Unlocking the door, she slips inside. Warmth, glorious warmth; praise be to the ladies of the manor. She should have put her coat on before she left the guesthouse, but that's by the by. She'll always be forgetful with an end goal of food.

Raid the kitchen, raid the pantry. Why so much food? The house is shut for winter. It's marvellous, of course, but way too much, even for ravenous beasts like Harvey's friends on their trips to London. What a luxury.

What a life.

Romy fills the hamper with a greedy glee. Pungent cheeses, honey crackers, little jars of who-knows-what with names she can't pronounce. If they're gross, they'll be a drinking game. A tropical fruit bowl, sliced meats, olive-flecked bread; she shrugs and takes it all. Maybe there's an elf topping off the fresh supplies.

Thank you, little elf. Red wine from the wooden wall-rack, and she's done, navigating her hungry way back to the door. The rush is kicking in, her grin a buzz from ear to ear as she lumbers out to the cold. Goddamn, the hamper's heavy; god*damn*, it doesn't matter. The sky is pure and scudded with clouds, the sparkling grass alight with frost. Pop, pop, pop. Proud trees, the brittle river, glinting in the night. Smoke coiling up from the guesthouse chimney. Dusty. Perfect. Peace.

Distracted by buzzing beauty, at first, nothing seems wrong.

The door, though.

'Marnie?' Romy calls. The door stands open. After her cheeky mudslinging, she'd cheekily kicked it shut. 'Harvey?' Pausing on the threshold, she peers into the dark. 'Hamza?'

It's not just dark; it's silent. Even the fire is shrivelling, despite Marnie's talent for making it blaze. Romy sets the deadweight hamper down by her feet. Are they—

Music bursts into life in the dark. Romy flinches, swallows her gasp, and rolls her eyes; yes, they are. They're trying to scare her. 'You realise this is stupid, right?' Shuffling the hamper inside, she shuts the door behind them. It *is* stupid; she's Romy McFadden, king of Hallowe'en. She spent enough years terrorising

Kira, a fact of which they're well aware; last year, they became the new recipients. They can't expect to make her scream.

And if they do, and think she won't execute terrifying, pitiless revenge… well. Romy places a hand on her hip, fixing her face into fully fledged scorn. As her grandma used to say in her old snooty Britishness, *Darling, more fool them.*

'Harvey.' She bats at the wall for a light switch. *Papillon of winter light,* the song growls. To add insult to injury, it's her favourite; it couldn't scare her in a decade of Sundays. *Are we dead when we have died?* 'Game over. I brought food for everyone, but I'll eat it by myself. Gladly. Aha.'

The lights flick on. Romy folds her arms, set to throw contempt like darts.

The words never drop. Her eyes widen, to moons, planets, galaxy clusters. 'Fuck.' Stumbling backwards, she trips over the hamper, collides with the door, and crashes down. 'Fuck.' Her voice cracks hoarse. She can't breathe. *'Fuck.'*

She's Romy McFadden, king of Hallowe'en, and she screams, and screams, and screams.

6

The chill

0:07.

'He's beautiful.'

'He's gone.'

'He's boyfriend material.'

'He's *gone*.'

Macy smiles, all mischievous eyes and teasing. She hasn't let up since the movie finished, when Sutter followed Aimee like he should have all along. 'But I heard him invite you to stay.' She bats her eyelids sweetly. 'Will you?'

Kira takes a swallow of beer. 'Maybe.' Her treacherous lips twitch up. Dammit. 'I've not *not* been thinking about it. It's just—'

'Just nothing!' The smile becomes a beam of light, and Macy flings out her arms. 'Just *nothing*, Kira. Look at you!' She nudges Kira with her slippered foot. 'I've seen you smile about a guy maybe once. You don't even smile at Peter Kavinsky, and that's a travesty.'

'Peter Kavinsky's sixteen.'

'Not the *point*, Kira. Message him now and tell him.' Macy leans over precariously, batting at Kira's pockets. 'Go, go, go! Tell him you'll come.'

The doorbell rings. With a melodramatic sigh, Macy tosses her ringlets and gets to her feet. 'I expect to see the message when I get back.' She wags a stern finger. The beer bottle sloshes. 'I'm serious. Serious as death.' She shoots Kira a pointed look. 'The snakebite kind.'

'Not all snakes are deadly.' Kira leans back to switch on the lamp, shaped like a pixie's hat. The red, muted glow is soft in the night, and stretching out her legs on the sofa, she reaches for the plate of Oliebollen. Empty. *Dam*mit.

'Macy,' she calls, in her best wheedle, 'can you bring that ginger cake? We're out of sugary death.'

'I already promised you the snakebite kind.' The door opens with a jangle of bells. 'Send that message, woman.'

Kira tips her head back against the armrest. She won't be sending messages; she's not that hasty. Even if she was, she's not confident enough. She couldn't take Callum's hand, so how can she take his offer?

God, this morning could be years ago. Taking another swallow of Corona, Kira slips into memory. It seems unreal that they were huddled up here, with the new year's light pouring cold through the windows. His solid arm around her. Their deepening almost-moment. The pitiable melancholy that kept her in bed until three.

Well, that, laziness, and the hangover. Kira huffs into her bottle. She couldn't realistically expect him to stay, to drop his whole life for however long, no more than she can drop hers and quick-march to Spain.

But if only he'd come back along the street. Hammered on the door, declared he couldn't leave her, and then…

Then what? That's the point where she starts to feel stupid, and severs the fantasy. They had a batty, dark adventure, for a handful of days, a year ago; pining for a big romance is a trope from teen dramas. Aimee and Sutter proved that ten minutes ago. It's not real.

Or maybe she's being cynical. Watching the pixie hat warm up, she shuffles toward hope. Callum could be here. Curled up on the couch, in a room that smells of Christmas candles, sleepy in the lamplight and eating takeaway. It's not so different from the cabin in the—

'Kira!' Slamming the door, Macy bounces down the hall. One arm lags behind her, towing someone along. She beams. 'Look who's come to play.'

Shock belts through Kira's chest. 'Romy!' she exclaims. Clutching at the sofa, she works herself upright. 'What are you…agh.' Shoving the Corona between two cushions, she gets clumsily to her feet. Her eyes flicker as she looks at her sister, as if she's been staring at something too long. Shock. She hasn't seen Romy since August. 'What are you doing here?' she manages. 'Did you message? Did I miss it?'

She moves her hand to her pocket, but there's no point checking now. Macy slips away in a waft of peach. Staring at her waiflike sister, Kira reclaims her status as household goldfish. They've never hugged; it's not what they do.

With Romy in front of her, though, Kira aches. No matter how much they fought to the bone, she's missed her sister like hell.

'No.' Romy gives her a pale-lipped smile. Kira hadn't noticed she was tense, but relaxes. It was inching toward being awkward. 'Sorry. I should have, but it was last-minute, and you know I'm not good with messaging.'

Kira folds her arms, and smiles. 'I do.' It's like dragging blood from Hadrian's Wall. 'What triggered it, though? I mean, I'm glad to see you, but...'

Now it's awkward. Kira tightens her arms.

Thankfully, Romy catches the baton before it hits the floor. 'I was watching the fireworks in London,' she says. Flicking her fingers, she works her mouth. 'And, you know. Remembering. I wasn't far from the park where it happened, though I didn't know that when I planned it.'

Romy frowns. It pinches her bony face. Kira nods. 'So you thought...'

'I thought, well, it's been a year.' Romy shrugs. 'We've been talking more, and getting on more, and I thought we should be together.' She shrugs again and draws herself up. It seems to inflate confidence into her chest with a pump. 'So I came.'

Kira smiles. It stretches wide. She almost wants to hug her sister. This is unheard-of. This is un*real*.

'Um, please. Come in properly.' She waves at Romy's coat and boots, leading them into the kitchen. 'Beer?' She crouches to open the fridge. 'All we've got now is Sagres.'

Romy's boots click on the kitchen tiles. 'Sagres is fine.'

Kira fights her way through the yogurts and cheese. They really should go shopping. 'I think you're right, by the way,' she says. 'One year on, we should be together. I was dwelling on Wh—'

She catches herself, her face a mask of horror, clenching the cheap fridge door. 'What happened to our parents,' she finishes. Winded, her heart throbs bloody, her cheeks an oven of heat. Hopefully, Romy didn't notice. They only talk about the present or the future, and apparently, that makes it too easy to forget what rots underneath.

'Or what didn't happen,' Kira adds, keeping her head in the fridge's glow. Her flush is cooling. She was distracted. That's all. The fridge is bonkers. 'Everything, really. Trying to remember anything beyond setting off after you.' She straightens up, in possession of two beers and a calmer countenance. 'Here.' Twisting off a cap, she hands the bottle to her sister. 'I'm not sure what happened to mine, but I have an unfortunate suspicion it's all over the couch.' She grimaces. 'Let's stay in here. I do not want to know.'

Romy shrugs, and with a clink of bottles, they sit. 'You've got a nice house.' She nods at the small, square kitchen. 'From what I've seen, anyway. It's a lot better than Harvey's. You know, he goes to Petroc?' She takes a swig of beer. 'His room doesn't even have a window.'

Kira chokes, and splutters. 'What?'

'No'—Romy holds up a finger—'I lie. It has a really nice window. It just opens onto the dining room, like you're ruled by a panopticon.' She rolls her eyes. 'No privacy, no air, and the sense that you're always being watched. Because, you know, you are, and curtains and a rail are too much to ask for.' She raises her bottle high. 'Anyway, cheers. My point is that your house is nice. Very you.'

She nods at the Kay Nielsen print on the wall, and the lack of cooking equipment. The bobblehead turtle on the windowsill, the glinting, empty wine bottles lining the tops of the cupboards. Scarlet, violet, midnight blue. Any artistic glass, Kira kept. 'Thanks.' She leans back in her chair, watching Romy take it in. It's still a wonder that her sister's here; that she showed up, after what's never been between them. That, on the outside, she's so unchanged.

Her blonde hair, stretching its spindly fingers toward her belly button. Limbs that her year five teacher dubbed 'apelike,' her face so pointed it looks ready to cut. Light eyes ringed with dark, from both makeup and fatigue. She could be an ice queen, ruler of a forest, and bestower of glass to the minds of underfed kids. Or is that a mixed reference? Kira gestures for Romy to drape her coat on the back of an empty chair. Black coat, black jeans, black vest, black boots. She may be more upbeat, but she's still the sister from their life together, destroyed in a matter of days.

Kira blinks. That was a twist; now is *really* not the time. Swallowing the rest of her tiny beer, she pushes herself to her feet. Distractions. Romy's surprise is great, giving hope for some kind of sisterly future, but at the same time, she's the past. She's already accentuating the ache—the dampened nostalgia, the sad float back—that was meant to end last night.

'More beer?' Kira yanks the fridge open. Catching her mistake just in time, she shoots out a hand to halt it mid-topple. Romy laughs.

'Please…?' she says, as Kira bends down. 'Does it do that every time?'

'Try to plummet to its death?' Beers in hand, Kira straightens up and kicks the fridge shut. There; punished. 'Yeah. And the washing machine'—she nods at the hulk beneath the dark window—'vibrates so much that we have to clear the counters before we use it. It broke a pile of plates by vibrating them onto the floor. Oh, and if you need the toilet'—she flicks a hand at the stairs—'stamp your foot by the sink first. Don't ask me why.' She drops into the blue metal chair. 'Assuming you're staying, that is.'

She propels a beer across the table. It wobbles into Romy's waiting hand. 'I am if you'll have me.' She spreads her arms wide. 'But term starts in ten days. Ish. I think. I mean, I didn't bring anything.' She throws a glance at her battered handbag, drunk beside the table. 'I didn't think it through, but if I can borrow some stuff, and you don't mind me being here, I'd like to stay. Holland looks fun.'

Kira leans across the table. Romy's fingers are cold, and masking a flinch, she runs a thumb over the knuckles. 'Stay for the next ten days. Ish.' Her vision flickers as she meets Romy's eyes, but she blinks the bright little jerks away. If it's not shock, it's dehydration. Last night was excessive. 'Seriously. It's about time we bonded.'

She sits up. Tipping the chair back, Romy snorts. 'I suppose it is.' The chair clatters down. 'And I've been thinking.' She clunks her elbows on the table, wagging her bottle in Kira's direction. 'We should go away for my birthday. A girls' holiday, somewhere hot. Got to start the bonding off right.'

She winks. It's jarring. Kira lifts her eyebrows. 'A girls' holiday, somewhere hot? Like where?'

'Spain?'

'Spain?'

'Why not?' Romy grins. 'I'm sure Gran and Gramps will be over the moon. Their distant, wayward charges *getting on?* Alert the bannermen, stop the press.' Her eyes glitter with mischief. 'Also, my childhood's going out with a bang.'

Kira laughs, high and bursting. This is insane; this whole day has been insane. 'Wow. Um.' She combs a hand through her hair, wishing for a beat that it was blonde. Oh, nostalgia. 'You know this is strange for me, right? To not see you for however long, then you turn up wanting a girls' holiday? Our whole existence used to be avoiding each other, because I thought you were too emo and you sniffed at my life-loving artist vibes.' She lifts her bottle. 'But yes. Yes! Where in Spain?'

A grin splits her face, and they clink their bottles. Callum, Romy. Romy, Callum. All things considered, the new year is starting off pretty damn well. Why not go on holiday? God knows they deserve it.

Even if Romy doesn't know how much.

'Somewhere sunny but barren.' Romy pats her stomach. 'With stellar food. I don't suppose…'

'Help yourself.' Kira does a mental sweep of the cupboards. 'There's a good chance you'll find crumbs, and a slim to fair chance of scrounging up more.'

Romy stands. 'There's always sofa beer.'

Kira smiles, following her sister's gaze as she glances out of the window. Fat white flakes fall, spiralling tight-knit circles above the lamplit streets. Night has left the town deserted; it's an eerie antithesis to the previous evening, slumbering behind tiny doors and smoking, fire-warmed chimneys. A world within a world, muffled by the weight of clouds and snow.

No wonder Romy's been transfixed. The moments pass, and still she stares, motionless and watchful. She's lived her whole life in a bricked-up wilderness. A cobbled winter street, as a place to call home, must seem like Narnia.

Kira's phone vibrates. She digs it out quickly. With Romy quiet, turning to the cupboards, her thoughts are treading on dangerous ground.

Sorry it's so late. Callum. Kira's heart hops. She tells it off. *The snow screwed the flights up, then they go and lose Andre's case. He's still having kittens because of this morning, so if this is the last you hear from me, he's set them loose on my balls.*

Delightful. Kira shakes her head, wistful and wry. *Death by kittens…* she replies. *After the crazy things we've survived, it's pretty anticlimactic. Also—* She pauses. Considers. *Messaging you is weird.*

'New boyfriend?' She looks up to Romy watching her playfully, a banana in one hand and Oreos in the other. 'I know that smile.' Dipping her chin slyly, she sits. 'That's the "Peter asked me out" smile, or the "Andrew's taking me to London for my birthday" smile, or even'—she leans low across the table, as Kira's cheeks disobey her and flush—'the "I kissed José and we're back together" smile from many, *many*—it is!'

She throws up her arms, dropping the banana. Kira bites back a guilty grin. 'It's not.'

'It is.'

Kira shakes her head with all the fervour of denial in front of a judge. 'It's not.'

'It *is*, though.' Romy rips into the Oreos. 'You think I wasn't listening, if you talked about it when I was there? I was the master of superficial disinterest. That smile is the guy smile. Come on.' Knotting her fingers together, she rests her chin on their net and blinks entreatingly. 'Who is he? We're being real sisters now, right? Bonding? Well, that starts with talking about guys. And eating.'

Kira snorts. 'Okay, then.' She waves through the door at Vero as her housemate slips inside, blowing kisses to someone on the doorstep and smoothing down last night's dress. 'If that's what we're doing, you start us off. We'll trade. What happened to Ryan?'

Her phone lights up, and she glances down. WhatsApp audio: Callum Reeve. After a brief hesitation, she slides to reject. They can talk later; as much as Romy's a persistent pest, this snowballing strangeness is something to savour.

Looking back up, another guilty grin fights to break through. Romy's eyebrows are raised, the eyes themselves flicking between Kira and the phone. It lights up again. WhatsApp audio: Callum Reeve. Kira dismisses it quickly.

'That's him?' Romy nods at the screen. It lights up a third time, and her eyebrows almost hit her hair. 'He's nearly as dogged as Peter. Woof.' She scoffs a strawberry cookie. 'Confess.'

Locking her lips, Kira tosses the key. 'Not until you tell me what happened with Ryan. You've been holding out for a month. Think of it as payment, for the upcoming board and lodge.' She turns her phone face down, ignoring the message flashing up on the screen. Their newfound contact can be revelled in later. She sips her beer. 'I'm waiting.'

Romy purses her lips. 'Fine.' She crooks her arm and points a finger. 'But I'm warning you, he makes Peter look like an imprinted gosling. You know how Ryan was perfect?'

Kira bites into an Oreo. Ew. They do *not* go with beer. 'Yes?'

Romy arches her eyebrows meaningfully. 'Well, he flipped the honeymoon-phase switch, and became a bat out of hell. He started talking about *marriage*, and *kids*, and how it was time I started going to fewer parties and, you know, learned to cook, so that when we finish sixth form in July, and get an apartment, I can be ready with tea when he finishes work.'

'What?'

'Yep.' She nods slowly. Kira stares, lips apart. 'What, indeed. We're seventeen, and he's trying to make me a housewife. No buildup. No hints I was blind to. Just suddenly, "Hey, I've been thinking, shouldn't you see your friends less and take out your nose ring? If you're going to be a wife and mother soon?" And that was that.' She mimes an explosion. 'Boom! Perfection gone. I kicked that son of a bitch to the curb.'

'He proposed?' Kira plonks her bottle down. The flimsy table shakes. 'What—he—god.' She pulls a face at the slopping beer. 'I see why you kept it to yourself. I didn't think guys like that existed.'

'Well, they do.' Romy lifts her bottle. 'To losing Peter and Ryan. The worst little goslings to ever trap women.'

They clink their cheers, and shaking her head, Kira drains the rest of the beer. 'Seriously, though. He *proposed*?'

Romy screws up her mouth. 'Not in so many words, but yeah.' For a second, she almost looks nostalgic. 'It was strange, how he pulled such a total one-eighty. He really had been perfect: paying for our tickets to Download, carving me a little meerkat because I said I liked the adverts. I actually miss that side of him. But anyway'—she gestures to Kira—'that's all over, and now I have Harvey, who is less perfect, but lets me stay over every weekend. With Gran and Gramps so pernickety, it's needed.' She pushes up from the table. 'Where's the bathroom?'

She throws a look at the open door. Veronica is finally tripping upstairs, giggling into her phone. Kira smiles. She could be five years younger, home from her first date. Her first date, her first kiss, standing on the porch in the evening mist. In a perfect world, there'd be a summer breeze, a night right for sandals and a flowery dress. A diner meal in her Arizona hometown, pancakes and syrup and thick red booths. A date with a dark-haired, 1950s—

'Kira?'

Kira blinks, and the image pixelates. Romy. The bathroom. A creative writing module does wonders for the mind, but nothing for reality. 'Sorry. Yes.' She blinks again. 'Up the stairs, first door on the left.'

Cutting her a curious, bemused smile, Romy obeys. 'Yes, *mein führer*.'

'And don't forget to stamp!' Kira calls after her. 'To the right of the sink, or it makes it worse.'

'Yes, *mein führer*.' Romy laughs. The words echo back down the stairs. 'First star on the something, straight on till morning.'

'Precisely.' Kira's phone buzzes. Ducking her head in exasperation, she tips her groaning chair legs back and scrolls through the notifications. They've reproduced like rabbits.

Answer your phone.

It's important, Kira.

Disquiet unfurls like a flower in the dawn.

Goddammit, Kira, are you even alive? I NEED TO TALK TO YOU.

Okay. I had a missed call from Mum when I landed, and only just called her back. There's trouble with W, and it involves you. Now bloody hell, answer me.

He's still typing. Before she can reply, another message comes through, and for a second, Kira can't breathe. It stills her blood, and chills her bones. No. No, no, no.

I give up, it says. *I really didn't want to type this, but you need to know. Let the FBI think I'm a fruitcake or illuminati. Whatever. A huldra's escaped, and it wants you and Romy. No one knows why, but Mum's been told it's looking for you. If I don't speak to you soon, be careful. She says Huldra stay dangerous, right until they're fully human. Warn Romy.*

Pause. *And fucking call me.*

Kira lets the chair drop. It hits the floor with a juddering bang. The screen blurs as she stares through it. Whiteland. Huldra.

It's starting again.

7

The talk

1:42.

Bring on fifteen years of sleep. Callum collapses into his desk chair. In his pocket, his phone quacks, and he yanks it out. Gods of whatever, let it be Kira.

It's not. In a slump of disappointment and a stab of concern, he slings the phone to his desk. Dammit, Kira. It's been far too long.

The quacking stops, and restarts at once. Callum rolls his head toward it, on top of dog-eared photocopies and dissertation notes. It's a UK country code.

A sleepy interest stirs. Callum bats the phone onto his knee. They've got ten seconds to prove they're not a wine merchant, a weirdly specific wrong number, or a relative from Scotland.

'Hello?' Yawning, he spins around on the chair. The flight was delayed, the train was delayed, and it's snowing. *Snowing.* In *Spain.* Jesus.

'I…' the person on the other end tries.

Callum yawns again. 'Hello?' he repeats, eyeing his rumpled bed like a rösti. The interest is disintegrating; he'd really rather sleep.

He has time for a stretch, a thought of a snack, and a full look of longing for his two duvets, before the caller stutters her way to a sentence.

'I'm sorry,' she says. She sounds as steady as a twelve-year-old boy, breaking voice aquiver. He'll give her ten seconds, or maybe even twenty. Just because she's so damn slow.

'Why?' Bouncing on the springs of the chair, Callum idly flicks a folder named "Morality in *The Divine Comedy*." And, tatty and bitter underneath,

"*The Bible* and Ethics." It's the biggest regret of his life, and the bane of his existence. There's probably some irony there, for Professor Santos to hate.

'Because…' The girl gulps, and swallows. Callum hauls his attention back to her. Her seconds are tick-tick-ticking. 'Are you Callum Reeve? I'm really sorry. To call, I mean. To call like this.' She swallows. He can hear her lips, her tongue, her breath; the sounds of someone fighting for calm. Tick, tick, tick. 'I've been told to, I guess. Advised to. I'm not sure. I don't *know*.' She takes a deep, shuddering breath. 'I don't know anything.'

Intrigue drips through Callum's fatigue. Raising the back of the swivel chair, he kicks his feet up to the bed. The girl has passed the attention test; he'd like to know why sentences are so hard.

'Who is this?' He stifles another yawn. Time to play detective. 'You're English, right? Who told you to call me? Someone from the UK?'

Lips, tongue, breath, teeth. Thick earrings clink against the phone. The sound harks back to most of his girlfriends. Callum's intrigue is marred by a twinge of concern.

With another long, slow sigh, the girl clears her throat. 'Kira.'

Callum goes rigid.

'Kira told me to,' she says. 'Kira McFadden. She said I need to go to you. She didn't tell me why, or who you are, and I don't know what's happening, but she said she's in trouble. I'm in trouble, too, but apparently hers is worse. I'm sorry.' Her words grow harder, high, frustrated. The earrings clink and scrape. 'This explanation is shit. Problem is, that's all she's told me. I don't understand what there is to explain.'

Callum's hand hovers over his folder. 'Go on.' His eyes burn holes in the mottled carpet. Her tremulous breaths sound more and more like carefully managed hysterics. Kira's in trouble. Two hours after he warned her, after he heard about the huldra. He could have been there. He should have been.

'She sent me a message.' The girl is speaking again. Callum makes his mind slow down, and listen. 'We were on the phone, and something happened. On her end. I don't—I don't know what, I've no idea, but I heard a load of distorted noise, and shouting, and—and a while later she messaged.'

She swallows again, breathes. One, two, three, vibrato. One, two, three, again. 'Just once, about an hour ago,' she continues. Her rising voice is a tad more controlled. 'I've been trying to call her ever since, but it gabbles in Dutch and cuts me off. Every time.'

'Read me the message.' Removing his legs from the bed, Callum slowly leans forward. There is a pause, a fumble, a series of taps, and her tinny voice returns like wind in a tunnel.

'She forwarded your contact,' the girl says. Callum holds the phone closer to his ear, resting his elbow on his knee and his mouth on his fist. A suspicion is sneaking in, and it's not one he likes. 'Then said, *"Call him. Tell him I said you need to go to him. I'm in trouble. Probably more than you."* She clears her throat. Her voice is a leaf. *"'I'm leaving now, and I'll try to get to you, but if—if it's okay, stay with him until I can. He might be able to explain what happened at Harvey's. Same thing just happened here. Run, Romy."'* She inhales shakily. *"'Something's coming for us.'"* She puts the phone back to her ear, clinking. 'That was it. That was the last I heard. Does it make—'

'You're Romy?' Callum asks sharply. His sneaking suspicion was right: the girl he found under a tree, half-dead and possessed. The girl he and Kira followed into Whiteland, who kidnapped and killed her own dad. The girl, he thinks with a shuriken of dread, who remembers nothing, and has never been told. This is the girl he's talking to, sent to him by Kira.

Oh, she's put him in the shit. 'Kira's sister?' he continues, playing for time to think. He somehow needs to avoid the edge of this hellish, bottomless pit. 'Her little sister?'

Romy's earrings clink and scrape, clink and scrape again. 'Yes,' she says. 'Sorry. I didn't say. Kira's mentioned me? She's never mentioned you.'

Of course she hasn't. She thought he was dead. 'Yes,' he says. His mind is a river, swollen by rain and bursting its banks; as soon as it thinks the deluge is over, another torrent falls. Jesus, Kira. He can't take it in. Not as fast as he needs to in order to act. 'She's told me about you. And in answer to the question I didn't let you finish, the message makes sense. At least a bit.'

An image of Romy flickers like a deleted scene in his mind. Scratching. Flailing. Growling. Wild. Callum blinks it away. He really needs to act. To think, to plan. Kira must be right about the link to the huldra, but he hadn't expected the fallout so soon. His mum only found out this morning, and sensed he'd found Kira this afternoon.

'Tell me what happened,' he says. 'Then tell me where you are.'

Romy's words come in fits and bursts. Callum's face grows taut. His stomach muscles clench. She was explaining all this to Kira, she adds, because she didn't know what to do, who to call. There was a crash, though, and then nothing. It was like Kira had dropped the phone and walked off.

'I could hear the shouting, though.' Romy sounds as though she's swum the Channel, with dumbbells in each hand. 'And music that sounded like that Ragnarok song, you know. Or maybe you don't.'

Callum rubs his forehead. 'I do.'

'Okay.' Romy swallows. 'Okay. Yeah. And then—then the call died. Like I said, I never got back through. She sent one message, like twenty minutes later.' She sighs. Callum has a flash of her waving her hand, searching for words like her sister. 'And, I guess, here we are.'

Here we are, indeed. Callum shuts his eyes. It's as clear as the shit, and the bottomless pit: manipulation and murder, repeat. What's not clear is why, and what he should say. What he should *do*. He can see why Kira told Romy to call him, but everything inside him has sunk through the floor.

He's lost. More lost than paradise, but Romy is waiting for him to respond. Until they can contact Kira, she needs him.

'I need to figure this out,' he stalls. Getting up, he moves over to stare at the night. Snow flings itself at the window, like desperate summer moths. *Snow*. In *Spain*. He draws the paisley curtains shut, frowning at the pattern. Ugly. He should have changed them months ago. 'Listen, Romy,' he tries again, hoping for inspiration. Maybe, if he keeps talking, the words will form themselves. 'There's a lot you don't know.'

The line bubbles. His Wi-Fi is dire. 'What's coming for us?' Romy asks.

Callum suppresses a groan. Of course she'd start with that: the question he absolutely shouldn't answer. Sinking into his bobbing chair, he tilts his head to the ceiling. 'I'm not the best person to answer that.'

'But Kira said you can help explain.' Romy's voice is quiet, but there's a kraken underneath. Turbulent and straining, it hates being cowed. 'Do you know what she meant?'

'Kind of.' Anything he says, no matter how cautious, will probably blow Kira's secret apart. Callum grimaces. What did she expect? For him to explain what he can to Romy, protect her, whatever—but without the unpleasant details? They're the only explanation he has. Callum scrapes his hand across his head, leaving it a bristled surprise. 'Kind of,' he repeats. He's already said it once; if he backtracks, it only spawns more lies. 'But there's a lot you need to know before you'll understand.'

Romy's sigh sounds like relief, and he winces. She wouldn't be so relieved if she knew what was coming. 'So you'll tell me?' she asks. Callum screws up his face. It's not just relief; it's hope. How has this fallen to him?

'…Yes.' He pushes the word through his teeth. 'But not on the phone. After what you've told me, it's a bad idea. I guess Kira thought so, too, if she wanted you to come to me. I'd come to you, but…' He glowers round at a knock on the door. 'But you need to get away. Once the police find out what happened at the guesthouse, they'll want to talk to you, and keep you nearby, if they don't arrest you straight off.' Another knock pounds. 'I'm busy!' he shouts. 'Sorry, what?'

'I said I figured that out.' Romy skitters into sarcasm. Annoyance flares inside him, and gutters. She's been through hell. 'I look guilty. I know. I left after I talked to Kira, and got on the Tube. I'm in Hyde Park. I…' It's there again, the roiling kraken. Carefully managed hysterics. She takes a quaking breath. 'I was waiting to see what you'd say, if you'd say anything, but I took all my things with me. Where are you?'

'Wait.' Callum lifts a hand, as if she's there to pause. 'Don't come here. I've changed my mind. If the police do want to find you, they'll start by tracking your phone.' He pinches his eyebrows together. 'I think. They'll look at your call log, see my number, and track it here, so if you're with me, you'll get caught. They'd know you were in Spain from your flight, but that'd make you a sitting duck.'

He taps on the table, jiggling his knee. 'I'll meet you somewhere neutral, and we'll leave our phones behind. I have another one. All right? I'm getting a plan. Right now. Finally.' He waves a fanfare at the air. 'Stay on the phone.' He tugs his Mac from the folder volcano. 'I need to figure this out. It should work. But Romy?'

The girl breathes in, a hesitation. He probably sounds like he's springing a curfew. He certainly feels like a guardian. 'Yes?'

'You realise I'm not some superman?' He opens the Mac and starts to search. 'I can't fix anything. All I can do is help you understand. I'm the only one Kira can trust, because I'm the only one she knows who knows, but I can't make it go away.' He slots the phone between his ear and shoulder, typing with both hands.

Romy laughs, a humourless burst. Callum flinches. 'And I know nothing, so you're one up regardless.' She sounds like a cannon, about to get loose.

The deleted scene returns: scratching, breaking, screaming. Kira's gouged face. 'I thought the guesthouse was isolated, but from what you're both saying, it's this whole big thing.' She pauses. 'I don't need Superman. I need…' Another pause. 'Yoda.'

Callum stops typing. 'Lower the bar.'

Romy huffs. The sound is damp. 'Tyrion Lannister? You drink and know things?'

Despite himself, Callum snorts. 'Good enough.' He focuses back on the screen. He helped Kira a year ago, and he'll help her sister now. If Whiteland's breaking out, she needs it. 'I'll do what I can.'

'Tha—'

'On one condition.'

'What?' Romy asks at once.

Callum's humour fades as fast as it came. How did things change so quickly? 'You help me find your sister.'

8

Unreal

0:31.

It's not possible. It can't be. Kira's heartbeat flutes and quickens. Whiteland is the past, left in other countries. It's not meant to touch her here. She's here to get *away*.

Kira shoves her chair out from the table. What could Whiteland want with her? She was only involved because of Anna, and it got what it wanted. It took her. Now, forever, it should leave them alone.

Blindly crossing the tiles, she leans over the sink. Arms stiff, face set, gripping the kitchen counter. She stares down the drain. Breathe. Whiteland let her go. It let her leave. Could Callum and his mother be wrong?

Something brushes Kira's senses, and she looks up sharply. The indigo night outside is changing; she can feel it, as sure as the draught around the edges of the window. Across the street, the moon hangs full, illumining the white, narrow gables and the snow-cloaked cobbles underneath. Bright behind the witching clouds, shining through the mist.

Mist? Kira's heart dips, and swoops back up. Low along the curving street wind drifting wisps of mist, straggled and floating like gathering graveyard ghosts. A gothic Christmas spirit, the future yet to come. They're eerie, lonesome, slow in their meander. The hair on her arms lifts, thin and electric. The world is closing in. Reduced to the swirling glass, the moon, the thickening atmosphere; it's not a stretch to think she's the only one alive.

No people walk by. No pub-goers, bowing their heads against the cold. No students, back early with bulging cases, leaving drunken trails in the snow. No cats, no dogs. No sound. Even the sound in the house is muffled.

It's like it was in the forest. Kira's breath stutters. Drifts of snow surrounded them. Her jittery senses moved her back, until she pressed against Callum and the trunk of a tree. Perhaps one; perhaps both; perhaps neither. She can't remember. It doesn't matter. What she does remember, with perfect clarity, is the weight of the mist as it crept like a sandstorm, and the animal rawness that shrieked in its wake.

Kira swallows. Her skin is too warm, her chest too cold. The white wisps twist past the glass, glowing in the street-lit amber. She turns away. Stop. Digging her nails into the counter, she rests her coccyx on the sink. Just stop. There are no creatures, no threats, and there's certainly no forest. Her memories have made her paranoid.

Kira's phone lights up. Her eyes cut to the table, her heart turning skitters into bounds. Blinking past the afterglow of staring at the night, she slowly moves toward it. FaceTime audio: Rosemarie McFadden.

The phone buzzes to an aggressive stop. Kira stares at the screen. Romy? Has she fallen down the toilet?

FaceTime audio: Rosemarie McFadden. The screen lights up again. Kira jumps.

'Romy?' She holds the phone to her ear. Her heart thuds like a pounded door. 'Is everything okay? I thought you were in the bathroom?'

'Kira!' The voice jars her ear, loud and high and terrified. 'Oh, my god, Kira, I'm so sorry for calling you like this, but I didn't know what else to do, oh fuck.' She gulps a breath that the air avoids. When she gasps again, she's more shallow-lunged than ever. 'I don't know what happened.' She sobs. 'I really don't. I mean, I do, because anyone can see what happened, but how and why, I don't know, oh, my god, Kira—'

'Romy.' Kira digs her nails into the counter so hard they almost bend. 'What are you talking about? I thought you were upstairs?'

'Upstairs?' Romy sobs again, higher still and bubbling. 'Upstairs where? I'm not upstairs. The guesthouse is a bungalow. But that doesn't matter, Kira, listen to me—'

Kira holds the phone outstretched. She's a disconnect. The house is silent. No voices, and certainly not the gasping panic gusting down the line. She narrows her eyes, straining to listen. There should be two stories pouring out, one here and one upstairs. Stories of staying with friends in Harvey's parents' guesthouse, of losing a bet and being sent to the main house for food, of returning to find it dark and silent until the music started, even though they don't have speakers in there, but she didn't think of that at the time, she thought it was a trick to scare her, but when she turned on the lights, shit, when she turned on the lights—'

'What?' Kira tunes in, electrified. Her mismatched nails pierce the crappy counter, but she can't have heard right. She can't. 'What did you just say? What did you find?'

'They're dead, Kira!' Romy's words pitch close to a scream. 'They're all *dead*. I went in and saw them sitting there, Harvey and Marnie and Hamza, oh, god, and then I recognised the song that was playing over and over and over and it was the one I messaged you with yesterday, the one that goes "are we dead when we have died," you know, and it was like some sick game because they were all sat up on mine and Harvey's bed—they're still on our bed, I don't know what to do, it happened while I was in the house and they don't look that dead—'

Her voice sticks in her throat, but she doesn't stop. The scratching words must hurt like hell. 'They're sat up,' she croaks, 'like they're still alive, lined against the wall, but they're not. Their faces are turning blue and they're not moving or blinking or speaking and their necks are bruised and I don't know what to do because it wasn't me, Kira, it wasn't me, but everyone's going to think it was because I'm the only one still alive and they're on my bed like a sadistic display case—Kira?' She breaks off jerkily. 'Are you there?'

Disconnected, floating outside herself, it takes an age to respond. 'Yes.' Tentative, she steps toward the kitchen door. She'd been listening for a sound from upstairs, for her sister's garbled horrors. Her mind has got stuck, somewhere unreal and giddy. Romy here, Romy not. The house can't be silent. It can't be, but it is.

Then it isn't.

A thumping bassline starts above her. All the air leaves her lungs, sucked away by a gasp. Pulsing through the ceiling, down the stairs, through the walls. Macy wouldn't listen to it; neither would Veronica.

Besides, she knows that beat. She knows the music, the lyrics. *"Are we dead when we have died," you know.* The phone slips from her hand.

The kitchen is too bright. The overhead lights sting her eyes, glittering like a migraine. The phone cracks on the tiles. She passes it with pillars for legs. Past the table, where the lost beers warm. Listening. Listening. Filling up with nauseous dread, so numbing she can't think.

Murder.

The song thumps on. Romy's voice trembles from the floor. One palm pressed to the doorframe, Kira steps into the hall. Her body is made of concrete. Romy in the bathroom, Romy on the phone. The song, *this* song, the song she mentioned, thudding and shrieking through the ceiling. Death. Three dead friends. Murder.

Murder?

What Romy's been saying finally sinks in. At the bottom of the stairs, Kira stiffens; murder. If it's true, her sister's friends have been murdered. If it's true, her sister's in England.

If it's true, someone else is upstairs. And if it's not, and Romy's the one upstairs, whose voice is shouting her name from the floor? Kira swallows. Her lips have gone dry. It's impossible. One thing or the other can't be happening, unless it's an elaborate trick, and she'll reach the top of the stairs to see her sister jump from hiding. *Got you!* she'll yell. *Did you like the ruse? The song worked well, right?*

New year, new tricks. Like when they were young.

But this is a terrible trick. Years ago, they'd leap out at each other, or make gasping noises in the attic. Jump scares; minor thrills. Spider-walking in the dark after illicitly watching *The Exorcist*. Nothing like this.

'Veronica?' Kira calls. The music chews the word and swallows, as she fully thought it would. The bass throbs in her eardrums. 'Macy?'

Kira breathes in, and out. It judders. Her foot seems further than the end of her leg as she places it on the stairs. Even if this *is* a trick, it wouldn't explain the silence when the phone girl was speaking. That kind of mania can't be kept quiet, and the walls in here are like leaves.

Another slow step. Another. The song ends, and starts again.

It takes her an age to reach the upstairs landing, the stairs shrouded in gloom. Kira stops. The music surrounds her, thumping through her skin. If all is as it should be, she'll open her door to see Romy by the boom box, as smug as all eternity at such a fine reaction. Nothing else explains the situation; nothing. You can't be in two places at once.

One more step. One more. Anger roils with fear in her gut. To think Romy had changed; if this *is* one of her tricks, then she hasn't changed at all. And carrying it out on the anniversary of…briefly, Kira shuts her eyes. Thoughtless doesn't cut it. Romy's waging war.

This is what she tells herself; this is what must be true.

The narrow hall's light is unlit as she passes, the windowless walls making everything dark. She should have changed the bulb when she thought about it; now, she's a typical horror movie heroine, slowly approaching through the shadows.

'Macy?' Kira tries. If they didn't hear her before, they certainly won't hear her now. The roaring song is inside her rib cage. She can't even hear herself.

The smiling canvas on the wall leaps out, cheerily screaming affirmations. A memento of the last tenants. *It'll never fail to make you laugh, or at least roll your eyes*; Eva's case for keeping it had beaten their disdain, but now, it's clownish and wrong. Its backdrop of grinning cannabis leers. Kira lifts her hand as a barrier.

Does she really have to go further? The bathroom door is open, the pink fluorescent off. Kira tugs her sleeves down, twisting her fingers into the cuffs. The only other open door is Eva's. She went out hours ago, so it's not much comfort, and the other three are black and closed. Kira balls both cuffs and fingers into fists. She knew this was the case before she started looking, but she couldn't bring herself to face it: the muffled music, thumping in a pulsing, malevolent tunnel, blares from the room straight ahead. Her own.

You're living in a dream now; can't you taste it?

The words shriek, obnoxious and angry.

You live what you believe now; don't you hate it?

Kira balls her fists tighter, and breathes. It's a trick. Get the proof over with, and start waging war. She could delay, go into Macy and Vero, confirm that they're not the ones doing this…but there's no light beneath their doors. Kira shuts her eyes, and reopens them. The sooner she knows, the sooner she can get angry, and the sooner she can turn it into whiskey, or wine. She just has to open the door.

Stopping and starting, starting and stopping, she grasps the handle. One, two—no. One—no. Kira shakes her head sharply. There's nothing in it. Turn the damn handle. Cool metal beneath her fingers. Breathing hot through her mouth. Nothing's wrong.

Then why is everything dark? Why is Macy not complaining, or Vero blaring rap in competition?

Get it over with. In a rush that feels like ripping off a plaster, Kira opens the door.

Hunting wolves in curtained skies. Men screaming over raucous guitars. She liked this song a while ago, but now it's deafening, violent. *Are we dead when we have died?*

Dead. Kira stumbles backwards, clutching at the door. Romy stands in the centre of the room. One hand holds a knife, and the other…

The other curls around Macy's throat.

Kira's spine hits the doorframe. She staggers, palms slapping the walls, eyes filling up with horrors. Her chair of clothes has been knocked over. Her crocheted rug is skewed. The frosted wind whispers through her window, sprinkling sugarcoated snow on the floor. The fluttering curtains are speckled with red.

They used to be white. They used to be delicate, and Kira hated them. How could she have hated them? Now the edges drag along the wood, laden down with—

Kira's throat closes up. When it opens again, she can only choke. Beside the curtains lies Vero.

Blank. Staring. Convulsing in throbs. Kira gags, slapping her mouth with her hands. Vero's life drains away into stains on the lace. A gash slits her neck, her graceful body graceless in the lilac party dress. She's gulping, gulping. Gulping, gone.

The song loops round.

'What have you done?' The words stick like spokes. Fixed on Vero, Kira feels like an earthquake. Her friend's lips are parted, about to call out. Wide-eyed, terrified, about to save herself. How did this happen in silence?

The music. 'Oh, god.' Kira blurs. Her stomach broils and threatens to rise. 'Oh, my god, Romy.' She can't hear herself. *Papillon of winter light.* 'What have you done?'

She drags her eyes up—from the curtains, from Veronica, from Macy's tainted feet—but it's worse, so much worse. The knife, almost lovingly, has pricked Macy's skin. A dewdrop of blood beads bright on the blade, but breathing, swaying, staring, Macy doesn't seem to care. She stares at the doorframe, as empty as a sleepwalker. Her freckled hands droop limp.

The knife inches deeper.

Kira can't breathe. The lack of air gasps at her temples, and she forces it up through her clotting throat. Deeper. Deeper. Blood trickles down Macy's neck, mingling with her hair. The room smells of metal and peach.

'Stop.' Kira pushes off the doorframe. She didn't know she was going to, and dizzily, she stumbles. 'Romy, please. Stop.' She lifts a hand. 'Let Macy go.'

Animals in stolen hides.

Romy flicks her wrist. The knife slashes out, slicing at her fingers. With a small scream, Kira jerks away.

'Romy!' Her voice is hoarse and catching. The blade returns to Macy's neck, casual, almost caring. Kira cups her burning hand. 'Romy—'

Romy smiles. Kira's vision flickers. Her sister's face shimmers, blurs, and is gone. Back again, gone again, blurring into someone else. The smile becomes a grin.

Higher cheekbones. A heart-shaped face. A wicked, curving stranger fills out her sister's clothes.

Hunting wolves in curtained skies.

A wolf in sheep's clothing. More accurately, a wolf and a lesser wolf, or a coyote in the night. Perhaps they were never Romy's clothes at all; anyone can hide in black. Oh, god. Kira's chest hammers. The heat in her fingers blurs with her eyes. Swaying through it all, Macy stares.

Macy. Kira sharpens into horrified clarity; the someone else, the woman, is caressing with the knife, moving it across Macy's pale, freckled skin. No. No, no, no.

Kira lunges forward. Desperation lunges with her; she has to grab Macy, shake her limbs, shake her bones. She has to wake her up, and then they have to run.

The woman's animal grin grows. 'Too slow.'

She jerks herself and Macy away across the room. Kira staggers off-balance. The woman's speed is intricate; she wasn't even close.

'Stop!' Kira yells, hoarse. The song is so loud, tearing off the roof. Her lurching feet knock something soft.

Veronica. A silent scream surges up. Kira claps her hands to her mouth. The taste of blood. The smell of blood. Her feet are wet.

A door slams.

'Guys!' Eva calls, and Kira's heart stutters. Faint as she is, she sounds jubilant. 'Guys, guys, guys! This music is perfect.' The strange woman arches an eyebrow. 'I suggest tequila, but amaretto works, too…'

Let's become a carnival now Ragnarok is visceral.

'No,' Kira breathes, as the stairs begin to creak. 'Jesus, no.'

The woman yanks Macy's head back. 'Perfect.'

Kira's mind roars and rushes. She lunges again. She has to do something, anything, *anything—*

The knife slits skin, and her friend starts to die.

'No!' Kira screams. The light sparks back into Macy's eyes. Confusion, horror, terror, pain. She lets out a sputtering gurgle.

'Kira.' It's a bubble. Blood dribbles from her lips. Her glazing eyes find Kira's. 'Kira—'

Her face contorts. Slowly, her chin droops to her chest. Her sagging body goes limp.

Murder. Kira screams again. Ripping, strangled.

'Guys?' Eva calls. 'What's going on?'

Let's become a carn—

'There's three.' The woman tilts her head. 'How nice.' A pause. 'Take this.'

She lets Macy fall like a bag full of rubbish. Her lifeless body slumps forward, and as her weight buckles Kira's legs and screeches her arms at the sockets, the woman slips lithely to the wall behind the door.

In an unfocused, horror-scarred flash, Kira understands. 'Eva!'

The bedroom door opens. 'Eva!' Kira screams. The words are an unfocused, horror-scarred gabble. No, no, no, no— 'Eva, no, don't!'

Too late. Eva stands on the threshold. 'Kira?'

Doubtfully, blinking, she takes in the room. Veronica. Macy. Her lipsticked mouth drops. 'Oh, m—'

The woman steps neatly away from the wall, and snaps Eva's neck like a matchstick.

'No!' Kira's arms turn boneless. Macy crumples to the floor. In the woman's arms, Eva sags. 'Eva!'

I hope the wilderness will call.

The song loops round again.

'All yours.' The woman frees Eva to the air.

Kira doesn't lunge. She can't think, can't move. Her dead-eyed friend collapses to the floor.

The bright-eyed woman snorts. 'Your reflexes need some work.' Sweeping toward the window, she salutes. 'Thanks for the beer.' A wink. 'I'll see you.'

Flicking the bloody curtains aside, she perches on the sill. Moonlit, ethereal, she jumps, and is gone.

9

The walk

Let's become a carnival now Ragnarok is visceral.
The music dies. Kira's ears are a buzz. The room recedes, tunnel vision without the tunnel and starting to lack in vision. Black butterflies bloom, and flit before her eyes. She stretches out a hand, but there's nothing to steady her. Nothing but the fruity, bloody air.

Swaying, Kira lifts her shaking hands. Blood. She lets them fall. All she can do is stare, seeing-not-seeing the same bit of floor. Auburn hair spills over one corner, brightening up her indigo rug. A flutter of maiden curtain does the same. Shock, horror, terror pales, tuned out by the white noise shielding her from life. Stare. Sway. Stare.

As she stares, one thought trickles in like blood: she has to leave, and fast.

Woodenly, she pivots toward the door. The movement sends her swaying again, and biting back bile, she slaps her bleeding hand to the wall. Her arm jars. The butterflies coalesce. Breathe.

The shock of the impact rings through her body. Slowly, the darkness dissipates, and so does her numb protection. It leaves the room with a bruising void, an uncomfortable shedding of senseless skin; her perception, her awareness, tingles back to life. The scene slots back into the world.

Before, it was a movie, harrowing, overintense, and deep; now it's unavoidable, stark. A crime. Murder?

Murder.

It won't end. It won't even pause. Blinking around, she's anaesthetised, dread rising dully as she struggles to think. Eva, eyes hooded and drunk. Mouth open, lipstick smeared, red on her snaggling tooth. Veronica, her dress hitched up, frozen in fear like a victim of Medusa. And Macy; Macy, barefoot, clad in clashing pyjamas, who'd been drinking beer with Kira such a tiny time ago.

Kira's head clears like the death of the music. With it comes adrenaline, and whipping round, she runs.

Handbag by the shoe rack, ankle boots beneath. She pulls them on, shoulders the bag, and wildly looks around. Coat?

Living room. Sofa. Beer stains the cushions, stale and reeking. The glow from the pixie lamp is dim. Kira fights into her thick blue coat, forces up the fluffy hood, and runs to the kitchen. The front door shakes with knocking. Concerned voices call through, but they're trapped in a bubble, far away. Kira snatches up her cracked phone, and stalls. What if they're coming round the back as well?

No time. She whirls around, back to the living room, yanking the French windows open to the dark. Should she ditch the phone? Kira ducks her head against the wind and shoulders through the mist. Will people look for her? Can they find her with it? Will calling the police make it better or worse?

Worse. *Definitely* worse. Here, everything points to her guilt. In London, it points to Romy's. Maybe Romy could lie, but she can't; she can't pretend she came home and found her housemates dead. The people outside the door would have seen her.

She could double back. Kicking the creaking garden gate, Kira pauses. She could loop around to the front of the house, and—

She's covered in blood. A strangled whine slips from her throat. Her mind is colder than winter. She can't lie, and she can't tell the truth.

The truth? Biting her lip so hard she can feel her bottom teeth, Kira kicks back into motion. Out of the gate, left down the road. The raw pain is sharp, and she squints at her phone, damp already in the mist. The splintered screen unlocks on her second fumble, loaded with notifications. Romy, Callum, Romy, Callum; *Where are you? Are you okay?* She bites harder, and dismisses them, battling hard to think. The woman in her house was not her sister. The girl on the phone *was*, terrified because her friends had been killed.

Callum's warning was real. Something's targeting them. Kira starts typing, her fingers losing feeling in the freezing, muffling fog. She has to warn Romy, to tell her to run. To get her to safety, get them both to safety, somewhere they can find out what the hell's going on. Hiding the past is over.

Forward contact: Callum Reeve. *Call him,* she writes, before she can overthink. *Tell him I said you need to go to him. I'm in trouble. Probably more than you. I'm leaving now, and I'll try to get to you, but if it's okay, stay with him until I can. He might be able to explain what happened at Harvey's.* She swerves down a narrow, sweet-smelling alley, the bricks glinting bright. *Same thing just happened here. Run, Romy. Something's coming for us.*

The message sends and delivers. Kira takes a breath, braces herself, and hurls the phone at the wall.

It slaps the bricks like breaking bones, but she's already moving on. Walking as fast as she can without running, she burrows into her coat. The night is barren, but no chances will be taken. Not after what just happened.

Clouds thicken over the moon. The cobbled streets lurk in darkness, softened by the snow. Down another alley, and a residential street. The mist lifts in a breath, a veil, hovering innocuous over the roofs. Droning into life, sirens start to wail.

Panic seeps into her throat. Kira's thoughts scatter, and break. Faraway sirens. Don't know where she is. Can't. No one followed.

Did they?

No. Kira whips her head around, but the winter street is bare. She's alone, and she's innocent. Even if they find her, she has to remember that.

Despite how guilty the woman made her look. Killing in her bedroom, soaking her in blood. *Macy's* blood. Panic heats her eyes with tears. Oh, god. How guilty she made her*self* look by running…but what else could she have done? Try explaining to the police that, although she was found alone, stained and bleeding, with three dead girls at her feet, she was framed by a woman who could change her face. Best-case scenario, she'd be committed.

No. She can't be caught. She can't leave Romy. She shouldn't have involved Callum, but she has, and she needs to get to them both. Sending Romy his way was an impulse, a knee-jerk reaction because of his warning; she'll find them, un-involve him, and run.

Especially considering the deaths upon deaths. Kira's insides writhe, a roiling reminder that tastes like vomit. Deaths upon deaths upon sirens.

They wail louder, shrill in the mist-damp air. Kira ducks into a side street, pressing herself into a glass-fronted doorway. They're not passing here, the beginning of the modern town, but again, she's taking no chances.

A minute passes. The sirens fade, dipping and whining to a halt. Kira tucks her flowing, frosted hair into her hood. No chances.

With a hundred different plans piping up and facing ruin, Kira heads into town with her eyes on the ground. Tall, narrow alleys, slushy backstreets, the dirty, unpopular trails. It's a holiday, and although her street is tired and old, the centre is certainly not. A new year, a new vigour, for love and lust and beer; music, laughter, flashing lights, street food, and dancing. Kira avoids it as much as she can, panic pounding knuckle-duster punches on her sternum. Unbelievably, last night, all of this was her.

Dutch pancakes, strawberry wine, girls' heels catching in the gutters. Bottles drained, bottles dropped, missing the roadside bins. Sounds of a jaunty fair, ride music, screams. Her panic splits to course through her body, leaving no vein untouched. It's hot. Viscous. Too many people; too much noise. If panic set the fuse, and anxiety lit the match, her cranium would explode.

In comparison, the station is a peaceful embalming. The doors slide shut behind her, and she almost breathes without effort. It's grey and white and minimalist, clinical, clean, glass. No shadows for anything to skulk in. Starbucks, with a single customer. The smell of coffee. Banks of benches. Leon, with its luminous menus. It's safe, familiar.

Her footsteps clap and echo. Kira stops, the panic rushing hot up her throat. All at once, it's not safe, not familiar; by leaving the busy streets, she's made herself stand out. Conspicuous. Guilty. In a crowd, she'd be anonymous, but here, alone by the ticket machines, she's more jittery, more antsy, more clearly not okay. The one that security would spot check at airports, that train staff would question as a runaway.

Helpful. Kira goes through the motions of a normal traveller, but it winds up worse than an act. She feels like a puppet stabbing the ticket screen, putting on an unskilled show. They'll think she's more than a runaway; they'll think she's a victim of trafficking. They'll think she's committed a crime.

They? With a split-second decision, one-way to Schiphol, Kira woodenly walks away. Who's they?

Guards. Cameras. She's too false, injecting too much bounce in her step. They'll see her strings. They'll think she has a master.

For the love of God, shut up.

The next train out is waiting. Kira boards as calmly as she can. Her boots are loud on the scratchy carpet. She sinks into a seat, sighs in a shudder—

And feels her stomach pump and convulse. Stumbling down the empty, sickly aisle, she barely makes it in time to retch. Hands on her knees on the bathroom matting, she upends her stomach's acrid contents, foul and surging, a purge. Her clammy skin shivers and sweats. Shock, horror, revulsion, the lot. Putrefying scenes of night and blood.

Crouched in the poky toilet, Kira bursts into tears.

Her eyes are puffed and bee-stung when she finally looks up. Her knuckles cramp from gripping the basin, the bathroom bluish and hard to see. Her friends are dead, as sudden as a dart in a board or a riptide. Throat-slit and bleeding out, broken-necked on the floor. *Her* floor. Her mind shrinks back, from the sight, the sound, the smell. From the evening as a whole, looping like a pedal.

Like that vicious, goddamn song. Kira shuts her eyes again. Her stomach thumps once. Her thoughts are running races, rhetorical questions for all the seven seas. Did the neighbours hear this, should she have done that, and on, and on, and on. She needs to stay calm, take stock, and make a plan, or both Whiteland and this world will catch her.

That's the opposite of calm. She's a moron. Oh, god. Kira grits her teeth, drags her bag toward her, and drags herself up with the sink for support. First things first: passport. She can't find Romy and Callum without that.

Her eyes find the mirror, and the mirror finds blood. Kira's lungs miss a breath.

Spots and splashes, drying in crusts, from her breastbone to her neck. Scarlet swathes, trailing out of sight. Shell-shocked, Kira stares. Lights sparkle and dance. She could faint.

No. Blinking fiercely, she rips her coat from her sticky arms and faces her reflection.

Pale skin paler than ever, as sickly as second-day flu. Her blue eyes are fading bulbs. What beckons the tears, though, is everything else: her baseball shirt, treasured for its memories of Route 66, has darkened from white to crumbling bricks. Her hands are staining the sink.

Kira recoils, but the damage is done. Blood—mostly hers, from the weeping wound—finger-paints the basin. The toilet is ruddy with smudges. She cradles her throbbing fingers. Even the ends of her hair are painted, curling in on themselves. Everything, tainted. Fouled. Disgraced.

Kira bites her cheek hard. She can't think like this. For now, she needs to be clinical, detached, as much as she possibly can. Turning on the filmy taps, she rinses the ends of her hair, knotting it on top of her head and firmly out of sight. Off with her shirt. She scrubs at her arms, rubbing her chest to pink. Running her hands in cold water, she numbs the gash to nothing.

Plasters. The pads of her fingers are cut, but not deeply, and she grapples for her bag. One step at a time. Plasters, then—

A knock raps the toilet door. Kira's nerves fly out of her body. The train rocks, and she stumbles. Her knee clashes with the sink. She looks guilty, and feels it, but at least the door is locked. Have they found her?

A dispassioned voice calls for tickets, but Kira's tension only grows. She's injured, half naked, and scrunching a bloody shirt. She looks around, wide-eyed, stranded. It's dizzying, having no clue what to do. She's only attached to her body by a thread, watching herself in a TV thriller, waiting for a saving grace.

The flimsy handle rattles. The woman calls for tickets again, faintly impatient. Kira takes a frail, bitter-tasting breath. She's not in a TV thriller, and there is no saving grace. She's all she has. She's all she's going to have. Clearing her scratched, sour throat, she swallows, and grimaces. Her chest is a rock of period pain, but bundling back into her coat, she swills water into the pinkish sink, buries the shirt in her bag, and leaves.

'Sorry.' She squeezes out of the toilet door, holding out her ticket. After an uncomfortably close inspection, both of Kira's stilted smile and the crumpled slip of paper, the angular woman moves on.

Sinking into the nearest seat, Kira lets out a gusting, trembling sigh. The window is cold on her temple, cooling her sticky skin. Through the glass, the night is empty, the train too blasted with chirpy, saccharine light to see anything. Flecks of snow trail to water, whipped away by the speed. Her tired reflection is shadowed.

And then the impulse hits. Glancing up and down the carriage, Kira delves into her bag and yanks down the window. Winter air billows in. *Wh-up-whup-whup-whup*, it rocks to the train's pace, sharpening her every sense and colder than a brain freeze. Darting another glance around, she screws up her baseball shirt and throws it to the night.

The wind whips it out of sight. A few rogue snowflakes settle on her lashes, and blinking them away, Kira drags the window shut, resting her forehead against it. Her heartbeat bellows. The action shot adrenaline back through her chest, and she's jittery, giddy, too hot. Disposing of evidence; it's unbelievable. Now she really is in a thriller.

A heroine without a plan. A heroine without a *shirt*. Carefully coating her fingers in plasters, Kira stares through her skin and thinks. Plan first; shirt later. Shirts are so last year.

After far too short a time, a voice announces Schiphol. Kira dredges up her eyes, to the static-filled speaker. She must have spent an age in the toilet…and there's still no plan in sight. Is she on the run?

She slumps back into the seat, as slow and steady as her sinking heart. If she is, then she needs to turn invisible. Can her debit cards be traced? Can her passport? Outside the window, the lights multiply, heralding the late-night city. Kira grits her teeth. God, she has to think. No amount of media prepares you for this; you watch things, read things, hear things, and think you'll know what to do; you think you'll keep your head, step up, and rationalise, but in reality, the madness is a blur. An endless stream of microseconds, with you, her, anyone whirling from one to the next to the next.

The train judders in, and Kira's stomach bottoms out. *What is she going to do?* She should have seen more films, read more books, emptied her bank account. Or would that make her look more suspicious?

Stop, stop, stop, stop, stop, stop, *stop*. Despair flutters a threat, but Kira firmly slams its door. What matters now is that she's quick and anonymous. Invisible. Untraceable. The worlds and their dogs can know where she started, as long as they can't work out where she'll end.

It's such a cliché, too Hollywood and brash, but it goes some way toward clearing her head. Kira swaps the train for a gleaming bench and delves back into her bag. Rationality: first things first.

Pocket mirror. Swiss Army knife, an old gift from her dad. Neither of any use right now. Pulling a face, she delves deeper. Her purse, containing cards she likely can't use, a fifty euro note, and a pocket of change. A pair of thick socks. She pushed them in last night, in case she took her heels off. It's trivial now, but at least she won't be cold.

A wry sadness twists as she puts it all back. Anything else?

Yes. Tucked inside a hidden pocket, where it always is: her passport. Logistically, she's good to go.

At the bottom of the bag, something else clinks. *Vintage*, she's always claimed, ancient and battered. Her iPod.

Her *iPod?* Slowly, Kira pulls it out, trailing by the headphones. A frown carves lines in her face, seeping through to her bones. She stills. It can't be here. It shouldn't be here. If it is…

The music stopped when the woman left. Her iPod is here, in her hand. Maybe the song was playing from the air.

Maybe it never played at all.

Whiteland. Up to its mind-bending, air-bending tricks. With a shiver, she buries the iPod and hastily closes her bag. She never thought it would find her again.

It has, though. Breathing deep, Kira grounds herself. Icy metal bench. Robotic announcements. Garish yellow ticket machines, the faint smell of bleach, the headache threatening behind her eyes. Whiteland found her, but she's here, in the world. *Her* world. As heavy as if her clothes are drenched, Kira stands. She needs to get money, get a ticket, and get out. Find somewhere she can think; somewhere that doesn't need passports, security guards, or planes.

The next train out, then. Schengen's a godsend. The next train out of the country is hers.

Full of fearful drive, she walks.

10

The girl who can't be seen

Kira huddles in a humming seat as Amsterdam retreats. All of her money is squashed in her bag, which she squashes in turn on her lap. Tears still threaten to scratch, on and off. Her headache is a state of being. It put down roots in the internet café, when she started squinting at the news. She shouldn't have done it, but she had to do something. Now, at last, she's away.

At *last*. The night passed with the hollow anxiety that comes from drinking coffee too late, and her whole body, not just her skull, is ready to pop like the weasel. The only news item was a snippet concerning an "incident," to which both the police and ambulance were called. Kira's skin grows hot at the memory. The words still scald the front of her mind, even when her eyes stay open. Even now, hours later, with the train speeding away. It listed her *street*. It asked for anyone who had been in the area, between eight and nine, to contact the police. And it promised a report in the morning.

Kira forces her toes to stop tapping. A report. The morning. The tension of not knowing gnaws. She's a tree worried by a beaver, shoelaces tied into double, triple knots. Exhaustion smothered her hours ago, but she can't sleep. She shouldn't; the police might come. They might drift out of the greyscale dawn, boarding the train like Dementors. She might have to run.

Technically, she's already running.

Shut up. Kira squeezes the straps of her bag, and breathes. At least she's doing something. Acting on an awful plan is better than waiting for capture.

It's what she told herself when she settled on the ticket. It's what she told herself when she realised that, if she *is* checked by security, she'll need to remove her coat. It's also what she told herself when she begged a man for his shirt.

No shops would be open before her train; she trailed round them with mounting despair, mixed with gross resignation. The man was changing in a corner, and feeling like the lowest of the low, she asked if he would sell it. *Excuse me?* he said, and she felt her body burning, in places where she'd never felt embarrassment before. She mumbled it again. He stared, his face twisting. Part bemusement, she figured, part pervert-addict-creep.

But slowly, he handed it over. Offered it for free, after snorting, deriding, and advising more caution with the things she asks. She walked off with the shirt in sweaty palms, humiliated to the marrow.

It's better than waiting for capture.

And capture must be close. Kira's eyes scan the carriage, as they have a dozen times before. How can she have got this far without attracting attention? Something has to go wrong. The man across the aisle; he could be watching her. The woman opposite got on out of breath. Was she late? Or did she make a last-minute booking, to follow, catch, and arrest?

Is she on a watch list? Will she be?

Oh, god. Kira squeezes her bag so tight the zip bites into her palm. Nobody's watching her. Nobody knows who she is, over and above the fidgety girl in carriage two, seat twelve.

The fidgety girl in carriage two, seat twelve, in a pungent T-shirt. She wrinkles her nose, and not for the first time. No amount of bathroom soap has made it any better; if anything, the smells have mixed and made it even worse. But at least she's wearing something, even if it's an XXL. With her lack of luggage, it turns her into a tired student traveller, less focused on hygiene than life-enriching sights.

That's such a pretentious stereotype that Kira almost smiles. It even starts to twitch, until she remembers.

Death. Whiteland. Murder. She's alone, hunted, tainted, both inside and out.

Stop. Snatching at the window blind, Kira jerks up her legs, pressing her mouth to her knees. Stop, stop, *stop*. She needs calm. She needs sleep. There are no Dementors. There are no police. She's had next to no rest for next to two days, and her brain needs the break.

She'll need all its power, and strength, when she pulls into the village.

Faultlessly changing in Paris is the zenith of relief. The next train whisks her out of France, and she tries to keep her chin above terror. Is the village the frying pan, or the fire?

Either way, no one will look for her there. Why would they? Nobody's heard of the place. Once she reaches obscurity, in the form of tiny, toy-town trains, she'll be invisible.

She hopes.

Another change. Another. The train eases into its lakeside stop, and with her limbs crying for rest, Kira gets to her feet. Christmas decorations linger on the streets, unlit but cheerily festive. Giant golden baubles loop between buildings, reflecting the sunset descending on the lake. Multicoloured fairy lights link up balconies, Chinese lanterns, ribbons, stars. Red, green, yellow. Red, green, blue. The neat pattern continues, past Christmas trees in windows of stores and light-up snowmen on walls.

Kira folds her arms tight, tighter. Sale signs bray. A fifteen-foot reindeer glitters across the road. The train screeches to a rubber-scented halt, and she shivers. The town is pretty, magic in its winter, but it's inextricable from her life going wrong. Her father combed it in the car for her mother; Romy attacked her in its hospital's walls. It hosted the fireworks they planned to attend, and it opens the gates to the mountain.

On the steps of the train, Kira falters. Is she making a colossal mistake? Memories, dangers, *Whiteland*? She could sit back down, carry on to Italy, and get blissfully, invisibly lost.

No.

A guard barks. Kira starts back to life. He's glaring impatience at her from the platform, and before she can cower back into the train, she hops down to the platform. She's been through this five hundred times; it's here that she'll figure things out.

'Sorry,' she murmurs, as she passes the guard. It's English, but she never could speak in tongues. Muttering something about *touristes*, the guard waves her on.

That's actually not a bad thing. Forcing herself to appear unhurried, Kira trips down the steps to the station. If he thinks she's a tourist, she's doing okay.

Just about. Bowing her head, she lowers her eyes, and cranks her brain into weary gear. She needs to change her money, and get rid of this shirt. She can't turn up at Callum's house smelling like a buffalo and looking like a beast. Bank; shopping centre; mountain. Go.

The winter air hits her like a thousand shards of ice. Holland was icy enough, but *this*... Kira pulls up her fleecy hood. The cutting cold stabs her lungs. Her breath plumes in clouds. Across the road a bank glows green, and thanking all the merciful gods from every possible creed, she dodges a whirring tram and slips in.

'Bonsoir.' She nods at the clerk. The woman looks her over, and smoothing her features, Kira lowers her hood and smiles. Her stomach knots tighten, but she's only changing money. No one's looking. No one cares.

Nevertheless, it's a vast relief to leave. With her head spinning from exhaustion, she makes for the shopping centre. One out of three.

The reindeer is bigger than it seemed from the train. Normally, she'd smile and take photos, marvelling at the white wires and lights; it sparkles in the sunset, and would dazzle her at night. Now, though, she hurries past, every step a conquest. Across the square selling roasted chestnuts, through the revolving doors. She's never been so isolated, but quickly plucking a basket from the ranks, she prays to be left alone.

As a dot in a bustling, hustling crowd, that shouldn't be much of a problem. The sales shoppers engulf her, a black hole sucking up a star. Kira plants a thoughtful look on her face. Normality. Normality. She drifts about the store, an imposter, a pretender, the obvious, cliché spy. Heavy perfumes hang in the air, made for evenings and winter. Students mill around her, screaming children, mums with prams. Laughing girls trying out makeup. Trying to seem innocuous, Kira starts to sweat. The stuffy building is far too hot. Migraine-bright. Too intense. The lurid decorations, the bounding music, trilling New-Year-new-me-new-life. The butter-yellow, sparkling lights, like knives in her fatigued eyes. She skirts a group by the hair dye, brash and yammering. Far too loud. Backing up and into her, they laugh and apologise.

Oops-a-daisy. The leering creep rears in her mind. Kira blinks him away. Get on and get out.

A bag full of toiletries. Change shop, find somewhere selling clothes. Nausea churns in the back of her stomach. Lack of sleep, constant worry, crushing, crashing stress. Normality. Normality. Breathe.

Finally, a store she knows. Kira drifts into H&M in a daze. Reduced Christmas jumpers scream: polar bears and penguins, innuendo-laden pies.

Anything cheap goes over her arm: vests, leggings, thin black jeans. A slightly ugly cardigan, underwear, socks. A denim jacket and canvas shoes, too thin for a Bengal tiger in the summer rains, but whatever. They're cheap, untainted, and not her style.

Are they staring? Are they staring? It fast becomes a mantra, and when she drops her bags in a toilet cubicle, she'd kill to drop herself, too, and never be revived. Jesus without the resurrection.

Is that blasphemous?

Probably. Her brain doesn't work. Nothing wants to work, but after a moment of eyes closed, head in hands, she's as grounded as she'll ever be. The cubicle smells of pee. A song plays tinny above her head, echoing round the bathroom. It's old, something by Coldplay, maybe, or David Bowie. Who knows. Tugging her fraying threads, Kira makes her puppet move. If she sits too long, she'll rust.

Clothes on, products in hand, she peeks out of the cubicle. The shiny row of sinks is empty, marble-topped and gleaming. Kira sags. Thank God. She couldn't be subtle if she tried.

Showering in a shopping centre sink? Why yes. It's a habit, a fetish. I do it all the time. Lamenting to every god she thanked that she had to grow so much hair, Kira cricks her neck, holds her breath, and sticks her head under the tap.

Water splatters everywhere. Batting for the shampoo bottle, she grimaces. The cold water tingles, and faintly tastes like metal. This was not thought through. Lathering as fast as she can, she rinses, covers her scalp in conditioner, and, easing out from the tap, scoots back into her cubicle. Her heart thuds to a marching drum. Please, just let it end. Shampoo stings her eyes. Water drips down her neck. Twisting her fingers together, she swallows. This is crazy.

Please, just let it end.

A full song passes on the bathroom speakers. Something from the eighties. It might be a meme. Two girls enter, two girls leave, and with her heart somewhere around her jugular, Kira scoots out again. Rinse. Wring. Water and soap, crudely slapped on whatever she can reach, without standing naked in public. Hair blasted in the sci-fi dryer. Scoop up bags. Go.

The boots and rancid T-shirt meet the bathroom bin. Up the escalator, out to the cold, underwear slipped in another bin while she fiddles with her bag. Alone in the station lift, she drops her coat and jeans, and stepping onto the platform, wintry and windy and barren and brown, she leaves herself behind.

11

And so they echo

Callum's plan isn't complex, which is just as well. If it was, her shock-addled, semi-drugged brain would undoubtedly do something wrong.

Crash in Heathrow overnight, fly to Milan in the morning. *It's cheaper,* he insisted. *Trust me. Your bank account will praise you.* Bus-train-whatever over the border. Describe themselves perfectly beforehand, to keep any tricks at bay. That was it, and now she's here.

Stiff from a night on plastic seats and hours of juddering transport, Romy tumbles from the train to a crisp winter dusk. Snowcapped peaks soar high from the station, their blankets of trees all dusted in white. The buildings are few and far between, nudging each other up the slope. Slowly spinning, she stares. On her other side lies the lake, lined with mountains stark and severe. The sky is a starry, cold blue.

People file past. Romy shifts in place. It's a whole other world, and one she didn't like the first time. There's too much open space; too much scope for the world to be wild. Wilderness is within, not without.

After what happened at the guesthouse, though, she's not about to complain. She would have eloped with Callum to the Outer Hebrides, if it would get her away from the chorus in her head, and the stench her nose can't shake. Withering branches and frosted air. Death, dying, bleak earth, rot. Or just death and dying. She can't blame the winter; she can't blame the trees, or the air, or the cold. The cackling, stubborn smell of blood, that's barely lessened since she ran from Harvey's, can only be blamed on pale, blue skin.

On faces that haunt her like Marley and Marley, choked in a Victorian Christmas. On lifeless marionettes, woodenly human but not quite real, worsened by memory. The living dead. Romy pinches her hand, but the faces stick. They sneer when she looks between them, their limbs twitching in the corners of her eyes. Grotesque, mutated. Dead.

Three little children, sitting on a bed. A killer came in, and now they're…

In the name of all that's holy, *stop*. Romy kicks her mind like a sleep twitch. Never mind complaining; she's not meant to be thinking at all, and certainly not like this. Sadistic, maudlin idiot. Seizing the fire of her scorn, she slams last night back in its box. Locked, chained, and booted out of sight. She shifts her rucksack, and smooths her face blank. That, kids, is how to cope with crisis.

On with the plan. All of the signs are blue and foreign, most of the trains either striped or gold. Romy raises an eyebrow at the carriage in the corner. Emblazoned with marmots and edelweiss and moored on a cogwheel track, it snuggles by the rock face, smug and unique. She shakes her head and makes for the steps. It looks like a toy.

This country is *strange*.

She'll say one thing for marmots, though: they make her think of spring. As she sinks into the station's bowels, her box inches away. Cherry blossom, new green. Light blue skies and—

'Romy?'

The voice reaches her over the crowd. Pausing on the stone steps, she scans the arching tunnel. People are rushing, gushing past her, a slipstream to the escalator waterfall, but no one's looking her way. No one she can see, at least; she's tall, but not tall enough. There are so many skis, so many skulls, heading toward the twinkling café or the glass-fronted world outside. Jesus Christ, it's cold.

And my, her clothes are feeble. Standing still, buffeted by draughts, it hits her in a groan. She only packed what she had at Harvey's, and clearly, the Alpine January is taking the upper hand.

'Hello?' she calls. A kid with a giant schoolbag scowls as he passes, but wrapping her arms around herself, Romy stands on the tips of her toes. 'I'm here.' Tightly, she orbits, bumping dancers stuck in her lobster quadrille. 'If you can find me, that'd be great. It's way too bloody cold.'

A gloved hand lands on her shoulder. 'Romy?'

Knocking the queue for a vending machine, Romy swivels. The man has a couple of inches on her, brown eyes narrowed as he looks her up and down. His thick, sweeping mess of hair hovers by his ears, his face held with the ease of one who casually knows he's attractive. His ski jacket screams planets and nebulae. His jeans are just looser than a diet-girl's latte, and Romy relaxes. Callum.

'Howdy.' She shakes his glove with a frozen hand. She's frightfully, wickedly dressed. 'Your portrait was perfect, especially the jeans. Thanks.'

She steps to the side. A man with a Saint Bernard clumps down the stairs, both hands gripping the leash. His mouth is glued in a permanent *sorry*. 'The quote.' Romy looks back to Callum. He's still examining her, looking for the jade leather jacket, the nose ring, the black ear-stretchers that Gran and Gramps hate. The endless blonde hair and the figure that, as she commented dryly, comes from a new love of wine and cheese. 'The night…' she begins, with a twist of her lips. It may have been her idea, but it sounds like a secret handshake, or a key to the lair of a presumptuous cult.

'…Parrots are speaking,' Callum finishes with a smirk. 'As weird as it is. You and Kira aren't that different.'

He nods toward the escalator, burying his hands in the pockets of his coat. 'She's always given the impression that you are.' He frowns. 'Although a liking for obscure books doesn't say much. And I guess that's the only thing. Except for the hair.'

Romy lifts her eyebrows, slow and deliberate. He touches his own hair absently, before shaking his head. 'Sorry. Ignore me.'

Romy shrugs. 'I will.'

Callum snorts, and dryly meets her eyes. 'How kind of you. Blame sleep deprivation. It's a heartless son of a bitch.'

'It is.' Romy balls her sleeves up over her hands. Leaving the station for the slush of the road, it's only going to get colder. 'Me and Kira are different, by the way.' She sticks her fingers in her armpits. 'I want to make that clear. And the quote's a cultural reference.' She shoots him a smug look, a match for any smirk. 'At a push, it's a poem. But yes, it's obscure.'

Glancing at her sideways, Callum cranks his eyebrow. 'And you say you're different.' He offers her a smile. A little vexation, a lot of amusement. My, he's attractive as hell. 'Kira also takes pleasure in proving me wrong.'

'Clearly, it's easily done.'

'How kind.'

He turns down a steep flight of icy steps. Grateful for her Docs, Romy follows. 'Have you heard anything? From Kira?'

Callum's joking fades at once. 'No.' He tightens his mouth. They cross another rush-hour road before he sighs, 'Have you?'

Romy hitches up her rucksack. 'No, but I left my phone in a bin. And I thought using the airport Wi-Fi would be a terrible plan.'

She looks across at him. He nods, and she looks away again. Whatever he's feeling, it clenches his hands into fists in his pockets, bringing him to a hazy-faced stop before the lakeside wall. She wants to stare, to fire curiosity pellets at the side of his head, but at the same time, his disquiet is private.

No; his pain. His worry. All three. Why did Kira never mention him?

Plopping onto the low wall, Romy drags her gaze toward the lake. She can quiz Kira later, when they find her.

Last night's box rattles its chains. They'll find her. They will.

Romy drags her thoughts away. That *lake*. Black beneath the evening, it's empty of boats, the town lights rippling amber and blue. Mountains hulk in the distance, the stereotype of an Alpine loom. It sends her mind soaring back, revisiting places she'd rather not go…but Callum's not speaking, and they're better than the guesthouse.

Faintly disgusted, Romy lets them in.

From the angle of the lake and the flames of her memories, they're uncomfortably close to last year's town. Another box rattles, deep in a vault. They must be close to the village, too; maybe that's the link between Kira and Callum. Maybe her sister met him here, and said nothing because of The Christmas That Was.

Which would mean that Kira's keeping secrets. That became stupidly clear last night; but hey, it's another box. They're stacking up fast enough to give her an embolism.

Distractions. She swims her eyes back into focus, and lets the memories fall.

Same lake, different town. The mountains on the other side sighed with snow. Down here, there was only frost on the ground and a snapping in the air. The summer pedalos were quiet, moored for the winter by the water's edge. It was too bleak even for Dickens, but they embarked on a family outing regardless, stubbornly sitting outside beneath parched, leafless trees. Freezing on the lake path, down from the market square. They drank the same beer, from the same plastic cups, that she gets back home, in the warmth, on her own.

You're missing the point, her parents said. It was always jovial, always light, always full of hope. She ignored them. Kira was flicking the rim of her cup, watching the quaint, mismatched street. Why is that the thing she remembers? Kira quiet, Kira flicking, probably painting in her head.

Because she stared at Kira staring, trapped inside her own. She probably missed a thousand points. Her mind was a ball and chain. Then it became The Christmas That Was, and she shut it all away.

Until now. Now, it peeks through cracks, split by the lake, the season, the dark. The dark she's been fighting again, especially since last night.

Distractions. Another memory slots down, and it's the night before Christmas. Thinking about it, she *has* been here; the town's unbending, humming street is growing more familiar, merging with the memory as she looks left to right. Christmas Eve, when they walked a busy market into the night, buying mad amounts of food and trinkets that never got home. She almost enjoyed that day; the spiced cider was hot, with cinnamon and rum, and her mum's face at the mulled white wine was absolutely priceless.

Hot piss! Anna exclaimed. *Oh!*

She clapped her hand to her mouth. Passersby smiled, and Mathew hooted, Kira emitting a shouting 'ha!' Anna's guilt became fresh disgust, and Kira doubled up shaking. *Oh, wow,* their mum kept saying, beckoning for one of the neighbouring beverages to take the taste away. *This is—oh, god, oh, wow. Au secours!*

Nobody would, preferring to laugh, and wide-eyed, she seized Romy's drink. A waft of fragrant cider replaced the wine, and Anna drank with a sigh so grateful her shoulders actually slumped. *Heaven.*

Yes, it was, Romy muttered, although she had to grin. A snowflake landed in the wine, and she cocked her head. Its ivory arms were already melting. Peering at it, she thought for a second, and lifted the glass to her lips.

An odd hint of cold and sweetness, before the revulsion rose like bile. Sour everything, hot vinegar, alcohol gone so *wrong*. Romy swallowed with a graceless gag, shoving it blindly into Kira's hand, and from then on it was a game. Laughing through the cold sunset stalls: who can stomach the most?

It turned out to be Kira, though she very quickly fled. In urgent need to drown her nausea, she came back with rösti, Canadian crepes, and hot dogs made of cheese. Romy's stomach gurgles. They'd moved on with the delicacies, into a fur-lined model of an old Canadian village, clustering in a low yurt with fires and cushioned seats. They'd seen stalls upon stalls of rose petal candles, wooden reindeer, Alpine tea…and then, like the Edmund Fitzgerald, she sank.

Back at the hotel, she couldn't stop it. No longer drunk on the sparkling, otherworldly, rustic Christmas Eve, on the sights and smells and lights and magic of the last day of the market, it didn't take long for her happiness to die.

'Romy.' Callum's voice is a head rush, a come-down.

Dizzily, Romy blinks. Deep blue twilight. A honking bus. The cold, pock-marked wall. 'Yes?'

Her chilled cheeks heat, and she scowls them away. He's peering at her like she peered at the snowflake. How long was she staring, picturing a market?

'Are you all right?' Callum motions to her, to the street she was watching. At some point, he joined her on the lakeside stone, his emotions tucked away. Usually, that efficiency's hers.

'Fine.' She stands. Goddamn boxes, do your job. 'Memory lane took a shot.' She flaps a hand at him. Her vision flickers, and blurs. She must have risen too quickly. 'I didn't realise I'd been here before.' She shakes her head sharply. 'Shall we go?'

She takes a step, and stops. God*damn*. 'Admittedly, I don't know where we're going.'

Fleeting and ironic, Callum smirks. 'That way.' He nods to the several-storey shops. 'My mother's got a flat.'

Romy stares. 'Your *mother*?' She lifts her hands, moving back. 'No. Hell, no.'

'Trust me.' Callum drops his voice, approaching as she retreats. He looks like a lion-tamer, calming the cat. 'It was always part of the—'

'No, it was not.' Romy's voice is a hiss. There's nothing beneath her but air. 'Are you mad? She could call the police. She could hear my story, see me on the news, decide I'm lying, and call them. What then?' She lifts her shoulders, spreads her hands, juts her head forward. 'You moron! I could be all over the news. The British news, if nowhere else. You're British. Is your mum British?' She shakes her head, contorting her lips. He needs to see her disgusted. 'No way.'

'Being British is important?' Callum's words are unoffended. In fact, with his eyebrow arching, he even looks mildly amused. 'There's no un-patronising way to say this, but you're definitely overreacting.'

'Yeah?' Romy's laugh is jagged, disbelief and fear. Her heart has started to thrash. 'By wanting to avoid the police?'

'My mother—'

'Is not the reason I'm here,' she snaps, clenching her fists in her sleeves. 'I'm here because Kira trusted you, not your mother. Neither of you, at any point, said anyone else would be involved. I refuse to let that change.'

Swiping a newspaper up from a bench, she throws herself down in its place. The rucksack rebounds, and she wrestles it off. She can't speak French. It doesn't matter. Setting her face into stubbornness, she glowers down at the page.

Off to the side, Callum opens his mouth, shuts it again, and ducks his head. Good. Satisfaction stabs her chest. He must have realised he's a dolt. A pillock. An absolute, dim-witted, blockheaded *tit*.

'My mother can help more than I can,' he mutters. Ire stabs Romy's satisfaction dead. 'Say we don't go to her, okay, whatever. I'd still call her for advice. She's been caught up in this from…'

Callum trails off. Romy wrangles her face into concentration, aloof in pretending not to hear. After a second of sighing, he plunges on regardless.

'She already knows what's happened.' He lowers himself beside her. She bristles, turning the page, and he sighs. 'I called her last night, after we spoke.'

'Callum.' Romy's fingers whiten on the paper. Every wisp of air is leaving her lungs, a balloon popped with a pin. The image in front of her burns. 'Shut up.'

'Honestly, she can help more—'

'Shut up!' Romy jerks her head up, eyes wild. Callum flinches. A nearby pigeon alarm-calls, *ooorh!* 'Shit, Callum.' She brandishes the paper. 'Look.'

'Why?' Callum's voice pitches, squeaky Tenth-Doctor-style. 'What is it?'

'Holy *shit*.' She can't think. That disconnect before something sinks in, the jarring when you wake to night terrors. She thrusts the paper toward him. 'Translate it. Now. Can you?'

She drags her attention, kicking and screaming, back down to the photo. It dominates the page: a candid image of Kira, pushing her hair away from her face. Laughing, looking over her shoulder. An autumn leaf drifts past her head.

Callum's expression closes in. Romy's lungs close with it. As stunning as the photo is, the article must be its antichrist. 'Callum?' She grits her teeth, balls up her toes, tensing every muscle and bone. 'Can you read it? What does it say?'

In a rush of violence, Callum screws up the paper, lobbing it into the lake so fast that his arm whips the air like a lash. Romy recoils. 'They want information on Kira.'

He slumps back against the bench. Romy waits, but there's no more. 'They?' She spreads her hands. 'Who's they?'

The crumpled bundle sinks into the ripples. Callum knots his knuckles in his lap. 'The police.'

Now she really can't breathe. *'What?'*

'The Dutch police.' Callum stares through the pavement. 'They want information on her "movements." Her friends are dead. They were found in her room.' He meets her eyes in a daze. 'Christ. She's disappeared, and from the sound of it, the police can't decide what she is.'

Shaking his head, he leans forward, resting his arms on his knees. Romy can only stare. 'What she is?'

'Whether she's a missing person, or a suspect.' Callum scratches his head with both hands. 'Agh. This is—someone thinks they saw her leave. There's a handprint at the scene that might be hers.'

Romy's vision flickers as she watches him. Kira. Oh, they're in so much trouble. 'So…'

'So anyone who knows where she is,' he continues, pressing his teeth to his knuckles, 'or where she's been in—'

'Romy?'

Romy's spine stiffens. The voice comes from behind her, an echo in an alley, the spit of the man on the bench.

'Romy,' it repeats. Closer now, sure of itself. 'Romy McFadden. I've been looking for you. Did you forget where we were meeting?'

With her scalp prickling, Romy turns. A man steps toward them. Her stomach slowly drops. Planetary snowboard jacket, lightly stubbled face. Wild hair, matching eyes.

Holy shit. Callum.

12

Out, I say

The flames at her back are blue. To one side flares a wall of fire. To another lie furs in haphazard heaps. In front of her stands her mother.

At least, what's left of her. She's paler than the wretches of the Kyo, and a ghost compared to the women by the wall.

One has a look of revulsion. One sags unconscious. The first strains to support the second, splaying her hand flat on the stone. This is where the fire sparks. This is where it starts. As the woman drops the younger girl, Kira grows cold.

Thin and alive, the flames form an image. A sketchy tree, four lines for branches, and one slashed for the ground. Whiteland.

Kira wakes with a cry half-formed in her throat. Whiteland?

Yes. No. Maybe. Kira rubs her eyes viciously. No. It doesn't have her. She's on a train, facing two blue seats, and her cheek has numbed from the window. She was asleep.

Thank God. Whistling out her breath, Kira slumps into the seat. Her cheek really is numb. Rubbing it warm, she clears her fog from the glass. The world drifts by through panoramic windows, but the panorama is black. It's nearly six: night has settled. Lights glint by the distant lake like match-heads in the dusk. The tiny train tilts round a bend, and they twinkle out of sight.

Great. Now she's left with nothing but herself. Reluctantly, Kira scans her reflection. In the shopping centre, she didn't look properly, and she certainly didn't *see*. She didn't want to face the train toilet's mania, warped and bloody and pale and cold. Even though she's clean—clean, nice-smelling, and dressed like a hipster, the springtime antithesis to everything she loves—in her mind, there's only the madness. The taint, if not the blood, seeping out to stain her skin.

Out, damned spot! Out, I say!

Lady Macbeth committed murder. Kira presses her fingertips into her forehead. She did not commit murder; she witnessed it, but—

That doesn't help. One breath, two breaths, three, and she dampens the melodrama. Look at your reflection. There won't be any blood.

Focusing on one thing has never been so hard. Of course there's no blood, but her eyes betray her fear. Too much of the whites are showing. The darkness drains her, shaded like a ghost. Her new clothes are gallingly thin.

The queen of the unprepared. The thought is so worn, so comforting and normal, that she tries to crack open a smile.

It's weak, but normal. Everything is normal. Her face is normal, her skin is normal, her drying hair is normal. Barely damp in the train's inferno, it falls in its waifish, straightish way. *Normal.*

There's snow on the ground when the train pulls in. Slowly descending into the cold, Kira holds her bags tight. The open-air station is familiar, and crawls with unease in her gut. If they left the hotel, after fifteen minutes, they'd end up driving past it. It's the next village down the mountain.

The mountain. Above her, it towers, grand and white. Kira's breath plumes. Unease isn't right; not when she's looking up. It's sickness. It's sweat, in her armpits and palms. In twenty minutes, she'll be there: with the hotel, the train line, and the long, snowy road to the forest. There with the forest itself.

That's a bridge she won't be crossing. If she comes to it, she'll burn it. Bobbing on the balls of her feet, Kira hugs herself for warmth. She'd forgotten how *different* this village is: the station is smaller than a gym hall, run by one-carriage trains. Kira tries her rickety smile on them. The Mystery Machine, or pods from space: there is no in-between. Christmas lights glow in the dark. Stars hang from lampposts, stockings stuck on walls. Despite her unrest, the air is festive.

A Santa hat on a ticket machine. A dawdling train on the final bend, *joyeuses fêtes* pixelating its destination screens. People painted by pools of light, talking, breathing like dragons. The hillside houses are painted, too: watching the village, they're postcard-perfect, looking beyond to the lake like she'd scan the horizon for ships. It's beautiful, mystical…and nothing has changed.

That, more than anything, curdles bedlam with her fear.

Which was not the intention. The starry train whines, sparks, and chugs to a halt. *Les Plèiades* flashes on its screens. It's okay; she's nearly there. Soon enough, she can stop.

Soon enough, it'll start.

Shut up.

Boarding the train with a smile for the driver, Kira rests her head on the window. *Thunk.* She's never been good with conflict.

And she's getting sick of trains. The worry that comes with trains, at least; the doors slide shut, and she starts in her seat, knocking her head on the glass. The thoughts swoop before she can stop them: this is it. She's been caught, cornered, trapped. The huldra's back. The police are coming. She tried so hard, and got so far, but in the end, it didn't even matter.

'For God's *sake*,' Kira mutters, to make it sound real. The doors shut because they're leaving, rumbling up the cogwheel tracks. No one's looking at her. No one cares. Not the man with a briefcase and a squat, squashed hat, straight-backed and sombre; not the young woman in bright leggings, with hair as wild as *Brave*; not the leggy teenage girl, dark braids gathered high on her head and the toe of her sports shoe tapping. Kira's attention drifts away.

Mouse.

What?

Her eyes snap back to the girl. Crawling from her hood is a mouse. Really?

Yes. Perching on her shoulder like the king of the castle, the dappled mouse is real. Kira blinks, frowns, and checks herself: eyes working, brain awake? The girl doesn't even glance around; the toe keeps tapping, and the mouse starts to snuffle. A *mouse*.

She's such a long way from home.

The mouse distracts her well enough until the girl gets off. They're high among the mountains now; the train winds through pine trees, a star-scudded sky, and snow, but the duo made the journey timeless. The mouse crawled everywhere; behind the girl's neck, down her leg, onto the blue-gold table. Only then did the girl replace it on her shoulder, without changing rhythm or looking around. Watching them vanish, Kira almost smiles. She should be a writer; she'd use them in a book. As it is, she's a painter, and she's lost the will to paint.

She's tried. Last time, all she saw was grey. The time before was worse: pines, snow, and two lost figures, staring at the sky.

Then, she never thought she'd be here. Now, she can't believe she is. The wild-haired woman presses the button. The doors beep, and Kira steps from the train, into the frigid night. The driver whistles away with a wave, and there: pines. Snow. One lost girl, staring at the sky.

It feels as though she should be squinting, as she would for a horror film she's already seen. She shouldn't have this light bulb expression, drinking the mountain in.

'*Bonsoir.*' The wild-haired woman jogs up the steps, vaulting the hotel gate.

Vaguely, Kira nods. Nothing's changed: the dark-wood train hut, the postbox battalion, the train trundling up and away. Kira's legs are lampposts. She heads for the road, glazed with ice. On one side is the little car park, on the other the track to the field. Two of the hotel's windows are lit.

Kira peers through the gloom. Okay, then; one streetlight is disillusioned, but the murky sign has changed. The hotel's become a school. A dorm. With her belly twisting, Kira turns away. At least something has moved with the times; it was feeling like Groundhog Week. In the world she found a year ago, stranger things have happened.

Stranger already is how little she feels. A sneaking, snaking guilt slips in: she should feel more. God, she expected to, but setting off is more like stepping from a picture, leaving *Mary Poppins* instead of entering *It*. She jumped into a painting and cavorted with the carousel, while in reality, nothing changed. Dreamland let her forget for a year, and then it threw her out.

Reaching the devious Jack Frost stones, Kira carefully makes her way up. Through the arch lies Callum's house, but the emotion still doesn't come: no desolation, or devastation, or dread. Her mind doesn't scream. Her mind does nothing. Halfway up the garden, Kira stops, breathing hard. The moonlit ghost of the window lights her slow, weighted tramp. She can certainly blame lack of sleep for this: the weakness trembling through her limbs, the dizziness behind her eyes. Pressing a fist to her booming heart, she glances over her shoulder. The evening outlines the peaks in black. A dusky bank of cloud nestles in their bellies, the valleys masked by floating wisps. Wheezing more easily, she turns back around. If Callum's mother lets her enter, soon she can drop.

Drop. Sleep. Sweet, safe sleep. Pushing on her knees, she climbs.

A memory flits in front of her as she reaches the giddy house. Another night when she came here, seeking sanctuary: she'd exhausted herself then, too, and was bending over, puffing into the snow, when Callum's mum appeared. In ten seconds, she was banished.

Rainbow lights rim the windows now, and a berry-laden rowan grows by the door. Otherwise, though, the nights could overlay and you wouldn't know the difference. Kira's lungs steady. The world stops drifting. Stiffly, she straightens. Okay.

Are we ready? No. Are we steady? Ish. Brushing back her sweaty hair, she flaps her arms to air them, and takes a soft step toward the door.

The snow squeaks. Of course it does. Hastily, Kira knocks. This time, she wants to announce herself of her own wavering accord.

The door opens. *'Bonsoir?'*

Kira's chest flip-flops. There'd been a tiny, ignored part of her that wondered if, when she arrived, she'd find a different family; but the silhouetted woman is the same.

It's *all* the same.

'Est-ce que je peux vous aider?' The woman folds her arms. A querulous eyebrow arches, a true imitation of her son. *'C'est un peu tard, non?'* The eyebrow plunges. 'Oh.'

Thick brown hair falls in front of her face, and she pushes it back. Recognition is a plague. 'You're Kira.'

Kira can't help a fleeting grimace. She'd been too preoccupied with getting to this point to plan what might come next. 'I'm sorry.' She fiddles with her jacket sleeves, rocking onto the sides of her feet. Mistake: her bare ankles hit snow. 'I know I'm not your favourite person, and even if I was, you hardly know me, so you have no reason to help…' She lowers her eyes, the better to avoid the upcoming rejection. 'But Callum sent me your warning last night, about something escaping from Whiteland. I didn't know it then, because I thought it was my sister, but it was already inside my house, and…'

She braces her shoulders. It sounds beyond lame, and definitely fake. 'It's hard to explain.' She digs her nails into her sleeves. 'But Callum told me you're involved with Whiteland.'

Callum's mum takes her arm. 'And you didn't know where else to go.' She sighs, tugging Kira into the chalet. 'Of course you didn't. Like any sane person, you put Whiteland behind you and never thought you'd have to look back. Tea?'

She heads toward the kitchen. 'Please,' Kira murmurs, self-conscious as she follows. Her voice is distant from her lips, her mind. 'It doesn't feel sane right now, though. Maybe if I'd been on guard…'

'What?' The woman snaps the kettle on. 'Maybe you'd have protected yourself? No one could have expected this.' Her smooth forehead creases. 'When was the last time you slept?'

Kira shrugs. Her head pounds. The kitchen around her is vaguely detached, tidier than before; then, she had to share a chair with teetering pasta boxes. Now, it's clean, uncluttered, and bright. Far, far too bright. She drops her speckling eyes to the floor. She needs to sit down. She needs to pass out. She needs to not see the drawing on the wall: a sketchy tree, four branches, and a line for the ground.

She needs to not think about where she is, and where she shouldn't be.

'Kira?'

The voice breaks through her daze. Hazily, Kira looks up. 'Hmm?'

'I said, when did you last have anything to eat?' The woman rifles through a cupboard.

Cups clink. Kira's face twitches, and she tilts away from the clatter. 'Um.' Consciously, she rearranges her tired facial muscles. For such a minute movement, a frown is a lot of work. When *did* she last eat? 'I had some pizza yesterday…'

No wonder she feels like this. She'd had far more important things to think about than food, and with no sleep, she's running on empty.

'Okay.' Callum's mother plops tea bags in cups, tightening her Aztec cardigan. 'How about this: you leave your bags in here, find a cat, and go sit on the sofa. I'll bring the tea and something from the fridge. I'm worried you'll fall over.' She eyes Kira up and down. The crease in her forehead cracks some more. 'And you weren't my favourite person last time, but at this point, that's by the by. I'm Carol, by the way.' She raises her hands to shoo. 'Now go.'

Kira does as she's told. God, she's tired; sinking into the red cloth sofa, she could easily fall asleep. This room isn't helping. The fire isn't lit, but the air is warm, the mismatched curtains drawn. The chequered armchair houses a contented curling cat. On the cream pile rug dozes another, purring like a machine, and on either side of the sofa stands a candlelit table. Kira rubs her hot eyes. What chance does she have of not drowsing? Even the canvas by the corner door is sleepy, a smiling Buddha with half-lidded eyes, and as for the oils depicting the moon…

'Tea.' The stupor retreats to the trenches as Carol comes in with a tray. 'I don't know what you like, but you need to have something. We'll eat properly when the troops get back. I have to fetch the twins in'—she checks her watch, a witch on a broomstick—'fifteen minutes. Here.' She sets a cup on each candlelit table, nudging packets into Kira's lap. Her accent is more distinct than Callum's. If only he was here, too.

'Thank you,' Kira murmurs, morosely considering her hoard. Slices of sausage, slices of cheese, half a pack of blueberries. It could be a picnic, were her stomach not churning. 'I didn't know you had twins.'

'I don't.' Carol sits beside her, tucking one leg beneath the other. At once, the dribbly tabby appears, frailer and even more dribbly. 'They're Lena's. They barely spoke English when I took them in, but thank God, they're very quick learners. Speaking French at nursery and Swedish at home, I suppose languages are their strength.'

'Lena's?' Kira extricates a slice of cheese and nibbles at the edge. She can show willing, at least, although the meat is too far. Since Whiteland's cooked little bodies, she's been unable to stomach the thought. 'Where's Lena? I knew she was following us.' She swallows. Her throat is as stubborn as her belly. 'Did she stop?'

Mid cat-lift, Carol pauses. The tabby lets out a piteous mew. 'You don't know.' Slowly, she settles the cat in the folds of her skirt. Her eyes have put up barriers. 'Callum said you spoke about everything.'

A siren starts up in Kira's head. 'We didn't talk about Lena.' Calm. She nibbles at the Gruyère. 'I don't think he mentioned her, but we didn't have much time.' She pauses. 'Is she still in Whiteland?'

Carol hesitates. 'Kira.' She sighs, shaking her head. It's less of a no and more to herself. 'Lena died in Whiteland.'

The cheese turns to sawdust in Kira's mouth.

'Sorry.' Carol looks up, her fingers stalling on the tabby's ears. Her eyes and mouth slope down. 'That was unkind.' The cat purrs indignation. She continues her soft massage. 'I don't mean to be unkind, but I'm surprised. Shocked, really; I thought you must have known.' She stares at her gentle hands. 'Callum found out from a man you met. A man that brought supplies.'

Erik. The skier. He came in the night, with coats and food, when his village had chased her out. 'I remember,' Kira whispers. Her lips barely move. 'But I didn't know he said anything.'

'He did.' Carol's chin hardens. Kira knows that look: the forcing down of feelings. The swelling in her throat of a hot, fleshy knot. Carol swallows. 'He said Lena froze to death.'

Froze. Whiteland. Died in Whiteland. Kira's own fleshy knot swells, churning in her belly. Her mouth tastes like acid. She's a whirlpool, lava. A hot stew rising. Swallow. She can't vomit here.

But Lena's dead, and Callum didn't tell her. Did he think she couldn't cope? Did he think she'd blame herself?

If he did, he would have been right. Lena died because of them. Because of her.

'…Whispers confirmed it,' Carol is saying. 'And at least the Kyo didn't get—'

'I'm so sorry.' Kira throws up words rather than vomit, choking emotion welling in a burst. Macy, Eva, Vero…and Lena. 'I had no idea. I'm so—sorry.' She takes a rasping breath, swiping angrily at her eyes. Tears will make her seem like she wants to be pitied, a damsel or a crocodile child. 'Sorry. For everything. For—for involving Callum, and ignoring Lena's warnings. Everything could have been different, oh, *god*.'

She swipes again, rougher and knuckled, biting her lip until it tastes raw. It's barely had a chance to heal.

'Kira,' Carol says.

'If you want me to leave, I will.' Kira painfully squeezes her thighs. 'Callum always said you were friends with Lena, and now you have her kids…I must seem…' She makes a move to stand. 'I shouldn't have come here. I need to stop involving other people. I need to find my sister, and work it out with her.'

'Stop.' Firmly, Carol tugs her down. She lands on the couch with a whump. 'Not everything in the world is your fault, and thinking it is will kill you.' She pincer-grips Kira's wrist. 'Sometimes, things just happen. I tried to get Lena not to go, and from what Callum kept repeating when I found him in Croatia, his involvement was as dogged as hers. At the time, I blamed you, but I needed a scapegoat; this all happened because of your mother. And now that your…'

She pauses for a lightning flicker. Something flutters in her eyes, but Kira doesn't chase it. She feels like a fly in a storm.

'And I'm already involved.' Carol dips her chin. 'I'm a watcher; so was Lena. Getting involved is what we do.' Her mouth twists. 'It's as much a part of me as Scotland. I'll explain that later, unless Callum's done so?'

Dumbly, Kira shakes her head. What else has Callum not said?

For a moment, Carol is quiet. 'If you want my help, you've got it.' Her tone softens, as if Kira's a child after all. 'The Whispers told me to watch for trouble, and report, as it were. They don't know what the hell's going on. We all need to figure it out. But'—she returns to stroking the tabby—'that wasn't why

I warned Callum. I had a sense he'd found you, and I wanted you to be alert. You're not to blame for your mother's mayhem.'

She offers Kira a tired smile. It's probably meant to reassure, but her words buzz around Kira's head like oh-so-many flies. She can't speak. She can't think. The Whispers. Her mother. Trouble. Mayhem.

Hell.

'More than anything else'—Carol touches Kira's leg—'you're a scared young woman with nowhere to go. On top of *that*...' She taps the tabby. It squeaks. 'You're being hunted by a huldra.'

Kira's mouth winces.

'So no.' Carol reaches back for her tea. 'I don't want you to leave. If it were my children in this position, I'd hate to think of them kicked to the curb. What I do want you to do'—she nods to the picnic—'is drink, eat, and tell me what happened. If you want me to help, I need to know why you're a scared young woman with nowhere to go.'

She settles into the sofa. 'The twins won't mind the delay.'

Nevertheless, Kira hesitates. Reliving it all will empty her out, but beyond the barriers behind her eyes, Carol is surprisingly comforting. With her legs curled up in a long black skirt, her waiting expression a mirror of Callum's, and a purring, drooling cat on her knee, the urge to confide is a burn.

Kira inhales the whispering candles. Pumpkin spice; she bought the same. 'The huldra,' she says, and stalls. Pokes the pack of blueberries. 'Last night, she found me.'

Cradling her Eeyore mug, she lets the horrors fall.

13

The shapes that shift

This isn't real. She's not real. Romy stares. Should she pinch herself until she wakes up, or run and never stop? Time has trickled through the filter, the coffeepot is full, and now, nothing can move.

With his mouth still open, the roadside Callum grinds to a tensing halt. A young boy swaggers past, his smart blue uniform spattered at the ankles, chattering into his phone about when to kiss on a date. A tramline bus meanders, sighing through the slush. Over the water a lake gull cries, and for a nightmarish span of time, that's all the life in the world.

The wind has dropped. The atmosphere chills. As still as the air in a freezer, fogging up the glass.

But then the Callum beside her stands up, and time kick-starts with a bang.

Romy's off the bench at once, poised and ready to run. Her rucksack tumbles to the ground. 'What the fuck?' Backing away to the lake wall, she scrabbles for the cold, pitted stone with numb, clumsy fingers. The men are identical but for a satchel, carried by the one standing shocked by the road. Which one is real? Either? Both? 'What the *actual* fuck?'

Her senses swoon. Unreality crashes down, blooming with a need to either sink through the ground or awake from this two-day shitstorm. She should live in the nineteenth century; her corset would be so tight, and her sensibilities so taut, that she could collapse where she stands and break the tension. She wouldn't have to think, then; she'd have passionate male admirers, and they'd do it for her.

Yeah, that's really useful. Romy grips the wall tighter, sharpening her mind. No one's going to save her unless she saves herself.

She looks between the Callums. Neither one is moving. It's like she's told an anecdote in too low a tone, so no one hears, no one responds, and she wonders if she spoke at all.

The blood thumps in her ears. Her chest inflates, and sticks. The lake's behind her; she could swim for it. The cold might knock her out, and Callum could save her. At least she'd know which man was real.

'Romy.' The roadside Callum steps forward. The bench man's face grows dark with the night. Romy cuts her eyes between them, one to the other to the other. They're tauter than cats with their hackles up. 'Do one thing for me.'

Romy's gaze darts to the Callum by the bench. For a hair's breadth of time, he blurs.

'Run.'

The world stops. Romy's breath stops with it. She sees rather than hears the word, in a film's distorted mouthing. Slo-mo, right as things go wrong.

Propelling herself off the wall, Romy runs.

The lakeside path becomes a blur. Past withered trees and grassy squares, barren benches and ice cream stands left for dead until May. Crisp air slaps her face. Wind buffets her back. Feet pound behind her, fuelling her adrenaline, crooked and washing her cold. Someone's catching up.

She doesn't look round. She's Romy McFadden, king of Hallowe'en, but the fear might knock her flat.

Train station. The idea bursts, and she veers to the right. Trampling lifeless flower beds, she skirts a writhing sculpture, a branch-woven humanoid looming in her path. Men with prams. Piles of slush. Barrel past, across the road, and back the way she came.

She flies. Rich shops, Swiss clocks, lots of fancy clothes. The yellow storefront awnings are down. Romy ducks to avoid them. Shopkeepers pulling in their stands jerk back. The clock on an alley wall is wrong, stuck at ten past four. The last time she ran was…fourteen? Twelve?

Either way, she's tiring, and the footsteps hammer on. Closer. Louder. Horns blare. People yell. Romy's lungs are ragged.

A gloved hand grabs her, and she spins around. 'Fuck!'

'No, no, wait!' Callum throws up his arms. His satchel slams into her hip, and she staggers. Satchel Callum. Roadside Callum. And behind him… 'The station's up these stairs. You were going to run right—'

Romy doesn't wait. Freeing her arm, she wheels toward the steps. They're being chased.

And not by Callum.

She takes the sheer steps three at a time. Whoever she was with before, she's with the right man now; consuming the stairs beside her, his face is just as manic, and beyond him, the woman—the woman, the *woman*—is dangerously close to their tails.

Crest the staircase, storm the road. A car screams to a beeping halt. 'Calm your tits,' Callum shouts, slamming his hand on the bonnet. 'Twat.'

The driver swears, and then they're across, barging into the station. Romy falters.

Callum grabs her. 'Come on.' He charges up the escalators, dragging her behind him, up to the platform she arrived on. A train groans to life on the rails, creaking its red-and-white bones. Ignoring the bellowing guard, they hurtle toward the door.

The steps are retracting. Callum launches himself. Hauling Romy after him, he shoulders through the door, scrambling into the carriage. The train speeds up. Romy's shins smash the metal. The door's trapping her arm, oh, Christ, and in a burst of terror at dismemberment, she grapples for the metal bin and heaves herself inside.

Her back scrapes the doorway. Her shoulders pop and screech. Frantically kicking her legs to her chest, she crumples into Callum.

The automatic door slides shut. Shoving her off, Callum climbs to his feet.

'Hey!' Romy cries, tumbling back. The bin that saved her clangs. *'Ow.'*

Callum doesn't seem to notice. Pressing his hands and face against the window, he peers at the receding platform. 'She missed the train,' he informs the glass. 'The woman.'

Romy rubs the bruised knobs of her spine. 'The woman that used to be you.'

He casts her a look like a chick with ruffled feathers. 'The me-clone. Whatever.' He offers her a hand. 'She's still on the platform, all creepy and smiling.'

'Thank God.' Romy ignores his hand, standing with the aid of the bin. Her chest is sputtering. Everything hurts. If the chase was being dragged through a hedge, the leaves were made of screws. 'But how do I know you're real?'

She frowns. Callum leans on the toilet door, hands sliding into his pockets. He *looks* real, and doesn't blur, but the other one didn't til the end. 'That—

thing.' She waves at the outside. It can't roar past them fast enough. 'It wasn't you, but how do I know that *you're* you? There could be loads of…' She flounders, uselessly flapping her hand. 'Shape-shifters.'

Callum snorts. 'Shape-shifters.'

Romy's cheeks rush hot. 'Yeah, you laugh.' She glowers at him. 'What is she, then?'

'Not a shape-shifter.' He cranes his neck to peer out of the window. 'If she's what I think she is, there's only one of her. Out here, at least. And as for knowing I'm real'—he cranes his neck the other way, squinting at the approaching tracks—'if we're honest, I'm far too annoying to be fake. The first day I met her, Kira called me a wazzock.' He smirks. 'No half-arsed imitation comes close.'

Romy cranks an eyebrow. 'Really.'

Before she can slap him with snark, he lifts a thoughtful finger. 'Didn't you have a rucksack?'

Romy frowns at him. 'What?' Her eyes snag on his satchel, and widen. *'Shit.'*

She slaps her hands behind her back. Nothing. Groping her shoulders for the straps, she looks up, down, around and around their closed-off cube of the carriage. Her chest sinks through her Docs. Her rucksack is a goner.

'Why?' Spreading her arms, she shuts her eyes, an appeal to a hidden deity. 'Why is life cruel?' Romy lets her hands drop. They *whap* on the sliding door. 'What kind of god, from any creed, would let me lose a bag from my *back?*'

'Bit more dramatic than Kira, aren't you?' Callum lifts on his toes to peer over her head. 'Though she had her moments. Is there anything in your coat?'

Hope, glorious hope. 'Maybe.' Romy starts to scavenge. Wallet and passport in her jeans. Hip flask and packet in her coat. 'Yes.'

'Good.' Callum nods behind her. 'Because we've got bigger problems.'

Romy jerks her head around. Through the glass in the sliding door is a train guard. Solid, brusque, and discontented, he's marching down the carriage. Romy's face contorts into fifteen shapes. He should be in a tattoo shop, with a red bandanna and a Harley.

He's also the bellowing platform guard, and his blood has fully boiled.

'What are the bets he's pissed because of us?' Callum lowers his voice to a murmur.

'And you called me dramatic for saying life is cruel.' Quickly, Romy steps out of sight of the window. 'If anything, I was understating. What do we do?'

She leans out a little, chancing a look. Two blocks of seats remain, and then the guard is on them. His ticket clicker clicks at a menacing pace.

The train starts to slow.

'Oh, you beauty.' Callum's face smooths. 'You know, we might be okay.' He flicks his eyes outside. Racing trees, distant water, scaffolding, walls. 'Come on.' He drums his fingers. 'Come on, come on, come on.'

Romy tugs her sleeves over her hands. 'What happens when you're wrong?' She cuts a look at the sliding door, biting her nail through the fabric. 'He's nearly here. What's the plan? Hide in the loo?'

'No.' Callum peers around her, pulls a face, and beckons for her hand. On some bewildered instinct, she gives it to him. 'We're going to power walk'—he wheels around—'and hope for the best.'

He wrenches open the opposite door. 'And if it comes to it,' he adds, 'i.e. if he catches up, I'm Brian Doherty and you're Shannon Hart. Ready?'

Callum yanks her through the gap. 'What?' Knocking her thigh on the same damn bin, Romy scorches it with a glower. It's going to be one of those idiotic things that stick in your mind for life. 'Those are the shadiest names you could have thought of.'

'I was pressed for time, Romy.'

'Ah!' Romy stubs her toes on a protruding case. She trips, but Callum pulls her on. 'Jesus, Callum! And *Shannon*? Really? Do I look like a Shannon?'

Her foot catches an outstretched leg. The sloth-like boy sighs. 'Callum!' Romy's yelp rings out. 'Slow *down*. I'm pissing off the world.' Twisting her torso, she scrapes through a door, the rubber catching her belt. 'And as much as I love excitement, this is a terrible plan. I'm just saying, you know'—she bangs into an armrest—'so that when we get fined in a foreign country, I can say I told you so. Why didn't we just buy tickets? Agh!'

She shoots an old lady a breathless apology. Into another carriage, her foot snagging a tote bag, dragging its spilling contents several metres down the aisle. 'Blame him!' she shouts over her shoulder, staggering, kicking it free. 'Oh, *Christ*.'

The guard has entered the carriage, all bluster, ire, and noise. 'Callum, we're screwed. We're really, truly screwed.'

'Nope.' The train squeals its way to a halt. Shouldering through the sliding door, Callum bashes the button to let them off. 'Come on, you stupid, slug-like—'

The door beeps, and trundles open. Callum jumps down to the platform at once. Romy stumbles after him. 'Where—'

'This way.' Grabbing her, he breaks into a run.

With masterful resonance, they clatter down a staircase, into the sweeping station. 'I know,' Romy gasps, 'how to run by myself.' They barrel through a tunnel. It echoes like a church. 'I was'—up the stone steps at the end—'taught as a child. Oh, great. More fines.'

Callum stops beside a train barely bigger than a bus. Jabbing the button, he ignores her, bobbing on the balls of his feet. The doors beep.

'I've got this one.' Snatching her arm out of his grasp, Romy follows him onto the train. 'Where are we going now? The moon?' She clutches her chest, breathing like a bellows, collapsing into a seat with a sigh. 'Or does this munchkin form of transport not do tickets?'

She waves about her. The floors glitter grey. The doors are glass. Blue seats press against panoramic windows, and Callum points to a group of four.

'You and your tickets.' Reclining across two of the four, he rests his head on the glass, shoves his satchel onto the floor, and shuts his eyes. 'Jesus.'

'Yes, me and my tickets.' Dragging her aching, burning limbs, Romy plops down opposite. 'Because, you know, it's the law. To buy tickets.'

Callum holds up a finger. 'Which we're not doing.'

Romy ignores him. Condescending git. 'Correct. And while it might inconvenience you, *sir*, I could do without a fine. Being wanted in two countries is not on my to-do list.'

Eyes shut, Callum waves this away. 'I know the driver,' he says, lacing his hands on his stomach. 'If he comes round to check, I'll write an IOU. Chili chocolate, Drambuie, and shortbread.'

'I see why Kira called you a wazzock.' Romy kicks her Docs up beside his legs. 'Your choices are questionable at best.'

Callum cracks one eye. 'Feel free to get a ticket. Or…' He holds up a second finger. Whistling, the train shudders into life. 'Or don't. I knew we didn't have time.' The eye clicks closed again. 'Good day.'

Romy curls her lip. What a git. What a wazzock. With a sigh, she flops back in her seat.

Whistle, whir, squeak. Whistle, whir, squeak. The train creaks up in the dark, away from the small-town lights. *Bing-bong*. The robot announcer gabbles. Callum stays shuttered and silent. Everyone on the train is quiet, staring at phones or out at the night. Romy props her head on her hand.

Let's become a carnival now Ragnarok is—

She jerks upright. No, no, no. 'Where are we going?' she blurts quickly. Whenever she stops, the song is there. Blood. Bodies. Death.

Callum opens his eyes. She looks away, but his gaze lingers, frowning at her face. 'My mother's house,' he says at last. He tips his chin at the window. 'Up that mountain. She doesn't know it yet, but it's a bit late now.'

That mountain. It hulks at the edge of her vision, lit with clustered chalet lights and snow-brushed hints of memory. It's a sick familiarity she'd kill to avoid; up there, she fed her demons. Up there, her parents vanished.

Up there—and it feels like her guts are crawling—something started, and didn't stop.

'The other you said she was expecting us.' Romy turns her back on the devilish night. 'He—she—it—said that's where we were going. To your mother's flat.'

Callum snorts. 'He-she-it is a fool. My mother would never leave the mountains. And even if she wanted to, she can't. Well, she could, but she'd wind up in a similar place, so she doesn't really see the point.' Abruptly, he swivels, righting himself with an arm flung over the back of the seat. 'I'll explain that when we get there. I know I said it before, but there's a lot you need to understand.'

He looks at her. His jokes have gone. Surprised, Romy nods. 'Okay.' She offers him a smile, as sincere as she can muster. After all, he *is* helping her.

As the train whistles, whirs, and squeaks, they rattle through the vineyards and up into nowhere.

14

A merry chase

He doesn't break and enter. They never lock the door. He enters, and watches their faces drop, wrinkle by wrinkle, sag by sag. *Oh, my,* they say.

They don't for long. Blood on a cupcake-printed apron, bright against the plastic. It clashes with the knitted jumper, with the baggy cords beneath.

Before the wife can scream, there's more. Blood blending with burgundy leggings, her white-wool poncho turning red. Two thuds, and four glass eyes. He places the knife on the chessboard floor and drags the bodies away.

The living room table is laid. How quaint. Three plates, three knives, three forks. An orchid in the centre. Two candles. Pretty cups.

He hoists the couple onto the sofa. Their heads lean together, and he leaves them that way. Doomed, ancient lovebirds. He turns the TV on. Doomed, ancient lovebirds, forever enshrined in a lack of meaning. The voices inside him cackle and keen.

A clean shirt and a thick pen: one, two, check. He drops his old shirt on the stairs, makes his mark, and considers. The scene is set. All is as it should be.

The knife he deserts on the chessboard floor. Let them find his fingerprints; they'll never lead to him. Rebirth changes more than death, and what a merry chase.

Besides, soon enough, he'll be gone. Lifting his coat from the peg, he snicks the door shut. No one, returning to nowhere.

Happy New Year.

15

All today's surprises

Kira sits in silence after Carol has gone. Going through it all out loud has made her feel abhorrent.

Again.

Cradling the black cat, she smothers her fear in its fur and tries not to listen. The creaks of the chalet could be someone on the roof. They could be sneaking through a window, or already upstairs. The thumps of logs shifting on the fire—Carol lit it before she left, with instructions to add wood and prod—could be the first notes of a bassline. Alone on the mountain that devoured her family, who knows what anything is.

This is ridiculous. Kira gnaws at her cheek, worrying the ulcer. She finished her tea a while ago, and ate as much as her curdled belly could. She has to do something.

Preferably something apart from dwelling. Brooding. *Listening.* Imagining phantom intruders, and not so phantom Huldra.

Hugging the sleeping cat, Kira wearily, warily leaves the couch.

Whoa. Black spots sprinkle. Her whole body sways. She clearly needs more than a sit-down and cheese.

But not now. Right now, she needs distractions. Blinking the head-rushing spots away, she slowly starts to wander.

The door by the crackling fire is fairly disappointing. Leading to a tiny, spiderwebbed toilet, it's the homely home's antithesis, and Kira moves on. Past a squashy armchair, huddled by the front door; past a rustic pair of raquettes, crooked on the wall. Down the hall to the kitchen, but oh, there's nothing *here*. No distractions.

None she likes. The symbol stares from the wall, and she hugs the cat tighter. The tree has invisible eyes, haughty and blinking when she looks away, watching wherever she goes. It's far more disturbing there than on her arm.

Avoiding its gaze, Kira lifts the window blind over the sink. The cat shifts in sleep, but doesn't protest. In the moonlight, a strip of snow shines blue, crammed between the house and a hedge. She drops the blind again. Nothing. The chalet is tiny, but still. There must be something *somewhere*. A mystical mark, in need of analysis. A sword in a corner, or a crystal in a cranny. A secret room for her to find with a thrill, then quickly close the door on because anything else would be prying.

Kira huffs to herself. She'd make a terrible adventurer. The Famous Five wouldn't sniff at her; the kids from *Stranger Things* and *It* would laugh her into shame.

She can hear them now, cycling and crowing. Leaving the kitchen, she peers up the stairs. A dark landing, a beaded curtain, and four half-closed—

The front door opens.

Kira's head swoons hot. Her chest floods cold. She'd been trying not to listen, but to not hear at all? She should have heard the squeaking snow. She should have been prepared. Instead, she's the victim of a basilisk, frozen at the bottom of the stairs.

'Who are you?'

A breaking voice. An accusation. Kira's mouth is dry. 'Um.'

The boy narrows his eyes. 'And why are you holding Nibbles like you're Gollum?'

Sense rockets back. Kira's body sags. God, she needs to sleep.

'Hi, Jay.' She steps fully into view, trying to look neither guilty nor afraid. The boy is a bundled-up Michelin Man, tufty brown hair escaping from his hat. He's a few inches shorter than her, but in a ski coat, ski trousers, and hefty moon boots, he looks like a yeti come in from the cold. With a tentative half-smile, she moves toward him. 'I'm Kira. Please, don't shriek "stranger danger." Your mum said you were walking the dog.'

Radio silence. The boy's suspicion radiates. The dog in question snuffles in, flopping lackadaisically onto the rug with a throaty exhale and a thump. Kira frowns a little. Gone is the large, hairy beast she met before; this is a heartily jowled Labrador, chocolate-coloured and dribbling. Why does everything dribble?

Her chest pangs for the beast of old. She only met it once, but apparently, today is her day of feeling bad for the world.

'Your mum's gone for the twins,' she tries. The nearby train rumbles past, lumbering up the mountain. Jay disrobes and shuts the door. Silence. Too much silence. 'She's letting me stay.'

'Yeah.' Kicking off his boots, he makes for the stairs. 'I know. When she gets back, tell her I'm done. I'm never walking Diego again.'

The stairs thunder. 'That insolent, shelf-mounted mammoth of a—'

The rest of the griping drowns in a slam. Kira flashes her eyebrows. Okay, then; gone is the old dog, and gone is the old boy, repeating village gossip with a cheeky, nosy grin. In a year, he's become a preteen.

A grouchy one at that. Nibbles starts to wriggle. Kira carefully sets her down. Nibbles and Diego; what a pair. Kira tilts her head to regard the dog. He's the least Diego-like pet she's ever seen.

'Hi, Diego.' She sighs. Bring Me the Horizon starts up above her, their dulcet tones raging mid-song. For a second, she feels like an out-of-touch mum.

For several more, she's back in Holland, climbing the stairs in the dark.

No.

'How was your day?' Kira bumps her hip against the couch. Diego is already sixty-percent doze, but she's not letting that back in. No way. 'Really?' Stubbornly, she shakes her head. 'Same. I don't suppose you fancy sharing how you've pissed off Jay?' She glances at the thumping ceiling. *Are we dead when we have died?* She looks hastily back to the dog. 'You've lumped me with one very disgruntled—'

This time, she hears it. The crunch of snow, the echo of voices, bickering exclamations. Kira stiffens to listen. Are the twins back already? Carol didn't say how long she'd be, other than not long, but this doesn't sound like young children. Kira tries and fails to twist her sleeves. The cardigan is too short, too summery. She's naked, lost, exposed.

Tucking her hair behind her ears, she roots herself in place. She's the adult here. She'll face the door. No cowering, quailing, or running away, hiding behind a cat. She assumed the twins were young, but they might not be. Who else would argue so close to the house?

Someone trying to fool her. Real stranger danger. The huldra, posing as somebody else. Kira wavers, gripping the sofa. On second thought, not hearing

Jay was good. Great, even. The blood flutes in her temples. Her chest stretches, tightens, taut, a balloon ready to pop.

At least with Jay, her panic was brief. Now, the crunching snow crescendos, the squabbling louder but mostly obscured. Please. She could disintegrate. Let today's surprises end.

'You have to be fucking kidding me.'

Under the snow-laden arch, Romy stops. Looks up at the garden, down at herself. Turning to him, she gapes. 'It's vertical.'

Callum shoulders past. She badgered him about tickets at Blonay, even though the last train was leaving, *now*. She badgered him throughout the journey, sighing at the driver's door as if asking to get fined. On top of that, she refused to believe that the service stopped at seven, and combined with an intermittent humming, not to mention the Lost Rucksack Lament, he's thoroughly had enough.

Sure, she's suffered a horrific shock. Sure, she's fled the country, and sure, she's worried to death about Kira. He's cut her slack, but his patience has limits. He's barely slept in days.

'I preferred you half-dead,' he mutters, slapping his hands to his knees. Up through the snow, the mighty push. The house lights are on. Jay's music roars. All the metal wrath in the world is better than Romy McFadden.

'Oi.' Ploughing after him, Romy puffs and pants her pique. Callum commits to snubbing it. 'What do you mean, you preferred me half-dead?' She falls behind, wheezing. 'When was I ever half-dead?'

Silence. Callum doesn't wait.

'Is this another wild-man mystery?'

Silence.

'Of course it is.' Quickly, Romy ploughs up to his side. Five blissful seconds, then, 'How do I know you're not fake?'

Snap. 'You asked me that already.' Callum swivels to face her. Unsteady in the trampled snow, he teeters, glaring. 'And you'll never find out if you don't shut up. I'll lock you in the attic and pretend you're a poltergeist.' He jerks back, digs his hands in his pockets, and climbs. Everything about him is stretched too thin. 'The amount you moan, no one will know.'

Five more seconds. Maybe six. Then, reflectively, 'Shrek. Yeah!'

She speeds up, the better to gasp at the side of his head. Powder from her boots coats his jeans. Her clouding breath is lemony. He grits his teeth. 'It's like you're Shrek'—she grins—'and I'm Donkey.'

'*Shut up.*'

But her humour is infectious, and a part of him relents. At least she knows she's annoying. 'So basically, I'm Scottish.' He squints in the glare of the Christmas lights. 'And you're a pain in the ass.'

Romy claps, slow and deliberate. 'Well done.' Reaching the top of the upward slog, they trudge toward the chalet. 'You're Charlie Chaplin now, as well.'

Despite himself, Callum snorts. 'Hilarious?'

'No.' Breathing hard, a fist to her chest, Romy rolls her eyes. *'A literal pain in the ass.'*

'Not literal.'

'Shut up.'

Close to smirking, Callum opens the door.

He expected to see his mum and the twins. He didn't expect to see Kira.

16

Home.

The meal smelled nice. Shepherd's pie, and toffee pudding. He should have had some; the voices forget that living things need food. They've been too dead, for far too long.

He walks through the evening drizzle to their cackles. A sign pixelates into view. It sways, creaking fish and chips, and only then do they stop; the smell of sustenance trickles up his nose, faint to them but there. Five minutes later, he exits with food.

The witch is good. No one will remember him. Small, unnoticeable memory blips. Melting into the shadows, he's away.

Time to come home, girls.

17

The sleep

When the door opened, Kira turned away. She was almost sure it was the twins, but still; she couldn't face such boisterous bodies, couldn't face reacting. If she wasn't looking when they entered, they could react for her, and she could pretend to be lost in the day.

That's what she was expecting; that, or a posse of bitter dangers she tried to block from her mind. What she wasn't expecting was her name.

'Kira!'

It's almost a scream, a raucous yell, exploding in a thunderclap. Kira turns.

A catapulting girl engulfs her. 'Kira,' Romy cries, as they stagger together, caught by the shifting couch. Wrapped in the scent of winter, Romy hugs her. It's the first time in years. 'You're all right.'

Crushing Romy to her, Kira lets relief crash in. '*You're* all right.' She inhales her sister's staticky hair. Somehow, Romy's here. Romy's here, and she's okay. She's animated, curvy, with black ear-stretchers, smelling of the Nina Ricci she loved to hate; and she's far more full-on than the huldra's imitation. That Romy was a carbon copy, her sister from a year ago: thin and tired and eaten by her mind. This Romy seems real.

'We're both all right.' Pulling away, Romy fans her face. 'God, it's hot in here.' She glances over her shoulder. 'I think you know my annoying friend.'

Instead of flooding with cold, Kira's chest stutters and leaps. A bike backfiring, an engine stalled. This Romy must be real; hanging up his coat by the door is Callum.

'I thought you'd gone back to Madrid,' Kira blurts. 'I mean…'

Her skin surges hot. Of all the things she could have said, *that's* what comes out? *I thought you'd gone back to Madrid?*

Callum slides off his boots. 'Hello to you, too.' Shadows brush beneath his eyes, but he musters an arching eyebrow. 'Long time no see. Actually, no.' He almost smirks. 'That was last time.'

His eyes and mouth wryly combine. He really hasn't changed: the *Am I Alive?* shirt, the instant teasing. Closing the gap before she can doubt herself, Kira wraps her arms around him.

He hugs her back at once. His skin is hot from climbing, the scent of cold fading fast. She presses her face to his shoulder. Rumpled, weary Callum, holding her too tight. Tearfully, she shuts her eyes. They're here. They're both okay.

'I don't suppose you speak?' Callum asks, resting his smile on her head. 'Mmm.' Her hair lifts as he inhales. 'Coconut, honey…and a hint of mortal danger.'

Kira laughs. It comes out fairly manic. 'You're right about the danger.' She pulls back. 'As for the rest, I've not slept, eaten, or showered since the end of December. See?' Pushing her hair away from her face, she widens her eyes. 'I'm a walking zombie.'

Callum flashes her a grin. 'All zombies are walking. Also, neither have I.' He rubs his eyes with the heels of his hands. 'Not that that's saying much. What are you simpering at?'

Kira turns. Draping her jade jacket over the couch, Romy regards them fondly. Her black-lined eyes are studying, thinned. 'Not such a Shrek with her, are you?' She huffs. 'Don't worry, Petals, it's cute. But is anyone planning on dishing the dirt?' She sweeps her arms around. 'Letting the cat out? Spilling the beans? Especially the beans. I'd love a burrito.'

Outside, snow crunches. Faint voices drift. Romy's head snaps up.

'Ah.' Callum's face puckers into guilt. His eyes slide to Romy's. 'That'll be Mum.'

Folding her arms, Romy dips her chin. 'I'll put the burrito on hold.'

Silence. Callum taps his fingers on his leg. Romy stares at the floor.

Kira narrows her eyes at them. 'Why do you both look shifty?' she asks, as the snow and voices swell. 'It's Carol and the twins, not the mafia.'

Romy *humphs* in her throat. 'Well, that's the thing.'

Understanding blooms in a bloodstain. 'Oh, for crying out loud.' Kira rakes her nails through her hair. 'Callum, you—' Openmouthed, she gapes at him. 'She doesn't know you're *coming*?'

With a wincing look, Callum shakes his head. 'And Romy—'

'Callum!' Kira's eyes fly wide. God, don't let her find out like this.

'And Romy?'

Kira's eyes sink shut. Of course Romy wouldn't let that slide. For crying out *loud*, she could throttle him.

Callum sighs like the world is ending. The voices are right outside the door. 'Ladies, hold on to your hats.'

'No.'

Kira opens her eyes. Romy is cutting glances between them, and where Kira would start to fiddle and fret, her sister looks ready for a fight. 'And. Romy. *What?*'

Her very aura seems to darken. Belligerent, trustless, oily, and red. 'Callum.' She snares him with her eyes. Suddenly, they're danger. 'Is this linked to what you said?'

Foreboding floods Kira's chest. 'What?' She looks to Callum. He can see her watching; of course he can. Studiously, he won't meet her eye. 'What'—she turns to Romy, flat and accusing—'exactly did he say?'

For a second, Romy looks unsure. 'That he liked me better half-dead.'

Kira's mouth pops open. 'You *what?*' she hisses, rounding on Callum. 'Do your feet actually live in your mouth?' Throttle, hang, draw, and quarter. She'll do them all. 'What's wrong with you?'

Callum shrugs, helpless and slow. 'I was annoyed.' His tone is defensive. The door swings open. 'She wouldn't stop whinging, and… Mum, hi.'

He straightens up, guilt levels shooting sky-high. With one hand rising to scratch his head, he looks like a teenager caught doing drugs. 'Fancy seeing you here. How was your New Year?'

Carol stops, half-in, half-out. The twins snake past her. 'Callum?'

'Callum!' A bounding jack-in-the-box, the girl explodes toward him. 'You're here, you're here, you're *here*.' She beams a ruddy, chubby beam, bounding into his arms. 'You're here!'

'You are.' Carol's eyes wither to nothing. Callum scoops the girl twin up, peering with suitable awe at the wielded party bag. 'Who've you brought to tea?'

Her attention skims over Kira to Romy. Kira glances at Callum; he's examining the party bag contents, first the cake, then the fudge, making her uncomfortable as he buys uncomfortable time. She opens her mouth, ready for a damage-control introduction. Better her than—

'I'm Romy McFadden.' Still puffed up, if a little less belligerent, Romy steps forward for a handshake. Kira's heart skips. Oh, no. 'Kira's sister. I don't like Swiss kisses, but you don't sound Swiss.'

Oh, no. Oh, Romy, no.

'I'm not,' Carol says slowly. Her face could be iron.

'That's fine, then.' Romy returns to leaning. 'Callum said you can explain what's happened to us. I have literally no idea, and he'—she pointedly indicates Callum—'has refused to tell me anything. "Wait, run, I'll tell you later," is like his mantra.' She digs her hands in the torn-up pockets of her woefully torn-up jeans. 'So, yeah. I'd apologise for the intrusion, but no one's said if I should.'

Kira could disintegrate. This is Romy being nervous, but Carol won't know that. Between them, Romy and Callum are wrecking her hard-won trust.

'Indeed.' Slamming the front door shut, Carol yanks off boots and coat. Snow cakes her long skirt. 'Callum, put Julia down.'

Callum opens his mouth.

'I wouldn't argue with me.' Carol's mouth is set. She's a stone-faced snake, and Kira twists her fingers. 'Put Julia down and start talking. Yes, before you say it, I know how old you are, but that clearly doesn't mean you're intelligent.'

'Mum—'

'Julia,' Carol snaps. The girl slides from Callum's arms. 'Karl. You're not in trouble, but go upstairs. Please.' She looks to Karl and Diego. 'And tell Jay to stop that godforsaken music. How was he when he came in?'

It's Kira's turn for flying words. She almost backs away. 'Grumpy?'

Julia clomps toward the stairs with a sighing, pouting cabaret. Quietly leaving the dog, Karl follows. Their dad must have been the happiest, most Swedish man on Earth. They couldn't be less like Lena.

'Grumpy,' Carol repeats.

Jay's sullen words stamp back. 'He's never walking Diego again,' Kira adds. 'I don't know why.'

Carol lifts her eyebrows, staccato. 'I do.' She does it again. 'I met a neighbour in the car park. Apparently, Diego was after his Yorkie. It's a boy, and smaller than a cat, but Diego didn't care. Jay got very cross.' A bedroom door slams upstairs. Carol sighs. 'Thanks, Kira.'

She turns to Callum, breathes out through her nose, and lifts her chin. 'Okay.' She jabs her finger at Romy. 'Why did you bring her here?'

Callum opens his mouth again, but too slow.

'Kira thought you'd stay in Madrid.' Carol glances at Kira. 'Didn't you?'

Kira nods apologetically. She hadn't thought past getting Romy out of London. She hadn't thought they'd turn up *here*.

'So why is she in my house?' Carol's voice pitches high. Swallowing, she drags it back down. 'I have three children, Callum. After what happened at the hotel, what screwed-up delusion made you think this was wise?'

Tipping back his head, Callum groans. 'It's completely different, Mother.'

'Stop.' Romy pushes off the couch, hands up. 'Just stop. Stop talking about me like I'm not here, and stop talking so I don't understand. What's going on? Why am I the anti-Christ?'

Her eyes slice them up. Kira's heart retreats behind her spine. Romy's face is icily familiar: fury masking fear. It was there each time she fled to get wasted. It was there in the hospital ward, as the Kyo tore her up.

'I'll keep on asking.' Romy shrugs, in a vicious, rictus jerk. 'I'll get an explanation. You all know something.'

Kira can't speak. Her mind has shrivelled.

'It's not that easy,' Callum tries. Even he sounds cowed.

'Of *course* it's not.' Romy claps her hands with a pout. 'Poor things.' She flicks her fingers at Callum and Carol. 'And you two! I barely know you two, but you've got a worrying amount of opinions. I've been thinking it since I met Callum, and now I'm thinking something else, too.'

She shifts her slashing gaze to Kira. Kira's heart skips again. Dropping her gaze, she works her throat, and scratches out a whisper. 'What?'

Romy's face warps. 'You lied.'

It hits her like her chest is a gong. The reverberation resonates, resounding through her body. *You lied.* Kira's throat closes up. Lies. Guilt. She knew this would lead to the truth, but...

Realisation seeps in like oil, or blood: the tall tale is over. Broken. Dead. Panic flutters through her, whispery and hot. It was over as soon as Romy walked in, but some things don't become real until they're pointed, unavoidable, glaring and looking betrayed.

'Kira.' Romy's voice is barbed.

Kira lifts a hand, and lowers it. She needs to vomit. She needs to pass out. Too bright. Too hot. 'Yes.'

'It wasn't as simple as you said it was, was it?' Romy juts out her chin. 'You remember way more than you told me. That's why we're here, right? Instead of, I don't know, running to Greece? We could have fucked off to Bali, or something, or gone to the police, but no. No, no.' She laughs. It sounds like a splinter. 'Instead, we're here, where it all began. I don't know these people, but these people know me.'

'Romy,' Carol says.

'You sent me to them because you remember.' Romy stabs a finger in Kira's direction. Kira drops her burning eyes again. Hot. Bright. Disintegrate. 'You do! And it's all connected. The thing coming after us? What it's doing? It's all part of this *bull*shit. What happened a year ago, Kira?' Romy flings out her riotous arms. 'What happened to our parents? What happened to *us*?'

'Romy,' Carol repeats.

Romy rounds on her. *'What?'*

'Be quiet.'

For an eyeblink, nothing happens. Then, snatching the distraction, Carol's hands dart out, seize Romy's cheeks, and Romy slumps into sleep.

'Hey!' Kira's heart hits the ceiling.

Callum groans again. *'Mum.'*

Carol shifts Romy's weight. 'Kira.'

'Ah—' Kira gasps, as Romy lands in her arms. The huldra, she thinks in a horrible shimmer, falling, smiling, dying—

'One of you could have done me the honour of saying she had amnesia.' Carol's voice is brusque, and brusquely, she leaves, swishing toward the kitchen. 'Put her on the couch. She'll wake up tomorrow.'

Kira staggers, limbs clicking. Romy feels like a cannonball, peacefully asleep. 'What did you do to her?' she cries. 'Why—is she okay?'

'She's fine.' In the kitchen, Carol sighs. 'I've actually done you a favour. When she wakes up, she'll know everything I do.'

Kira hugs Romy to her. 'About what?'

'About what happened in Whiteland.' Carol taps her nails on the fridge. 'Ideally, it'll trigger her memory. Do you like pizza?' The freezer door bangs off the wall. 'It's all I've got to feed the army I've managed to amass.'

Incongruous. Unreal. Kira's voice is a bubble. 'Um.'

'You need to eat,' Carol continues, 'so I'll take that as a yes. Callum, you can either have some or not.' She slings four boxes onto the table. 'Right now, I really don't care.'

The oven door joins the freezer. Kira's arms start to tremble.

'Here.' Taking Romy from her, Callum lifts her onto the couch. 'Sorry about that.'

Kira drags her vacant self to Earth. 'Sorry?' She moves her hair off her face, a slow, sticky tingle. 'Why?'

Straightening, Callum looks at her. Kira's cogs clunk. 'Oh.' She presses her hands into her cheeks, pushing them up to her forehead. 'Did you really know your mum could do that? Subdue people at will?'

Skirting Diego, Callum crouches. 'Unfortunately, yes.' He scrapes a poker out of the basket. 'She told me last year, when she said she was a watcher. It was fun. She put me to sleep, and explained it later.' He shakes his head. The fire doesn't need his help, but he prods it regardless. 'I'm annoyed for Romy. Your sister's a pain, but that's rude.'

Kira huffs. He's not wrong, and it buys them time.

It buys them time. Kira twinges. Her face drops. Is that all she can muster? Romy's been put to sleep on the couch, and the shock is already wearing off?

Returning to the uncanny is easier than it seems.

'I know this sounds harsh'—Callum reaches for another log—'but I think Mum's actually helped us. It's…'

He draws a circle with the poker. 'A helpful plot device?' Kira murmurs, brushing Romy's hair from her face.

Callum frowns at her. 'If you want to call it that.'

Perching on the arm of the sofa, Kira folds her hands on her thighs. 'I've thought about it a lot.' She sighs. 'And I never worked out how I'd tell her the truth. Should I be more surprised?' She looks up at Callum. 'I'm surprised, but not like the-end-is-nigh. Your mum put my sister to sleep.'

'And you're okay?'

One second. Two. Four. Hesitantly, as though the *okay* might up and leave, Kira nods.

Callum stands, replaces the poker, and drops a chipping log on the fire. 'All right. Let's sum up all of the madness you've seen.' He sinks into the chequered armchair. 'Romy was possessed, and we ran from mist beasts. Twice.' He screws up his face. 'Fun. I got kidnapped by a siren, the air took your mother, and we followed light-up birds to a cabin. Yes?'

Kira nods, almost smiling. 'Yes.'

Callum counts on his fingers. 'Already, that's six. To add to that bundle of joy, a ghost appeared in said cabin, you were taken to a lair of crazy dead women, and you encountered a talking fish. By the way, I'm supremely jealous of that.'

Ducking her head, Kira shakes it. 'Don't be.'

Callum spreads his hands wide. 'Either way, *then* you rode on a wolf, for a supernatural showdown. My mum planting a helpful dream isn't the strangest thing you've seen.'

Their eyes lock. Kira says nothing, but Callum's head droops. 'Ah.'

Kira smooths Romy's puckered blue sleeve. 'You realise what you said?'

'Yeah.' Callum digs his knuckle into his lip. 'I'm sorry. I am. It's been a long few days.' He frowns. 'Which is as insensitive as what I said before, considering how yours have been.' He rubs his face, up and down. 'Ignore me. I'm a pillock.'

'You're not.'

Callum looks up at her. 'I am.' His lips twitch. 'Good intentions don't make it moot.'

Stroking Romy's hair, Kira almost smiles. 'The present's enough of a nightmare,' she says. 'We don't need to get stuck on the past.'

Callum prods the chequered chair. 'Still.'

'No *still*.' Scraping a hand through her hair, Kira holds it up in a knot. 'You remember when Romy was in hospital?'

Callum flashes a frown. 'Yeah?'

'Lena did a similar thing to what your mum did.' Twisting her mouth, Kira lets her hair fall. 'Somehow, she put Romy to sleep. I didn't see it, but one minute she was laughing, and the next, she was out.'

Callum stares off. 'I remember you saying.' He tugs on his knuckles. 'According to Mum, all watchers have some kind of...' A headshake. 'Power's too superhero, and I'm not twelve, but they have *something*. The something draws them to Whiteland entrances, and then it draws the Whispers.'

In the kitchen, oven trays clatter. Kira meets his eyes.

'Yeah, I know.' Callum waves a weary hand. 'I'm explaining it like I'm actually twelve. But that's what it's like: the watchers come here because of a feeling, discover themselves, and stay.' He pulls a face at himself. 'Sorry. That was even worse.'

Kira lifts a shoulder. 'It lightens the mood.'

'Ha.' Callum scratches his head. His hair stands to attention. 'Anyway. After Dad left, Mum left. She wanted to start again, and because of this pull, or whatever, she wound up here. Turns out there are deadbeats everywhere.'

'Why?'

'Jay's dad left, too.' Callum's tone grows an edge. 'A few years ago. This time, though, Mum stayed where she was. It's…' He shrugs. 'Her place. I don't know. I don't understand, but I'm not a witch woman who "senses" things, and sends people to sleep.'

'Callum.' The kitchen echoes Carol's warning.

Callum's moodiness brightens. It's not his usual grin, but closer than a shadow. 'Just seeing if you were listening.'

Kira doesn't need to be a witch woman to sense her rolling her eyes. 'In despair,' Carol mutters.

Kira doesn't laugh.

Callum does. 'It wouldn't be right, Mum'—he grins—'if I wasn't driving someone to despair.'

Gravity descends as he looks back to Kira. Her perch on the couch arm, here, unreal; her hair, falling in front of her face; her toes propped on the rug. The firelight catches her, watching Romy, glowing golden-red. She's so much like her picture. It tugs inside Callum. The picture in the evening news that shocked him to the core.

'Kira,' he says softly.

She doesn't look up. 'Mmm?'

He pauses. She's tired. She's beautiful. The hollows of his body ache. 'I'd like you to sit on a chair,' he says. 'And then to tell me what happened.'

18

The peaks

She should have nose-dived into sleep. She should have welcomed it like a long-lost lover, reunited in arrivals. Instead, bone-tired on an air mattress, all she can do is think.

Just before nine, she started yawning. It was constant, whale-worthy, and prompted a military basement scavenger hunt for an air mattress and pump, but now, she stares at the beams with a pumped-up steroid mind. The glow from Jay's monitor doesn't help, not to mention the fractious mutters, epileptic clicks, and frenetic bashing of keys, but still. She might no longer be numb with horror, but her world has grown too strange to compute.

Cramped with pizza in Callum's kitchen was utterly bizarre. She and Callum haven't had the chance to do normal, and an oddball feeling unravelled. They had a cup of tea once, in the same tiny kitchen, but then, it looked more like a junkyard. Their hours at New Year don't count.

Yawning wide, Kira rolls over. The velvety mattress wobbles. Those hours were too much of a shell-shocked blur to even hint at normal. This was a snippet of family life: the twins clamoured at the table, Carol sat between them as a barrier to bickering, and she, Callum, and Jay (who would rather stand sullenly with youngish people than sit, more sullenly, with kids and his mum) leaned against the counters, gobbling. Such an everyday scene was jarring, strange. Is this what it would be like if they'd met at school, in a bar, or on the street?

Technically, they did meet in the street; just not in a normal fashion. If they'd met in a normal fashion, would they ever have met again?

She was wondering this when she started to yawn, but before it unfurled, she was banished. As soon as she lay down, though, it slunk on back.

Kira rolls over again with a thump. Jay's mouse is going haywire. Blue and purple flashes light up the screen. Next door, the twins murmur, less stealthily than they think. Kira smooths a wolf-patterned patch of pillow. It's so low on the important-scale, and the thought makes her cringe, but…Callum's feelings. She buries her face in the musty fabric. *Feelings*. In this context, the word is embarrassing. Does he have *feelings* for her? Does she have *feelings* for him?

They've never talked about it. She's never let it in. Last year, they kissed in a cave and slept, kissed on a hill as a temperature experiment, and then he disappeared. This year, other than yesterday's not-kiss, she's going on nothing.

Granted, they've not been alone. Also granted, she's been here four hours… but still. *But still*. It'd be nice…

With a sigh, Kira flops onto her back. What would be nice, exactly? She pulls a face at the ceiling, all bulging eyes and warring lips. At this point, everything is so confused that relief, surprise, gratitude, whatever blend into wanting to be near him. She drops the face, and sighs again. He's warm with her, affectionate, so maybe there's something; but maybe he's like that with everyone. Maybe that's *him*. Really, this is the first time she's seen him with anyone else.

A brooding huff escapes her lips. Maybe, from her, he wants nothing at all.

Pushing out her mouth, Kira stares through the ceiling. Faded spots speckle it, shaped like little stars. Jay must have had those stick-on things, the ones that glow in the dark. Romy did, too.

It's not enough. Her mind keeps stubbornly plodding along, and she twists her face into knots. Why can it not shut up? Even if Callum did want something, they're probably unfeasible. They live in different countries. They lead different lives. They barely know each other, at the end of the day, even if the end of the day is being snared by a second supernatural mess. They bonded in the first place over their predicament…and at the end of another day, she's half a wily huldra.

'He's in love with you.'

Disconnected, Kira blinks. Once. Twice. The keys have stopped bashing. The mouse is asleep. Jay's impatience is weary, as if they've been hashing this out for weeks.

'What?' She works herself up on her elbows. His headphones glow on his desk, leaving a dent in his hair. 'Are you talking to me?'

He snorts, Callum-esque. 'Yes.' He taps a picture on his screen. 'Turtles with jetpacks. You should watch it.' He swivels on the chair, kicking one leg over the other. 'And stop worrying about Callum. He's different with you than with other girls, and he doesn't care about feasible.'

Feasible. Kira frowns. An odd feeling slinks in, potent and dark. She used that word. She *thought* that word.

'How *old* are you?' Her voice pitches, plucked by disbelief. 'When I was twelve…' She shakes her head. 'Actually, no. I won't go there. I'll date myself.'

'You already have.' Reclining in the chair, Jay slots his hands behind his head. 'Your thoughts are extremely loud.'

He grins.

If Kira had a drink, it would splatter.

'My *what*?' The odd feeling spreads its wings, bursting from its cocoon. 'You're not—no.' She struggles up to sitting, her hands palms-out. 'You're pulling my leg, or my arm, or something. That's impossible.'

Jay grins on. 'Shout something in your head.' He swivels side to side in the chair. As smug as Callum, as chuffed as can be, he lets out a breaking giggle. 'Go on.'

Kira stares at him, nonplussed. It's a game, a prank, a trick, a tease. If-I-have-to-share-my-room-then-it-might-as-well-be-worth-it. He can't be reading her mind.

Women can't change faces. Whiteland can't exist. Carol's a watcher, and watchers have abilities.

She looks at Jay. He looks at her. *Shout something in your head.*

Okay.

'"Let's become a carnival now Ragnarok is visceral."' Jay waggles his hand. 'That's an okay song. Try again, so you know I'm not a fluke.'

The world is slipping. The mattress is slipping. The stuffy, boy-smelling dark is slipping. Before all sense and reason slips, Kira does as he says.

'"A few days away and you're nothing but sound, with your feet in the air and your mind on the ground."' Jay cocks his head. 'What's that?'

Kira's mind bends. 'How…?' she stutters. 'You—how? It's the only song I ever wrote. No one's heard it. I was learning guitar, and my sister was—'

Shaking her head, she cuts herself off. 'You know what, forget it.' Dropping flat on her back, she throws up her hands. 'Callum's right; I've seen too much to be surprised.' She angles her gaze toward him. Her mouth hovers open. Astonished doesn't cut it. 'How many people know?'

Jay swivels back to his screen. 'Two.' Click: a cat dressed up as a pug. He snorts. 'It only started recently. The twins know, because I practice on them, and they love having a secret. Callum has no idea, but he's got the supernatural skills of a spud.'

Kira laughs. Jay grins winningly over his shoulder. 'Mum probably suspects.'

'Mothers always do.'

'They *do*.' Jay thumps his fist on his knee. 'Also, she has her own "power-ups."' He quotes in the air. 'You've seen those already. I've learned a lot from listening to her.' He shrugs. 'Not personal stuff, because no way in hell, but the weird stuff.'

Kira cranes her neck to look at him. 'All of this counts as weird stuff. You're inside people's heads.'

'Yeah, but the really weird stuff.' He clicks on a GIF, too small to make out. 'I was freaked out at first, but I listened more, and then I kind of felt it was normal. If someone's thoughts are all "hey, this is fine," then it starts to be fine for you, too.'

Astonished *definitely* doesn't cut it. Kira laughs, high and slightly mad. She's slammed straight into gobsmacked; the moody, skater-dressed, metal-loving preteen, holed up with games of medieval magic, is the one with the magical secret. Who would have thought he could be so—

'Wise.' Jay taps his head. His eyes stay stuck to the piano-playing parrot, but his voice is a satisfied smile. 'Yoda. Savvy. Intellectually gifted. I'm nearly thirteen; I'm complex.'

Kira rolls her eyes, and huffs. 'I'll give you the complex part.' She pauses. 'But why did you tell me?'

Jay shrugs. The room is darkly moonlit, the screen painting the side of his head an eerie, bluish white. With her in it, the space is boxy, fat beams slanting at all angles and edges jutting from nowhere. Books upon mangas upon memorabilia. You couldn't swing a tadpole for fear of destruction.

'Didn't think you'd freak out,' he says. 'I don't hear everything, and I try to block a lot, but your thoughts are so *loud*.'

Kira's face warms. 'And that means you know what freaks me out?'

'No.' He swivels on the chair again, his round face falling into shadow. 'It means I get an idea of what won't, considering everything you're trying not to think about. You're, like, covering it all with pictures of actors.'

The warmth in Kira's cheeks rises. 'Great.'

Jay lifts his shoulders: *why not?* 'It means I can't see it, which is probably good, but I get this idea of craziness.' He swishes his hands through the air, like the craziness in question is a roaming fireball. 'What I *have* seen, though, are all the other things, the things you let yourself think about. What you're going to do next, and Callum, and your sister, who I know my mum put to sleep.' He thickens his accent into his mother's. '"She was exhausted."' He huffs. 'Sure, she was. And…'

He opens his mouth, shuts it, and looks away.

Kira puckers her forehead. 'What?' Silence. Jay shifts in his seat. 'What, Jay?'

Jay's eyes dart to hers. 'In Mum's head,' he says. 'And yours. I've seen…' He hesitates incrementally. 'Whiteland.'

Kira's body stills. Whiteland does it, every time, like smoothing the head of a beer. Jay knows close to everything, from her head and Carol's. Whiteland, and all that comes with it. How is he so…fine?

'I told you.' A yawn muffles his answer to wool. 'When people's minds think things are normal, you start thinking they're normal, too. Like…' Jay tilts his rumpled head. 'Like if you grew up and your mum licked her toes every hour. It'd be weird, but also kind of ordinary.'

Kira smiles, small. 'That's a pretty good analogy.' Her own words become a yawn. Rolling over, she curls up to face him. 'All the things you'll know, though. Things that people think are private.' She tucks her hands under her cheek. 'Do you—'

She breaks off. *He's only twelve,* part of her says. *He's opened up,* the rest argues. 'Do you know a lot about Whiteland?'

Jay smiles sleepily. 'Quite a lot, yeah.' He stretches wide, with a satisfied grunt. 'When Callum's here, he thinks about it. It, you, the quest, repeat.' He twirls a finger. 'It's kind of good, though. It means I know the reasons for what happened last year.'

Leaning over, he shuts down his computer. 'Like Callum coming with me?' Kira asks. He'll see it in her head anyway. 'To Whiteland?'

'Yeah.' Jay switches off his monitor. 'The excuses for that? Wow. And Lena? The trip to Croatia? I got a three-day sleepover, so I didn't care, but it all makes so much *sense*.' He stretches again, intent and catlike. 'I like understanding. Eleven and nearly thirteen are pretty different.'

He glances down at her. Kira nods into the musty pillow. 'You do seem a lot older.'

'Thank you.' He tilts his head. Whatever her mind confirms, he smiles, and gives her a double thumbs-up. The urge to bristle sparks, and dies. At least she knows he's in her head; think of all the people that *don't*.

'Exactly.'

Kira narrows her eyes at him. 'I can retract that acceptance.' She wriggles down in the wolfy duvet. Finally, she's getting tired. 'Please go back to last year.'

As smug as Callum, as chuffed as can be. 'Okay.' He grins. 'I was a bit like the twins are now.' He waves at the wall of their room. 'None of this bothers them at all. Two strange girls and their wonderful Callum, turning up and making Mum angry? But *pizza*.'

He bugs his eyes. Kira huffs. 'Wise. Yoda. Savvy.'

Jay clicks his fingers at her. 'With all the secrets I hear, you shouldn't be surprised. At school, on the train, in the village…'

'No, thank you.' Squirming, she smushes her face in the pillow. 'I really don't need to know. If it was me, I'd end up hating humanity. Either that, or howling at the moon.'

'Oh, but *Kira*,' Jay says. 'How else would I know about my German teacher's drunkenness?' His voice is the deliberate picture of youth. 'If you're lucky, he does a Jesus on the lake. Or pole dances with streetlamps.'

'Gross.' Kira screws up her face. 'But whatever floats your weird little boat.' She wriggles onto her side again. 'It'll get you through lessons, at least. But what did you mean when you said…?'

She stops. He's twelve. She should let it lie.

'About Callum?' Getting up, Jay skirts her air mattress. 'I literally know what you're thinking, even if you're hiding behind it. It's like a captcha.' Opening the window, he latches the blinds. 'And I didn't say it because I've read his mind.'

Closing the window, he skirts around her to the door. The moonlit night has gone, shrouding them in gloom. Kira hesitates. Her heart is inching up her throat. 'Then why did you?'

Fingers on the doorknob, Jay pauses. 'I guess…' He frowns. 'I guess because he's not had a girlfriend since he met you. Which is insane. He wasn't like a player, but he used to have a lot. Oh, and he says he never got over someone. It's you.'

Kira's heart drops away. Suddenly, she's grateful for the dark; her face feels like it's simmering to a boil. 'It's not.'

'It is.' Jay opens the door. '*That* I know because I've read his mind, along with the whole feasible thing. You were different in his head before today, but it's you. And not because you're some kind of siren.'

He snorts. Kira curls her toes. Never mind a boil; she's on fire.

'Go on the internet,' Jay continues. 'Google it. Anything anywhere will tell you: that kind of feeling goes away with the siren.' He shrugs. 'No, he's in love. With you.'

He pads away down the hall. Uncoiling her body, Kira shakes her head.

The padding stops. 'You think he barely knows you?'

Kira shuts her eyes. God, this is crazy. 'Maybe.'

'You thought it, though.' Jay's voice, calling quietly, holds more of Callum than ever. 'This is what I think.' Kira opens her eyes to him arranging his fingers in the shape of a photo frame. 'After what happened to both of you, he probably knows you best.'

The bathroom door clicks shut behind him. *He probably knows you best.*

Echoes after echoes, riddling her mind. *That kind of feeling goes away with the siren. He probably knows you best.*

And the one she edges around, that's the craziest of all. *No, he's in love. With you.*

By the time Jay comes back, she's asleep. He smirks; her dreams are out already, like sunset clouds, immersive, vivid, swirling. He could easily watch them, but he won't. Discarding his jeans, Jay clambers into bed. She believed him. She didn't act like an all-knowing adult (which is such a stupid front; adults have power, but not a lot of knowledge), and really, it's not worth it. People's dreams are meaningless.

Once or twice, when he was angry, he watched his mother's dreams. Once: people filing through a room, disturbing her on the toilet. Twice: choosing a sandwich in a shop. It took forever, and he hasn't watched since.

Callum's were even worse. He dreamt about documents full of assignments, or kittens he wanted to catch and bring home. Grinning in the dark, Jay fumbles for his phone. He's pinched himself so many times, holding back jokes about kittens. Two ginger fluffballs, evading Callum's grasp, making him growl in despair…

Kira sighs in sleep. As Jay loads 9GAG, he can't resist a peek. Pictures, like thoughts, are easy when they're loud; and Kira is so, so loud. She probably has no idea—why would she?—but if all he's learned about Whiteland is true, it's not surprising how easily it got in her head.

For a second, or two, or three, he watches. Kira, on a stretch of snow. A woman fading away.

The image flickers, and changes: Kira, running through a funfair. A funfair, then a forest, and suddenly, she's flying. Leaping into the air and soaring through the trees, past fields of narcissi and mountain peaks, until she reaches a cottage.

'What took you so long?' a friend is asking. 'You should have taken the Tube.'

Pretty, nonsensical, and vibrant, the dreams lull Jay to sleep.

19

The sun

'Hey.'

The voice accompanies a hand on her shoulder, Kira's least favourite wake-up. 'Mmm,' she mumbles, and wriggles away. Her brain wants oh-so-much to dally: she was skiing in the glittering Himalayas, with each ski pulled by a Pomeranian and each Pomeranian dressed in skis. 'Mmm. I'm sleeping.'

'That wasn't English, and I don't speak Dothraki. Wake up.'

Kira unsticks her grainy eyes. She's already far too awake. 'Not fair,' she groans. The room is bleary. Her head is fog. 'What d'you want, Callum? Beautiful. Beautiful sleep.'

'I'm sure it was,' the voice says, and suddenly, she's moving. Kira grunts. It's like stopping the world from spinning when you've had too much to drink: dizzy, unpleasant, and completely unnecessary. 'You're awake.' The hand becomes an arm, a vice round her waist. 'It's okay. I want to show you something.'

The wolf duvet drops away, along with her tangled blankets. Cold air rushes in, and she shivers. 'No wonder you've not had a girlfriend lately.' Kira's grumble comes out thick. 'Is this how you treat them? Like dug-up cadavers?'

Carefully, Callum guides her from the room. 'Not as far as I'm aware.'

Kira stubs her toe on the doorframe. 'Dammit. Victorian doctors, Callum.'

'What?'

'You're taking me to…' She flaps a limp hand. 'I don't know. It's the dead of *night*.'

Just as well she doesn't sleep naked.

He was probably hoping she did.

'It's not.' Callum holds her steady on the floorboards. The stairs loom daunting in her groggy eyes. 'And I'm sorry for the manhandling, but you'll miss it if we don't go now. I only just had the idea.' On the top step, he hesitates. 'Trust me. It'll be worth it.'

Will it, though? she wonders, thumping her hazy way downstairs. She was happy. She was living the dream. Kira smiles, blurry. Literally.

'You can't wear those.' In the grey-blue lounge, Callum nods at her shoes. Canvas, flowered, and totally useless. Kira shrugs. It doesn't matter. She'd rather adopt the Pomeranians, or at least go back and try.

'What does Mr. Explorer suggest?' She yawns. Stretching, she yawns again, rubbing clogs of sleep-muck out of her eyes. 'Shock me with your—your—' A third yawn, cavernous. 'Wisdom. Yoda.'

Callum shoots her derision. '"Shock me with your Yoda."' He shakes his head, looking around. 'You're witty in the mornings. Let's not get started on "Mr. Explorer." Aha.' He delves into the shoes by the door, retrieving two fat snow boots. 'Wear these.'

'Mmm.' Kira stretches again, squinting at the sofa. Romy's sleep looks fit for kings. Hair splayed like Sleeping Beauty, her pale face smooth, serene. What's more, Callum's blankets lie mussed on the floor, fuzzy and crooking a finger. They're *there*. So *close*. If only she could crawl in, and rejoin the dogs. Callum can come, too, if he wants. She's not fussy.

'Kira.' He taps her shoulder.

She turns to him with a pout. 'What?'

'You can't wear that denim thing, either. Take this.' He pulls down a ski jacket.

Black and dwarfing her, she pulls it on. She's clearly not going to win.

'Okay.' Callum fastens the nebula coat, running a hand through his hair. You couldn't calm it with a tranq gun. Kira stamps into the beasts of blue, using the wall as a prop. Through another yawn, she smiles. He's like a dog himself. 'Away.'

The morning is blue, shadowed, and blank, brushing light behind the mountains. Nighttime fog sinks into the valley. They could be floating away in a cloudland, lost on a misty sea. Everything silent. Everything still. Everything frozen and bright. She burrows into the coat. Every breath is an image in the air, and the morning frost, crisp and crunching, sparkles over the snow. It's the kind of postcard winter that you don't expect to exist.

And the kind of cold that shouldn't. Outside the tiny train stop, Kira bounces on the balls of her feet. Callum's gloves are beautifully warm, but still, her fingertips tingle. Really, everything tingles; the winter might have woken her up, but its pale-blue air is piercing. She'd forgotten how icy, how sharp and clear, the world up here could be. Its magic takes her breath, but she'd love to run for the hills.

'Late.' Stamping his feet, Callum shoves back his sleeve, wiping mist from his watch. The light behind the peaks is spreading from cream-tinged white to streaks of orange, lifting with dreamy speed. 'I bet,' he says, sighing. 'It's Guillaume. He's always late. Aha!'

Down the line, the train tracks whir. He grins. 'Speak of the French.'

He turns his grin on her. 'Where are we going?' Kira asks, slow, numb, impatient. He can look as smug as he likes, but she's freezing to rigor mortis. 'I can't feel my mouth.' She frowns. 'Also, I don't have a ticket.'

Callum's laugh is a bursting 'ha!'

'What?' Kira throws out her arms. 'Can I not enjoy legality?'

The little train trundles, whirring and whining. Stepping close, Callum bends to her ear. 'Live dangerously,' he whispers, and it heats her like a touch.

The trundling stops. The doors creak open. Winking, he hops up the steps.

Kira's chest is a shiver. Ducking her head to hide her cheeks, she follows him onto the train.

It must be a hundred years old. Taking a seat by the radiator, she sceptically looks around. It's rustic, rectangular, cute, quaint…but as an elderly man, it'd walk bowlegged, carry two canes, and totter off the tracks.

'I was right.' Callum cranes his neck toward the cabin. 'It was Guillaume. Therefore'—he glances back, as smug as a cat—'and as I told Romy when she complained, I'll trade tickets for chocolate.'

'Callum?' the driver calls.

Callum tips his head back. *'Ouais?'* He sidles into the cabin. *'Salut.'* Callum switches into fluid French. Kira rests her head against the window, watching the glass mist up with her breath. Eight again on car journeys, she traces a smiling face.

Through the eyes, Callum's house creaks by. Through the mouth, unknown chalets, volcanoes of firewood, towering trees. A fox streaks past. The ski slopes are closed, and he bounds across them, vibrant against the snow. Kira smiles.

The cogwheels groan. The glass mists over a second time, reducing the vanishing fox to a smear. Yawning, Kira looks elsewhere. Her eyes land on a sign: *100 ANS*. What?

She peers closer, as though that'll help, but the title doesn't lie. *100 ANS: 1911–2011*. Years. 100 years. Unease pokes out its wormy head. Great. Great, great, great. Her scepticism was justified, and should be applauded; tacked beside the cabin is a poster, and above a photo of the train itself, mooching through a glory of autumn, this fact is proclaimed with pride.

Kira pushes out her lips. Her elderly man was correct; this cute, rustic rectangle has lived for a hundred years. More. Smooth, wooden insides, small, wooden compartments. As much as she loves the old, the scenic, the *real*, she'd prefer it to be safer. Wobbles, moans, and creaks…how does it cope in a storm?

Kira dashes the hurricane from her mind. She'll never find out. No way in hell. It's one thing to live dangerously; a danger-free death, in an antique train crash, after all that's happened, is a step too far.

Mercifully, the ride is short. A few minutes later, silently relieved, Kira follows the men from the train. It wasn't as bad as the gargoyle—that steep, tilting, god-awful hulk that masked itself as a chairlift—but getting back on? Not a chance. She'd rather wait a lifetime for puppies pulling skis.

'Forward march,' Callum announces, as soon as Kira's boots touch snow. Catching Guillaume's eye, he salutes. '*Chocolat, je te promets.* À *tout.*'

'*À tout.*' The bearded man checks the station clock, grinning and lighting up. His trilby is slightly too small for his head.

Turning to Callum, Kira bites back a smile. 'Where are we going?' she asks. If you're wearing a hat, just wear it. Don't perch it on your head like an egg-and-spoon race.

'Just up here.' Callum wanders away, toward a low, snowy hill. 'Not far.'

Warily, Kira follows. 'I'm not getting on the chairlift,' she says, as he leads her around the dark-wood station. 'Just putting that out there. It was, believe it or not, the least fun.'

Trudging up the slope, Callum laughs. 'You refused last time, if you recall. It didn't go that well.' He reaches the top, turns around, and spreads his hands at the world. 'Behold.'

Hands on her thighs, Kira climbs up beside him. 'I've been learning Krav Maga.' She lets out her hitching breath. This mountain is far too hilly. 'I can fight back better than—'

Her words steal back down her throat. She's been here before.

The mountain's summit is flat. It's an outdoor exhibition, weather-beaten models of the solar system, and memory ghosts across her mind: she and Romy, swinging on the sun.

It's huge, and it looks like a climbing frame. Romy pointed this out with a shrug, adding that they wouldn't find a better one for adults; Kira was hook, line, and sold. They swung like children while Mathew perused, peering through telescopes and studying maps. Anna sniffed out the restaurant.

And Kira had forgotten. It was early on in the holiday, and while Romy hadn't abused in months, their parents watched her beer like falcons. *I'll live here,* she said, with one of her rare, glittering smiles. *None of this waiting to turn eighteen. Find me a shack in the woods and I'll stay.*

She very nearly did. Kira blinks, but the holographic images linger. Later, Romy redeemed herself, neatly returning to normal: growing angry at something small, storming off and camping out to fume and watch TV. She refused to speak to anyone, faking a love of football for back-to-back games, but up here, she'd been chirpy, alive. Smirking at her beer and swinging on the sun. Sadly, faintly, Kira smiles. For once, her sister had had fun.

The image fades, to shadows, ghosts. Romy, hanging upside down, trying to cover her stomach; Kira herself, sat on a pole, dizzily flipping around.

'Are you beholding?' Callum asks, bobbing once on the balls of his feet. The orange sun is on her left, now, a play park on her right. He stands with his hands in his pockets. 'My personal magic trick won't last.'

The last of the past pales. 'Sorry,' Kira murmurs. Trailing his gaze instead of her memories, she stills.

The morning's on fire.

Her breath flies away. Behind the peaks, the sun lifts up, streaking the horizon, the snow, the sky. Colour. Light. Winded and wondering, Kira stares. The creamy orange has billowed and bloomed; washes of crimson bathe the snow, in swathes of amber, butter, rose. The blue has burnt up, the civil twilight exploding at dawn, and standing before it, they're small.

Dark specks on the mountainside. Pink-cheeked, and nothing.

'Wow.' Kira shakes her head. 'Definitely worth it.'

The comment is quiet, meant for herself, but the morning is soft and still. Watching the sky, Callum nods. 'I thought it would be.' He crooks a smile. 'Is the gallant Mr. Explorer forgiven? Does he get a cookie? A star?'

Tearing her eyes from the sunrise, Kira looks around. 'He gets…' Her gaze lands on the play park. Perfect. 'A slap for methodology, but a Flake for results.' She starts across the snow. 'Maybe an extra pinch, for the jokes.'

'My jokes are top of the range.'

'They're not.' Heading for the climbing frame, Kira grins. A hoist, a jump, and she settles herself, wriggling onto a platform. The metal is ice…but the vista is hers.

Also, she gets to sit down. She's still not reached full charge.

'Trying to pretend we're not short?' Callum saunters over to join her. Kira bats at him. 'Sadly'—he dances out of the way—'we still have T. rex arms.'

Kira's kick falls short of his back.

'And legs.' Balanced on his toes, he bends his elbows, flopping his hands at the wrists.

'We do not.' Kira rolls her eyes. 'And that looks more like a meerkat.'

Callum snorts. 'Fine.' With a T. rex flourish, he drops the act. 'I wake you up to show you a sunrise, and you won't let me dream I'm extinct. You're a monster.'

Kira bats at him again. 'A monster,' she says, as he leans out of reach, 'who does not have T. rex arms.' Brushing the sleeve of his coat with her boot, she sits back. 'There. Satisfied. Did you have a reason for showing me a sunrise?'

The words skip inside her, but as nonchalant as possible, Kira looks back to the sky. *Live dangerously,* he told her. It flustered her then, and flusters her now, swooping through her chest like anxiety, or hope. They're alone, on top of a mountain. He brought her here at dawn. She needs to speak. She needs to act.

Callum leans back against the climbing frame. 'What would be your theory?' he asks, tilting his head toward her. His tone bounces slightly: he knows exactly what she thinks, and they both know where this will go.

Kira pretends to consider. Her brain is flitting with moths now, fluttering down to her belly. 'Oddly executed romantic gesture?' She throws him a teasing look. The moths are a murmuration. 'Sorry to break it to you, but the dinosaur lets it down.'

'You cut it off in its prime.' Callum smirks, tutting through the peeling bars. 'My stegosaurus is killer. Even *married women*'—he taps her knee—'the most loyal of wives, no less, fall at my feet when they witness its charms. It's not my fault you're immune.'

Only to the dinosaurs, is Kira's first thought.

Nothing's changed, is her second. Sarcasm. Stupidity. She gazes at the blazing sky, wrestling with herself. The fire has spread to fill her vision. The iris of the sun peeks over the mountains, a peacock, kaleidoscopic, breaking into day. For the first time in months, her artist's mind clicks. Sunrises are overdone, but this, she has to paint.

From its beauty, she decides.

'Callum.' Kira lifts her chin. If Jay was having her on…

Arms folded, he inclines his head. 'Yes?'

Live dangerously. 'Come here.'

Callum snorts. 'Yes, ma'am.' Pushing himself away from the bars, he places himself before her. 'Better?'

Kira's stomach twists. She's hot inside. 'Much.'

'Good.' Resting his hands on the rusty platform, he tilts his head like a puppy. His thumbs brush her thighs. For once, he's barely taller. 'And how may I be of assistance?'

He meets her eyes, his eyebrows raised. He knows full well.

Live dangerously.

Leaning in to catch his collar, Kira kisses him.

It's clumsy, he's not really close enough, and for a plunging second, she thinks she was wrong. He doesn't react. If anything, he stiffens, and she lets him go.

'No.' This time, he's fast. Taking her face in his hands, Callum pulls her toward him. 'No.'

He kisses her.

Her body burns. Her hands turn to arms around his neck, her legs wrapping round him as he moves in closer. She could lose herself. Could, can, will; his fingers grip her waist, tangle in her hair, holding her fast, and her breath grows short. Everything slowing, deepening, thrilling, heat rising like the fiery sky. Stopping isn't possible. Kira digs her fingers into his shoulder blades, gripping him tighter, tighter. The burn spills through her body, her mind.

Her mind. Her body. Her *body*. The press of him is maddening, kissing so they sigh. A low moan escapes his throat. Her leggings are flimsy. His jeans—

Abruptly, Callum pulls back. 'I can't…'

He ducks his head. Kira's everything is racing. 'Can't what?' she manages. Body, mind, burn, *need*.

Sliding his hands up her arms, Callum grip her shoulders. 'We...' He shakes his head. Breathing ragged, eyes like sparks. 'If we carry on, it...'

No, no, *no*. 'I know.' Shakily, she rests her forehead on his. 'I know.' Dragging herself away from him, Kira sits up. The racing everything aches to continue, to lean back in, to kiss him hard, but, 'It's a children's play park.'

Brushing back her hair, she drags in a breath. Uneven, sheepish, smiling. The new space between them is sharp and cold.

'Yeah.' Callum scrapes a hand over his head. Taking in the frozen swings, the frosted slide, the monkey bars, he huffs a wavering laugh. 'Yeah. Um. Jesus. You...'

Kira bows her head in penance. 'You did ask how you could help.' She peeks up at him, under her lashes. 'It would have been rude to disappoint.'

He stares at her. 'You...' A laugh bursts out, incredulous. He shakes his head. 'You're full of wonders. If we ever get any privacy, you'll have all the help you want.'

In his pocket, his phone starts to quack. With his eyes lingering on her, shooting heat from her chest to her thighs, he fumbles in his pocket. 'Hello?' He listens. 'Ah.'

With a rush of foreboding, Kira knows what's coming. 'What is it?' she mouths.

Callum's forehead creases. 'Not good,' he mouths back. 'Okay,' he says into the phone. 'We're coming back.'

He hangs up. Warily, Kira watches him. Her heat is draining fast. 'We have to go.' He grimaces. 'Romy's woken up.'

20

Repeat

From the other side of the field, Freya watches them go. She has to leave, herself; she didn't come back to be a third wheel to erotica.

Being first wheel wouldn't be too bad. In the three days she's been out, Callum is by far the most attractive man she's seen. Not that she's been looking at men for their aesthetics…but it helps. Assessing thoughts is so much nicer when the faces that hide them are pretty.

Sadly, Callum's mind has sentries. Kira's, though…her guards are dead. Freya's lips twitch. How easy it is to crack Kira's head, to pluck out what the women need. Once they found her in her little white house, it was a walk through an open door. Pinpoint her mind in an *augenblick*, extract her memories of Romy. Even then, behind it all, she sang to the tune of Callum.

Freya stood in the snow and listened. Pluck, appear as Rosemarie. Pluck, a song that links them both, and Taika worked her magic. Pluck, file Callum away for later, and crack his mind in person.

Along with everyone else. *Sorry to bother you, sir, but would you mind if I stayed the night?* Eye contact, sparking irises. The man stepped back to let her in, and never spoke a word.

Repeat by the road, in shops, on trains. *No, I'm afraid I don't have a ticket; no, I won't be paying for that.* Eye contact, sparking irises. *Oh, could you give me a ride?*

Think of it all as a kind of magic. We have ours; the outside has theirs.

This is what the voices hiss at anything unknown. God, the noise, the fouled land. The number of people, living in boxes, travelling in more. Buying things, looking pretty. Talking to the air. The bags of food she's bargained for, and vomited back up. Burgers, chips, and acid drinks. Nothing in them was real. Her gut scrambled and died.

How did Anneliese do it? She left their world alone. No whispered guidelines, no instructions. Freya would go insane.

Freedom. She came to this conclusion, stooping in the dark, as her insides cramped and pulsed. Anneliese craved freedom more than any other life, so she dug herself in and survived. Freya was small when Anneliese escaped, but she grew up on the stories: Anneliese fought from the day she was born.

Born and abandoned, left in the snow. Solveig found her caterwauling, and brought her to the village. Once she got older, and realised they were ostracised, she itched for retribution, vindication. Life.

Freedom. Freedom, freedom, freedom. Listening incessantly to tales of how to get it, until, at seventeen, she started her own. She did what others tried to resist. She killed.

And she liked it.

Freya started for freedom, some form of excitement, and the gratification of beating the world. No, she's never burned like Anneliese, but Taika and the Kyo meant free reign. Seduce, kill, repeat. Men were a dark-lit passion, and the Huldra rage with violence. When the Kyo roped her in, it was perfect.

Men still have their pull. The rage, though…it's only been three days, but the longer she's human, the more the rest is vile. Her ruthlessness, her wicked pleasure. Away from the wilds of being a beast, a reviled, ruined monster, she sees what others did. She didn't when she killed in Holland, but her mutation is fast.

Everything is waning. Manipulation is hard. Mild persuasion is doable, along with easy minds, but where the echoes were loud, now they're like whispers. Even Kira, the braying mule, will soon return to silence. She's losing her abilities, and losing herself.

They said, at the end, that Anneliese was weak. Maybe this is what they meant.

Watching Kira and Callum, though, weakness could be worse. If she's becoming human; if she can live as Anneliese did, with a husband, two daughters, and an uninhibited existence; if she can have what these two have, then does her monster matter? Once everything is over, she'll be free. She can brush away the past, learn from Anneliese, and never, ever go back.

She has to hurry up, though. Freya shifts in the snow, numbing in the cold. If she's mutating this fast, the end result could scupper the part she has to play. Either that, or the whispering women will drive her to despair. They never stop talking. *Never.*

In silence, Freya stands. Kira and Callum are trudging off, down the hill to the train line. With a smirk for their thwarted lust, Freya heads the other way. Her jeans are soaked. Her hands are a bruise, an unhappy human colour. She pushes them under her shirt to her stomach, slipping away through the snow. Under the eaves of Karliquai, she'll focus, eat, and rest; this morning won't see violence.

Later, though, Callum will die.

21

Tell me the tales of old

Traversing the icy railway tracks, she had to concede that the way up would have been nothing short of lethal. Snow has buried the path to hedge height, and walking on the line, as Callum pointed out, would have meant being squashed by Guillaume.

He thinks he's on the home stretch when he gets to this point. Callum settled into a determined impression, hunched in a fictional cabin. *Wild and free, a horse on the plains, that guy on the bus in* Speed—

Then the chaos caught them. For a moment, they stared, stopped literally in their tracks, and now, Kira's insides are gnarling.

'I mean…' She lifts an aimless hand. She can't tear her eyes from the chalet, the way she'd watch an oddly acting dog. 'I know you said Karl was upset, but…'

Callum rocks back on his heels. 'Yeah.' His face would suggest the dog is rabid. 'I thought he was overreacting.'

'Clearly not.' Kira glances at him sidelong. 'You said you heard arguing? This is not arguing. This'—she waves a hand at the chalet—'is full-on war.'

Leaving the trenches, all guns blazing. Nothing quiet on the Western Front. Arguing? The Battle of Carol and Romy doesn't know the meaning of the word.

'Goody.' Callum narrows his eyes. The voices echo and clash. 'I think we should have told her the truth last night.'

Kira flashes her eyebrows. 'Too late for that.' Extending her arms for balance, she continues down the line. 'Your village grapevine will quiver with joy. Again.'

'Don't worry.' Callum jogs, unsteadily, to catch her up. 'We've dealt with scratchy-bitey. We can handle a bit of rage.'

At the crossing with the road, Kira stops. 'Scratchy-bitey.' Deliberate and slow, she turns. Her voice is as flat as her gaze. 'Really, Callum? You studied philosophy. Where are your lofty words? Your'—she slips, and Callum's arm shoots out—'esoteric ideas?'

'Define them, my dear, and I'll let you know. Up.' He hoists her off the line, through a patch of knee-deep snow. 'And down.' He lowers her onto a stepping stone. She barely had time to inhale. 'I'll give you some good words.' He motions for her to go ahead of him, through the arcing hedge. 'Joviality.'

In the sun-streaked garden, Kira glances back. She should be annoyed at being manhandled, but he's just so *Callum*. So *here*, in his frosted, breeze-blown village, somehow keeping her sane. 'That's not that good a word.'

Callum shrugs. 'It serves a purpose.' He shoves his hands in his pockets. 'It's a bit of a shit segue, but I've been wanting to say it for a while. Don't think my joviality means I'm taking this as a joke.'

Surprised, Kira cuts back her humour. If their habits were reversed, he'd be fiddling with his sleeves. 'I don't. I don't think that.'

Callum looks away, his eyes tight. 'Good.' He sighs, and looks back. 'Good. Because from what you and Romy have said, it's really fucking scary.' He shrugs. 'All of it. You know. But if we don't joke, or forget for a while, our minds will end up scarier.'

Inside Kira's chest, something twinges. Drawbridge down, open gates; offering her a serious smile, it's the frankest he's looked.

'It's why I took you up the mountain.' Closing the distance between them, Callum brushes her shoulder. 'I know I'm on the verge of sounding very unmanly, but I felt like you needed a reminder. The world can be revolting'—he kisses her forehead—'but it can also be pretty as hell.'

Up above them, the battle pitches. 'I see what you mean.' Putting her arms around him, Kira leans into his chest. 'Thank you. For the sunrise *and* the unjovial philosophy.' She squeezes him. 'They're both kind of pretty as hell.'

Pulling back, she musters a rueful smile. His face creases into a frown. 'It's a compliment.' She taps his arm. 'And I'm the king of brooding, so I get it. I don't know whether you've noticed, but I'm trying to follow your lead.' She lifts one shoulder, dropping it slowly. 'I never thought you weren't taking anything seriously. If we were constantly serious, then yes. We'd be worse inside than out.'

Inside the chalet, someone bursts into tears. Kira flinches. 'Oh, dear god.'

She makes to carry on, but Callum grabs her wrist. 'Hey.'

'What?' Kira glances back, bracing for the bedlam.

Callum lets her go. 'We've come across worse.'

Arching one eyebrow, Kira lowers the other.

'We have!' Callum spreads his hands. 'I refuse to indulge your idiocy, but I will say this: "Whiteland."' He brackets the word with his fingers. 'On the scale of what we've been up against, two angry women don't chart.'

The crying steps up to a wail. Kira nods at the chalet with a wince of her lips. 'And that?'

Callum thins his lips. A door slams. 'That sounds a lot like Julia.'

They head inside in silence. The voices rage from the kitchen, and the kitchen door is shut. 'You find Julia.' Kira sighs, hanging her coat on an overflowing peg. Muffled now and gulping, the crying has moved upstairs. 'I'll go see what's happened. Once more unto the—'

'No.' Callum stops her before she can enter the fray. 'You find Julia'—he nods at the kitchen—'and I'll tackle the breach.'

His strange dog expression is a copy of hers. 'Why?' Kira frowns, watching him eye the door. 'Surely that's the wrong way round.'

'Not…if you think about it.' Scratching his head, Callum lets her go. 'Romy's woken up knowing that you've lied to her for a year. What's more, you've lied about something huge, and listening to her, she's furious.' He angles his head at the kitchen. 'You going in there might make it worse, but if you go hug Julia—in case you haven't noticed, she loves hugs—by the time you see Romy, she'll have hopefully calmed down. I can talk to her.' He glances at Diego, snorting in sleep on the makeshift lounge-floor bed. 'She has no grounds on which to hate me.'

Kira hesitates. Run upstairs, go, go, go. 'Are you sure?' she hedges. 'You're really willing to bare your throat?'

Callum nods. 'Absolutely.' With a smile, his look turns sheepish. 'And as much as I love my surrogate sister, I'm lost when it comes to comforting kids.'

That's enough. Heading up the stairs, Kira tries for sombre over relief. It's cowardice to run from facing her sister, but Romy's fury is a landslide. A forest fire, a runaway train. No tail doesn't mean no monster.

She's known it in herself. It's awful to admit to, and barely occasional, but its ugly maw is there.

Flash. Sports Day, year five, when a girl elbowed her out of the way so she could overtake. Her mother looked shell-shocked, pale and wordless, when Kira started to scream. Fists balled at the finish line. Her throat felt razed for days.

Flash. A time when Kira was younger, vowing in detail to butcher the seagull that flew off with her chips.

Flash. She was fourteen, she'd gone to a party, and the punishment for a sip of beer seemed way too harsh. (Even if it was three sips, or most of two pints.)

Flash. Slapping Callum with all her might, for no reason at all. Something may have been messing with her mind…but she'll never know for sure.

Romy's anger is far more rational than hers has ever been. It's uneasy, a disquieting flutter, and as Kira pauses on the landing to listen, she shuffles it under the rug. Jay's door is shut, patterned with stickers. The twins' is the same, with *KARL* and *JULIA* in spaceship decals. The crying is coming from the bathroom.

Forcing her face into optimism, Kira opens the door. She's not the best with kids, but she'll try.

Julia, clad in a Star Wars nightdress, sits in the bath and cries.

'Hey.' Kira drops to her knees at once. Clutching her legs to her chest, the little girl is shaking. 'Hey, Julia, hey. What's wrong?' Reaching for Julia's buried face, she brushes the hair from her temples. It's wet and hot, her skin pink. 'Julia? What's happened?'

Julia shakes her head. One-two-three, frenetic. 'Okay.' Resting her chin on her hand, Kira rests her hand on the bath. 'That's okay.' She squeezes Julia's shoulder, rubbing with her thumb. The girl smells sharp and acrid, and she fights the urge to grimace. 'You don't have to. Just as long as you're all right.'

One-two-three-FOUR, frenetic, fervent, dizzy. Without lifting her head, Julia points at the door.

A thrill of fear fizzes through Kira. Knocking her chin on the bath, she whips her head around.

Nothing. The dim hall, windowless and cramped.

Windowless, cramped, and empty. 'You want the door closed?' Kira guesses, after a close, peering scrutiny. This near to Whiteland, she can't be too paranoid. 'Okay.' She heaves herself up.

Julia looks up. 'I don't want anyone to see,' she mumbles, as Kira shuts the door. Her voice is thick and woollen, an almost-Scottish lilt. Returning to the cold tiles, Kira's heart pangs. Julia's eyes have puffed like beestings, her hair sodden and stuck to her face. This is breakup crying, or witnessing-murders crying; it's absolutely not chubby-children crying.

'See what?' Kira asks, peeling away more tear-damp hair. 'You crying? Do you want me to go, too?'

Sniffing, Julia wipes her nose. 'No.' She shakes her head once.' I don't want anyone *else* to see.'

She lifts her hot palm, damp on Kira's cheek. Kira's eyes flicker dark, flicker out, and she sees.

It's a film reel, vertigo, falling into the Pensieve. Julia woke to Callum clumping Kira down the stairs. She lay for a while, trying to sleep, but the sound of the rumbling train, and Karl's tossing and turning—more like thumping and bumping—was too much. She slipped into her slippers and shuffled downstairs.

She was hoping for a hot chocolate, and maybe a packet of pancakes. She wasn't expecting a woman on the table.

Sitting cross-legged, the woman was twisting the top off a big glass bottle. Julia knew her fast enough, the woman from the sofa, but for a skipping second, she was scared. Sleeping people look different, and being up alone makes her chew on her hair *without* strange people around. The gloomy chalet seems gloomier; the fireplace could be hiding boggarts. Tomtes, even though they're friendly, might be snickering by the door. Sometimes the garden is scary, too, depending on how dark it is; the front could be home to goblins, dancing round the rowan. The back—

'Morning,' the woman said, and Julia jumped. 'You're around early.'

She glanced up. Her face was round, all carved in lines from trying to open the bottle. What was her name? Rosie? No. Something new. 'Um.' Julia nibbled her finger. Romy. That was it.

'Aha!' Victorious, Romy dropped the bottle top, pouring the liquid down her throat. Julia watched in a kind of awe. No stranger had ever come to the house and sat up on the table. No strangers came at all.

'What's that?' she asked, pointing to the bottle. Coughing quietly, Romy pulled a series of ghastly faces. 'It doesn't look very nice.'

Red like a ruby, the bottle seemed to glow. 'Astute little thing, aren't you?' Romy held it up, peering at its contents. 'And it's Pure Hell.' She swallowed another mouthful. 'Ah.' A sharp exhale. 'Yet at the same time, it's beautiful. Come sit.'

She patted the table. Julia hesitated. She could drown her pancakes in treacle, make her hot chocolate, and go watch *PJ Masks*—but this woman was far more interesting. She had a twisted, angry face that didn't exist when she was asleep, and she was sizing Julia up with cold blue eyes. She could be the Snow Queen, or Elsa; she was *exciting*. Kicking her feet up onto a chair, leaning back on one hand, tipping the Pure Hell into her mouth; exciting, exciting, exciting. Retrieving the treacle-less pancakes, Julia hopped up to join her.

'Want some?' she asked.

Romy raised an eyebrow. 'Sure,' she said, with a shrug. 'Thanks. You know'—she wagged her new snack in the air—'you're the best person that could have walked in. Kira's an *unbelievable* liar. Callum annoys me to the moon and back, even if his lies'—she crammed the pancake into her mouth—'aren't as shameful. That woman, who I now know isn't your mum, because your—'

She stopped like a statue. Julia blinked. 'My?'

'Never mind.' Unfreezing, Romy waved a hand, drinking again from Hell. 'Whoever she is, that woman put me to sleep and gave me a creepy-ass dream. No, a *wonderfully informative* dream.' She curled her lips. 'Forgive my Freudian slip. But you—you're an innocent little chicken.' She patted Julia's head. 'You want pancakes and to sit on the table. After the nightmare I've just woken up from, the nightmare that oh, how delightful, is shifting around up there into memory, you're the cliché breath of fresh air.'

Julia smiled around her pancake. Most of that didn't make sense, but Romy seemed to like her. 'What nightmare did—'

'Imagine finding out you've been lied to for a year.' Romy interrupted as if she hadn't heard. Her mouth distorted in dour disbelief. 'And the lie is so colossal—so appalling'—she threw her arms wide, the bottle sloshing—'that you can't believe it exists. Not only that, but it's been hidden for so long. For a *year*. Can you imagine that?' She bugged her eyes. 'For me?'

Julia stuffed the rest of the crumbly pancake into her mouth. It really could do with treacle, or Ovomaltine spread. 'Yes,' she replied, in a spraying mumble. Romy said nothing. Julia warmed to her even more. 'No one tells me and Karl what happened to our mum. They say she disappeared and never came back, but they're all'—she moved her hands in the air, like the man kneading dough at the market—'jumpy, and weird. They never look at us when they talk about it.'

Romy started to laugh.

'What?' Julia looked up at her, wounded. 'Am I imagining it wrong?'

The laugh was as sharp as her eyes. 'No.' Romy shook her head. 'The opposite. That's exactly—*exactly*—the lie I was told. Now, thanks to the sand-woman, I know the truth. Exit light, enter night, all that bullshit. Smell?'

She held out the bottle. Julia hesitated. If it tasted bad, it couldn't smell too good. 'Okay,' she said anyway. Today was a day to be daring. She'd already sat on the table.

'That's my girl.' Romy held the bottle closer. Squinting, Julia sniffed.

'Ew!' She jerked her face away. It hurt her eyes like onions and smelt like loos. 'That's horrible.' She wiped her nose, rubbed her eyes, and turned back with a swaggering grin. 'Can I try?'

The Snow-Queen-Elsa's eyes were quiet. Four, six, eight, then, 'Sure.' She handed it over. 'I don't care. Serves everyone right.'

Whatever that meant, Julia ignored it. Taking the bottle, she held her breath, copied Romy, and upended it down her throat.

Fire. Fire, fire, fire, fire, fire, fire.

'Ah!' she cried. Coughing, she clapped her free hand to her mouth. 'It's hot! And it's *gross*.' She screwed up her face, coughed again, and clasped her gurgling, churning stomach. 'I think I'm going to be sick.'

'Nah.' Bracingly, Romy patted her knee. 'Just don't tell your mother.'

She was taking back the bottle when Carol walked in.

Kira returns with no big shift. She could be opening her eyes mid-dream, and from scowling at the drink, acidic on her tongue, she's back in the bathroom, kneeling on the tiles.

'What the…?' She narrows her eyes. Staring through the shiny bath, the Star Wars nightdress, and then, the world jolts back. 'Oh, my god!'

She flails backwards, loses her balance, and topples onto the floor. 'How did you…? I—oh, come on, this *house*!'

She scrabbles to her feet. Julia's expression is desperate, wide, as wounded as she was with Romy. 'Please don't tell anyone,' she pleads, shifting to cling to the porcelain edge. 'Please. Only Karl knows. He likes me showing him things.'

She gulps back a sob. A sniff, and she wipes her nose on her knuckles. 'Please don't tell Carol.'

'I'm not going to.' Scraping a hand through her hair, Kira holds it on top of her head. Eyes closed: breathe. The rage she was recalling is gas around her ribs. 'It's…' She leans down jerkily, squeezing Julia's hand. 'It's not you. I'm not angry at you. When everything's calmed down, though, I want a full report. I want to know how you do that. Okay?' Pressing the chubby fingers again, she whirls from the room.

She doesn't bother knocking. 'You gave alcohol to a child?' she yells, barging through the kitchen door. They might have been shouting; they might not. The gas is turning red. 'What the hell, Romy? Are you a psychopath now? I thought you were over this.' She flicks her fingers in disgust, at Romy, languid with her chin on her hands, poking the half-full bottle. 'What happened to "Oh, I'm okay now, I haven't binged in months, I'm not depressed anymore, I'm fine, I'm dandy, I'm *great*, Kira, *great*?"'

Romy bats lazy eyelids. She can't have been shouting; she looks almost asleep. 'Well, aren't we high and mighty?' she drawls. Her hair is a tangle, her makeup smudged. 'Pull up a chair, sister. Tell me the tales of old, where our mother is a succubus and I killed Dad.'

The wind leaves Kira's lungs. Her angry sails deflate, and she stares, full of blood, rushing and throbbing in her ears. She'd thought of Carol's sleep as a helpful plot device, but seeing Romy, burdened and burning…

This is so screwed up.

'Oh, by all means,' Romy continues, when the struggle of anger and guilt leads to silence. 'Take your time. Amass your excuses. You've got a year's worth, after all.'

'I told you, that's not fair,' Callum warns, tense in front of the oven. 'She was trying *not* to hurt you. Leave her alone.'

'I can spar with her myself,' Kira snaps. 'Sorry.' She holds up her hands. 'I'm sorry. This is all just insane.' She casts him an abashed apology. Hands back in his pockets, he nods. 'But he's right, Romy.' She looks back to her sister. Lazing on her hand, Romy blows out her lips: *I'm drunk, and I don't care.* 'You didn't remember anything, and I didn't want to hurt you. Now you have to know, because it's the only way to explain why we're here, but back then you didn't. What would it have done to you?'

The stairs behind them thunder. Kira glances to the side. 'It would have been too much,' she continues. 'It was too much for me.'

Through the kitchen window, Carol shifts. Staring at the sky, her outline could cut, resting the knob of her skull on the glass. She's escaped. Lucky her.

'Which is why you left.' Romy's voice is dead. 'How brave of you.'

'I don't pretend it was brave.' Fixing her eyes on Romy, Kira swallows. 'I'm sorry, but I wouldn't take it back.' The words surge, and she pushes them out. It's true, but is it selfish? 'I wish you'd never had to know at all.'

The stair thunder ends. 'You've got bigger problems,' Jay blurts, colliding with the doorway. His face is paler than a horror-movie patient. 'Right now. You really do.'

In the silence that follows, Romy laughs. 'And what might they be?' She scoffs, lifting her hand to slap the table. The noise is jarring, but Jay doesn't look. 'Huh, little boy?'

'Shut up, Romy,' Callum snaps, Kira close behind. Their eyes meet, and they almost smile.

Almost. 'What is it?' Callum asks. Jay is fidgety, eyes darting, nails scouring the doorframe. Kira's stomach crawls.

'It's…' He glances over his shoulder. Scratches his head, glances again. 'It's really…'

'Hello?' Romy waves at them, screeching back her chair. 'Scarred-for-life memory bank over here. Can we focus on that? Yes, okay, I gave a child astonishingly strong liquor, but what the *hell* are these memories?'

Jay, the rock. Romy, the hard place. Kira pulls a gargoyle face at the fridge. Romy's not wrong; she deserves an explanation, and a damn exceptional one. What does she have now? Knowledge? Memories? Knowledge meant to trigger memories? The whole story? More?

Looking at her sister from the corner of her eye, another wave of guilt descends. Caught not talking, not spewing bitterness, Romy is open, blank, and far less drunk than she's choosing to act. A listening face, wide-eyed and aware.

Her eyes flick to Kira, and she reels it in at once. The sharp edge returns: the hooded eyes, the deliberate slouch, the smirk. Kira looks away. Romy can front all she likes, but she saw the slip. Her sister's hurt. Hurt, and terrified.

'What's going on, Jay?' Callum asks, touching Kira's back. Jay's still dithering, rocking on his heels. 'How do you know we've got bigger problems?'

Jay stops his fevered rocking. 'Wait.'

Spinning in the doorway, he disappears. A moment later, the TV chatters, full of bounce and sparkle. Kira frowns. The channel changes, from an over-bright kids' show to a stroppy tween show, to the drone of a British parliamentary debate.

'Guys.' Jay's voice wobbles, up and down and back. 'Guys, I've found it. Come here. Now.'

His urgency belies his age. Kira does as he says. Her stomach is no longer crawling; or rather, it is, but the creature inside has a hundred jagged legs. She tunes in to the TV with a breathy sense of dread.

A British channel, breaking news.

'…Links between these murders, and those of two days ago in the Dutch town of Middelburg. The whereabouts of nineteen-year-old Kira McFadden, resident of the house where the Dutch murders took place and granddaughter of James and Helen, are still unknown. Anyone with information on either case is asked to come forward, via Devonshire police or Crimestoppers. In other news…'

Kira's stomach bottoms out. Her hands hit her mouth. Jay's channel-hopping, but her picture, taken by Macy in the autumn, is branded on her retinas. *DOUBLE MURDER IN DEVON.*

Granddaughter of James and Helen.

Another channel, breaking news. Kira's head rings like a pretty little bell. She barely sees Callum, stepping up beside her. The breathy dread is an iron lung.

'…Were discovered on the sofa, at 7:04 p.m. Police found this on the living room wall.'

The world collapses. Oh, god. Oh, hell. Kira gasps, or cries out, or both, buckling, clutching her stomach. Pain. The picture; the *picture*. She's crumbling, exploding out, shattered, destroyed. Neat in black on the wall is a tree.

Sketchy, four branches. A line for the ground.

That would be enough, but no. Beneath it is a message: *time to come home, girls.*

Beneath that, the rocking chair that Romy came to love.

Whiteland. Her grandparents.

Granddaughter of James and Helen.

Time to come home, girls.

'Police are looking for the couple's granddaughter, Kira McFadden, who hasn't been seen since the murders of her housemates in Middelburg, the Netherlands.' The news presenter clears her throat. 'Once again, in what looks like an unprovoked attack, an elderly couple have been stabbed to death in their home in Woolacombe, Devon.' Another pause, for a serious face. 'The victims have been named as Helen and James McFadden.'

22

The grief

Every breath leaves Romy's body and returns like a kick in the head.

'I said you had bigger problems,' Jay mumbles. She ignores him. Everyone ignores him. 'I'll go keep the twins upstairs.'

He scoots away. Romy stares at the TV, through the screen. She could be a head and nothing else. Her body doesn't actually exist, a series of numb lumps crudely sewn together. Tug her and the stitches tear. Tug again, she's ash.

'Gran…' she mouths, lifting a hand to her hair. It shakes like she's back in withdrawal. 'Gramps…I—Kira—'

The TV's moving on. 'No.' She scrapes her nails from her hair to her face. 'It's wrong. They're—no, they're *not*.'

The remote, thrown on the sofa. Romy lunges for it. Flick: the next channel is *The Big Bang Theory*, the next a squealing cartoon, the next an old repeat of *Top Gear*, but on the next she finds it.

It's a cheap thrills news show: *DEVON SLAYING*. A sleepy beach town, slapped with gore. The theme from *Midsomer Murders* wobbles into her head, a jaunty, countrified *X-Files*. Seventy-five-year-old Helen McFadden and seventy-nine-year-old James, found murdered on the living room sofa. Above them, an odd symbol, and a message telling some girls to come home. This was home to Dutch massacre suspect Kira McFadden, granddaughter, and her younger sister Rosemarie, so—

'Turn it off.' Callum spins around. Romy jumps; she'd forgotten he was there, forgotten Kira was there, slumping to the floor. Why is Kira on the floor? 'Turn it *off*,' he shouts, and it's close to a snarl. The remote is snatched from her hand, the television silenced. 'Jesus. Kira?' He crouches beside her. She stares at the floor. 'Kira, are you okay? Ah, that's *stupid*.' He rubs his chin. 'Jesus.'

'What's going on?' Carol sweeps in. Riding a rush of cold, stuffing a feather into her pocket, she tightens her dressing gown and fixes on Romy. 'You're upright. What happened?' She glances at the floor, at Callum holding Kira. She doesn't seem to know he's there. 'What *happened*, Romy?'

Earlier, Romy vented everything she could. This woman put knowledge in her head, of things she doesn't remember, and in the process, unlocked what she does. Although she gets it, as though she's watched a film and absorbed the facts, she doesn't get *how* she gets it. It's a distinct sense of déjà vu, like she never saw the film, though she must have.

Goddamn it all to hell, it's confusing. Fucked. Romy's heart thumps in her stomach. After she yelled at Carol in her overwhelmed tipsiness, and after Carol gave as good as she got, not to mention the Julia debacle, they should be at loggerheads, whatever those are…but as Romy looks at her, all she sees is worry, and all she has inside her is pain.

So much for the tipsiness. So much for the high.

'Our grandparents…' she chokes. Her voice catches, eating itself. 'Died. They *died*.'

The word is a feeling, and the feeling is a fiend. Now she knows why Kira's on the floor. *Papillon of winter light, are we dead when we have died?* Slapping a hand to the sofa back, Romy forces her lumps to move. They'll give out. All of her will give out. Fleshy piles of horror, puddled on the rug. She needs to sit. To fall.

Around the table with its burnt-out candles, around the cat-scratched arms. Three little children, sitting on a bed. A killer came in, and now they're—

'…Dead.' Callum forces his voice to work. Romy's collapsed on the couch, and Kira's starting to worry him. 'They've been killed.'

Romy gasps, the gasp of impending tears. Kira flinches into him. So she is still in there. Thank God. 'Sorry.' He hugs her to him, far too tight. 'That was—insensitive. Beyond insensitive. It was on the news. And Kira…' He shakes his head. Even with last night's paper, it's unreal. Unbelievable.

Carol could be cut from stone. 'And Kira?'

Callum rests his lips on Kira's parting. 'The police are looking for her. They've already connected it with Holland.' He dips his forehead to her hair. 'Maybe they were thinking she ran away to England, and now…' He closes his eyes. 'God, this escalated quickly.'

'But they're not looking for me,' Romy whispers.

Slowly, Callum looks up and round. He can just about see her, her mouth half open, a girl abandoned and lost in the rain.

'Should they be?' Carol asks.

Streaked with tears and mascara, Romy's eyes drift to his. One second, two, then the knowledge hits them both.

'The guesthouse.' He sees her realise, the whites of her eyes growing glittery and large. 'They're still sat there.'

Sat, propped, wooden dolls. The image knocks on his lungs with a thud. Three bodies, undiscovered, long past smelling of rot. Bloated, bloody, blue.

'Jesus Christ,' Callum murmurs. Romy coughs a sob.

'My god.' Heavy and slumping, Carol leans on the doorframe. The old wood creaks. 'Kira did tell me. I'm…I'm so sorry.' She pinches the bridge of her nose. 'I know that's not enough, but I am.'

Seconds pass, five, ten; so many that Callum starts to wonder how much her next words will be forced. 'You can…' she begins. Pursing her lips, she gestures limply, resting her head on the wood. 'You can stay. Here.' She looks as though she's lost a fight to win a wider war. 'For as long as it's safe for the children. On the condition that *nothing*'—she eyes Romy, biting, sharp—'like this morning happens again. I'll try and help as much as I can, because my god, you're in a mess, but I can't endanger them. None of this is fair on you—I'd call it downright evil—but the fallout'—she looks around deliberately, up to the ceiling and back—'is even less fair on them.'

She's just as insensitive as he is. Wrapped around Kira, Callum tenses. *My god, you're in a mess.*

But Kira, switching back on, whispers, 'Thank you.'

She straightens up in his arms. 'We'd be wrong to ask for more. And we'll leave as soon as we've got a plan.' Pulling away, she climbs to her feet. Her look is flat, a waifish thing, pared and paled from 3D to two. 'It must have been the huldra.'

No question, no spark. The dullness makes him ache. 'I don't see how it could have been.' Standing, Callum glances at the couch. Romy is staring through the cat on the carpet, wilted with silent tears. 'The tree means Whiteland, but it can't have been the huldra.' Edgy and hopeful, he looks to Carol. 'Unless she's kept some kind of…'

He waves a hand. He'd rather not say *magic*.

Carol folds her arms. 'That depends on why you're asking.' She watches him closely, picking him apart. He tries to stay blank, but his poker face is dross. 'Until this world takes over, which tends to happen fast, a small amount of energy will linger.' She keeps her probing gaze on his. 'Why?'

Kira turns her flatness toward him. She doesn't need to echo his mother; the question brushes his cheek.

On the sofa, Romy drags in a sniff. Callum puts a hand on her shoulder. It shudders. This is the part they've kept to themselves.

'Because…' Callum ducks his head. He's worse than Jay with negative news; if Carol hadn't, would he have brought up Lena? Now? Ever? 'Because the huldra was in Montreux.'

Beside him, Kira stills.

The silence is ringing. It feels like gravity. 'When?' Carol asks.

Callum keeps his eyes on the ground. A patch of shoe-print snow is melting, others crusting the rugs. 'Yesterday,' he says. 'Me and Romy ran from it. Her. Him. God knows. It…' He scratches his head. The question on his cheek has turned piercing. 'It met Romy and faked being me, just like it faked being Romy. If it was here last night, then it can't have been in Devon.' He frowns. 'I'm assuming.'

The leaky fridge drips. Romy sniffs, coughs, and swallows. A floorboard creaks upstairs.

Finally, Carol shakes her head. 'It can't.' She rubs her temple. 'But I wish you'd said sooner. I have to pass on that the huldra's come back.'

Now the roaring has died, Kira's mind is a sheet. 'If it's back,' she murmurs, 'someone else was in England.' Soft. Muted. Dull. 'Some*thing*.'

Slow and weighted, Carol nods. 'It can't be in two places at once.' She rubs her mouth, staring off. 'And it can't travel faster than anyone else. What it does'—the skin between her eyebrows wrinkles—'is continue to manipulate. If you look it in the eye, you'll end up controlled. It actually works better out here, because no one knows to be suspicious. Ticket collectors, men in bars, whoever the huldra needs.'

Callum shifts. 'Does it wear off?'

'Yes.' Carol pushes away from the doorframe. 'As does the rest of it. For now, it can appear how it likes, and it's strong. Not inhumanly strong, but stronger than you'd think.' Eyeing them all, she starts up the stairs. 'I need to check on the children. I was hard on Julia, and I've not seen the boys, but what I will say'—she pauses at the top—'is that the huldra is finding you far too fast. Someone, or something, must be helping it.' She clinks through the beaded curtain and away. 'Something the Whispers don't know about.'

Something inside Whiteland.

The words don't have to be spoken. They should be a volcano, but Kira feels nothing. They're ripples on the surface, far from the depths. They could be about a traffic jam, or snow.

The huldra's still here; it can't have killed her grandparents.

Her grandparents are dead.

The ocean depths beckon, but she forged a submarine. Locked the doors, bolted the hatches, barrelled through the goggling life. It roared too much, and she shut it out.

'This thing,' Romy says thickly from the couch. Turning around, she swipes at her eyes. 'If it can't be in two places at once, and can't get anywhere faster than us'—she wipes her nose, too, her hand smeared black—'how did it get to both Harvey's and Kira's?' She clenches her fists on the back of the couch. Teethmarks dent her lower lip. 'The two things happened at the same time. How the hell did it manage?'

'It didn't.' Kira's mouth precedes her thoughts. 'Something else left Whiteland, too.'

Silence. She stares through Romy. Romy stares through her. Suddenly, nothing else can be true: on New Year's Eve, two things escaped.

Romy's swollen eyes skitter upstairs. This doesn't need to be spoken, either; either Carol doesn't know, or won't tell them.

'So something escaped'—Callum severs their look—'and is ordering you to come home.' He drops to the armchair with a whump. 'Great. Something murderous, at that.'

Kira lowers herself to the sofa by her sister. 'We're assuming it meant us?' she says, unable to muster a tone. Stare at something, anything. Purple penguin socks, given to Romy by Great-Aunt Moll, who thought she was still eleven. The toes are holey.

It's not enough. Glazed, dazed, Kira looks around. Beside the toes, a wintry cushion, of bright-lit trees and an Arctic fox. The chalet is stuffy, the curtains closed. Sunlight fights to enter, caught and mottled by the fabric's hue. The room is bathed in blood-light. Fitting.

The world can be revolting, but it can also be pretty as hell.

Kira sags into the couch. How was that not years ago?

'It must mean us,' Romy croaks. Kira looks across at her. How was it not years ago that they were furious? How much everything pales. 'It's our house. Our grandparents. One day after the next. And that symbol.' She frowns. 'I've seen it.'

Callum catches Kira's eye. 'In Whiteland,' he says.

Reconciling, Kira adds. Romy's knowledge, memory, life.

'Yeah.' Still frowning, vacant, Romy scratches her cheek. 'Yeah. It's too much of a coincidence. God, what do we *sound* like?'

Bitterly smiting puzzlement, her cry is a thunderbolt. Kira flinches.

'Our grandparents are *dead*.' Throwing her arms up, Romy lets them slap. 'Dead, Kira.' Her eyes are raw. 'Sure, most of the time we wished they'd go away, but seriously? We're sat here wondering what it means for *us*? Shouldn't we be'—she slashes her hands through the air—'doing something for them? Planning the funeral, talking to family? Dad's family, I guess, which makes so much more *sense* now. We should at least be lying in the dark.' She flumps back into the sofa. 'Mourning. Screaming. Getting drunk.'

'I'm wanted in two countries, Romy.' Every word weighs more than her conscience. Kira bites both sides of her cheeks. Her throat is hot. Stay numb. Stay dull.

Our minds will end up scarier.

'She can't call anyone,' Callum says quietly. 'Or message them. They'll find you. Both of you.'

The heat scorches, from her throat to her eyes. Kira fixes on Callum's makeshift bed, and pushes down the roar. Numb. Dull. Flatline.

'It's not just about death,' she says, lifting her gaze back up. Numb. Dull. Flatline. Cold. 'If it was, we would be being callous, but it's not. This is aimed at us. It's about us. We need to figure it out.'

The stairs creak. Kira glances round. Karl and Julia tiptoe down, slipping into the kitchen.

'My brain hurts too much,' Romy mumbles, hiding her face in the couch. 'Let me grieve. Let me think. I'm overheating.'

'You can't.' Callum's impatience is terse.

Kira shoots him a look. 'I'm sorry, Romy. He means we don't have time.' She lowers her voice to a hush. 'If we don't work out what's going on, whatever comes next could be worse. It's already going to get worse, once the police find the guesthouse and link it to you. They'll link you to Devon, and come full circle.'

Romy groans, but sits up. 'It still sounds selfish.'

Kira cuts her an appealing look. 'It's not.' Is it? 'It's really not. Once the police link it all up, they'll be looking like crazy for us both. If we drop everything to cry...' She sets her jaw, and swallows. *Helen and James McFadden.* 'I mean,' she says woollily, 'if we don't try to...'

Getting up, Callum sighs. 'It's been done for you to see.' He wedges himself on the couch beside her, one arm pulling her in. Swallowing the burning, Kira lets him. 'For us to see. Whoever.' He drops his own voice. 'Maybe something worse will come, but I don't think we'll get hurt. At least not by the huldra.'

Kira clears her clogged-up throat. 'It could have killed us all by now.'

'Exactly.' Callum taps Kira's arm, one, two, staccato. 'And the other thing, if there is another thing, has been close to Romy. It's some kind of game.'

Romy tugs on a rip in her jeans. 'Amazing.'

'Not really.' Callum taps Kira again. 'You know how Whiteland toyed with us?' Beneath his jaw, she nods. 'That's what this feels like. Doesn't it? Being taunted, like a sadist with a dog. Poke it, see what it does.'

'Poke it again, and watch it dance.' Romy jabs her knee with a savage finger.

Humourless, Callum huffs. 'Yeah.' He rests his chin on Kira's head. 'The problem is not knowing why. Other than the huldra, and whatever wants you to come home, the rest of us are in the dark. The black hole kind, too, not some poxy midnight.'

'Fiona.'

Callum glances up, as if expecting someone new. 'The huldra,' Kira clarifies, sitting up to shift around. 'From now on, she's Fiona. All I heard in Whiteland was huldra. Huldra, huldra, huldra, so this one needs a name. Fiona was the first one that came into my head.'

Romy snorts. 'Fits with Shrek and Donkey.'

She catches Callum's eye. Something twists in Kira's chest.

Callum smirks, fleeting. 'Fiona it is.'

'And the other thing, assuming there is one?' Romy crooks her fingers, air-quoting. 'It can't just be "the thing."'

This time, she catches Kira's eye. *Peter*, she mouths.

Kira almost smiles.

'Liam?' Callum suggests. 'No.' He clicks his fingers. 'Milo. When has a good guy ever been a Milo?'

'In the *Tweenies*,' Karl pronounces, ghosting in from the kitchen. Scooping up the remote, he settles himself on the floor.

Callum raises his eyebrows. 'Were you going to ask?'

'I did.' Karl lays his waffle beside him. 'Carol said we could watch TV.'

Rudely shaken from its slumber, Kira's stomach groans. The stodgy waffle is coated with sugar, smelling of syrupy heaven like nothing has before. Romy's eyes latch on to it, too.

'She also said'—Karl starts to gobble—'to tell you that the bathroom's free. And to feed Diego. He's hiding upstairs.'

Callum cocks his head. 'So basically, Mum wants us out of the way.' He sniffs his shirt. 'And while we're at it, can we please stop smelling rank.' He casts his eyes heavenwards. '*Charmant. Trop sympa.*'

'They still show the *Tweenies*?' Romy asks.

The *Tweenies*. Milo. Kira watches Julia, edging in, scuffing along in her slippers. How much more did they hear?

'Yes.' Darting puffy eyes at Romy, Julia shuffles around the couch. 'On throwback thursdays.' She presses down on Kira's thighs. 'All they play is old stuff, like *Teletubbies*, and *Bagpuss*.' She tips forward for a clumsy hug, yanking Kira's neck. 'Thank you.'

The breath is barely there. Surprised, Kira strokes her back, gently kissing her temple. 'You're welcome,' she whispers.

Julia squirms back.

'Ahem.' Callum pointedly looks between them. Sitting on the rug by Kira's feet, Julia starts on her waffle.

Kira blinks at Callum. 'What? I comforted her well.'

'No, no, leave it on that.' Romy nudges Karl with her foot. To Kira's relief, Callum's focus diverts. Scowling, Karl obliges. 'Thanks.' Romy nudges him again. 'We'll watch princess Barbies later.'

'Hey!' Karl exclaims, batting at her socks. The holey penguins wriggle. 'I don't want princess Barbies. I just didn't want this.'

It's something they used to love as kids, robots and dynamite. Callum gets up with a murmur of a shower, and Kira shuts her eyes. TV. Teasing. Made-up names. What are they doing? All of them? Romy, bonding, in her cynical way, over an old cartoon. She, Kira, idly listening. It's trivial, insincere. Achingly wrong.

Which was part of Romy's point. Then, though, they were trying to think, to figure everything out; now, normality is slinking back, as if tragedy isn't a room. Four walls, encroaching. Ready to squash them all like bugs.

Denial. Survival. Shock. Or all three?

Romy laughs, and that makes it worse. When Kira left in August, Romy was improving, but now...Kira rubs her eyes. Something isn't sitting how it should. The drinking, erraticism, irresponsibility. She's lighter than she used to be, no sullen, spiteful zombie, but something isn't right. She's up and down, down and up.

Kira lets suspicion pool. She's seen it all before.

She rubs her eyes again, with the heels of her hands. Romy. Fiona. Julia. Callum. She'll work it out. She'll work it all out.

And she damn well won't come home.

23

Conceal

In the room beside his mother's, Jay tries not to hear. Usually, he can block her out, but wow, today is awful. Everyone's thoughts are so *loud*. Outrageously, hideously, gallingly loud. They feed off each other, sucking and slurping, ramping up the overall cacophony; how don't they make their owners explode? Slapping their hands to their ears, gasping at their brains to stop screaming? The distant ones can be tuned down low—Romy's white noise, darting up and down and back, round and round and round like an ancient fairground ride; Julia's niggling doubt over showing Kira her trick; Callum's…

Callum's are the worst. Climbing frames and fantasies, no, no, no, no, *no*. Jay blocks them out with *Overwatch*, vibrant on the screen. Usually, it works for his mum, too; usually, he knows the thoughts are there in the same way he knows it's winter, or that a half-eaten chocolate snowman lounges by him on the desk. Aware, but not currently conscious. Usually, it works, but today…

He gives up.

It happened last time she talked to the Whispers. Then, at least, he hadn't been surprised; the time before, he'd only just realised he could hear things, and his mother mind-talking to an eerie set of voices was the icing on a worrying, bittersweet cake.

Then, he didn't want to listen. He was panicky, overwhelmed, and actually chose to walk Diego, only to hear the minds of everyone he passed. *Did I leave the cat in?* a random skier wondered. *I wish Camille wasn't coming,* moaned a mother in an Audi. *Marjolaine deserves much better.*

DOG!

That was from a squeaky girl, like fireworks in his brain. His filtering system is better now, and he doesn't get so startled, so when he heard the unearthly voices sigh on New Year's Eve, he didn't run. It's ruder than eavesdropping, so he tried not to listen; but then, like now, he failed.

Everything's failing. Old-school *Doctor Who*, endless games of *Overwatch*. The only thing left is his list of facts.

Gleaned from other people's minds, they usually haul him through anything. Conceding a seventh dismal defeat, Jay quits the game, swivels in his chair, and starts from the very beginning. One: Julia thinks no one knows about her trick, but she's done it to Mum by accident. Two: Trilby Guillaume the train driver fancies his sister's boyfriend. Three: Luca broke his arm in a tussle with a T-bar, not skiing down a black run like he said. Four—

Tell them, the Whispers whisper. The thoughts bleed through his headphones, and Jay stops his listless spin. Tell who what?

Four: Karl—

It was not a suggestion, the Whispers whisper. *You have to tell them who else got out.*

Ripping off his headphones, Jay blows out his lips. For God's sake, *fine.*

He listens.

Maybe one Whisper, maybe more. Their voices are the sounds you hear in the night: not real enough that you're sure they're there, but *something* enough that they could be. That's the sense he gets from his mum, and that's what he feels for himself.

Unwrapping the crinkling chocolate Santa, Jay stuffs it in his mouth. He might as well have snacks.

His mum is swirling, reluctant doubt. *Surely it can wait,* she offers, ginger, rueful, soft. *They've got enough to deal with.*

The Whispers hiss inside her head. She spikes, and Jay spikes, too. *Fighting what's happening means knowing what that entails.* One voice, black ice on the road. *You weren't meant to handpick the parts that suit your purpose. We do not deal in deceit.*

In his real, physical hearing, his mother laughs.

Deceit! she cries. It's more than a thought, but less than a sound, a soft cut in the air. *Can you really talk about deceit? You chose not to tell me about Anneliese, and that you used her husband to lure her.*

She's trying to blend disgust with her upcoming chores, but it's as clear in her head as the morning. Jay shifts in his desk chair. The chocolate tastes of dust.

Not to mention, Carol continues, sending a squirm through his stomach, *that her husband's body vanished from the ice when he died. Correct me if I'm wrong, but you never planned on telling me. You wouldn't have spared it a thought, if he wasn't causing chaos with a huldra.*

Another thought, badly masked: *If you had, you might have stopped their escape.*

Jay screws the shiny paper up. It's as tight a ball as his belly.

Mathew is innocent, a different voice sighs. It swirls around the barb in a way that means it heard, a breath too close to his ear. His ear, or Carol's ear? Jay shivers. His arms have hairs like sentinels.

What do you mean, he's innocent? Carol's mind goes grey, grainy, blurred. *From what you said before, he dealt with the devil and faked his death. He's killing people.*

Mindless conjecture, the first voice murmurs, delicate, dangerous, daintily amused. *He was not a man to make a deal. He is being controlled, like Freya, but without Freya's awareness.*

He's a puppet. The Whispers roam together.

Like me, Carol thinks.

Oh, god, Mum, no. Jay scrunches his toes, creasing his forehead. They'll definitely have heard that one; she hardly even tried to smother it. The Whispers are nothing he can understand, but they smear a sickness in his stomach.

Whose puppet is he? his mother asks. Her mind is starting to roil, the frustration you feel in your gut. The kind that's hard to suppress. *All you said before was that he got out with the huldra.*

Before, that was all we knew. The second voice slithers in, snaking round the words. *It's still all we know, but our conjecture is mindful. Until Freya left, we were unaware that anything was taking place; someone*—and here it hisses—*went to great pains to hide it. Someone revived Mathew, concealed him, and somehow masked the process. He's a puppet, and there is a plan.*

Now, his mother's mind blackens. The light drains. Jay could drown.

So it was orchestrated. Carol's words are faint, her memories a gas: the girls' names exploding when the huldra got out, a shudder running through her like a bursting sonic boom. The Whispers rushing in, so dizzying it hurt. *I'd hoped to God it wasn't. I'd hoped it was a whim.*

The black deepens. Stifling, it sucks Jay's air away. *Who's...* Carol's mind coalesces. *Who's controlling them?*

The Whispers rustle, swelling around her. *We're blind,* they hiss. *Blindness is rare. Considering that...* They pause. *The Kyo.*

Falling. Carol's horror spirals, and Jay's head swoons. The game on his monitor lurches. His chocolate-coated tongue is sour, his belly lurching, too. He shouldn't have given in. It's too much.

It's far too much, but he can't pull away. The voices are hooks. He's dizzy, and dark.

Through a witch, the Whispers continue, nauseous in his mind. *Either they're protecting her, or she protects herself. Both are unsettling.*

Unsettling. Carol's echo is thin.

They feel cheated, we presume. Anneliese's girls escaped.

She takes a breath. Shuddery and stale, it passes into Jay. *Isn't that drastic?* she asks, so faint. *Chasing revenge through the worlds?*

The Kyo are inhuman. The swirl, the whirl is building. *They haven't been human in a very long time.*

Cracking necks, screaming mouths. Jay stifles a whimper. Too dizzy. Too hot. *And you can't make them stop?* Carol asks. Her hope is sicker than him.

We cannot see inside. The Whispers crackle; they're ready to leave. The mounting rush is familiar. *To stop them, we need to find the witch. And we will.* They're ready to swarm, to fade. *We don't want outsiders in Whiteland, and we don't want those already here to think they can toy with the worlds. It has*—they pause, tasting, savouring—*already provoked unrest.*

Wind through leaves, a rising storm. *Why would there be outsiders in Whiteland?* Carol's question pales in the hum. *Has someone else got in?*

No. The Whispers' storm increases. Fluttering energy, white noise, inches from her skin. Sweat sticks to Jay's body. *Think, Carol.*

His mum's mind teeters, and stops. The realisation hits her like a train. *They want to push the girls back in.*

Jay stiffens with her, stilling with her breath. The sweat prickles cold. His stomach thumps. His hand shakes on the desk.

The Whispers are weakening, whipping away. *That is what we presume.*

Carol's mind is a roar. *They don't want to kill them.* She ghosts her hands to her face. Oh, god. *They don't even want to find them, do they? They want to ruin their lives, until Whiteland's all that's left.*

If it works, the Kyo and the witch will be waiting. Weaker still, an echo in a tunnel. In Carol's mind, Jay strains to hear. *Tell the girls about their father. Help them make this stop.*

How? The question comes out quickly, before they disappear. She could focus and force them to manifest, drawing them to her like summoning ghosts, but they wouldn't take it lightly. They may be a feeling, in her thoughts, as a presence, brushing against her, deadening the air, but their anger deadens the world.

The Whispers don't reply. *What good will telling them about him do?* Carol tries, one last time. *He's killed his own parents, and for some sadistic reason, left a message telling the girls to come home. Knowing will only screw them up more.*

And prepare them for what they're facing. The first voice is barely there. *No one else can do it for them; no one else can get involved, unless you take it upon yourself. Better they find out from you, rather than Freya and Mathew's subtleties.*

And Carol… The second, sly voice slithers in. *You should pay more attention to your son.*

The Whispers shift. Turning to him, dead and creeping, a shadow in the corner of the room: *Jay.*

Jay's gut wrenches, and suddenly, he's back. Back in his own mind, run, abort, sick and giddy, hot and cold, but the Whispers are building, rushing, screaming.

With a roar, they arrive.

Jay. Pressure in his chest, filling his skull. *You have to learn,* and they're gasping, raging, no longer will-o'-the-wisps through the wall. Jay claps his hands to his ears, but they're in. *You have to learn,* they screech. *LEARN. You have to learn, you have to learn, you want to see?*

You'll see.

Split and shatter, splintering pain. With a yell, a howl, electric shocks, in a rush of colour, he sees.

A haunted, thinner Romy, snapping someone's neck. Wolves, Kira screaming, a naked woman running, emerging from the forest by Motalles with a grin. The dead man following, the same woman grinning, gutting someone else with staring eyes.

Lena, frozen beneath a tree. Shrieks harsh in a rumbling mist. Inhuman creatures, twisting to look at him, clawing and scraping and breaking their bodies. He runs and tumbles away through the mountain, lost in the dark, and they crow and they chase. A bloodthirsty clamour, he can't get away, he won't get away, and flowing light leads him astray, and now he's sinking. Inhaling water, mud, slime, the surface shrinks to oily nothing, and his throat is a pinhole, no air, no *air*—

The cosy house erupts. Pulling on a dubious pineapple vest, Kira stills. She'd taken a shower fit for queens—finally feeling properly clean, heating the water enough that nothing else could breach her mind—but now, someone's screaming.

'Jay!' Carol shouts from the hallway, with the ragged catch that comes from horrified surprise. Slowly, Kira straightens, buttoning her jeans. The screams continue, petrifying, petrified. 'Jay?' Creaking, thudding, pounding on a door. 'Jay, let me in. Let me—let him go!'

The sliding shriek is chills and thrills. *Let him go.* Let him go?

Kira jolts into life. With her wet hair slapping, she fumbles from the bathroom. 'What's going on?'

'Let him *go*!' Carol yells. Shoving Jay's door, rattling the handle, her voice hitches, pitching and hoarse. Her own door is askew, and Kira catches something move; a pulse in the air, rose petals fluttering, shifting in a vase on the desk. 'What are you doing?'

'Carol!' Kira cries, but her voice is lost. Behind the door, Jay's screams grow raw.

He sounds like he's choking.

'He hasn't done anything wrong!' Carol shouts, kicking with a slippered foot. 'Let him go, oh, my god, so what if he was listening?' The door doesn't budge. '*Jay!*'

'Mum?' The stairs thunder. Kira jerks her head around. Callum, taking them two at a time, Romy close behind. The beaded curtain clacks. Somewhere, Karl is shouting questions, Carol yelling, Jay screaming, choking, hacking, *screaming*, and under it all is a breath of a voice: *You'll see. You have to learn.*

The memory is physical, and whips her in the lungs. *You must watch.* The dead women, cracking their necks, sowing seeds of dreams and hoping she would die. The dank cave. The Kyo.

Kira thinks on hyperdrive. The hall around her slows, with its shower-scented steam, its chaos and its fear. The Kyo can't be here. They had to wait for Romy in the woods; they can't reach this far out. And why would they want Jay? Why would they know he exists?

The Whispers. It settles in her chest like a sandbag. *So what if he was listening?*

Rage bursts inside her. It's the flaring, burning beast, and barging past Callum, Romy, and Carol, she stops in front of the door. The floorboards stick to her feet. She roots herself in place. The Whispers took her mother, and then they took her life. They're not taking Jay.

In class, she'd picture dodgy men. She'd prepare for unexpected attacks, never wisps of ghosts and doors, but aiming high, Kira kicks with everything she has.

The rattle judders through her, but the room stays shut. She didn't angle it right, didn't use enough weight. The noise around her turns white. Rickety door. Adrenaline. Rebalancing, she coils her leg, breathes, and kicks again.

The door flies open and bashes off the wall. It wasn't locked, only jammed. Bouncing back with a battered moan, it slams her humerus.

'Ah!' Kira cries. It blocks her way, the bloody thing, and she shoves it, jarred with pain. The air mattress trips her up, and she curses. All these bloody *things*.

'What are you doing?' someone shouts behind her. 'You can't—'

Slumped in his chair, Jay gurgles. Through a dizzy patch of air, Kira grapples for him. 'Jay!'

His shoulders are fitting. He jerks from her hands. 'No, Jay, wake up!' She grabs him again, latching on, shouting into his face. His hands grip the arms of the chair, his eyes a sickly white. She wants to scream, faced with his shrieks, shaking and coughing and gasping for breath. His mouth is black and far too wide. *'Jay!'*

She shakes him once, hard. His head lolls, a scarecrow on a stick. 'Jay, wake up, it's not real!' Another shake, harder. 'Come on! It's not real, none of it's real. Please.' Another, another, panic in her throat. Bulging, smothering. It feels like she's floating, up among the beams. 'You have to wake *up.*'

Kira, wake up.

A hiss sounds behind her. The door slams shut. Her vest flutters, a breath on her foot. Her giddy head sways.

Whatever the Whispers are, they're here.

Get back. The thought is fire, and she flings it at the room. They may be here, and they may have trapped her, but oh, she won't be cowed.

A laugh tickles her ear. Get *back*, she thinks at them, fireworks and bombs. Muffled shouts from outside, thumping on the door.

Lurching forward, Jay begins to retch.

The laughter is soft, two strains, three. Kira flounders, wide-eyed, horrified, as bile spews from his lips. They won't stop. They're killing him, and she's letting him die. Dodgy men attacking, never wisps of ghosts and doors.

Kira wrenches her mind from the beams. Classes taught her fighting, but Whiteland taught her more. She has to wake him up.

Shoving Jay upright in the chair, she slaps him as hard as she can.

His head snaps to the side. His fitting shoulders still. Has she killed him herself?

'Jay?' Bending down, she touches his face. His skin is clammy. Her fingers shake. Her rage drains into dread. 'Jay?' Her ears ring. He can't be dead. 'Jay, wake up. Please wake up.'

With a rasping heave, Jay's chest bucks. Falling forward, he pukes with sour aggression on the floor.

'Oh, thank God.' Kira crouches, pushing Jay's hair from his face. He spits and coughs, dragging in air.

Kira, my, a dark voice sighs. It circles her neck like a choker. *How feisty.*

Another slips in. *Would you like a reward?*

The air lifts. She hadn't realised its oppression, but now it feels less pregnant, less wrong. 'No,' she spits. Her hand aches. Wrapping an arm around his shoulders, she pulls Jay to his feet. 'Fuck off.'

Pity. The voice is a smile. Hugging Jay to her chest, she ignores it. He's all right; he's awake; he's alive. His breathing is heavy, and his body quivers, but flopping into her, he just seems drunk.

Truly, Kira. The Whispers rustle. They're faint now, faint and fading, rising up and away. *Especially when we're giving it regardless.*

They pause. Their pleasure is tangible, slick and bright and sickening. Kira's rage flicks its tail. 'I'm not listening,' she says, heaving Jay toward the door.

No? the voices whisper. *But Kira, Carol hasn't said.*

A longer pause, teasing. *Your father is alive.*

24

The rage

She's taunting the Chlause. So close, yet out of reach—in theory, at least—she's baiting them. Goading them.

In theory. It's not dark, but still; she won't push it too far. The stories may be true, or halves of sly deceits, but either way, opening her arms to grin *come and get me* is a step too close to dodging knives with her soul.

Her soul. Arms folded on the flaking balcony, Freya watches the snowy outside. The nearby forest sways in a breeze, the same one lifting her hair. Somewhere, there's woodsmoke. Her soul. Her *soul*. Does she have one, now she's human? Did she have one before?

Her lips quirk. Such a human question. The women have been toying with it, since she stayed with the man who never spoke. Arnaud. Short, bald, wearing pink. He'd managed to convince himself he was guilty; he was riddled with heinous doubt.

Doubt, guilt, sin, souls. Save my soul; bless my soul; Lord, I'm going to Hell. He'd been unfaithful. He'd left his wife. He'd been unfaithful again, he was cursed, and now he couldn't stop hating himself. His mind was the colour of blood and wounds. Taika found it unsettling. The women listened with glee.

If Freya was the saving sort, she might have dragged him here, to Whiteland. Protect yourself, and you'll fade to Ørenna. Whether you think your soul is good, or whether you think it's cold, in Ørenna, it just *is*. If nothing gets you first, you sigh back to where you were born.

Inside her head, the women heckle. They want her to move; time is not to waste, sheltered by the chalet, a black figure blending with the old, dark wood. Pushing off the balcony, she creaks around the corner, past the carved heads and the animal skulls. Whoever decorated had the right idea; even in the breezy day, Karliquai is still. Freya skirts the edge of the buckled steps, down to the squeaking snow. There's something else here.

Something prescient in the rough walls, hiding in the gaps. If she had to choose a word, disquieting would do; Taika found Arnaud unsettling, but really, this is worse. The chalet is imbued with a breath of eerie magic, far beyond anything trapped beneath the snow.

With her frozen toes throbbing, Freya starts to climb. Dense trees straddle the mountain. It's a perilous slant, and she pauses, glancing over her shoulder. Through the branches stands Atikur, across the snowy field; for outsiders, it's magnificent. So picturesque, so pretty, backing onto the peaks. Shrunken, quaint, and tame, even she would walk through it, struck by the delicate branches and trails. She could wander at night and enjoy the silence. She could look out for animals as something more than prey.

She could, but would she? Freya smiles. She's a hunter. Lissome and languid and lithe, she climbs through the trees, quiet in the noisy undergrowth. Would she ever lose enough of her Huldra to—

Whispers WHISPERS move go

A collective, sucking gasp drains the thoughts from her mind. Freya's lungs shrivel. Her head expands. Slapping her hand on a tree, she staggers, jarring her shoulder on the greenish bark. Her eyes twitch, flickering, dusty. Just like that, she can't breathe.

WHISPERS

She knew they were out here; the women felt it. It wasn't a worry, to her or to them, but they must be raging. They always rage, but this is more. Freya staggers again, scraping her skull, jolting her back on a gnarl. The pressure bubbles through her, through the women in the Kyo, stripping her of layers of energy and self. The woods spin. She can't *breathe*. The Whispers—they're beyond rage. They embody rage, insidious with power, with spite.

An image, faint and lonely, floats to the surface, and she manages to wonder if this is what it's like. Is this what happens when you're thrown in the fire? Did the Chlause hear her? Were her taunts too much? Is it not the Whispers at all? If the scaretales are wrong, and they can take when they like—

In a second sucking gasp, the pressure lifts and leaves.

Freya heaves a breath to sweep the air from the worlds. Another, and a third, inelegant and desperate. On the fourth, she presses her palms to the tree.

They're angry, the women hiss, sinister and seething.

Freya closes her eyes. Her fingers are scraped. The bark is chilled. Its knobbles and knots are grounding, and she pushes herself upright. The shocks might never have happened.

'Angry.' She shakes her head at the snow. Numb ears. Stiff jeans. Twigs beneath her thin-soled boots. 'I wouldn't call that angry.'

With a huff and a grimace, she carries on climbing. The Whispers can do whatever they like, so long as it doesn't mean sniffing her out. They can rage. They can pretend to be crazed. All their storm has done is give credence to the Kyo.

The women were right. She has to move.

If the Whispers are out here, they're working with watchers. They're trying to uncover what's happening, and it has to end before they do; at the very least, she has to play her part and slip away.

Quick and quiet, she lengthens her strides, breathing hard as the mountain steepens. High above, a raven *craaak*s. Somewhere close, the whoosh of skis. It may be the message from the Kyo to the girls, but she damn well won't come home.

25

Reveal

'What?' Kira clutches Jay to her, crushing him on instinct. Jay grunts. 'That's not—what?'

She meant to be venomous, spitting like before. She means to, but the shock won't let her. She sounds the way she imagines they craved: breathy, stunned, and bested. 'That can't—I...' She flounders, swallows, her mouth half-open. 'I saw him die.'

You did, the Whispers croon. They're drifting back into Carol's room, whipping their wind to a moan through the wall. *And yet, he's alive.*

The chalet creaks. The wind lifts to a dramatised keen, throbbing, heady, hot. Kira could be underwater, a balloon outside her mind. Jay groans. A vein thumps in her temple. She plants her feet to stay upright. The wind moans. The Whispers roar. She could pass out, left by gravity, hit by unseen energy blasts. The pressure is a vice.

With a keening crescendo, everything drops.

The air leaves Kira's lungs in a puff, and she sags. In her arms, Jay slumps. The chalet settles around them.

The super sinks to the natural, and Whiteland slinks away.

'Jay!' The door slams open, and Carol flies in. Kira lets her snatch him. Her father's *alive*?

Her ears ring. She barely dares to think the words, to inch around the concept. The room around her blurs. If he's alive, where's he been? And why would Carol not say?

Time to come home, girls.

Tears barrel up her throat. Whirling around, Kira shoulders past Romy, colliding with Callum in her haste to leave. Jay's room is angular. The walls are too close. Too full of people, too small. Too warm.

'Kira!' Romy grasps her arm, but Kira jerks away. Down the stairs. She has to go. Her lungs are crushed, yet again, collapsing after a crash. Her head is a whine in a tunnel. Dad.

It's a joke. It has to be. Kira stumbles down the creaking stairs. The Whispers must be lying.

It hits her like a slamming door, shoved by a gust of wind. Staggering, she reaches for the wall. The house in Devon. Mathew alive. Gran and Gramps dead. *Time to come home, girls.*

He's the other thing that's escaped. He's Milo.

No, no, no, no, no. Anxiety billows up inside her, and she pushes off the wall. Thoughts upon thoughts upon thoughts rattle round. He's not. He can't be.

'Is Jay okay?'

Kira's senses rush back. She's stumbled into the living room. Karl and Julia blink from the couch. Why?

She's the adult. Kira forces her breath. Sharp bursts are not enough: In, two, three, four. Out, two, three, four. She's the adult, and after the bedlam, the twins need reassurance.

'Yes,' she manages, pushing her hair back. Heavy and wet, it drags her down, in curtains of orange blossom. 'He's okay, but he…'

She stalls. Julia bites her thumb. Karl's eyes are moons. How is she the adult? In the last few days, she's had less control than in the previous nineteen years.

'He had a horrible nightmare,' she finishes, in her best preschool voice. Behind her, Romy thumps down the stairs. 'I think you should give him a hug.'

With a nod, Romy hops out of the way. 'He fell asleep at his computer,' she says. 'And he didn't think he'd wake up. It made him start screaming.' She rubs her arms with a Scooby-Doo shudder. 'You've both had horrible nightmares, right?'

Fervently, Julia nods. A little more cautious, Karl does the same.

'Right.' Kira offers Romy a small, grateful smile. 'Everyone has. If you remember the worst dream you've ever had, the creepiest, scariest stuff, you'll know how scared he is.' Catching Romy's eye, she tilts her chin toward the stairs. 'He'll appreciate the hug.'

Scrambling to her feet, Julia thunders up the stairs in a one-girl stampede. Karl casts Kira a sceptical look, but obeys. Kira's chest twinges. He knows it's a lie, and not a very good one. It doesn't explain the slamming doors, or the wind inside the chalet, but the truth is more than a nightmare. The truth takes place in the day.

Upstairs, voices rise and fall. The television chirps to *Tom and Jerry*. Tom is doing his damnedest to lure Jerry out, and with a prick of disbelief, Kira shakes her head.

'You're a child charmer,' Romy remarks, placing a hand on her hip. Kira turns. Romy's earlier fury is muted, but its afterglow is clear, setting her face in guarded jags as they meet each other's eyes. 'What—'

Looking away, she opens her mouth, slowly letting it close. Her expression dulls and tenses.

'What happened up there?' The words are stilted. A decision seems to settle. 'Are you...' She stares through the banister. Her lips pucker, work, and smooth. Kira suppresses a hangdog grimace. Romy's trying so hard. 'Are you okay?'

She could sail in on a riptide of sorrys. She could, and maybe she should, but Romy needs to know. 'No.' Kira steps toward the couch, closer to *Tom and Jerry*. Her voice barely touches her lips. 'But not because of that. Well, kind of. What happened was the Whispers' fault. They're—'

'The ones that sucked up Mum.'

Kira blinks.

'I know, right?' Keeping the words low, Romy spreads a sarcastic hand. 'My new knowledge has no bounds. The Whispers, the ones that watchers talk to. Carry on.' She shifts her weight.

Kira shifts, too, toying less than idly with the loops on her jeans. Romy is cutting her eyes around the room, to the Buddha, the raquettes, anywhere but her. Kira twists her mouth. She can hardly blame her.

'I think that Jay was eavesdropping.' She lowers her voice to a breath. 'The Whispers were talking to Carol, heard him listening, and thought they'd teach him a lesson.'

'A lesson?'

'Yes.' A door creaks on the landing, and Kira glances up. Hurry. 'That seems to be what they do. Just before they left, though, they said something to me.'

Romy folds her arms. 'Like what?'

Kira's attention flicks to the TV. Fooled and tricked, Jerry is trapped, shut in an airless box. She chews on her cheek. To repeat it means validation, and validation means… 'That Dad's alive.' She drops her eyes. The words feel more like stolen breaths than things she's chosen to say. 'He's alive, and Carol knew.'

Tom forgot to weight the box; Jerry is peeking out. Kira tweaks her belt loops hard.

'Dad's alive,' Romy repeats. Slowly, Kira looks up. Her sister's face is very still. 'How?'

Kira tugs on the loops. 'I don't know.'

'Do you believe them? The Whispers?'

Pinching, harder. 'I don't—'

'Actually, it doesn't matter.' Romy blinks, swinging her gaze to Kira's. 'I think we should leave. Now.'

Pausing mid-tug, Kira frowns. This was not the response she expected. 'You do?'

Romy nods, twice. 'Yes.' Her stance hardens to confidence. 'If she's keeping things like that from us, I don't want to stay. Our crazy deadly peril doesn't hang around for liars.'

Liars. The word stings. Kira tucks it away. 'You believe the Whispers, then? About Dad?'

Romy regards her evenly. 'Is our crazy deadly peril worth the risk?'

Silence. Then, 'No.'

All of a sudden, the way is clear. She'd been wondering since liquor-gate if maybe they should leave; when she made this plan, she hadn't known about the twins, the police weren't after her, and her grandparents hadn't been killed. It's been less than a day, yet here they are, storm-blown and breathless; she can't keep this family boxed in her and Romy's chaos.

And if they can't be sure that Carol is honest, about Whiteland, the police, their *dad*…

'Let's go.' Kira's voice is hushed but firm. 'While we're alone, and—'

Up the mountain, the train starts to whine. Romy's eyes widen. 'And while the train's coming,' she says. 'Holy—go!'

She kicks into action. Kira follows instantly, boots on, coat on, cracking open the door. Collecting her bags, her last look lingers. She'll have to jettison the clothes upstairs, but other than that, she has everything.

Go.

Go, before she changes her mind. Before Callum comes down, to catch them sneaking off. Before the guilt can hit.

She'd feel worse if she stayed.

Romy is almost at the ice-crusted arch. Muffled curses puff in her wake, and Kira slides down after her. Sun-slick snow, glittering, blinding. Ice shards spray her ankles. Three feet to the hedge. Two.

'Hell!' Romy slips, sprawling. Grabbing the hedge, she scrabbles back up, slapping the snow from her legs. 'We're so...'

Kira skids to her side, colliding with her shoulder. The train is still whining...

...Straight on by.

'No!' Spilling through the arch, Romy lurches down the stepping stones. 'We're getting on! Hey! Stop, on my—'

'Stop!' Kira echoes, shouting over "life." She hoists up her bags, waving like a maniac.

The power lines crackle. A chaffinch calls. The trundling turtle trundles away.

'Sacrilegious wildebeest!' Romy runs after it, past the hut to the platform's end. She slips on a patch of ice, throwing out her arms, but it makes no difference; down the mountain, the whining fades. '*Dam*mit.'

With a gusting sigh, she folds like a camel, sitting where she stands by the hotel fence. Ditching her bags in a snowdrift, Kira does the same. Dammit. Dammit, dammit, *dammit*. Their fleeting action is scuppered...and by trying to leave without a word, they've scuppered things even more.

'We'—Kira drops her head to her hands—'are the worst runaways.'

Romy snorts. 'It's not like there's a handbook.' Plucking at the snow, she flicks it at the hut. '"How to flee when you're framed for murder."' She glowers as her missiles ricochet back. '"How to sneak out, perfect your timing, catch your connections, and never get caught."'

'We've exhausted our quota for that.' Kira drags her knees to her chest. She shouldn't have sat in the snow; Callum's right. Her clothes are the absolute worst. The jeans skim her ankles, and the skin there is pink. 'It'd be a cliché to achieve it again. Unless we walk, we're stuck for an hour.' She pauses for the shortest of seconds, then, 'Romy, what are you on?'

Romy's shoulders draw in like the strings of a corset. 'No time like the present, is it?' She shakes her head at the snow. 'What are *you* on? You're Wonder Woman. Or, I don't know, Buffy.'

'Krav Maga since the summer. Your turn.' Kira tilts her head. 'You know what you said about peril and liars? I know this isn't the best time, and I know I'm one of those liars, but I'm also your sister.' She shuffles closer. Romy tenses. 'If I know, you don't need to hide it. I owe you a hell of a lot, and by that I mean turning on Wonder Woman.' She pauses. 'Or Buffy.'

Romy looks at her under her lashes. 'Turning on Wonder Woman?'

Kira graces this with silence, and for a while, that's all there is. The exuberant chaffinch, chirruping away. The drone of a plane. The *whump* of snow falling from a branch.

'Same as before.' Romy finally sighs. Kira's insides deflate. One dejected balloon that she's right, one for relief it isn't worse. 'But now I have a hip flask.'

'Filled with…?'

'Red Label.' Romy tosses a shard of ice at the hut. 'Blame Ryan for that. The rest is the curse of ADHD. Before they diagnosed me, all I did was scavenge.'

Kira summons a tiny smile. 'You never had ADHD.' She shuffles nearer through the snow, resting her head on Romy's. Her chest fills with air again. They're never this close. 'But I'll blame the diagnosis. Happy to, in fact.'

Shifting a little, Romy's corset draws tighter. Is she pushing it? The closeness? Her sister has every right to reject her.

'Goddamn doctors,' Romy mutters. With a sigh, and another, she loosens. Kira's chest does, too. 'Back then, they hit me with anything. "Hey, your parents disappeared, you have this."' She leans into Kira, an inch, a tad. '"And this. Would you like some drugs? Oh, you've got history with drugs? Catch 'em all." You'—she taps Kira's nose—'got off lightly. Three months of anxiety meds, when you should have been on them for six. What a scam.'

Smiling, Kira removes the finger. 'Personally, I see it as less of a scam and more of a lucky break. Cocktails aren't my thing. And'—she nudges Romy with her shoulder—'at least they didn't find issues with my joints and put me on pills for arthritis.' Snow showers Kira's head, and she flinches. 'Hey! I only speak the truth!'

'Exactly.' Romy snaps out finger guns. 'God, they screwed around so *much*. I ended up prophetic.' She flattens invisible wallpaper, smoothing the air with her hands. 'The self-fulfilling kind. Roll up, roll up, I'm feeling ADHD-positive and in need of their drug cocktail. Go science.'

Rueful, Kira huffs. 'They were idiots to give you it. Actually, I thought they'd stopped.' She studies the side of Romy's head, and pauses. Further away, the chaffinch peeps. 'I thought you'd stopped.'

'Mmm.' Romy pulls a face. Extending her legs, she toys with the rip in the knee of her jeans. 'I had, which is why I said blame Ryan. Once he went supernova, I didn't know what to do. It took me too long to get rid of him, and in the meantime...'

She lifts her shoulders: *see for yourself*. Kira stares. 'So all of that's true?' She sits up straighter, sniffing the air. From the hotel drifts a cheesy aroma, decadent and dense. 'The housewife, chauvinistic, 1950s switch?'

Romy's mouth pops open. 'How do you know about that?' She plucks at Kira's clothes. 'Are you magic, too? Is it in here? That'd be the icing on the cake, that would.'

With a laugh, Kira wriggles away. 'No. You know the huldra—Fiona—posed as you?'

One, two, click. 'Ah.' Romy ducks her chin to her chest, and shudders. 'Aha. Ho. Creepy.'

Jarred, Kira blinks. *Aha, ho, creepy?* Considering her fury, this is close to uncanny.

Is it really, though? Or is it more Romy than ever? Shutters down, curtains drawn, every internal bottle corked. It's how she deals with the world and every dog it's ever owned.

'Creepy's one word for it,' Kira says.

'Yep.' Romy draws her chin back up. 'But it means I don't have to explain it.'

Kira huffs. 'Every cloud.'

'Exactly.' Romy waves a hand. 'So yeah. I started defying Ryan, going out more, binging like I used to, and after a while I thought hey, why not renew my prescription? The doctor didn't even question it.' She shakes her head. 'No wonder the country's going to hell. The whiskey, okay, I'm not really trying, but I'm slowly coming off the Dexedrine.'

She clicks her finger guns again, as if to say, *I've got you there*. 'I'm used to the effects, so it's not really worth it. Doesn't last long, and isn't fulfilling.' She nudges Kira, winking with a grin. 'A bit like Peter, eh?'

Kira's insides squirm. 'Thanks for the reminder.'

'Anytime.' The grin turns to amazement. 'God, what *are* we?' She spreads her arms wide. 'Everything's light-years on from screwed, and I'm joking about addictions and sex.' She drops her arms to the snow with a slap. 'Wow. What are we *doing*?'

Here it is, again. 'Coping.' Kira wriggles around with a frown. Her legs are bitten with cold, and she's lost all feeling in her butt. To top it all off, her hair is freezing. 'Denying. Putting our hands over our ears. Something tempting but unhelpful.' She tilts her head, innocent. 'A bit like your addictions.'

Romy flicks her arm. 'Oh, what a genius. I—who are you?'

Her voice pogoes. Kira looks round. Watching behind the hotel fence is the wild woman from the train.

Kira chills even more. From the way she stands, with her feet firmly planted, she should be shrouded in mist, or wearing a cavernous hood. *The Exorcist*, or *Assassin's Creed*. As it is, she's in combat boots, psychedelic leggings, and a cavernous jumper, and with her black *Brave* hair flying, she tenses and vaults the fence.

If she'd been gunning for murder, they'd both be dead. The newcomer sits beside them, cross-legged on the tiny platform, before Kira feels more than surprise. Mouth open, Romy stares.

'I was trying to look threaten.' The woman leans back on her hands, angling her curiosity toward them. 'Did it work? Would work more if...' She gestures at the cobalt sky. 'Blue not scary.'

Now, Kira stares, too. What planet is this person *from*?

Romy points a finger. 'I recognise you.'

The finger starts to wag. Kira curls her toes in her shoes. Please don't let this be the grand return of nervous cockiness. She could be an assassin.

She could be Fiona.

Kira shoulders this away. If they think like that, they'll never trust anyone.

'You worked at the hotel.' Romy glances behind her, back in its direction. Clearly, she doesn't have the same reservations. 'When it wasn't some weird dorm.'

The young woman shrugs. 'I still do. But yes, is not hotel now.' She waves a blind hand at it. 'Is...' She cocks her head to one side. 'For sleeping. For school. My mother got old and grumpy and sold. We live in house behind it. She one of cooks there, I help with organisation and kids. I know you, too.' She settles a flat black gaze on them, irony sparking like a torch in a tunnel. 'You made madness, then disappear.'

Romy grimaces at Kira. 'Thanks for the reminder.'

One, two, click. Kira's stomach drops. It's surreal no longer hoarding secrets; Romy remembers everything.

Including her crooked part. How is she possibly coping? A sick taste coats Kira's tongue. How is Romy dealing with the violence, with the ghost that lodged in her head? With losing control, causing chaos, snapping their dad's—

Their dad. The waitress. 'Our father always talked to you in German,' Kira realises, scooping up the distraction where it lands in her lap. Her heart was drooping to her useless shoes: their dad. Alive? 'He never remembered you were Turkish. You're…' She struggles for a second. 'Tanya?'

The young woman moves her head, side to side. 'Talie.' She readjusts her glasses, black-framed and thick. 'I don't remember your names, but not a problem. I help.' She leans forward rapidly, linking her fingers on her boots. 'You're in trouble. Me and my mother, we know. If we didn't hear shouting today, or see internet, we still know. We feel.'

Romy's eyebrows fly. 'You *feel*?'

Shivering, Kira hugs her torso. This damn, accursed *cold*. 'What do you mean, you feel?' She pauses. It's going to sound stupid, but this tired, and this cold, there's no better question. 'Are you psychic?'

Romy scoffs. 'That's all we need.'

'No, seriously.' Kira turns to her, defensive. Of course she sounded stupid; whether or not it's true, it sounds like a question from a dated kids' show. 'I haven't had the time to tell you, but there's a…' She flicks her fingers in the air. 'A kind of psychic bug going round, which makes me not sound crazy. I'll explain it later.'

Romy's eyebrows fly higher. 'Jesus Christ, you'd better.'

Kira turns back to Talie. 'Are you, then? Psychic?'

Talie's curious expression returns, unfurling like flower petals warming in the dawn. 'There are more things than watchers in this village, girls.' She taps her nose, a film noir conspirator. 'Did you never get bedtime stories? No.' Her face flits with shame. 'You grow up with these things, you forget others know some. Or none. My mother—you remember?'

Lowering her eyes, Kira nods, her chest pulling tight. How could she forget? They terrorised Hazal's hotel, triggered her wrath, and in return, received face-melting alcohol and an extension of their stay. She's more than flitting with shame.

'Yes.' Talie nods. 'She remember you, too.' Her eyebrows arc for the briefest moment. A frisson of heat flushes Kira's cheeks. Shame, shame, *shame*. 'Anyway, my parents are Chlause. They hide between worlds near Whiteland. The best word…' She screws up her face. 'Traitor. No. Devil? No.'

'This is sounding good,' Romy mutters.

'Outcast!' Talie claps her hands. The reverb echoes off the hut, off the mountains, off the snow. Kira winces. 'Yes. Outcast. Not quite Whiteland, not quite real. Human, but not all. How, why, someone probably tell you. Is long history. Anyway—'

'Wait.' Romy holds up her hands. 'You've lost me.' She glances at Kira. Kira shrugs, turning her mouth down. 'Us,' Romy clarifies. 'You've lost us. Klause? Whiteland outcasts? Whiteland *has* outcasts? I thought it was, you know'—she makes a thinking gesture with her hands—'literally do or die.'

Talie lifts one shoulder. 'Every place has outcasts,' she says, as if this should be plain. 'This world, that world. Chlause are both, and none, for a long time. Over the world, too; wherever Whiteland is, they are. And you say it wrong.'

She lets out an oddly feline hiss. Kira flinches back. 'What?'

'*Ch*.' Talie hisses again. 'See? *Ch*lause. They are your help. Me and my mother, we talk, after seeing the trouble. Like that, seeing, I think you say psychic. Feelings, dreams, *knowing*. We don't know, and then boom!'

She throws up her hands. Kira flinches again. Something about this girl is strange, melodramatic, vaudeville. As overdone as the hiss.

'Boom,' Romy repeats flatly.

'Yes.' Talie drops her hands. 'Then we know, like we always did. Anyway, we talk, and we think: if more trouble comes to you, you go to Urnäsch.' She pushes her glasses up her nose. 'Hidden place, for Chlause. They can hide you, too.'

A quick silence falls. The explanation appears to be over, and Kira stares, at a loss for a response. Talie looks pleased with herself; she could be a caricature of satisfaction, tapping one boot with a square-cut nail and staring out at the mountains. Are they missing something vital?

The silence stretches on. 'Did you know you see Mont Blanc from here?' Talie nods at the powdered range above the lake. Romy turns. Kira doesn't. She did know that, and this all feels off.

'Why would you want to help us?' she asks. 'I don't mean to be rude, but you're right. We're in trouble, and we don't know who to trust.'

Romy nods. 'Also, why would the Chlause help us?'

'And,' Kira adds, 'if they're hidden, how do we find...' She searches for the other name, but it's gone. Lamely, she finishes, 'Them?'

In an accurate imitation of Romy, Talie wags a finger. 'Too many questions.' She leans forward again. 'I am not interview. I help because you do nothing wrong. They help because you are close to outcast. And you find them near the forest.' She tips her head back. A lone crow coasts above the station hut. 'Bad weather coming.'

She points at it. Romy doesn't look. 'How do we find the Chlause?'

Talie eyes her shrewdly. 'Patience.' She nods toward the road. 'When it's dark, walk straight from car park. Walk past the chairlift, walk, walk, all the way to a chalet. Almost black, very old. Stop there. Wait there.' In one swift movement, she pushes up to standing. 'They find you, take you, and hide you.'

'Wait.' Romy scrabbles from the snow to her feet. She's just about taller than Talie's solid confidence, but somehow, she's frailer, small. 'Kira's right; you could be anyone. You could be Fiona. The huldra,' she amends. Talie settles into a look of amusement. 'We named her Fiona. Short, not very interesting story.' She folds her arms. 'Not to sound cliché, of course, but how do we know we can trust you?'

Talie glances behind her. Apart from them, the village is quiet, as bright as a Christmas snow globe. 'In one minute'—she swivels back—'Callum come down the garden.'

Guilt unspools in Kira's gut. Romy merely scoffs. 'That's easy.' She shifts her weight to one hip. 'And even if it wasn't, it doesn't count as trust.' She jabs her chin. 'What's next?'

Talie laughs, a short bark. 'Okay.' She mirrors Romy's stance. 'Then this: three days ago, your father left Whiteland.' She regards them both evenly. 'With *Fiona*. He is alive, and he is bewitched. You say this? I like it. Bewitched. In a spell. That is not psychic, but it is trust. Carol told my mother. Now, I need to go.'

As sharply as she arrived, Talie turns and walks away. 'Kids come back today,' she says, vaulting over the fence. 'Goodbye.'

She lets herself in through a side door. Kira frowns in her wake.

Romy huffs. 'Well she,' she says, 'was what I call weird.'

26

Bruised and barbed and cold

In the house behind the hotel, Talie's cheer drops. It used to be a nice, airy house, lighter than the village's old, grumbling gloom, until she came down after a shower to find her *anne* unconscious in the kitchen.

She knew at once who the other woman was. Standing smug over Hazal, she shimmered at the edges, a hologram from a B-list sci-fi. Carol, in a shocked fluster, had told them the day before: the huldra.

Talie's mouth ran dry, but she didn't blink. She knew enough about the uncanny to not be wholly thrown, and never, even if she was, to show it.

'What do you want?' she asked calmly. Once the English girls arrived, she'd expected it to turn up, but she hadn't expected it to come here. With her gaze wandering down to her mother, she fought her expression neutral. 'What have you done to her?'

Arms folded, the huldra leaned back against the freezer. She would, Talie thought in an odd daze, make a beautiful woman; long, pale hair, a heart-shaped face, curves only amplified by tight gothic clothes. In other circumstances, Talie might…

'Whatever that language is, I don't speak it.' The huldra's lilting accent brought her back with a slap. 'I'm becoming human faster than I thought. It's a bit of a shame, but it's worth it. I love not having a tail.' She stuck out her hip, patted it fondly. 'What am I speaking now? I think I'm stuck with it, assuming you understand. For a while, I could chop and change.'

'It's English.' Talie switched. Habit made her start with French; the locals got grumpy if you didn't. 'You're okay. Most peoples speak English. Before, I say what do you want, and what did you do to my *anne*.'

The huldra regarded her thoughtfully. 'Funny thing, for my language to be better than yours. Your mother's fine.' She flicked a careless hand at Hazal, bruised and propped against a cabinet. 'Go to her, if you like. But don't untie her, or I'll kill you.' She offered Talie a sweet smile. 'For now, I'm gorgeously strong.'

Neither words nor smile hit their targets. Talie dropped to her knees. Pulling her *anne* to her chest, she hugged her, feeling her spidery breath, her warmth. An ugly lump marred the back of her head. A webbed, purple bruise shaded one eye, but she was okay. Alive and breathing.

Her bony, tired mother, unconscious on the floor. Talie hugged her tighter.

'And what I want?' the huldra continued, though Talie wished, with all she had, it'd just shut up and die. 'In terms of this very minute'—she slotted one boot over the other—'that's not hard at all. I want you to help me, then I'll leave you both alone.' She smiled again. Talie looked away. It was candy floss and dirt, burning sugar in a cupcake. 'Fair?'

It wasn't fair. It was blackmail, bruised and barbed and cold. Forcing herself to carry on breathing, Talie shuts the front door. She'll be calm. Calm, and more rigid than a stick up its—

'Talie!'

Her mother's voice, coming from the lounge. Talie stills.

'*Anne?*' she calls, not daring to be hopeful. Stepping down the wide, uncluttered hall, she stills again to listen. 'Are you all right?' Another step, a pause. 'Has she gone?'

In a sharp bustle, Hazal appears, angles and worry in the doorway. 'Oh!' She releases her wrinkled shirt, folding Talie in her arms. They always make Talie think of crispbreads, thin and ready to break. 'She refused to say where you were, and only untied me if I promised to sit and keep my thoughts to myself.' She pushes Talie's shoulders back, small eyes scanning. 'What's happened? Where did you go?'

'I don't speak that language, either.' The huldra leans on the doorframe. Amusement and leaning; what a personality. 'Did you do it?'

Talie nods.

'Good.' The huldra nods, too. If it sees Talie's loathing, it doesn't seem to care. 'I'm getting tired of killing.'

'Do what?' Hazal steps back. Her purple spider is bigger than before, blossoming to blue, to an acid puke. Talie looks away. 'Talie?' She looks between the two of them, half-humans one and all. 'What did you do?'

Talie can't reply; not yet. She levels a dull look at the huldra. 'Why all this if not what you want?'

Hazal snaps her fingers—*girl, hey, what did you do*—but Talie ignores her. She has to. 'You got free.' She shrugs one shoulder, forced and casual. 'Can you run away?'

The huldra meets her eye, and in it, there are cracks. Hairline cracks, maybe, but some of this is a fluffed-up show.

'I made a deal. Freedom for this.' It pushes off the wood. Refusing to cower, Talie stands firm, and the huldra nudges past. 'Maybe I'd run if I could. But they're in my head'—she taps her skull—'and you can't run from that.'

Long after it's gone, Talie still hears the words. *They're in my head, and you can't run from that.*

You can't. If the huldra's being controlled, then nothing's black and white. Her parents told her that enough before her *baba* died, and her *anne* tells her now. The Chlause paid a price. The huldra paid a price. She herself is paying a price. She never thought evil had a conscience, but maybe, she sighs, as weighted as a cannonball, evil's as shadowed as the rest.

But she's the heat for the hurricane. She's the one bringing the storm. She's the heat, the fire, the fuel, but now, pinching her bruising skin in the shower, all she feels is cold.

27

And so they fight

Up in the garden, snow starts to crunch. Kira looks at Romy. Romy looks at her. 'Let's go.'

Callum thunders through the arch to find them by the train line. Kira drops her eyes, and inwardly curses. *Guilty*, it screams. Her heart is as rapid as his angry footsteps. Guilt bleeds through her veins, spidery on her skin. Guilty, guilty, guilty.

For a moment, Callum says nothing. Stepping slowly down the stones, he stops at the bottom. 'What the actual fuck?'

Sodden with snow, Kira's feet are intriguing. No; they're riveting. Utterly sublime.

'We were just…' Romy sucks in a breath through her teeth. From the hotel, the cheese melds with bacon, or toast. 'Going to get lunch?'

Kira's insides creep and crawl. She could wither, shrivel, return to the ground, hiding like the ostrich of cowardly shrubs. Shame. Shame. *Going to get lunch?* It even sounded like a question.

If only her brain worked faster. She could have said *going for a walk*.

'Going to get lunch,' Callum repeats. The flatness of his tone could rival Simon Cowell. 'You run out, saying nothing, leaving the door wide open, and you expect me to believe it's to go to lunch?'

Yes. No. His hefty boots fill the side of Kira's vision. Her spirit cringes even more. He'd be stupid to believe them.

'Yes,' Romy says. Lifting her chin, she folds her arms, just like she did with Talie. 'It was spontaneous. Nobody's perfect.'

Oh, god. Make it stop.

'Spontaneous, I'll give you.' In her lowered vision, Callum shifts his feet, planting himself more firmly. What would she see higher up? Bitterness, anger, hands in his pockets? A stare as pointedly flat as his tone? 'What escapes me, and I'm sorry for being dim, is the need to go to lunch with all of your things.'

Liars. Guilt. Shame.

No. 'We thought we should leave.' Kira looks up.

Rolling her eyes, Romy sighs. 'I had this,' she says, in the suggestive mutter that clearly states 'you're a fool.' 'It was under control.'

'No, it wasn't.' Dragging her eyes to Callum's, Kira opens her face wide.

A black sensation flickers through her. It's the type that lasts a second, the type that sways like déjà vu, the type that makes you wish you were stuck inside a dream. This is exactly why she ran, why she left the door open, why she tried to get the train *now*; this is what she didn't want to face. Callum's eyes search her, narrowing, but it looks like a struggle. He's not only angry; he's hurt.

'I'm sorry.' Kira lowers her bags. They're evidence, tainted, wrong. 'We thought it would be easier.'

'Why?' He's quick. 'I don't want excuses. Why is taking off easier, other than meaning you miss an argument?'

Kira twists her fingers tight together. 'You'd get back to normal quicker…'

'No.' Callum shakes his head, twisting his expression. He still looks like he wants to stare, betrayed and so confused. 'We wouldn't. We'd have been worried. Thinking of what's out there, we'd have been *scared*. Neither of you have phones. After what just happened with Jay, anything could have happened to you, too. Did you think about that?'

'But that's just it, Callum.' Kira folds her arms, as defensive as she can be in the wrong. 'What happened with Jay was not okay. It was far from okay. If your family's going to be put in danger, and especially *children*, we shouldn't be here. Maybe we should have told you, but—'

'Maybe?' Half turning away, Callum throws up his hands. 'Only maybe?' Openmouthed, he turns back, shaking his head at her. 'Of all the selfish—and after this morning?'

'Your mum's lying, Callum.' Romy snaps like frost. 'Wait.' She frowns. 'This morning? What did I miss this morning?'

This morning. Kira's guilt ramps up to live-wire shock. God, she didn't think at all; he's not just hurt because they left him behind. He's not just hurt because they didn't talk about it. He's hurt because of what it looks like: sneaking out, heels in hand, abandoning a one-night stand.

'I...' Kira takes a halting step. Her voice has almost shrunk from existence. 'I'm sorry. I didn't—I—I guess I didn't see it like that.'

'Clearly.' For a moment, he holds her gaze. For a moment, she thinks he understands, but, 'Jesus. You're impossible.'

Twisting his mouth, he turns away, back toward the chalet. 'Both of you. I think you're in the lead, though, unless Romy whips out an atrocity.'

'Rude.'

Kira ignores her. Digging grooves for her nails in her palms, she swallows. 'I thought we were being—'

'Helpful, unselfish, conscientious. Yeah.' Callum swivels on the balls of his feet. 'I get it. Go, if you want.' He gestures at the day, glittering, sprightly, and blue. 'Leave us behind, even though we said we'd help. It doesn't matter, does it? Now that I know you're all right, it's all good.' Roughly, he starts up the stones. 'You've clearly got it all figured out.'

Ducking through the arch, he disappears.

Kira stares through the frosted hedge until it starts to blur. Slowly, cold digit by cold digit, she un-crooks her fingers. Bring it back, reel it in. God, this day is hell.

An echo in the quiet, the chalet door slams. Kira starts. Romy is a mirror.

'I guess we've been left out in the cold,' she says. Shuffling her feet, she blows out her lips. 'Quite literally. Shit.'

'Pretty much,' Kira murmurs, through a distant tunnel. The garden snow is silent. Callum's smell has gone. 'Do you think he meant it?' She turns to Romy. 'Saying we should leave?'

Romy screws up her face. 'He's pissed.' She squints at the sky, as if scrying for rain. 'Lovers' tiffs will do that to you. I think he'll come around.' Hands in her back pockets, she starts to wander off. 'I'm going for a walk.'

Kira narrows her eyes. 'It was not a lovers' tiff.' She watches Romy mooch away, past the old hotel. 'Where are you planning on going?'

Romy gestures at the icy road. 'This way, I suppose.' She lifts her voice, almost over the rise already that slopes down to the field. 'We don't know what we're doing, and the introvert needs alone time. Thinking time, whatever. I'll see you back here in a while.' She pauses. 'And part of it was a tiff.'

Kira almost finds a hint of a smile. 'Stay away from forests,' she calls across the snow. 'And don't do anything overly mad.'

Beneath two kissing trees, Romy laughs. 'I'll save that for when we're together again.'

She's out of sight in a matter of seconds. The chaffinch has stopped. The crow has gone. The car park is quiet, and Kira's alone.

Alone, freezing, and frozen; the feeling has gone from her toes. She can't be sure she *has* toes. Bending for the bags, slow and aimless, dull and lost, she looks around. *Thinking time, whatever.*

Romy has a point. Kicking snow ahead of her, Kira scuffs her way to the train hut. She can't get the train for almost an hour, and unless she follows Romy, walking leads to the forest. Callum probably meant what he said, so what can she do?

Sit here and brood. Dropping her maltreated bags, she shuffles into a corner of the bench and draws her legs to her chest. Brood? No. Resting her head against the wood, she stares at the pointed roof. Shadows, crevices, a wispy, dead spider. Brooding is for hens and twelve-year-old boys. This is an existential crisis.

Her eyes are closed when the footsteps slap. Go away, she thinks at once, deep in an image of a fire. Its warmth is almost working, and she's close to having a nap. Cosy-ish, warmish, her mind white noise. Interaction will kill the mockingbird.

'Kira.' The voice shakes the nap by the shoulders, instantly quenching the fire. Opening her eyes, she turns to the wall. 'Kira, what are you doing?'

Her guilt strolls straight back in. 'Brooding.' With guilt comes shame, and banding together, they stick their fingers down her throat. 'Spiralling existentially. Feel free to leave me to it.'

In her peripheral vision, Callum folds his arms. 'No. What happened to Romy?'

Kira shrugs. 'Walking.' Low and thick, her head thuds. Please, just go away. 'She wanted to think.'

Bit by bit, she turns her head. His expression is close to a caged animal, wary and unsure. Either that, or she's the wild thing, breaking out of her cage. 'Why are you here?' She turns away, back toward the wood. It smells of smoke and must. 'I mean, I thought you were furious.'

Callum doesn't reply at once. 'I was.'

Down the mountain, the train line whines. Kira coils herself tighter. 'Then are you waiting for the train?'

She'd like him to be. She's not ready for this.

'No.' Callum sighs. 'Believe it or not, I actually came to find you.' Ducking under the open doorway, he sits beside her feet. 'I thought, if you were going to leave, you'd wait for the next train. Logically, you'd be here, and if you weren't, I don't know.' He shrugs half-heartedly. 'I'd wander.'

He's just like Romy. It's obvious, in the way he sits, so careful, so thought through. His anger simmers beneath the surface, at the mess she's making, and has already made. Her viscous headache throbs. She resists the urge to run. If two people in half a day have felt they have to do this, maybe she needs a spiral. A spiral, a crisis, and a long, hard, proverbial look at herself and all her choices. Something somewhere is going very wrong.

With the effort of steering a ship through a storm, Kira sits up. 'I'm sorry.'

Tapping a rose on her useless shoe, Callum stares at his knees. 'Mm-hmm.'

'I really am.' Kira shivers. Out of her corner, the air bites. She struggles on. 'I wasn't thinking. I'm not'—she tightens her mouth, waving her hand—'thinking. I can't. I'm not one of those people in books whose decisions are always right, and you think wow, she's amazing, what a strong character. I'm just a person, and I don't know what's going on.'

He lifts his eyes, and it may be wishful, but he seems just a little less hurt. 'None of us know what's going on.'

'I know, and it's not an excuse.' She shivers again, rubbing her arms. 'And I...' She falters. Heels in hand, a one-night stand. He has to know she's not that girl. 'I didn't sneak off because I wanted to leave you. I know it looks like I did, but I didn't.' She lowers her mouth to her knee. The denim is stiff and cold. 'I really didn't.'

Callum's voice is even. 'Then what did you want?'

'What I was trying to say before.' She fixes her eyes on her shoe. 'I wanted to protect you, and Jay, and your mum, and the twins. At the time, it seemed like a good idea. Most of my decisions seem like good ideas, until I get halfway...' She trails away. Unbelievably, he's smirking. 'What?'

Callum taps her flower, one, two, three. 'Sorry.' The smirk twitches higher. 'I am. I'm sorry. I'm not laughing at your reasons, but I...'

Kira bites her cheek. 'You what?'

'Can't imagine you as a protector.' Callum meets her eye, and this time, it's not wishful at all. The hurt and anger are fading. 'You're kind of small.'

Light and warm and lingering, he leans in to kiss her. Kira stills. Inside, something blooms. 'And you're one of those people in books.' She pulls back. 'The guys who say mean things, but sweep it away with romance.'

She rests her cold palm on his cheek. He inhales, and shivers. 'So I'm a cliché?'

'Pretty much. And don't'—light and warm and lingering, Kira kisses him in turn—'underestimate me. You saw what I did to that door.'

'Deal.' Gently, Callum laughs. 'If you promise me this: next time you get an urge to flee, let me know, and I'll come. I'd rather do that than go Braveheart. Also, Mum thinks you've just gone out to clear your—'

An ugly screech squalls outside, the scream and squeal of metal. Callum's words break. Kira jerks back. 'What the hell was *that*?'

The train. She hadn't noticed it sliding up, a spaceship-looking thing, but its back end lurks beside the hut. Her heart rate slows to a canter.

'Lovebirds!' A chrome door whirs open, and Romy hollers out. Banging her fist on the metal, she beams. 'Get on! We're going to lunch.'

28

The closing jaws

In the restaurant at the summit, they talked. After Romy's swaggering tale, of walking so far downhill she found another train stop, and no way in hell was she walking back up, they finally, finally talked.

About Whiteland, their parents, Callum's unique escape. Growing up in Devon, growing up on a Scottish island where everything was grey. *I ran away once*—Callum shrugged—*but only got as far as the harbour.* He forgot he didn't have a boat.

School, university, the last year of life. How going back to get their A levels, degrees, or *Masters* degree, as Callum smirked, seemed impossible. Romy's sporadic addictions, which she brought up sardonically, drink in hand, slapping the truth, the whole truth, and nothing but the truth on the literal and figurative table. She used this to lead slyly in to Kira and Callum. She grinned, relished Kira's squirming, and then, they were on to now.

Then came Jay. *He what?* Callum cried, coughing and choking and cursing surprise. His beer went everywhere but in his glass. *He told you this? He showed* you?

Then came Julia, before he'd recovered. Romy started laughing—*I get the psychic bug now*—and as Kira swore them to secrecy, Callum shook his head, mouthed like a fish, and spluttered for three more *chopes*.

The bishop-fish was the one thing Romy wouldn't believe. They talked about everything, absolutely everything—Mathew, dead and alive again, Anna, Huldra, and air—but that, she couldn't accept. *This isn't Narnia*, she said, very loudly. *Fish just do not talk.*

As the sky smudges pink and purple through mist, they still don't have a plan. Hours of run-throughs, food, and beer have lessened the horror of *now*, and warm with bravado, they pile their thanks on the owner and brave the dusk.

The haze turns to fog on the way down the train line. By the time they reach Callum's house, Kira is bravado-less, apprehensive, antsy, and cold. The colours may be stunning, kaleidoscopic pastels, but the silence is weighted, muffled, and unnerving, and the chalet is far too still.

The Whispers were here, she can't help thinking, as she follows Callum inside. Wicking off the wood and flitting through walls, attacking, scaring, air. The ghosts of the ice plains, who baited her mother, sat back and waited, and took her away.

Kira was so close to them, and Jay was almost lost.

And what a*bout* Jay? What about Julia, with her dizzying talent? Carol, with hers, not telling the truth? They're all here, or at least, they were. Everything is quiet and dark. The house feels like it's brimming.

'Mum?' Callum calls, flipping on a lamp. The tabby cat slithers past Kira's legs, and she jumps. Slipping off her coat and shoes, she nudges it away. 'Hello?'

'In here,' comes the dim reply. Light shines beneath the kitchen door.

Callum relaxes. 'Just checking,' he calls. Heading for the fire, he pulls out the grate. 'I'm guessing we'll want a fire.'

'Please.'

Romy loops her arm through Kira's, and Kira jumps again. Antsy is an understatement. 'Are you okay?' she whispers, turning to her sister. Romy is stiff but shifting. 'You're shivering.'

'Mmm.' With the air of a reluctant pet, Romy rests her head on her shoulder. Callum clomps back out with the grate. 'I'm unideal,' she murmurs. 'But no one needs to know. I'm a jack-in-the-box.' She squeezes Kira's arm. 'I'll be fine before the weasel goes pop.'

Kira frowns. 'I'm not sure that means anything.'

'Are you all here?' Carol calls.

Kira's attention shifts to the door. With its singular stripe, glowing in the gloom, it could be the stairway to Heaven, or Hell. 'Yes,' she calls back.

A pause. 'Kira? Romy?' Carol's voice is strained. 'Could you come talk to me for a minute?'

Kira exchanges a look with Romy. Two eyes wary, two white-hot. Kira and Romy. Not Callum.

Like a student sent to the head, Kira tugs her sister to the kitchen. Carol sits at the gnarled table, a tablet discordant in front of her. The screen is black, but the hand at her temple, the way her eyes and her mouth slope down…the last of Kira's bravado dies.

'What's happened?' Romy asks. Her words could fit in a matchbox.

Carol motions for them to sit. Callum clomps back in again, whistling a song about folding stars. Does he know anything that isn't Biffy Clyro?

At least you're breathing. What do you want? I know lots of Biffy Clyro.

Kira shakes the memory. 'What's wrong?' she echoes, resting her hands on a chair back. Through the window, the sunset mist enfolds them. 'Please just tell us. Whatever it is, it looks like we need to know.'

Carol nudges a cactus-patterned mat. Rubs her temple, shuts her eyes, tucks stray ponytail hairs behind her ears, more times than she needs to. 'The police…'

Kira grips the back of the chair. In the lounge, Callum whistles on. 'The police what?'

Carol clears her throat, but doesn't look up. 'The police found Romy's friends,' she says. 'And now they want you both.'

Romy makes a noise between a cry and a moan. Kira stares, even as her head swoops, struck by vertigo. Something about the woman's face, hanging like an interrupted exchange… 'There's more,' she says faintly. 'There's something else.'

Pulling the tablet toward her, Carol taps the passcode, and stalls. 'There… is.' Rubbing her forehead, she shakes her head, and slides it over. 'I'm sorry. I should just tell you, but I can't.'

Romy jerks her gaze away, burning into the soul of a cupboard splattered with swimming awards. On the tablet's screen is a bungalow.

Whistling, whistling. Kira steadies her breath. God, Callum, *stop*. He's not completely oblivious. Surely he's sensed that something isn't right? Whatever he's moved on to is dire.

Forcing herself to focus on the tablet, she scrolls down the screen. What else can there be? Romy's friends, as Romy said. The text leaves them cold. The link to her, to the house in Devon. And then…

Then, there's a picture.

Then, there's a name.

Animals in stolen hides. Callum's raucous song sinks in. *Dig the grave and watch them cry.*

Climbing the stairs to the pounding bass.

'Stop it!' Kira whips around. Staggering, Romy grapples for the fridge. Her face turns to ash; she's recognised it, too. 'Why the hell are you whistling that? Stop!'

Kira whirls from the kitchen, but Callum doesn't stop. The fire is lit, and he crouches before it, burning his hand in the flames.

I hope the wilderness will call. Kira's whirl falters by the sofa.

Let's become a carnival now Ragnarok is visceral.

'Callum!' She lunges, bashing the side table. 'What's wrong with you? Oh, god, your *hand.*' She rips his arm out of the fire. It smells like grilling. The whistling stops. 'Why would you do that? How is that not killing you?'

Wide-eyed, openmouthed, she pulls him up beside her. 'Callum?'

Glancing at his face, she stops. Her heart flutters. There's nothing there.

Nothing real. Nothing him. White skin, shadowed cheeks. His eyes are full, matte, black. A curdling rumble growls in his throat. His hand hangs limp and smoky.

Romy in the hospital. It's happening again.

Kira screams. Stumbling backwards, she hits the side table. It topples, and jabbed and tangled, she trips and crashes down. The not-Callum's eyes get wider, blacker. Its acrid smell approaches slowly. She whimpers, winded, scrabbling away. Away, away, a chair scraping, her head colliding with someone's shins—

As quickly as it darkened, the hollowed face clears.

It's death, and then it isn't. Callum's eyes are dazed and blinking. His hand is his hand again, scarred but nothing more.

'Kira?' He frowns. She sees the moment he focuses, flicking between her and his mum like a child who's just woken up. 'What's going on? Why are you—'

His mouth works, but his words falter. Kira can't help him, can't explain. Propped on her elbows, her heart a machine gun, it's all she can do to breathe.

'Mum?' Callum looks between them again. The waking child is growing alarmed. 'Will someone please talk to me? Kira?'

In the kitchen, Romy mumbles something.

'Pardon?' Carol asks, as faint as Kira feels.

'It's the mist,' Romy repeats. Kira turns her head an increment, keeping her eyes on Callum. Clinging to the fridge, Romy stares out the window. 'You said strange things came out of the mist, like ghostly things that chased you.'

She nods at the glass. Beyond it, the haze swirls, vague and grainy but *present*.

'Yes,' Callum says. 'But that was to keep us out of Whiteland.'

He lowers himself to the arm of the sofa. Kira's heart fires off another round, or five. Although he seems normal again, glancing between them with bewildered hurt that he probably doesn't think shows… She swallows, unsticking her tongue from her palate. He became so other so fast.

'It was a warning,' she croaks, and swallows again. Callum's hurt spreads like a bruise. 'We'd been investigating, and got too close. Far too close, seeing as we got in.' Stiff and unsteady, she struggles to her feet. She landed hard on her rear and her thighs, and now they feel battered to her bones. 'There's no—ow—reason to warn us off now.'

'Because there's no way in hell we're going back.'

'Basically.' Rigid, she leans on the wall for support, nodding through the doorway at Romy. 'And I thought it wasn't the Whispers anymore.' She aims this last at Carol. 'They were the ones who said there was trouble.'

Carol pushes off the door. 'It's not them.'

She moves to stand by the kitchen window. Kira looks after her; the outside world is hung with mist, the orange-blue garden a deepening shroud. It's stifling, potent, and she rubs her goose-bumped arms. The fire might as well have been left unlit; the house doesn't feel any warmer. Not when something *other* found a way to slither in.

'They want this collision of worlds to stop.' Carol turns back, looking to Kira, to Romy, pale by the fridge. 'And they have no interest in hurting you. They never did. I know you'll be thinking Jay, but that was…' Her mouth contorts. 'Different.' She wraps her cardigan tight around her. 'At least to them. He was eavesdropping. The Whispers are brutal, but they don't lie, so if they say they want to make this stop, then that's what they're doing. If I was to guess…'

She doesn't need to say it. Callum's face was too familiar, too close to the screaming effigy stuck in Kira's dreams.

'The Kyo.' Her voice is flat. Her eyes are still trained on Callum, returning to tend to the fire. He's either showing remarkable patience, or he'd rather not know what happened. Either way, she's watching.

'They're getting stronger.' Carol moves past her, skirt swishing in a sweep up the stairs. 'I thought it would be too much, to show you earlier, but now...' She dips into one of the open rooms.

Kira frowns. 'Show us what?'

A long, black feather in hand, Carol swishes back down to the kitchen.

'Could you...?' Placing the feather on the table, she nods at the light switch. Kira pushes off the wall. 'Thanks.' The lights go out. 'Just for a minute. You'll only see if it's dark.'

In the centre of the table, the feather starts to glow.

'Oh, wow.' Romy moves closer on a breath.

Kira feels like stone. 'It's from a Hyrcinian bird,' she says, her voice a field-mouse hush. A short way from the feather's tip, a cold light is pulsing, a delicate, electric, phosphorescent blue. She puts a gloom-veiled hand to her mouth. 'How is it here?'

Drifting in with woodsmoke and pine, Callum steps up behind her. She thrills with a frisson of fear. Silent and watching, tall and tense.

And the Kyo are getting stronger.

'I found it in the garden.' Carol regards the feather sadly. 'I'm assuming it's a calling card, or the dead edition of "look at my strength."' She touches the pulsing blue. 'Unfortunately, all of this ties in with what the Whispers suggested. That the Kyo are the ones who want you, and have somehow found a witch. Could you...?'

She nods at the light switch again. 'A witch,' Callum says quietly.

'Yes.' Carol tucks her hair behind her ears. Her under-eyes are purple. 'None of this is possible without one. An unbelievable witch, too, if she can reach out here.' She's quiet. Then, as the lights click on, 'The Whispers think they've sent the huldra to push you back to Whiteland.' She pauses, staring through the table. 'The huldra and your father.'

Romy's head jerks up. 'You're admitting it?'

Normally, Kira would wince, but the feather holds her still. Electric blue, tinkling to black. As it fades, her memories fly: buffeted off the path with Callum, wing tips pulsing with colour in the night. The two of them were breathless spectres, the magic pure and cold. The birds were silent, harmless guides, and now...a calling card. Kira drags her eyes away. Did one of them die for this?

'I heard the whisper to Kira.' Carol glances at the window. Kira follows her gaze; through it, there's the hedge, and a single, popping star. The mist has slithered away. 'When they're here, they're in my head. They don't have to be talking to me.'

Carol moves around the table, stretching on tiptoe into a cupboard. Romy narrows her eyes. 'Why didn't you tell us?'

'Because I didn't think it would do any good. As far as everyone knew, he was gone. Until'—Carol rummages around—'he wasn't. Suddenly, he'd left the forest with a huldra, for reasons no one would ever have guessed.' She surfaces with the ruby bottle Romy chose to skim. Romy looks away. 'I was going to tell you when you needed to know. The Whispers…' She sets the bottle on the table. 'Well, they had other ideas.'

Rubbing a fire on her arms, Kira shivers. She shouldn't chastise her runaway self, but she should have bought a sweatshirt. 'That's what they want? To draw us back to Whiteland? Why—actually, never mind.' She holds up her hands. The answer is obvious. 'It's because we got away.'

Romy bursts with a humourless 'ha.' 'Wonderful.' She rolls her eyes, picking at the back of a chair. 'Fantastic. Fab. And with a witch on board, they're strong enough to prod while their puppets lure.' She drops a splinter of wood to the table. 'Such amazing fun.'

This time, Kira winces; their dad's not a puppet. Talie said he was bewitched. That's a very different thing.

Is it?

It has to be.

'To a certain extent, they've always been strong enough.' Retrieving a handful of small, narrow glasses, Carol bangs them down. 'Their extent being the car park. You found that out before.' She bats Romy's hand away from further chair destruction. Romy scowls. 'I've never seen them reach this far.' Her gaze drifts up over Kira's shoulder. 'Speaking of.' Her face sags. 'Callum, are you okay?'

Kira had forgotten he was there. 'I'm fine.' He toes a chair toward him. Its spindly legs screech, and the last of the spell of the feather is gone. 'Are you cold?' He nods at Kira's arms.

She clutches her prickled skin. 'I guess.'

'The fire's blazing. It should warm up.' Sitting down heavily, he slots both arms behind his head. 'Now that we're done with birds and harpies, will someone tell me what happened? I'd lit the kindling, and then…' His lips turn down at the corners, and he looks at Kira. 'And then.'

Black eyes. Rumbling death. Kira looks away.

'You didn't hurt anyone, if that's what you're wondering.' Pushing a full red glass toward him, Carol attempts a smile. 'I didn't see all of it, though.'

Deferring to Kira, she gestures wide. Kira twists her mouth. 'It wasn't you.'

Taking a breath, she comes to the table, accepting the proffered glass. Not-Callum shook her badly, but that's just it: *it wasn't him.* Just like it wasn't Romy, and just like it's not their dad.

After the tale is told, Callum tips back on his chair. 'And I'—he runs his hands down his face—'had no idea at all.'

Romy harrumphs, sitting down with a thump.

'Yeah.' He drops his chair. 'Like you. And my hand…' He turns it this way and that. 'Were any of the kids around?'

Carol lifts the bottle. 'The twins aren't here.' She tops up the glasses, one eye on Romy. 'They're at a sleepover. After what happened to Jay, I wanted to get them out. Jay himself is walking Diego.' Wryly, she smiles. 'He can moan until the cows come home, but he loves that dog to pieces. If anything else happens'—the smile fades fast—'then he can stay elsewhere, too. Just while we sort this out. I'd hope nothing would, but…'

She gestures to the tablet. A spot of liquor blots it, raspberry, or blood. Frowning, Carol wipes it off.

Kira's memory jolts; the picture. Oh, god. The picture, and the *names*. The names, the names, the names. Callum and the Kyo shook them from her mind, but in a rush, in a scream, they sear back.

Trouble has teeth, and its jaws are closing.

29

Little heathens

If he could feel, he'd feel nothing. A numbness, a distance like the sting of depression, staring at the walls with not a thought in his mind. But he doesn't even have that.

London is cold, the British cold of cities. The grass frosts, the air is grey, the people are as dull as the trees, and everything looks thin. Mathew walks through it all as a blank.

Weaving through the web of streets, he could be braced for the winter. His head is bowed, as they willed it to be. His collar is up, as they willed it to be. He's nothing less, and nothing more, than the shell they've willed him to be. They are veins of voices, nestled in his skull. They pushed him into the outside, and now they're pulling him home.

He's clad in dead men's clothes. Being dead themselves, they find this pleasing; it was, and is, a nice touch. Causing death in the skin of the dead.

But now he's done, his part played out. The McFaddens, the teenagers; the voices shriek with glee. Three little children, sitting on a bed. A killer came in, and now they're dead.

They didn't scream; there wasn't time. One by one they were trapped, and one by one they died. Nicely positioned, and each engraved.

The Whiteland tree, the voices hissed. Into their wrists, quickly, now, before their blood runs dry. Make the link between the houses. And then…

A name on the wall, behind the bed, beside the bodies. *Romy McFadden.*

A note on the table, to tie it all up. *Callum Reeve. CH-1807.*

Connections made, if you know where to look. Callum reeled in. He didn't escape them, but he left their land, and caged forever, that's just as bad.

Sticking Mathew's hands in his pockets, they prod him off the pavement and into the park. The rusted gate yowls. Nothing here works. It's enough to make a child jump and a tiny dog yap, but the women are too eager to care. He's nearly back, and once he is, they return to being untouchable. Undiscoverable, untraceable. Freya is doing beautifully, and all is as they willed it.

The day smears into evening. The park is almost bare. Leaving the cold path to the playgrounds, Mathew crunches across the grass. He's so close to the trees. A firework crumbles under his foot, smudged, soggy, and burnt. The grey sky spits irritated rain. It smells of fumes and sickness. Roads clutter the land behind him, to the left, the right, and, if you're not wandering the worlds, beyond the trees. A squirrel as dim as the office blocks scuffles in the grass. By a scrawny bush, a man sleeps, reeking, putrid, sweet.

Oh, to leave this place behind. The voices sigh for release. They'd kill to be alive, but not like this. Not anywhere like this, with people like this, stuck in a stinking, miserable, meaningless, dead-eyed labyrinth of nothing.

Come, Mathew. Scurry home.

With the rain spitting and traffic blaring, Mathew's feet speed up. The shade of the trees grows darker, colder. Behind him, London fades.

The first thing to go is the noise. You don't realise how loud something is until it snaps clean off: traffic, pigeons, airplanes, fools. The voices hum at the silence, at the bare shift in the air. It sharpens so the light is bright. Migraine-bright, sparkled, metallic, a sheen of pollution lifted from the world.

The second is the grey of the chill. It, too, becomes less fuzzy, white and clever and calm. The sense of approaching snow, when everything grows wild. Mathew's body shivers. White is blooming underfoot, sprinkles, then splashes, then patches, and now, as he heads away from the outside, the trees are heavy with snow. Unfolding into the ice plains, Whiteland has let him in.

Surprising, with the Whispers wrathful, but the wide, knobbled trees thin, and the ice lies bare. The voices smile. He could easily have been turned around, flung at the desert, or Skarrig.

Or not; this isn't Atikur. There, tricks are as homely as the pines, but maybe here, it's different.

Either way, they're back. On the edge of the ice, Mathew throws up his arms, closes his eyes, and breathes. Triumph and air. Even by proxy, they were feeling stifled. It's good to be pure.

It's good to be home.

Time to come home, girls.

Oh, how inspired. The girls may misunderstand the message, mistaking their home for the lump by the sea, and that makes it all the more wicked.

Come, little heathens. Here, where you belong.

The women are starting to cackle, and their sense is starting to wane. *Run, Mathew, run girls, sssss. The world will end.*

Mathew takes a last look behind him at the trees. He's silent and alone; no one followed. No one saw.

But would it not have been fun if they had? Such fun, such *fun*, *sssssss*.

Move. Turning Mathew back, the voices shove him forward. They're not completely safe yet; the Whispers might—

Snow. Mathew stops again. The women tilt his head up; he's stepped not onto ice, but the foot of a mountain range, sprawling in a craggy, snowy mess.

The voices drop dead. It isn't the desert, and it isn't Skarrig…but dark in the peaks, a shadow looks down.

30

Human flaws

To the skies with danger. To the skies with Urnäsch. She should have gone back to the chalet.

In the draughty barn, Freya crouches by the fire. It's far too feeble; her skin has grown thin. She would have been cold by Karliquai, but at least it was atmospheric. Strong. Here, she's far too human.

Like the men she used to consume. They'd huddle this way, in forest shelters, holding their hands to the flames. They'd know there were dangers, but they wouldn't hear her coming, far too focused on warmth. It was pitiful.

And now, she's pitiful, too.

Fat chance. Hands on her knees, Freya stares through the fire, pushes to her feet, and stamps out the flames.

She was done with waiting anyway.

31

Killers, corpses, cops

When the bathroom door creaks, she's staring at herself. 'Sorry.' Callum makes to back out. 'I thought you were done. You're a mouse.'

'It's fine.' Kira's eyes stay fixed. Bleakly, she twists the ends of her hair. The startled mirror girl does the same, her cut hand bandaged tight. She wasn't about to risk chemicals near the unhappy gash. 'All I'm doing is wondering if I've made a grave mistake.'

In the doorway, Callum hesitates. Does she want to be left alone? After the way she looked at him earlier, and the guilty, detached apology streams after they all saw the article…

If he's wrong, she can tell him to leave. When she looks so little-girl lost, he'd rather err on the side of comfort.

Or try to. 'I like it.' He moves behind her. 'You look more like you did when I met you.' He tilts his head in the mirror; lightness. 'Maybe I should do mine.'

Mirror-Kira gives him a smile, as small as the mouse he thought her. 'It is approaching calamity.' She reaches back to tug at his hair. 'It's longer than mine.'

'It's not.' He taps her tiny fingers away. Tugging at a strand himself, he eyes it critically. 'None of it reaches my collar.'

'Yet.'

'I think of it as dramatic.' He runs a hand over his head, a thick mess swept to the side. 'Don't you?'

Kira's smile grows. He's somehow made it scruffier, a wild, untameable show. 'Not really.'

'Well, I don't like hairdressers. They talk about your life.' He pulls a face, maudlin and sour. 'Like I have an idea where it's going.'

Callum, the one and only. Kira leans back, resting her head in the hollow by his neck. He's well and truly himself.

To back it up, he snorts. 'So we like self-deprecation, do we?' He wraps his arms around her waist. Is it her, or is he hesitant? 'I can do one better. You know…'

Dropping his eyes to the scattered products coating the floor, he sighs. 'I've peaked. At seventeen, I had it all: a reasonable school record, a string of mildly attractive girls, a winter job that paid enough to fund my epic summers. I'd even hit the top five in ski competitions.' He shakes his head sadly. 'But as I said, I peaked. It was downhill all the way from there, and not in the skiing sense.'

'Poor thing.' Patting his arm, Kira tuts. A mournful aunt with her darling dog, an acting child with a doll. 'What happened?'

Callum drops his sad mirage. 'I realised I didn't give a shit about contests, or the people in them. Or snow.' He huffs. 'But that's not the point. I'm being self-deprecating.' He kisses the downy hair at her temple. 'You like self-deprecating.'

'If you carry on, I'll be forced to subject you to Kira's backstreet salon.' Dubiously, she fingers her hair. 'I might have some bleach left. Ignore the smell. It's not quite turning.' Maladroit in the mirror, she pats his puckering face. 'Are you in?'

'Absolutely not.' He buries the puckering face in her neck. 'No. No, no, no.' He shakes his head, again, again. 'I'm too young to be Justin Bieber. Or that dick from *Game of Thrones*. You know, I-want-my-crown-Mummy-ouch-not-that-one.' He makes a slashing motion. 'Death.'

Kira rolls her eyes. 'I do not know, and your culture is dated.' She frowns. 'Does it really look okay?'

She watches him appraise her, rolling out a maelstrom of faces. 'Hey.' She flicks his cheek. He grins. 'Stop it. Truth or bust.'

Splitting her hair in bunches, Callum flicks it up and down. 'Why did you butcher us, Kira?' he squeaks. 'We've lost our mothers, and our brothers, and our lovers…'

'Stop!' Wheeling around, Kira slaps his chest with a laugh.

'What?' As smug as a hearthrug cat, he grins. 'Am I hurting the stumps' feelings?'

'Yes.' Giving herself a double chin, she peers down at her chest. The newly bleached amputees are breastbone-skimming and sad. 'I'd feel better if Romy had stumps, too, but she thinks her lifeblood'—she waves her hands—'somehow lives in her hair. She wouldn't part with it for the world.'

Even when the world is against them, killers, corpses, cops.

Kira's humour breathes its last. The pictures. The news.

'Hey.' Callum must have seen the light crinkle from her face. 'We'll figure something out.' Taking her hands, he moves them slowly, a back-and-forth bump against his chest. 'When have we not figured something out?'

Kira frowns. 'We never figure anything out.' She drops his hands, running hers through her hair. The motion ends too soon. 'Our track record is terrible.'

Callum pokes her shoulder. 'Your point?'

'Really?' Kira raises her eyebrows. 'Last time, we made bad decisions, nearly died, repeated steps one and two, and lost each other for a year.' She lifts her shoulders, her hands palms-up. 'I survived because I was given a horse that ran really fast through a mountain.' She drops her shoulders. 'You survived because you punched a mermaid. "We got this" doesn't work.'

Callum snorts. Kira narrows her eyes. 'I'm sorry.' He tries and fails not to grin. 'But that's never not going to be funny. I survived by punching a mermaid.' He holds up a finger. 'Sorry, a siren. Seriously, though'—he taps her nose—'we'll figure something out. At the end of the day, you and Romy are innocent.'

Kira prods the bathroom tiles with her toe. 'That's not going that well for us.'

'Yes, well.' He taps her again. Pursing her lips, she moves. 'The Kyo are creepy buggers, but their research is poor. The way they've made this point at you? Jesus *Christ*, it's bad.'

He spreads his arms like wings. 'Here, a mystical symbol, mystically linking two crimes. Here, a spooky scrawl on a wall. It won't hold up.' He shrugs.

'It's not convincing enough, and none of it means anything. I've seen better set-ups in *Scooby-Doo*.'

'Does it have to be a good setup?' Folding her arms, Kira leans back. The sink is cold on her tailbone. 'They want to get us cornered, and in that respect, it's working.'

She glances out of the boxy window. The hotel lights glow dim through the steam. By now, the hotel itself is probably brimming with boarders.

Laughing children, mischief, and noise. God, she's old. God, she's tired. Cooped up, disguising herself, in a cramped, damp-stained bathroom.

And the pictures. The *names*.

'Doesn't it bother you?' she whispers. 'That the police have your name?'

'So what?'

'So *what*?' Kira turns from the night. Callum's gaze is steady. 'There's no way in hell you can say that, Callum. So what, they'll *find* you. They'll come here looking.'

'I suppose it makes us even.'

'No!' Kira clenches her fists in the air. 'Are you doing this on purpose? Do you want me to explode? That's not a good thing. It's a terrible thing.' She shakes her head, a temporary goldfish. 'Please, Callum, stop. You're trapped in the middle of this, because of me, and making blithe comments won't change it. I shouldn't have stuck you with Romy, and I certainly shouldn't have turned up here.' She bunches her hair on top of her head. 'We need to leave.' She lets it fall, dropped on a whoosh of a sigh. 'Alone.'

Callum scoffs. 'Stop being a martyr.'

Kira gapes.

'Yes, that's what this is,' he counters her unasked question. 'You're an unbelievable martyr. Did you drop my name in it? No. All you've done is involve me a couple of days early, and at least this way I know more of what's happening. Chances are'—he lays his hands on her shoulders—'once I'd seen the news, I'd have involved myself. The last thing you should be worrying about is my feelings.' He lets her go with a smirk. 'Not those feelings, anyway.'

Kira battles down her heating cheeks. 'It really doesn't bother you?' She looks up at him. Quiet, tentative, open, exposed. 'Not them finding your name, or this…' She tenses. 'Sadism? Fiona and my dad are creeping around, even when we think we're safe. Your names were added after Romy left, which meant she was being watched.' By the killer. By Mathew. Kira squashes a pulse of dread. 'It's sick, Callum. All of this is sick, and you're saying it doesn't bother you?'

Without a pause, Callum shakes his head. 'I'm saying it doesn't bother me.' He sounds as though he means chewing, or rain. 'It's sick, yes, but I'm not going to banish you, whatever I said before. There might be any number of Callum Reeves around.'

Along the corridor, something thuds. Callum glances at the door. It sounds like someone dropped a laptop, or tumbled off a bed.

Kira folds her arms. The noise, the presence of other people, only strengthens her case. 'Your family, then,' she persists, as the hall creaks with feet. 'We should leave for them, if not you.'

The door explodes with a wildfire knocking. 'Fine by me.' Callum pulls it open. 'As long as I come, too. However the hell they got my name, it's made it my fight, too. Till death do us part. Whatever. What's up?'

In the doorway, Jay's eyes are taken over by whites. He doesn't look like he's breathing. 'Someone's…' He rubs his head. As well as not breathing, he doesn't seem present, like his spirit is floating around his skull. 'Someone's coming. They're loud. So loud.'

Kira chills. 'Who's coming?'

'And what do you mean, they're so loud?'

Jay flaps a hand at Callum. 'You know. I know she told you. Ah.' He rubs his eyes now, vigorous. 'It's a she, an it, I don't know. It's full of other voices, and it wants…'

Kira folds her arms tight. 'It wants what?'

Dismally, Jay looks up at Callum. 'It wants to kill you.'

Kill. It snags Kira's organs like a hook. It's not a word that should apply to her, or any of them. 'Me?' she stutters. Now she's the one floating above her skull.

'No,' Jay growls. 'Damn, they're so…' He shakes his head. 'It's a woman. Well, it is, but it isn't, and there are others inside, and I can hear them, which means she's close.' He presses the heels of his hands to his temples. 'She wants Callum. She wants to kill Callum.'

The hook drags, and starts to gut. Callum goes very still. 'Why?'

Not *are you sure* or *don't be stupid.*

Downstairs, Diego starts to bark.

'Cornering,' Kira says. Hands pressed to his head, Jay nods. 'Pinning more things on me and Romy. She won't have thought we'd get a warning, though.' She tries to look appreciative, and Jay nods again. He'll hear the noose in her mind: *kill*. 'It gives us time.'

'But time for what?' Callum grips the sink. She's seen him this tense, but never this pale. 'If she's coming to the house, then we're screwed.'

Paws and claws clatter on the stairs. Slobbering and bawling, Diego barrels in, crashing into Jay's legs, slamming into Callum's. Kira's mind is blacker than ice. *Kill.*

The dog thumps away again, barking, yowling. 'Basement,' Callum says abruptly. 'Jay. Kira. Move.'

He starts down the stairs. Jay hangs back. 'Where are Mum and Romy?'

Grabbing his arm, Kira pulls him away. 'They wanted to clear their heads. Not together.' Down the stairs, around the dog. 'Romy's walking, your mum's on a drive. God, Diego!'

He barges past her, into the kitchen. Under the table, Nibbles moans. 'Why are we going to the basement?' she asks, snatching at Callum for balance. 'Flight over fight? Is that the best idea?'

'Yes.' Callum yanks on the door beside the fridge. Kira wavers. The black is deep and yawning. 'Go.' Callum tears her hand from his sleeve. 'There's no other way in.' He nudges her. '*Go.*'

Unwilling to be forcibly pushed, she goes. Jay follows, unresisting, but as the dark enfolds him, he stiffens and stops. 'Callum.' He swivels on the step. 'Callum, no!'

The door slams. A key turns. Kira's mind lags.

But then, as Jay starts to hammer on the wood, she knows.

'Callum, stop!' Kira struggles round, flailing in the black. Blacker than leather, thicker than tar. Handle. Where's the handle? 'Callum, let us out!' She slaps the narrow walls, the door. No; overbalance. Where's the *handle*? 'You can't do this!' Clearly, he can. 'Open'—bang—'the'—*bang*—'door!'

'She's becoming human.' His voice is muffled. 'Which means I can handle it.'

'No.' Kira shakes her head, again, again. Beside her, Jay batters the wood, shouting, pleading, breathless. 'You told me to stop being a martyr, so for God's sake, stop being a hero. I can help. I told you I learned—'

'You're safe in there.' Callum's voice is final.

'We're not just women and children, Callum!' She can hear him leaving, his socks on the floor, and she grapples again for the handle. *'No!'*

Raw, Jay hollers, *'She's here!'*

It echoes. *No, she's here, she's here.* Then, from the lounge, 'You're pretty, for a monster.'

To hell with overbalancing. Kira rams the door with her shoulder. *'Callum!'*

'She's surprised,' Jay says sharply. Taking her arm, he squeezes it, and she falls quiet to listen. 'I can see her through Callum. She doesn't know how he was expecting her. That's from her. She's so…'

He grips Kira tighter. She holds her breath, her heart goring, the hook dragging and gouging and red. 'So what?' she whispers. Her heart is orchestral, the hall of the mountain king.

Jay's breath is ragged, hot on her cheek. 'She has other things in her head,' he says. 'Shouting at, at her. "Kill him, he's right there." They're laughing.' His bumpy nails are spikes. 'And her own thoughts…'

'You knew I was coming.' The huldra's amusement sounds brighter than it should. 'Just how did you figure that out?'

'She thinks he's collateral damage.' Jay runs his whispered words into one. 'Her humanity's messing things up. She's confused. Like, he's a man, but he knew she was coming, and it's worse because he knows why she's here.'

Dragging, gouging, red. Kira forces in a shallow breath. Outside, Diego whines.

'Useless guard dog,' Jay mutters, in the same whispered rush. 'Fight her, or something. She hasn't got much magic left. Her strength is nearly human, too, so all she had was surprise.' Loudly, he swallows. 'If Diego chucked himself at her, Callum would get away.'

Would he? Not much magic isn't having none. Kira breathes even less, a memory splintering, digging like glass in her eyes. Her mother, holding a man by his gaze. Her mother, leading him through the forest, gutting him like a fish. He didn't even squeak until he screamed.

Callum, Callum, Callum, *Callum*.

'We're not puppets,' Callum is saying, matching Fiona tone for tone. 'Did you think we were?' He huffs a laugh. 'It really sucks to be you.'

'Why is he antagonising her?' Kira whispers. Forget the orchestra; her heart thuds like a panic attack. Where on earth does he get his bravado? If she didn't know it from Whiteland, she'd think he was unafraid. 'He sounds like my sister, and not in a good way. Those two really should bond. *God.*'

Frustration takes hold, and she clenches her fists. She's the daughter of a huldra; she should have been blessed with some kind of talent, but no, she's crouched in the dark. Locked in a basement by a hero complex, while Callum's facing murder. She should have been able to help.

He should have let her.

'He's trying to be distracting,' Jay says, but he doesn't sound too sure. 'It's hard to hear him over her, or the crazy things in her head. She must have an epic filtering system, because she isn't really listening to—oh, Jesus, Callum!' His voice pitches. 'That's a terrible—*Callum no don't Callum—*'

His mind explodes, and he screams. Pain from someone, maybe his brother, maybe the huldra, roars through his head, everything rushing and screaming and *pain*, and he skids away, backs out, out, out—

Outside the door, there's a crash and a cry, a thud and a thump, and then nothing.

'Callum!' Kira's shriek scrapes his ears. She slams the basement door with her fists, and he winces. 'Are you okay?'

Momentary silence. Jay's heaving breaths wrack his ribs, fighting the current to reach his lungs. The basement air is stagnant, as musty as an attic, damper than an underground cave. He wouldn't bet a cent that nothing's died further down.

'Jay.' Kira shakes his arm. He blinks back to life. 'Jay, can you hear him? Is Callum okay?'

His lips are thick. His ears whine. His head sears. 'I,' he mumbles. His own thoughts have blown away; how can he hope to find Callum's? 'Can't. I can't. Hear.'

His head thunks back against the wall. Kira's mind is wild, blurry, staring wide-eyed through the gloom. It's a nightmare. It's all a nightmare, an unholy ghost of a day that should never have been born.

But it was. It was born, and *oh, my god,* there are footsteps.

The blur becomes a gulping terror. The whole chalet feels stained and dark, dirtied by magic and fear. Steady feet brush the floor. Her breathing is off. Jerky, spasmodic. Kira strains to calm it, strains her ears to hear. She's weaponless. She's *use*less.

The footsteps stop outside the basement.

The key unlocks the door.

The light stabs and blinds her. Kira squints, shading her eyes, ready to fight, to flee.

'Oh!' Somewhere between a cry and a gasp, her breath rushes away. 'Oh, my god, you're all right. You're all *right*.' More heathen than girl, she tumbles forward, flinging herself at Callum. 'What happened?'

She hugs him fiercely. The chalet has tilted. Her body feels queasy and strange. 'Where is she?' She pulls away again. Light, her ringing ears. He's stiff. 'Jay screamed, and I thought—I don't know what I thought.' She pauses. Frowns. 'Why…'

The penny drops with the poker. Callum lets it go, and Kira flinches, scalded by the clang on the kitchen floor. 'Oh,' she says, soft and flat. Something smells like burning.

'Did you hit her with that?' Jay stares at the metal. His eyes widen. 'Oh, wow, you did.'

Slowly, slowly, as if he's a dreamer, Callum shuts his eyes. 'My best anecdote has changed.' Slowly, slowly, as if he's a dreamer, he links his hands on his skull. 'It used to be punching a siren in the face.' He sighs. 'Now, it's hitting a killer with a poker. A psychic killer, no less.'

Later on, it might be funny. Jay is quiet. Kira swallows. 'Is she…?'

'Oh, Christ.' Callum drops his hands. 'Christ, no, she's not dead. I just didn't want her to go for me.' He toes the poker away from him. His face is a clammy, washed-out twist. 'The heat probably did the damage. I took it from the fire.'

The burning. Kira blanches. 'Can we have a new rule?' She fixes on Callum, sicker than ever. 'If I promise not to sneak away, will you promise not to treat me like a damsel?' She nods at the basement door. 'No more locking me up, or forcing me to be safe?'

Diego slithers into the room. Callum ruffles his fur. 'If we get rid of Fiona. Now.'

32

Alone.

With the huldra between them, they slip down the garden. She's breathing, loud and calm, but no way will he look at her face. The red-hot poker line. The lump on her head, where it hit the side table as she fell. She hadn't hurt him yet, but he hit her all the same.

Jay read her mind: it was what she came to do, and probably would have been brutal.

Jay read her mind; that shouldn't be a thought. Briefly, Callum shuts his eyes, dazed in the winter dark. Yes, Kira told him, but it didn't ring true, not until, scared and babbling, Jay appeared in the hall. Not until Diego started barking. Not until the front door opened to a haunting, haunted beauty. Surely it's too much for anyone, let alone his twelve-year-old brother.

From the flashing lights of his screen, Jay shrugs. 'I'm learning to shut it out,' he comments, to no one but his dog. A big, cowardly lump, being cowardly under the bed, Diego snorts and grumbles. 'I think I'll be fine.'

If anything, it's comforting. He's the only reason his brother isn't dead.

Halfway through the frosted arch, Fiona slips from her grasp. 'God, she's heavy,' Kira gasps, shaking out her arms. Dropping the huldra's legs, Callum watches her slump to the snow. 'Why don't you have a car? Or a quad bike? Or a *bike*?'

Callum regards her. 'I don't live here.' Turning slowly, he looks around, scanning the spectral night. 'And'—he lifts a finger—'I don't know how to drive.'

Stretching, Kira ghosts a smile. 'I suppose those are fair.' She cuts a distasteful look at Fiona. It's getting late; the moon has risen. Everything is white and blue. They may be alone, but they should get on. 'Shall we…?'

Callum crouches. 'If you reckon you can hack it.'

Hoisting the huldra up again, he ghosts a smile, too.

Kira elbows him. 'I can leave you in there with her.' Her pale ghost grows, and she lifts Fiona's arms. 'How do you think she thanks people who knock her out with a stick?'

Callum's smile mirrors hers, soft, brief, but there, and bracing, they start down the stones.

Mercifully, the road isn't icy. The night may be cold, but not cold enough for that; instead, the silent chill echoes a long-gone day, when she and Callum supported Romy like this. Then, they struggled through the morning mist, hurrying to what they thought was safety and panicked that Romy was frozen; it's the same long, winding road, lined with pines and sleeping chalets, snow piled on the verges and woodsmoke scenting the air. It's as if time has passed for everywhere but here.

'Everything's the same,' she murmurs, a breath to herself. Even the caricatured tree stump is there: the *pièce de résistance* of a showstopping garden, the dark misshapes its thick-lipped grin into something from *Wallace and Gromit*. A dog barks. A donkey brays.

A donkey. Her memory sifts. The fête of St. Niklas involves a donkey; Hazal told them about the village tradition last year. Hushed children follow a trail, lit by lamps through the forest, in the wake of a grudging donkey and a man in the guise of the saint. It sounded eerie, magical. On this kind of ringing night, tomtes could peek out of hollows. Elves could dance by firelight, capering under the stars. You'd see anything, believe anything, until the trees let go.

A thin veil between here and somewhere.

There's a thin veil now. The past and the present merge, overlaid and gauzy; a gate tied with birthday balloons, the low field, the ski runs, the car park's amber glow. A chill shudders through Kira, as if snowmelt pools her insides. It's not in view, but it's there. On the far side of the car park, cold and forbidding: the forest.

Callum's eyes are on her, but she walks, and stares. Past the quiet, sweeping field, with its lift for sledging children; past the chipping commune hut, by which Callum cornered her, pinning her against it in a hope she'd see sense; past an abandoned cable car serving as a bench; past the frozen trickle masquerading as a stream; and there, there, there: it's there.

The power lines crackle. The air does the same.

'Are you all right?' Callum asks. Stopping by the snowy bank, they lower Fiona to the ground. 'Because honestly, this'—he nods at the trees—'is not a welcome sight.'

'That would be putting it lightly.' Tugging on the sleeves of Callum's old coat, Kira twists her fingers into shapes. Kings and queens of edgy nerves itch through her skin. 'Have you not been back?' she asks. Even her feet want to fidget. 'At all?'

Callum scratches the back of his head. He looks as antsy as she feels, glancing back and forth between the trees, the car park, her. 'Not inside.' His eyes dart to the huldra on the ground. 'Do you want to just…?'

'Yes.' He doesn't have to finish. 'I do.'

Hand over hand, Kira starts up the bank. She wants to get it over with, and then, she wants to leave.

With a wobble at the top, she turns to wait for Callum, climbing and heaving behind her. 'Thanks.' Grabbing Fiona's limp arm, she drags her the last few feet. 'She's still abominably heavy.'

Straightening up, Callum meets her eye. 'She doesn't have to be.'

Kira lasts a second, and she looks away. It's too direct, not shaming, but meaningful, as if he feels betrayed here, too. 'I know,' she says, to the night and the snow. 'But you can't come in with me.'

He could. As she takes a deep breath, grips Fiona, and turns a slow path toward the trees, it's all he can do not to follow. He only can't because she wanted to go alone. She insisted. She knows what she wants to do, and Whiteland saved her once; they don't know if it would save him, too, or if he'd get in at all.

What she didn't say, and he didn't ask, is how they know that she'll get in, or if she'll be let out.

The two figures fade to shades, and Callum shuts his eyes. She's not going far; the clearing isn't far. If the Whispers want to hurt her, they'd have done it in the chalet. The night is still enough that he'll hear if there's trouble. The crunch of the snow is still clear. She'll be fine.

You told me to stop being a martyr, so for God's sake, stop being a hero. Her panic comes back, pummelled through the basement door. Clenching his fists, he makes himself stand. Stay. Wait. Roll over.

Shut up.

All at once, his mother joins Kira. Last night, when Kira was in bed, and he was just going, she sighed, and asked, 'Would you follow her to the end of the world?'

His answer made her look so sad. Half-turning in the doorway, he carefully chose his words, shrugged with a twinge at her concern, and walked away. 'I already have.'

Finally, she's gained some bravado. Heading into the trees, dragging the huldra like a plough, Kira tries not to look back. Tries to remember her logic in going alone, as stubborn, too, as a mule and a plough, and with the moonlight from the car park fading, fainter than faint through the gaps in the treetops, she repeats it yet again.

One: Whiteland will let her in. It's let her in before, and it's also let her out. What's more, it's let her go, after Mathew died, Anna disappeared, and she was left with Romy.

Two: she remembers, with a new acuity, the shift in the air that means she's in, that this other world is wrapping its dusty arms around her.

Three: she's already survived it alone. And, although she kept it from Callum, this way no one else is at risk if her optimism fails. He got to be a hero; now she gets to be a martyr.

Maybe it'll stop her feeling so guilty.

Dropping Fiona's arm, Kira stops to massage her own. She could do with knowing the huldra's name; Fiona was a mistake. Too much associative ogre, and not enough wicked beauty. If the wicked beauty wakes up, she'll ask.

Right before Whiteland takes her.

There's the optimism. The Whispers held a grudge for twenty years, and in Whiteland, Anneliese was a demon; Fiona is hopefully a fresher, redder wound. A fresher, redder wound that will make someone, or something, leap at the chance for vindication.

Or maybe, once Fiona is back, she won't be able to leave. One shot at freedom, and then the doors close.

Which means that when her mother set off, she knew she would never return.

That might not be true. Kira checks herself, pinching the pulse of pain. She doesn't know how Whiteland works. This is nothing more than a sanguine plan she's amazed Callum went for. Man-protect-woman Callum. Lock-her-in-a-basement Callum.

Although what's the alternative? A humane alternative? Nothing else would allow them to live with themselves.

Because leaving Fiona in a land that turned her mother to air is humane. Kind, even. Compassionate. Charitable.

Stop. Pulling out a pen torch, Kira clicks it on, determined to sever her thoughts. Devices are temperamental in Whiteland, but she might as well try. Anything to take away the pressure of the dark.

Bending for Fiona's arm, she trudges off again.

It doesn't take long to realise that the torch has made it worse. Instead of stripping the forest of menace, it lets more shadows stretch, and leer. The blinding, electric flare turns the moon dull and hazy, and oh, it's far too quiet. Nights shouldn't be this quiet; her loud breathing and louder footsteps sound like a phone in a cinema, so blatant and disturbing that she longs to hide away. To not chance awakening the sentient, slumbering beast.

With a shiver, she sweeps the torch around. Black, towering trees, surrounded by bushes of thorns and snow. Low dips, little rises, sloping around a night-masked path. Somewhere, she remembers, with a sudden clarity, there's also an icy pond; it curves along the walking track, with boards, and benches, and DIY shelters woven from broken branches. It wouldn't be around here. Here, she's heading straight, off-piste, on Romy's year-old track.

The track she forged, drunk and stumbling, almost up to her knees in snow. Kira's jeans are soaked. Her calves burn. The scent of pine is far too strong.

Far too soon, the track bears fruit. Sweeping the torch around again, Kira stops. Her breathing hiccups, missing beats. To her left is the hollow, rotting tree, and straight ahead is the clearing.

Everything since she arrived in the village has triggered something, but this…this is the slap that knocks her down. This is where the footprints vanished, and this is where they met the first real, if dainty, trouble. This is where the forest tripled, and this is where they ran from the snorting, chasing mist. Above all, if you have a connection, this is where the outside shifts. This is where the world becomes the bitter, shimmering Whiteland.

Kira lets Fiona's arm fall. She's really back; she's doing this. In some inexplicable way, it feels like a tidy circle. Like the last year was a fraud, and this is where she belongs.

Oh, stop. That's self-pity, or masochism. Kira shuts her eyes, pictures a wall, and opens them up again. She'll need her thoughts, and all of her wits, when Whiteland lets her in.

So shush. The thought is close to an audible word, drifting like the Whispers. She can feel it, taste it, watch it travel.

And then the forest prickles.

Just a little, but enough. The snow grows sharper, overexposed. Kira stills. It's starting.

The forest cools, and straightens its spine. Birds or beasts or breezes rustle their way to watchful quiet. The night slips closer, prescient and awake. The pocket torch goes out.

Kira's balance sways, dipping in the dark. Fiona stirs. Kira glances down. Their boots brush, but there's nothing to see. Are they in?

Peering through the black, she listens. No hoofbeats. No weaving wisps that drew her sister in. Her heart slows from a gallop to a trot. She should be more afraid; this could be disastrous. Breathless, though, waiting, still, she's slowly turning numb. It's as if the worst is over.

It's hard to fear an unknown threat. Kira thinks this consciously, deliberately, forcefully, battening down the smaller voice that says *you're not masochistic*.

Sh. Kira blinks, and squints. Her eyes are adjusting, and nothing has changed. There's no phantom road, or multiplying clearing, shifting like a staircase at Hogwarts. No abnormal shadows, or creatures, or landscapes. Just the sensation of—

Nothing would be what it is, because everything would be what it isn't.

Exactly. It's not the first time she's felt like Alice.

'No,' Fiona mumbles.

Shot with shock, Kira starts. She'd almost forgotten the huldra was there, but Fiona is sitting up. 'No,' she slurs, her eyes lidded. Drooping and drugged, she shakes her head. 'No, no, no, no, no—'

She screams. A single birdlike keen, it pierces, and then, slashed off, it stops.

Dully, she levels her eyes at Kira. 'Enjoy the Chlause.'

Her head snaps back. Another scream rips from her throat, a sharp, razing howl. Rigid with horror, Kira can't move. Oh, god. What has she done?

Oh, god, oh, *god*. Her paralysis breaks. Behind the scream, a rumble builds. She stumbles back. Wind hisses through the trees, rushing, mounting, moaning. Fiona's scream strangles.

The huldra collapses.

The wind roars. Kira staggers. Now, in a cannonball burst, she's afraid. Her hair lifts, whipping her cheeks. The hem of her jacket slaps at her thighs. The wind steals her breath, knocking snow from the trees. She turns to run.

Merciless, the roaring takes her whole.

Callum is staring at the *ski de fond* tracks when Kira slips from the trees. Tumbling quietly down the bank, she lands in a rumpled heap.

'Kira!' he exclaims, skidding quickly down the snow. Woozily, she shakes her head. 'Are you okay? What happened?' Crouching, he takes her cold, gloved hand. His old coat shines on the tarmac. 'I didn't hear you coming at all. Has she gone?'

Kira blinks at him. It's as though someone's pressed fast-forward, and she's trying to remember, the morning after, what happened the night before.

'They threw me out,' she says, letting Callum pull her up. It sounds and feels petulant; she didn't think she'd be ejected. 'They chased me to the edge, and gave me a shove. I felt like a fox in the henhouse.'

Callum snorts. 'More like a daft hen playing with the foxes.'

Weakly, Kira bats him. 'Rude.'

'A bit.' He puts an arm around her. 'You're okay, though? No dodgy tricks? Fee, fi, fo, fum, they took Fiona and...'

'Made me run?' Smiling fleetingly, Kira frowns. 'Yeah.' She looks down at herself. 'I just...I don't know.' She shakes her head, ridding her mind of the bleary haze. 'I thought I'd get there, feel the change, leave Fiona, and hope for the best. Instead, she wakes up, screams, collapses, and I'm thrown out by a phantom wind.' She leans into him, twisting her lips. 'I felt like a puppet, or a rag doll. The usual image, you know, and once it took over, I couldn't move. I couldn't think.' She glances back. The trees are harder and darker than ever, an unimpeachable army. 'You didn't hear anything?'

He kisses her temple. 'Not a peep.'

'Not the screaming, or the wind, or me?'

Callum shrugs, small and sorry. 'Nothing, until you slid down the snow.' He cocks his head. 'There was screaming?'

Fiona's head, snapping back, the harsh, ripping keen. 'There was.' Kira pulls a face. 'Let's go.'

At the chalet, Carol hasn't returned, but Romy's guns are blazing.

'About time!' She jerks up from the couch, violently staccato. 'Where the hell did you go? All the little walnut said was that you were on a "mission."' She quotes in the air disdainfully. 'I kept asking, and asking, but he kept tapping his nose and pretending to stroke a cat. What a *boy*. Also'—she looks between them—'there's a poker on the kitchen floor.' Throwing out her hands, she slaps her hips. 'Answers, please. Now.'

She's the schoolmarm from *Matilda*, or maybe even Carol. 'You know'—Kira looks at Callum—'Jay's not exactly wrong.'

Callum huffs. 'No, he's not.' He meets her eyes, and her smile. 'I quite like "walnut," too. I might start calling him that. And in terms of our mission'—he hangs up their coats—'Fiona appeared and tried to kill me, so we took her back to Whiteland.'

Kira's eyebrows hit her hair. 'You—Callum!'

'*What?*' Romy's head pops forward, like she didn't quite hear. 'You did what now?' She stares at them with black-rimmed eyes. 'Mary, mother of god. You're not joking.'

'I'm as serious'—Callum slides off his boots—'as my brush with untimely death.'

Kira kicks him. Passing en route to the kitchen, he grins and musses her hair. 'Jay heard Fiona coming,' she says, dealing him an elbow. 'Then, Callum's basically right. He hit her with a poker, and we took her back to Whiteland.'

Callum laughs. Romy blinks. 'I'll say it again: you fucking what?' She opens her mouth, and shuts it. 'No. No, no, no.' She laughs, humourless. She looks like she's pouring all of her scorn into one incredulous look. 'You've been to Whiteland and back in the time it took me to *walk*? After everything that happened there? Didn't it try to, I don't know.' She pulls down the corners of her mouth. 'Eat you?'

Sheepishly, Kira lifts her shoulders. 'Not today, at least.' She can't help feeling sheepish; coming from her sister's mouth, it sounds like the worst of plans. 'I dragged her in, and it threw me out.'

'And the thinking behind it was what?'

'Um. I thought it'd want her back.' The worst of plans; the *worst*. Even to herself, it sounds feeble. 'I figured the Whispers had a thing about escaping, and as it turns out, I was right.'

'"As it turns out."' Gaping, Romy runs a hand through her hair. 'You're insane. Both of you. Couldn't you have—I don't know, buried her in the—wait.' Her head snaps in place. 'What do you mean, *you* dragged her in?' She narrows her eyes to spikes. 'It threw *you* out? He didn't—you didn't go with her?'

She flings this at the kitchen, aghast.

'She wouldn't let me.' Callum reappears, sipping from a glass of water. 'She was being self-righteous.'

'"She" has a name.' Kira frowns at her sister, as indignant as Callum sounds. 'No, he didn't come with me, and yes, I asked him not to.'

'Told,' Callum interjects.

Kira cuts him exasperation. 'Either way, it worked. Fiona's gone. What that means for everything else, I don't know, but…' The front door opens, and her brain jolts. 'Why don't you have a Christmas tree?'

She turns to Callum. Romy stares. His eyes flick over Kira's shoulder, to Carol sweeping in from the cold.

'We do when it's Christmas.' He sips his water, as casual as summer wind. Kira rests her hip on the sofa. She'd been wondering that, anyway. 'Come the twenty-seventh, if we're lucky, Mum packs it up and shoos it out.'

'Pine needles,' Carol says. Kira turns. Callum's mother is flushed but calmer, swirled around with the winter bite. 'There are far too many as it is, and getting the men to use a vacuum cleaner is worse than Psyche's tasks. Plus, with animals clumsier than sin, the baubles fall like rain. Now I think'—she pushes back her staticky hair—'I'm going to go to bed. Any fresh horrors can wait. How's Jay?'

She aims this at the room as a whole. Slumping into an armchair, Romy flips a hand. 'He's twelve.'

She yawns. The whale moan is contagious, and occupant by occupant, the chalet falls asleep.

33

Old clocks and cold shocks

When the voices disappear, he isn't anything.

Not just anyone; anything. They took him over a year ago, ingratiating their presence onto his, so his body and self grew used to being mindless.

They were used to being controlled; that was fine. What they'd never been was abandoned.

For a long time, Mathew is an old clockwork toy, in desperate need of winding. The wooden soldier in thirties films, dressed in blue with a key in his back, staring, ready to go. He's close to nonexistence.

Eventually, awareness of the cold drifts back. Mathew starts to shiver, frosted with shocks. Pushing his hands into his pockets, he hunches into his coat. His scarf. Animal instinct. No thought; not yet.

Then comes sound. The faint moan of wind over snow, of ice whipped up into clouds. Something lighter, pattering. Heavy breathing, his and more. Crunching steps. A rhythmic thud.

Then comes sight. Mountains rising craggy from the valley where he stands, as perfectly white and splashed with beige as every peak should be. The sky, matte and dusty blue, sifted soft with clouds. The creature walking toward him, thumping the snow with its staff.

Its green eyes watch, curious and light. A wolf prowls beside it, hackled and grey, its pupils bright and cutting. A metre away, they stop.

Then comes meaning, late to the rave. Cold, sound, and sight collide, and Mathew McFadden is back.

34

Following the fall

Kira's first thought is *not again*, as soon as the hand starts tapping.

Get off, or I'll punch you like a siren is her second. The owner of the hand doesn't know that she wouldn't.

'Kira.' The hand keeps tap-tap-tapping.

Kira screws up her face. 'Mmm,' she manages. 'Sleeping, Romy.'

Balling up the blankets, she screws her eyes tight. The air mattress dips regardless. 'You can sleep downstairs,' Romy whispers, as Jay harrumphs in a dream. 'I thought you might like to swap.'

Kira cracks her gummy eyelids. 'What?'

Romy leans in. 'I said, we can swap.'

She's a wraith pale with moonlight, her hair high in a bun. 'Swan,' Kira mumbles. White, long neck. Like a swan. 'Never see your neck.'

'Okay.' Romy flicks her, and again. 'Good to know.'

A third flick. Kira swarms awake. 'Hey.'

'Hey, yourself.' Romy bends her legs in a lotus. 'Someone's down there huffing and puffing, and now you're awake, you can ask what's wrong. Also…' She winks, wicked and cheeky. Her breath smells like chocolate. 'You've not been alone that much. This definitely isn't happening because he's driving me mad.'

Now you're awake. Huffing through her nose, Kira rolls over. She is now. 'Fine.' Nudging her cherished blankets down, she groans her bones upright. 'Did you eat all the chocolate?'

Romy flashes a grin. 'If I'm craving anything, I'd rather it made me fat. Even better, it's helping.' Settling into Kira's space, she sighs. 'Oh, so warm. By the way, that's a yes.'

In leggings and a vest, Kira shivers. Her feet are shrivelling. 'How nice of you.' Curling her toes, she hugs her ribs, skirting the air mattress to the door. 'You definitely did it for yourself.'

'You're welcome.' Romy wriggles contentedly, snuggling into the blankets. 'See you on the flip side, lovebirds.'

On the stairs, it strikes Kira that she could have said no. That it might look more than strange, intruding on Callum when he's trying to sleep. That Carol will probably hate them tomorrow, as she did when she caught them on the couch last year. That she really, really, really should start thinking things through.

Too late. Padding across the wooden floor, she perches on the sofa. Romy's blankets bunch at the end, and she pools them around her waist.

She's so *awake* now. Outside, the wind is gentle, creaking at the walls. The cuckoo clock ticks, the fire settles. It still smells of woodsmoke, mixed with carbonara. It should be gross, but it's homely.

We have seen his star in the east, and are come to worship him. Shifting the blankets to her shoulders, she smiles. She recited that line so many times that she'll probably never forget it; she only had the one, and damn, it would count. She clutched her cloak the same as now, but then, as far as she remembers, it was fashioned from a sack race reject. She made a good wise man.

Yawning, Callum rolls over. 'I see she sent the cavalry.'

Trust him to have falcon eyes in the back of his wildling head. When she came downstairs, he was facing the fire. 'I'm cavalry, now, am I?'

Her retort is hotter than his humour required, but suddenly, she's awkward. Awkward, and abashed, caught reenacting the wise man from her eight-year-old nativity. She wriggles around, avoiding his scrutiny. If only she'd woken up more before Romy got in her bed.

'You tell me.' He stretches wide. 'I'm not the silent ninja gremlin.'

Kira scowls. 'I'm not a gremlin.' She unravels her cloak, scrunching the blankets down around her waist. 'And I'm not the cavalry, either. Romy said you were huffing and puffing, and that I should ask what's wrong. She's taken over the air mattress, so'—she shrugs—'I guess we're stuck.'

She leaves out the rest. It's raw enough already, sat in the bare moonlight in pyjamas, without Romy's not-so-subtle hints. Her nudge-and-wink insinuations kissing Kira's skin.

The cuckoo clock strikes three. Kira's shoulders shiver. It all feels different, late and illicit. They've never had this; this quiet, this promise. They've always had to talk, to plan, to move, and if they haven't, they've not been alone.

'Can't sleep.' Callum scratches the side of his head. His hair is frustrated from tossing and turning; Kira just wants to stare. 'You'd think I'd be out like a light, but no. My mind won't stop. Are those roses?'

'Are what roses?'

His lips twitch up. 'Your vest.'

'Oh.' Kira glances down. Now they're both looking at her chest. Her cheeks heat. 'No.' She wills her fingers not to fidget. 'No, I think they're cherries.'

When she looks back up, he's smirking.

When she looks back up, she registers, for the first time, that he's shirtless.

For the love of God, stop staring.

'What are you smiling at?' she murmurs, dropping her gaze to the rug. She can only hope that the moonlight keeps her face a ghostly pale; she needs a temperature gauge, and by God, she needs it now.

Focus on something. Anything. The dream Romy dragged her from, something about a church; the night chill of the living room; the dribbling cat on the mat. She still doesn't know its name.

A shiver cools her skin. Good. She drags her eyes back up.

'You,' Callum says at once, as if he'd been waiting. Knowing him, he was. 'You're fidgeting.' He cocks his head. 'It's cute, but why?'

Kira shivers again. This room is *cold*.

'Oh, come on.' Callum shifts in his blankets, budging closer to the fire. 'You're cold.' He gestures beside him. 'You know you're cold, and I know you're cold. Whatever's making you awkward, it's not worth being cold.' He gestures again, more vaguely. 'It's the same as New Year, but not on the couch.'

It's not the same.

But it's what Romy wanted.

Kira quickly banishes this, but all of a sudden, the room feels charged.

Callum lifts a waiting eyebrow. The silence stretches out, and she wills her fingers still. Maybe she's imagining it; she's almost certainly thinking too much. A room can't feel like it's holding its breath.

'You realise no one's forcing you.' Amused, Callum watches as, with a sigh that sounds more cross than accepting, Kira slides from the couch.

'I know.' Lifting the duvet, she slots herself in. She seized the moment this morning; it shouldn't be different now.

This morning's the problem.

Stop. Shut up. There might be no moment to seize.

'So?' Kira lays her cheek on her palm. 'Seeing as I'm the cavalry, are you going to tell me what's wrong? Before the home invasion, I was nicely dead to the world.'

Callum's eyes widen.

'What?' she asks.

He starts to laugh. '"Before the home invasion."' His voice is level and dry. '"Dead to the world." How is that a better comment than mine? Not only did it nearly happen, but it came with a home invasion.'

Kira pulls in her lips. From under her lashes, she smiles a tiny '… Oops?'

'"Oops?"' Callum should have glasses, to lower in disapproval. *"Oops?"*

'Oops.' Kira smiles, coy. 'It sounds like I have an echo.'

The way Callum looks at her, the coyness almost quails. Her body warms, from the inside out. The pillows overlap. The blankets hold them close. Her skin is wired. Quailing isn't right; it leaves the ashes, becomes a phoenix, and flies to fire, to flames.

She should make thoughtless comments more often.

'That'—Callum leans in, with mock severity—'sincerely deserves a "woman."'

He's close, so close, so close. Kira's insides leap, like a foregone conclusion, the foregone conclusion they are. 'Nothing deserves a "women."' She rests a finger on his lips. Warm. Soft. Breathing. 'I'm not the one who made a joke about dying.'

'True.'

Somehow, he's closer still. The space between them is tangibly hot, and he's real, so *real*. It hardly makes sense; he's always been real, and hard to ignore, but now, he's more solid. More physical. More here, now, with her.

He cups her face. She shuts her eyes. She can smell him, taste him, feel him, pulling her in, kissing her slowly, full. Her hands are cold on his back. His muscles tense beneath his skin. He presses her to him, everything hot.

In the middle of the night, she falls.

35

The woman in the doorway

'Are you really telling me this won't be vile?'
Doubtfully, Kira regards the mugs, brimming in Callum's hands. Black mixed with nutmeg; even Eeyore looks perplexed.

'I'm really telling you it won't be vile.' Callum takes the chair beside her. Draped with her wise-man blanket, Kira reels in her knees, cups the mug, and lowers her face to the heat. If nothing else, it'll warm her up. The kitchen is draughty and cold. 'You said you sniffed at fancy coffee. This is anything but.'

At a buzz from the counter, he glances up. 'You should get it.' Kira nods at the phone, left by the bread bin and a bulging muffin tub. It's the third buzz in as many minutes. 'It might be important.'

'I doubt it.' Callum pulls a dismissive face. 'No one has this number.'

The phone buzzes a fourth time. 'Apparently, someone does.' A fifth vibration. It jitters close to the counter's edge. 'Right, I'm going.'

Untangling herself, she scrambles up, before the device can plunge to its death. 'Here.' She holds it out. 'Embrace your popularity. Hey!'

Callum pulls her down toward him, half on his chair and half on his leg. 'Rude,' Kira mutters, graceless and skewed. He takes the phone with a grin.

'Just keeping you on your toes.' Curling an arm around her waist, he starts to scroll, and tenses. 'Ah.'

'What?' Kira twists her neck, frowning at his frown. 'What is it?'

Wordless, Callum hands her the phone. A stream of messages, all in French.

All of them but one. Kira stills from the inside out: *Callum I saw your name in 20 minutes. It says your connected to murders, they want to talk to you are you ok???*

She stares until the screen blurs, until her voice returns from its trip beyond the sun. 'What's twenty minutes?' she asks, oddly. The words feel lumpy and gnarled.

Callum sighs. 'A Swiss newspaper. Oh, my—'

The phone buzzes again. 'Mary, mother of god, no.' He covers his face with the groan. 'Whatever it says, I don't want to know. I'm already quoting Romy.'

'Mmm.' The words coalesce around her. Her brain is starting to fog. 'Who sent the one I read?'

How tight is the net?

'A girl in the village,' Callum mumbles through his fingers. 'Cupcake?'

He shifts her from his leg to the chair. Out in the dawn, snow is falling, pattering at the window. It should feel soft and cosy, even through the cold. The early kitchen bursts with home: a cloth witch, a chalkboard, scrawled with MUM, WE NEED BEER. It should be safe, but it feels like a door.

'The village?' Kira watches Callum snatch the portly tub. To think that mere minutes ago, she was frowning over coffee. 'As in, this village? Your village?'

'Yes.' He nudges her over, dropping the tub on the table. 'Which means that news is spreading, and as much as I like our bubble'—he sighs—'it also means we should check it.'

Kira sighs. 'I liked our bubble, too.' The Fiona debacle distracted her from their other, wider fiascos, but if Callum's name has crossed the channel, then their ignorance is a threat. 'What do the other messages say?'

She prises the lid off the tub; banana. Disappointed, she sits back.

'The same,' Callum says, into a mug shaped like a Russian doll. 'Three of them are Guillaume, the train driver. He said the police are looking for me, and obviously focusing here. The rest are from people I went to school with.'

Gulping his coffee, he sets it down. It sloshes over the side. 'Dammit.' He flexes his fingers, breathing slowly, into a fist and out. 'Basically'—he stares at his knuckles—'it's "what the hell's going on?" When I said no one had this number, I didn't think my old life would—' A buzz. 'For the love of *Christ*!'

Kira jumps. Snatching a muffin, Callum rips off the paper like he'd rather be crushing skulls. His face has angles she didn't know existed, and no wonder; they're getting close. The police, the walls, the world. Maybe, although it's always been real, it didn't feel real to him. Maybe now his friends are involved, it's finally smacking home.

The phone buzzes, yet again. Bulldozing the muffin, Callum sits and stews. 'Fuck off.'

Grimacing, Kira picks the phone up. His anger makes her edgy, but someone has to know.

Hey Callum, I know we've not talked in forever but have you seen what's in the news? If you haven't you really need to. Like really. Does it mean you?

Meurtres?? Vraiment?

Je t'ai vu hier c'est quoi tous ça??

Kira is steeling for internet search results when Romy breezes in.

'Lovebirds!' Spying the muffins at once, she neatly pilfers one from the tub and plops into a chair. 'If Carol's not up yet, my scheme will have gone unnoticed.' She grins between them. 'Eh?'

Kira says nothing. Quietly shredding the muffin wrapper, Callum stares away.

Romy's grin fades. 'What's wrong?' She looks between them again. 'Trouble in paradise?'

'No.' Kira holds out the phone. 'Just trouble.'

The search results loaded, and now, her mind judders. The police—which police? All police—want Callum. Well, they want to *talk* to Callum, which is possibly just as bad. Callum Reeve, with potential links to the murders in Devon, London, and Middelburg. Callum Reeve, thought to reside in the Riviera region of Switzerland. She found several articles in several languages, and they're all saying the same: they're coming.

They're coming.

Romy sets the phone on the table. 'What do we do?' she murmurs, a breath of dead air in a desert. 'We're being—'

A knocking shakes the house. Romy's words freeze.

'Cornered.' Slowly, Kira turns toward the door. 'We're being cornered.'

'Upstairs.' Breaking out of his stupor, Callum screeches back his chair. Kira stands to keep from falling; surely not. They can't be here. A hot-glue fear sticks to her bones, but it can't be the police, it can't. Can it? The timing is impossible, comic and cliché, and they can't have found Callum already. Speak of the devil, as if by magic—

'Upstairs,' Callum repeats, as the knocking comes again. 'This isn't the same as locking you up. It's a preemptive strike. Please.' Taking her elbow, he steers her none-too-gently from the room. 'Just go.'

'Oh, don't worry.' Romy is up, clumsy in her haste. 'We're gone.'

Her hip bangs the table. Seizing Kira's waist, she propels her forward. The cold hands spur her, and Kira wakes up; what is she doing, waiting? Freezing? She didn't run for—and from—her life to end up trapped by headlights.

They snick the bathroom door shut to a nasal French drawl. 'What if,' Romy murmurs, right in Kira's ear, 'it actually is the police?' The whisper lifts the hairs on her neck. 'If they search the house, they'll find us.'

'Sh.' Kira presses her ear to the door. Rigid, she keeps her breathing minimal, but all that drifts up is the fact it's a woman. A high-pitched woman.

She slumps with relief. Her funny bone catches the door handle, but she hardly feels the pain. A high-pitched, *laughing* woman. Casual noises, casual words, and a short while later, the front door shuts.

'That,' Romy says, 'didn't sound serious.'

Kira wouldn't count any chickens just yet. The stairs start to creak. Footsteps on the landing.

'Wherever you are, it's fine.' Callum. His voice is weary but relieved, disbelieving. 'I heard them trip in the garden. They've gone.'

Kira could crumple. Relief, relief; the ordeal only lasted a minute, but there are so many reasons to panic. Warily, she opens the door. 'Who was it?'

'A neighbour.' In the hall, Callum leans on the gloomy wall. His hair sticks up at angles, as if he was scraping it with both hands. 'A nosy one by all accounts, but yeah. Bad timing.'

He tries to smile. His cheeks don't move. Someone smells of sweat.

'What did she want?' Romy asks, starting back downstairs. Glancing at Callum, Kira follows. It's okay; they're okay.

For now.

'The same as all the rest.' Callum crashes on the couch. He looks about ready to knot a handkerchief, up his sticks, and walk through the Earth. 'To know if the papers are telling the truth. I told her I hadn't the foggiest, looked bemused, and that was that.'

He rubs his forehead. Kira folds herself beside him, Romy on the rug. 'Really?' She crosses her legs like a leprechaun, scooting across to Nibbles. 'She took you at your word?'

Callum shrugs. 'She kind of had to. I'm pretty sure she was peering around me, but I made sure I filled the door. I'd bet good money'—he sags into Kira—'that she was the forward guard. There'll be a troop of gossips out there somewhere. Greedy bloody vultures.'

Romy snorts. The sound is feeble. 'I love when they hunt in packs.'

Nobody speaks. The room is heavy, as dense as clouds of snow. Kira's mind replays the messages, projecting them on the air: *I know we've not talked in forever but have you seen what's in the news?*

Meurtres. Murder. The Riviera.

An overarching wrongness fires inside her, lodged between her ribs. They damn well won't be cornered; enough is enough is enough. They won't freeze up, caught by headlights, and they won't sit here and wait.

'We need to make a plan,' she says. Her voice is sharp, and Callum flinches. Romy turns. 'We're starting now.'

36

The thoughts behind a wall

'Christ!' Mathew careens away, with force enough that he trips. The packed snow is a hard landing, jarring an earthier curse. 'What the…?'

The watching wolf grumbles, and Mathew scrabbles back. The ground numbs whatever it touches. His heels kick up white shards, but still he scrabbles, and still he stares, and still the eyes watch on.

Somehow, he's in the mountains. Nothing grows here; nothing can. The motley three of them cluster in a central, powdered valley, and all around, on every side, are peaks. The wind whips, as it only does at dizzying altitude. The air is so cold it has flavour.

'Stop.' The large creature's voice is quiet. A tug inside Mathew halts his scrabbling. His limbs burn while he wheezes, unfed and unfit, and the creature blinks its crinkled, sleepy eyes. 'Thank you.'

Thank you? Mathew's mind is madness. Never mind how he got here; what fresh hell is *this*?

'It is not,' the creature says. 'And I do not believe you need to escape.' It taps its weathered staff. 'The minds inside you decided it would be best to depart.'

The wolf yips. Mathew glances at it. If anything, it looks amused. 'What?'

'The undead seem to be frightened of me.' With a chuckle, the creature wrinkles its eyes. 'I must say, it's very wise. I would have torn them out of you and severed their claims to existence.'

High above, the wind moans. Powder eddies off the peaks. Mathew tries to seize his breath. 'Whatever that means,' he gasps, 'it's not comforting.' He runs a hand down his face, three rapid times. A scrubby beard is taking hold; he's never grown one in his life. 'Christ.'

Blinking hard, he pictures a cord. It's how he taught his daughters to lift from a dream: find the cord, follow it, and wake up in your bed. He'll lift. He'll drift. He'll wake to sense.

The cord disintegrates. The snow soaking his gloves is real. The wild smell of the wolf is real. He can't lift. He can't drift.

'Everything is real.' The creature taps its staff again. 'As real'—it rumbles another chuckle—'as you are truly observant. You do not, however, understand where you are.'

It's more of a curious fact than a query. Mathew looks around him, flit, flit, flit. Snow. Sky. Wolf. Thing. Glaciers and chasms and visible wind. 'Should I?' he asks, disquieted. He feels like a lost little boy.

'No.' The creature's eyes unfocus, before sharpening like a lens. 'The leeches used you, and spat you out. You've had no thought of your own in…' It tilts its head toward the wolf. Watching Mathew, it doesn't blink. Its yellow eyes are thoughtful. 'A year.'

'A year?' Mathew scoffs at once.

The creature meets his eyes. 'Yes.'

'That's not possible.'

'Why?'

Mathew's derision stutters. 'Why? Because…'

Because…because what? He strains, but his mind is chalk, wiped clean from the board. Where he is, why he's alone, who or what is in front of him; there isn't so much as a smudge. He struggles through the nothing like a swimmer in a dream. Thinking is harder than punching a wall, and his knuckles are bloody. Does he know himself?

Mathew McFadden. It drips in droplets, beads of rain, but concern swamps relief. Concern that he had to forage, and it wasn't just there to be found.

But at least he *did* forage, and it *was* there when he looked. He's Mathew McFadden, forty-seven. His wife is Anna. His daughters, Kira and Romy, are eighteen and sixteen. He doesn't smoke, has never smoked, yet reeks of cigarettes. The last thing he remembers is—

'A year ago,' the creature says.

Mathew starts. How…?

'And,' it continues, 'I'd be much obliged if you'd slightly alter your thinking. Consider me less of a creature, and more of a nebulous spirit. I am not a spirit, either, but I prefer the touch of whimsy.'

Mathew's brain chugs in silence. The creature—the nebulous spirit—the esoteric giant—is probably right; it's not a creature in the sense of a beast, but how else was he meant to see it? Its head is a chiselled, wizened man, wide at the cheekbones and narrow at the chin; its eyes glint green, dug in a skull with plastered, greying hair. The thin, elongated body is shaggy and mostly bare, and a brown tunic hangs over feet to crush a house. They're truly, madly, deeply incongruent, and when you have a body that dwarfs a swarthy wolf, that's truly, madly, deeply saying—

Before his eyes, the creature—giant—man begins to change. It's as if he looked away, for a finely spliced second, and a ghost slipped peripherally by; in a blended blur of movement that he doesn't quite catch, the creature is suddenly *not*.

A nebulous spirit. He's close to human.

Mathew's mind bends back.

37

And so she hides

'Yes, yes, I know her. I was with her on New Year's Eve.'

Kira taps stop; play; stop. Seb's round face is a visceral shock, and no matter how much she watches the clip, the shock wave doesn't lessen. Her friends are being interviewed; her *friends*. Cheery, innocent Seb, so baffled by the questions.

Kira jabs play.

'She always seemed lovely.' Stop. Rewind. 'Yes, yes, I know her. I was with her on New Year's Eve. She always seemed lovely. No, I never met her sister, but I can't believe they'd do that.'

Stop. Loudly, gustily, Kira exhales, drooping back in the armchair. This is unhealthy, and she knows it's unhealthy, but there's nothing else to do. Romy and Jay are Diego-walking, Callum's chopping wood, and Carol's gone to see the woman who's looking after the twins. Moodily demolishing pretzels and grapes, how can she not sit and mull?

Especially when there's so much to mull over. Romy's flight to Milan has been found. Kira left blood on the wall of her room. They both made a call to the same Spanish phone.

Refresh. Refresh, refresh, refresh, every news site she can find, every update posted live as the story goes viral. They came up with a last-hope plan, but it just seems so…

'Screwed.' The pretzel muffles her mutter, and she reaches for another, refreshing her search yet again.

It's almost reached her mouth when she stills. Oh, no.

KIRA McFADDEN SEEN IN SWITZERLAND.

Kira's nerves fly out of her chest. Dynamite, a sonic boom, and out of panic, preservation, she jabs the other tab.

Seb's face fills the screen. *Yes, yes, I know her. I was with her on New Year's Eve. She always seemed lovely.*

Kira clicks back with a clacking nail. She's seen it too many times, and the same words, the same round eyes, twist ribbons of fleshy nausea deep inside her gut.

KIRA McFADDEN SEEN IN SWITZERLAND.

But this… She lifts a hand to her mouth, squinting at the link. Snow crunches outside. Is it true? Is it *likely* to be true? She skims the page. She was seen on a train.

Her nerves fly higher. A train? A fevered laugh flutters up. Who could have the memory to see her on the news, run through their recent life, and realise she was there? It was rush hour. She should have blended.

Clearly, she didn't. She fidgeted, or smelled repugnant, or something else that stood out.

Probably that: fear of standing out.

KIRA McFADDEN SEEN IN SWITZERLAND. More snow crunches, voices murmur, but they barely make a splash. *A train from Geneva Airport, through Lausanne to Brig.*

The bear trap is springing. The net is closing in.

Through the window, something moves. Kira looks up. It's blue.

Oh, god.

Out of the armchair and into the kitchen, all in a scrabbling breath. Grapes fly from her knees, pretzels grinding into the carpet, and she slams her back too hard against the wall. The police have come. They've found her. Oh, god. Nibbles eyes her from the tabletop, haughty and disdainful. She's winded, and not from the wall.

Two policemen, talking to Callum; she so nearly got caught. Caught reading a tablet, surrounded by childish snacks. Kira swallows, frozen by the basement door. The chalet is so bright in the dark; she was clearer than the midnight sun.

If one of them had turned, if one of them had seen her…she'd have been clueless until they burst in. Kira swallows again, fighting the urge to barrel out the back door. They didn't see her. She's fine.

But they're here, the police are *here*. They've found Callum. Will they believe him? That he ran into Kira on New Year's Eve, left on New Year's Day, and lost contact? That her sister called him, worried about her, but he said he couldn't help? That he flew back here so out of the blue because his mum is fighting depression?

It's not the tallest tale they've woven, but will it be enough?

What if it actually is the police? Romy whispered earlier. *If they search the house, they'll find us.*

Kira flicks her gaze around the room, a jangled, glittery blur. Her heart hammers so fast she feels faint. She needs to hide. Where can she hide? She discovered the other day that the nooks and crannies are lacking.

Her gaze zeroes in on the window. Jack-Frost glass, watching the garden, as bare as the ones in the living room.

Shit.

With a sobbing gasp, or a gasping sob, Kira pries herself off the wall, lunges for the basement…and slams the door behind her.

Shit, shit, *shit*. Sliding down the damp wood, she perches on the step, a scream trapped in her throat. At every turn, she's stupid; she's been *seen*, yet she stood in front of two windows, and slammed a heavy door. If anything's going to alert police, it's a loud attempt to hide.

Slowly, Kira swallows her scream. The crashing echo fades, and becomes the sound of silence. She could be alone in a vacuous void, and she hugs her torso tight. The basement might be dank, personified despair, but she's absolutely out of view. You can't see me, I can't see you.

Kira shivers, breathing, staring through the black. She never thought she'd spend so long hiding underground. There's sweet mould somewhere, and stagnant water, with a hint of animal kennels. A draught like a paper cut touches her ankles, tiny and slicing and sly. Outside the door, a cat click-click-clicks on the kitchen floor.

Click-click-click, then silence. Kira's chest fills. The black. The rot. It's a giant maw, filled with spit, ready to chew her up.

It's not. Resting her chin on her knees, Kira plunges into memory. She's nineteen; she won't be afraid of the dark.

The first thing to come swims up from nothing. She was three, maybe four, and her father was laughing, urging her into the bathroom. *Show your mum, Kira.* Her mum was by the sink. *Anna, listen. Where's Nina-Bear?*

Kira was bemused, but she spread her arms wide, pleased to have someone so pleased. *I've got* no *idea!* she exclaimed, and they laughed, at her puffed-out chest and something else. Something she couldn't quite figure out then, and still isn't sure of now.

Click-click-click go the cat's sharp claws. The tiny draught slits, nuzzling her skin, in-between her socks and her jeans. The rose of memory fades, and another takes its place.

One from around the same time, of a seat behind Mathew's bike. The tentlike canopy was rainbow-patterned, and lounging while her father pedalled uphill, she sucked Hula Hoops from her hands.

Another, from only a few months back. Biking home from campus, drenched by the rain, frozen with Macy but laughing. Where will her bike go now? What will happen to any of her things, or Macy's, Eva's, Veronica's? Romy's?

Out in the living room, the front door shuts.

It's faint, but definite. Kira stills. The police; not charging, but creeping, sneaking. The click-click-click has stopped, and something else is coming. Something measured, moving closer, like—

'Kira?' Callum calls.

Kira doesn't twitch. He may have come inside, but that doesn't mean it's safe. It doesn't mean anything at all.

'They've gone.' He waits for several uncountable seconds. In the damp, musty dark, time is nothing. 'I heard the car, too. Just now.'

Still, Kira doesn't move. Callum's footsteps retreat, and the stairs start to creak. 'Kira?' he calls in the distance. 'Where are you?'

Kira listens so hard her ears feel strange. No other sounds; no other voices. Inch by stiff, silent inch, she slides back up the door. She's being paranoid; Callum wouldn't trick her. Nor would he meekly let the police in, and, if they forced it, he'd probably think, say it was fucking ridiculous, and thereby tell her to run.

Nice, unhelpful logic. Every sense is on edge, every shivering goose bump, every hair that sprouts from her scalp. Inch by stiff, silent inch, she cracks opens the door.

The creak is too loud. The room is too bright. She's acutely aware of the scrape of denim, of her thighs touching as she moves. It's far too open to attack out here; she feels like she's fleeing Dunkirk.

'Kira?' Callum jogs back down the stairs.

She jumps. 'Yes.'

'Good.' He's alone; of course he is. 'I thought for a minute you'd legged it. Over the hedge or something.' He hugs her once, tight. 'Who knows.'

Kira forces her limbs to loosen. 'I considered it,' she croaks. Her mouth has turned to dust.

'Can't say I blame you.' Callum heads for the lounge. The room is empty, the front door closed. Everything's normal but her. 'How much did you hear?'

'None.' Following him to the fire, Kira bites her cheek at the scattered grapes, at the crushed, smushed pretzels. 'Well'—she crouches to pick them up—'I heard the snow, and voices, but I saw them through the window and hid in the basement. What did they want?'

'What we expected.' Crouching beside her, Callum removes three red grapes from the rug to his mouth. 'If I knew you, if I knew Romy, if I knew why my name had come up.'

He picks up a pretzel.

'Gross, Callum.' With a frown, Kira flicks it away.

Callum huffs. 'Charming. Anyway, I gave them the story, said they could look around. With their predictable Swiss decorum, they refused.'

'And then they left?'

'And then they left.' Pushing back up to his feet, he moves to poke the fire. Kira's eyes linger on his unburnt hand. 'They said they'd come back if they had more questions, but they mostly just looked confused. I'm not surprised.'

Emptying her hands in the grape container, Kira drops onto the sofa. The armchair is unpleasantly covered in crumbs. 'No?'

'Not really.' Woodsmoke settling on his skin, Callum sits beside her. 'Imagine it from their perspective: their orders are based on tenuous links, relate to foreign murders, and include driving up a mountain, in the dark, to question a student. The whole case must look mad.'

Kira flashes her eyebrows. 'It is,' she murmurs. A pause. A hush. A whisper, then, 'Callum, I've been seen.'

She's watching the churning flames when he sighs. 'Then I guess we need to go.'

38

Light and bright

Charging in from the cold with Jay, the first thing is the luggage. The second is Kira, straight-backed, pale, tapping her knee up and down. The third is Callum, guarding his woman like she's just been crowned the king.

'Mary, mother of god,' Romy says, unclipping Diego's lead. 'Who's died?'

It was meant as a joke, but only Jay laughs, a 'ha!' that chokes *bad taste*.

Callum ducks his head. Kira does nothing, tapping that goddamn knee. Romy nudges the door shut. 'What's going on?' she asks, guarded, looking between the mannequins. 'No one *has* died, right?'

Stiffly, Kira stands. Callum looks at her. 'We're going to Urnäsch,' he says, so naturally that it jars. 'To the Chlause.'

Romy blinks. 'What?' Her insides gnash their teeth, but less. Her packet went down the loo. 'Since when?'

'Since I was seen on the train.' Kira moves to the bags, and the clothes on top. Christ, she looks ill. 'And since the police turned up, with the fun fact that Callum's postcode was on the note with his name. The news left that bit out.' She yanks a hoodie over her head. 'They'll come back, and soon. If one person says they've seen me, I'm sure others will, too.'

'Probably people in the village,' Callum adds. 'We should have been more subtle.'

Tugging the hoodie down, Kira pauses. '*I* should have been more subtle.'

Callum frowns, but says nothing. 'Either way'—he tosses Romy a sweatshirt, patterned with Stark wolves—'we need to leave, before Mum gets back. I figured she wouldn't approve.'

Slowly, heavily, Romy slumps, thumping against the sofa. The police were here, asking questions. The police were here, and now they're running, to an unknown, supernatural exile. Through all of this, it's finally real: they're in trouble. 'Callum, too?'

For the briefest moment, Callum hesitates. 'Callum, too.' He catches Romy's eye. She looks him dead in the face, and shifting, he looks away. 'I don't want to be arrested, and someone wants me dead.'

At least those last two things are true. Romy nods. 'Okay. Let's go.'

'Good luck, musketeers,' Jay calls. Through the frosted arch, they leave the chalet lights behind, out to the black-iced road. The frozen dark is colder than last night, but wrapped in a tumult of Callum's clothes, she's relatively warm.

Not that she needed it, after Jay's comments. He saw her and Romy in their oversized jumpers, with old ski jackets over their coats, and laughed: 'You're Callum's groupies.'

'Only one of us.' Romy winked.

Jay winked back: 'Yeah, I know.'

Oh, how Kira burned, and burns again at the thought. He could have heard anything, but now at least, her mind is hers alone.

Alone to worry, and question, and dwell; on her unspoken doubt over what they're doing, on her dawdling guilt over Callum coming, too. On her grief about her grandparents, padlocked in a bawling box. On her grief, her confusion, her longing over Mathew.

On the news reports, looped in her mind. On the horror of the huldra, and the Whispers, and the Kyo. On her earlier terror, her current fear. Now that her thoughts are private again, she can feign bravado with the best.

'Can trees watch you?' Romy asks, when they reach the deserted car park. 'It feels like they're sizing me up, and don't much like what they see.'

'That depends.' Kira watches her sister shrewdly eyeing the trees. She looks like she's sizing them up and doesn't much like what she sees. 'In some books, they speak Latin.' She runs a gloved hand through her hair. The ends are frosted white. 'Is there…?' Her gaze snags on a shadowed cabin. 'There is. I thought there was. Does anyone else need the loo?'

Romy tuts, wagging a finger. 'Should have gone before we left.'

Her dad-voice is perfect, and it hurts. Kira turns away. 'I'll see you in a minute.'

The flickering striplight is automatic, and for a moment, she's perfectly still.

'Here.'

He turns Kira to face him. A burning overrides her indignation, and she squeaks. 'Sorry.' He lets go. 'I didn't realise.'

Kira flexes her fingers. In, pain. Out, relief. 'Neither did I.' He motions for her to look up, hold still. 'And I'm getting the feeling I should learn first aid.' A little dry, a little rueful as he tends to her cheeks. 'This is the second time in two days you've had to fix my face.'

Kira closes her eyes. The past settles around her, a fluttering sheet on a summer's night. She was lighter then, and younger. A year isn't long, but thinking about it, Callum was lighter, too.

'It's not normally like this, trust me. The most exciting thing that happened before yesterday was...' He screws up his forehead. 'Actually, never mind. Nothing exciting has ever happened. It's all bickering neighbours and figuring out why there are so few people, yet so many cats.'

Kira opens her eyes. Right.

'Never again.' Callum shakes his head the second she exits the toilets. 'I'm forbidding you to leave me alone with your sister ever, ever again. Ever.' He glances at Romy. A wry smile plays at his mouth, but he looks like she's dragged him through the forest by his hair. 'There's been some...questioning.'

Romy shrugs. 'Honestly, I'd go full hog and call it interrogation.'

Kira's eyebrows fly. 'Romy!' she cries. The burning threatens to reawaken; if this doesn't stop, she'll start to steam, like a bubbling winter Jacuzzi. 'Why?'

'I had to be sure of his intentions.' Romy spreads her hands at once. 'Make sure he's pure of heart, you know. Honourable and true.' She prods Callum with a bitten nail. 'We can't be going on a magic trip with a scallywag and a rogue.'

Aghast. Exasperated. Cringing. Proud. Caught in the riot, Kira stares. 'Great.' She sighs, and lets them slide. She'd love to moan, but despite herself, her gravity is lifting.

It's more surprising than it should be. Last time, they were light, and bright, even in the depths of Whiteland; there's nothing to say they can't be now. Maybe fighting the sense of *wrong* will help them all survive.

'You're forgetting some vital points, Romy.' Sardonically, Callum regards her, the way he'd humour a toddler whose argument is flawed. 'Not only did this rogue jump through hoops in your hour of need, but, and correct me if I'm wrong'—his lips twitch at Kira—'he's already been on a magic trip with your sister. I think I've passed.'

Planting a hand on her hip, Romy pouts. 'But *Ca*l*l*um,' she moans. 'You're ruining my turn.'

'Your turn at what?'

Kira rolls her eyes. They're all lightening, brightening, sticking their heads above water; either that, or they've all gone mad.

'I wanted to be the older sister.' Romy tugs on her rucksack straps like a child. '*She* does it all the time.'

Lower down the mountain, an engine growls. 'Being the actual older sister, I get all the turns.' Kira cuts her gaze to the road. 'And I'm sorry to end this really good talk, but if we're going, I think we should go.' She gestures vaguely. 'That could be Carol.'

Turning to Callum, she glimmers with guilt. Carol will let herself in, oblivious, and one of her sons will have gone. She'll stand and stare at the cutting dark. Her stomach will drop, and she'll think of Whiteland, of how she lost him once before.

She'll curse the cops. She'll curse the Kyo. She'll curse the girl who took him away.

'You know you can still go back, right?' Kira's guilt balloons to black. She can't look at Callum, so she squints at the road, at the glinting ice and the trees. 'You have your home here, your family.'

Callum lifts his chin minutely. 'I do.'

The engine growls louder. 'And,' Kira says, shifting her rucksack. His steadiness is throwing her off. 'And we've no idea what'll happen in Urnäsch. We could end up anywhere, for any length of time. Time we can't predict.' She sets her jaw. '*Things* we can't predict.'

'All the more reason to start the introductions.'

'No.'

Callum nods at the road. 'Come on.' He starts toward the field. 'The more I hear that car, the more I'm sure it's Mum's stress-driving. Any minute now we'll get the dulcet tones of Korn.'

Romy snorts. 'Your mum does not listen to Korn.'

'No.' He spins to walk backwards. 'It's often James Blunt, but Korn is a better image. Ah.' He cocks his head. 'Wrong James.' Humming an off-key version of "Hold Back the River," he spins back around. *'Allons-y.'*

He heads across the car park, humming. It could be Korn, or any number of Jameses; above the engine, the music is faint, barely more than strains.

Kira follows Callum's lead, and makes for the field. Either way, they need to go.

'Hey.' Tapping her arm, Romy falls into step. 'Remember how you doubt everything?'

Kira blinks. 'No?'

'Yes.' Romy drops the words beneath her breath. 'You shouldn't. Not with him.'

Kira skirts a stack of logs. 'You're being vague.'

'I'm really not.' Romy nods ahead. 'You know what I mean. The scallywag. The banter bus, the rogue.' The car hits the corner, and they step off the tarmac, shadows in the shadow of a tree. 'He has my seal of approval.'

A smile starts in Kira's chest and winds its way to her face.

Romy elbows her. 'That's cheered you up.'

Playing not a James at all but something just as weepy, the car snarls around the bend. 'No,' Kira lies, biting at her grin. 'I'm smiling at the seal of approval.'

Technically, she's smiling at both, but no one needs to know. It's nice to keep the fluttery little feelings to herself.

'Oh!' Romy claps her hands, stepping from the shadows. 'The seal of approval! Arf, arf, arf!'

'Precisely.' Kira mimics her, with somewhat less panache. 'Remember when it embarrassed us?'

Romy grins. 'Very much.' The grin wavers. 'That was the point.'

It was. The seal was Mathew's speciality, after he'd met a boyfriend, or seen a school play, or when Anna was getting dressed up. Kira's own smile slips.

'Ladies?' On the edge of the field, Callum stops. 'Are we taking this magic trip?'

Thank God for Callum. Latching on to the subject change, Kira hooks it with both hands. 'Talking of the seal of approval.' She bumps Romy's hip. 'What suddenly made you his champion? I thought you annoyed each other.'

'Hello?' Theatrically, Callum taps his wrist. In the moonlight, he looks like an otherworldly visitor, bright, white, and washed out. The night itself is ghostly, electric: crackling wires, an unknown journey. Back where it all began.

'Without you to mediate, we do.' Romy drops her voice. 'He's sarcastic, and buffoon-y, but he cares about you. I reckon, deep, *deep* inside, the Boris thing goes away.'

'Boris?'

Sagely, Romy nods. 'Johnson. Boris Johnson, oh hel*lo*, watch me ride my bicycle.'

'Romy.'

'Aren't I funny, la-di-*da*, I'm having a jolly good jaunt discombobulating the world.'

'Okay!' Lifting her hands, Kira battles a grin. 'Ten out of ten. I get it. You and Jay are saying the same, so I'll be gracious'—she eyes her pointedly—'and let those nuggets pass.'

Romy emits a bursting 'ha!' 'Jay? You talked about romance with *Jay?*' She gawps at Kira. 'Jay's like, *twelve*.'

The pointed look becomes a glare, and a spirited one. 'He reads minds.'

Romy laughs. 'Oh, yeah. Of course he does.' Crouching, she scrapes for a snowball. 'How could I forget? It's a circus up in here.'

'I think you mean freak show,' Callum says, as they finally reach the field. 'The worst thing in circuses are clowns.' He smirks. 'Thanks for joining me, by the way.'

Romy tosses the snowball up in the air. 'Eavesdrop much?'

'Not usually.' Somehow, he looks both innocent and smug. 'Don't worry. I missed the rest of the chin-wag.' He turns to the field. 'Where to?'

He sweeps his arm around the snow. A flash of last year's disbelief darts through Kira, from when the abnormal was strange; they're seeking salvation in a moonlit field, from knights in outcast armour. Is that better or worse than relying on branches, or the whims of phosphorescent birds?

'Talie said there's a chalet, and it's pretty much straight ahead.' Kira twists her mouth, at the winter trees, at the bare, vacant land. There's not so much as a fox, or a shadow, let alone salvation. 'Her instructions were very fairy-tale, but that was the general gist.'

'Like getting to Neverland,' Romy says.

'Or following special branches.'

Kira looks across at Callum, open and surprised. 'Yes.' She smiles. He dips his chin. 'Like that, and everything else. Don't talk to the bishop-fish, but the rest taste delicious.'

Callum tilts his head toward her. 'Or—'

'Yes, yes, the good old days.' Wedging herself between them, Romy slaps their shoulders, grips them tight, and steers them across the snow. 'Murderous worlds and crazy people: the nostalgia gets us all. Sadly, though, we're stuck in the first, and the second won't find themselves.'

Callum shoots Kira a crooked side-smile. Romy continues to chunter, and they let her push them on.

39

Dust and ashes

Guilt hits Talie with the force of a tanker.

She'd been calming a pupil after a nightmare—which is no mean feat when you're naturally brusque, often explicit, and this isn't your job—but she did it, and was closing the door to the dorm when the girl spoke.

'Yes?' She turned back to the nearest bed, wrestling down her impatience. This was really *not* her job, and the school were going to know it.

The girl propped herself up on her elbows. 'Thank you,' she whispered, with a timid smile. Despite herself, Talie softened; squirrel-small, with pools for eyes, she couldn't be more than eleven. 'You're nice.'

That's what did it. Talie smiled back and left, but now…out in the hall, consumed by the honeyed, pinewood fire, her insides contract. Cramp, sicken, gasp, repeat. She'd dealt with this already; she was sure she had.

She'd had to. The past two days had been busy, settling the kids in after Christmas, and she'd not had time to think. Besides, she said what she said and did what she did to protect herself and her *anne*. It wasn't malicious. It was natural.

But then a scared little girl called her nice. It was unrelated; it shouldn't have affected her; but it did, and it does, and it *hurts*.

Go. Propelling herself off the wall, Talie bursts from the hall like a bomb. Loud enough to wake the kids she's just put to sleep, she catapults down the groaning stairs, grabs her coat and combat boots, and barges through the suitcases crowding the restaurant's cosy light. Most of the staff are there, toasting the new term, and although they watch, aloof or bemused, she kicks past the obstinate obstacles and ignores them, one and all. No time.

There's *less* than no time. Wrenching the thin door open, Talie pelts out into the snow.

On the second frozen stepping stone, a voice stops her short. 'Talie?'

She stalls. Shit. Her heart writhes. No time, no time, no *time*.

'I thought it was,' the voice calls. 'Is everything okay?'

Forcing herself not to flee, Talie turns. The snap is on her lips—'It's fine,' or something less polite—when she sees the voice's owner. Locking her car, walking over, peering through the streetlight: Carol.

'Where are the English girls?' Talie blurts, before her brain can think. 'I go to your house to see them. I need talk to them. Are they there?'

Carol falters. Frowning at the chalet, she looks back at Talie, poised like a greyhound ready to race. 'I suppose so,' she says. They're on a level now, almost passing on the stones. 'I don't know where else they'd be. What's—'

The race begins. 'Oh!'

Shouldering through the arch, Talie powers up the hill. 'Talie!' Carol shouts. 'You can't—'

She can. Breathless, determined, she crests the garden and lurches toward the door. 'Kira!'

The yell emerges as a wheeze. Talie flings the door open. 'Kira! Romy! I need—' One hand on her chest, she blinks back dizziness. 'I need—talk to you.' Her heart is thunder, her blood the storm. 'Kira?'

She staggers inside, colliding with a chair. The house is gently dark, as it would be so late, but her storm makes it desperate, abandoned. Tumbleweed blown across an empty desert. A singular church bell. Death. *'Romy!'*

'Stop twisting your knickers, goddamn. They've gone.' Carol's son thumps crossly down the stairs. 'Are you here to kill them, or arrest them?' Leaning on the banister, he looks her up and down. 'Personally, I wouldn't try either. Callum's a pro with a poker.'

'No.' Talie flaps this away. 'No, no. I'm not—I need—'

'Whatever you want'—the boy yawns—'can it wait? I was going to bed.' He bats at his mouth, stretching and slow, sleepily smacking his lips. 'The last few days have been worse than school. Come back next week. That'd be great.'

'Talie!' Carol puffs up behind her, buffeting in the cold. 'Explain what on earth you're doing, or leave. You nearly knocked me over, and now you're yelling?' She slams the door. The chalet rattles. 'Jay's right; every day at the moment is one of Dante's Hells. Ten seconds.'

'I told them to go to the Chlause.'

The words fall over themselves. Talie shuts her eyes. It doesn't sound real; it shouldn't be real. After this, she'll think and think again before she speaks, or acts, or breathes. Carol will kill her. She should have been stronger.

That's the fucker; she should have been stronger. She should have fought for her mother, instead of instantly jumping through hoops. Even if she was terrified, and had it sprung upon her, she shouldn't have sent them to Urnäsch.

That's the fucker: thought by thought, they're going to be torn apart.

One second. Two seconds. Six seconds. Eight. The quiet is frailer than cobwebs, and gingerly, when it stretches on, Talie opens her eyes.

It's worse than murder; it's shock, and fear, and it twists into ropes of terror. Talie's heartbeat stutters. Her stomach plummets.

'You did what?' Carol lifts her hand to her mouth, to her hair. It falls back aimlessly. 'Your parents are… You—you *know*… Is that where they've gone?' She looks up at Jay, distant and dazed. He nods, and the ropes go slack. 'Ten Hells. We've outdone Dante. How long ago?'

Thumping down to Jay's side, Diego starts to whine. 'An hour?' Jay offers. Ignoring the nose bashing his thigh, he looks from woman to woman. 'Maybe less? I—' He fixes abruptly on Talie, and his eyes shoot wide. 'Mum!'

Talie flinches. The noise is too much, and his horror is worse; now she's told them, she can't help crumpling, cringing into herself. She needs to fade, she needs to drift. She needs to no longer exist.

'Mum, we have to go!' Skittering down the remaining stairs, Jay barges past for his boots. 'We have to get them back!'

'I know.' Car keys in hand, Carol turns. 'Except there's no "we." Absolutely not. Take Diego, and go to bed. But you'—she rounds on Talie—'God help me, you're coming. This is your mess, and I swear on all ten Hells that I'll make you fix it. I can't *believe*…'

Talie's towers are crumbling. 'I did for my mother.' It sounds like she's whining. 'The huldra—'

'I don't care.' Grasping Talie's wrist, Carol hauls her from the house, a forced, awkward convoy down the hill. 'There are always other ways. Ways'—she throws out an arm for balance—'where you don't throw people to the dogs.' She jerks Talie harder, and they skid through the arch, sparkling in the dark. 'Especially when one of them's my son.'

The towers, and the bridges, and the castle in the centre, rubble to ashes to dust. 'Your son?' Talie's voice is hoarse. She needs water. She needs air. 'Callum? He go with the girls?'

Unlocking the car, Carol shoots her blue murder. 'If Kira's there, then so is he.' She cuts her eyes to the arch. 'Jay, I told you to stay behind!'

Her words are close to a flint-edged shout. Hastily zipping up his coat, Jay is jogging toward them.

'You did.' The boy arrives beside the car, out of breath but sure. 'I ignored you. I can't sit there on my own.'

'*No.*' Carol shunts Talie into the car. 'You're not going anywhere near the bastards—Jay! Jay, get *out!*'

It echoes off the mountaintops. Disobeying as boldly as if he were deaf, Jay climbs in, slams the door, and firmly fastens the strap.

His challenge is clear, even to Talie: take the time to make me stay, and the Chlause extinguish Callum.

40

Parasites

With every cumbersome, tramping step, more and more comes back. The chairlift, closed and creaking, creeping steeply from the trees, each chair lifeless, a shell. She dodged careering children there, bargaining with Callum; on the way up, she saw him with reasonable hatred, but by the way down, he was bearable. Ish.

Not counting the fireman's lift.

Then, it was loud, and the air was boisterous. Now, as her uncertainty grows, it's silent bar their footsteps, painful, glittering squeaks in the moonlight. An irrelevant flood lamp illumines the ski slope. Where its beam meets the trees, Kira tumbled from a snowdrift, breathless with Callum as they ran from the chair. She was trying to stay aloof and annoyed, but it was already doomed to fail.

In a blink, the memory flees. As they follow a newly groomed piste, skirting a less stately tree line and a tilting, half-buried path, a chalet squints from the night.

'Oh.' Callum stops. The chalet nestles in a pocket of the forest, watching from a rise like a warden. 'Karliquai. I completely forgot about Karliquai.'

Kira's brain swoops. It's déjà vu, or free fall of the mind.

Romy stares at him. 'What?'

Whatever Callum says, it burbles into static. Kira lifts her hands like a camera. From this angle, the chalet is a hulk shot with silver, but if she takes a mental step back…

'It's your painting.' Romy turns to Kira. Her mouth is an o-shape. 'The one from the show. What the *actual* fuck?'

Slowly, Kira lowers her hands, but she can't lower her eyes. 'Believe me,' she murmurs. 'The feeling's mutual. Did we…' She shakes her head. 'No. We didn't come here as kids?'

Romy looks off to the side. 'Don't think so. We used to go to Italy. You know, Eurocamp, and the bunk beds made for mice? "Wake up, campers! Volleyball!"' She rubs her arms distractedly. 'We never came here.'

Suddenly, the night feels awake, and alive. 'You're sure?' Kira curls her toes. They're far too exposed.

'Yes.' Romy nods, and again. 'I'm sure. Last year, Dad was hyped to be going somewhere different.'

'Okay.' Callum taps Kira's arm. 'Hello. I'm confused. Have you been here before?'

In the foreground, Karliquai listens. Kira looks at Romy. 'No?' she says. 'I just…I *painted* this. I dreamt it, and I painted it, and then it won a prize.'

It was an urge. A grappling need to capture the feeling, of beauty on a star-crossed night, where there were few colours but a deep, aching purity. The world was rich, and real, and shone. She hadn't understood it, but she'd ached to recreate it, and by the end of the October holidays (in three days of frenzied design), it was done.

Because it wasn't just the scene she clung to; it was the sentiment, and the emotion. While she didn't know why she was stood in the snow, what she *did* know was that the people with her were more important, more stingingly vital, than anyone or anything else.

Romy, which was strange enough, with their unhinged relationship, and a man she'd known forever. A man she *felt* she'd known forever. A man who stirred up all kinds of feelings, that she couldn't exactly pinpoint, but never wanted to lose.

Again; lose again. She'd known that, too, as they stood before Karliquai. It matched the ache of the need to paint, and regardless of how long she spent with Peter, it took days to fully subside. The man was something else. The dream was something else. Now, after over two years, it's real.

It's a puzzle she hadn't seen as a puzzle, and now the pieces fit.

'You need the shooting star,' Romy says. Advancing through the deep, dragging snow, she tilts her head. 'There was a shooting star, right? In the sky above the people?'

Kira moves her hand from side to side. 'Falling,' she says. Her foot sinks, and she heaves it out, ice crusting her boots. 'And the people were us.' Despite the cold, she smiles, pleased. 'I didn't know you'd paid that much attention.'

Romy shrugs. 'It was all anyone talked about. What do you mean, the people were us?'

Curling the ends of her amputated hair, Kira glances at Callum. 'No, you carry on,' he says, dryly trudging on. He's slightly breathless; the snow is a slog. 'What's a magic trip without a little magic madness?'

Kira frowns at him. 'I'll push you over.' She turns to Romy. Beneath her clothes, sweat prickles. Her thigh muscles moan. 'I probably said at the time, but the people were me and you. I'm thinking…' She wobbles. 'That the third was Callum.'

Callum lets out a cross between a snort and disbelief. 'That's not magic madness! That's—'

'Hey.' Kira holds up her hands. 'I'm not just being weird. It was a man I didn't know, so I don't really remember him. Everything else is the same, though, which is why it was probably you.'

'Ah.' Callum flops an arm around her, and squeezes. 'How touching. You psychic stalked me.'

Suitably withering, Kira rejects the patronising limb. 'I did not.'

'You did.' Callum winks. 'That's not weird. It's downright creepy.'

'It's creepier when you think that she dreamt this, too.' Romy sweeps an arm around, at the field, at the snow-hidden path, at the sky. Beneath the stars, the chalet grumbles closer. 'Though I'll tell you what's really, *really* creepy.' She hits Callum with a mocking grin. 'Having your brother read minds.'

Callum scoffs. 'Nah. That falls on the weird end.'

'Mmm.' Romy taps her temple. 'I wouldn't be so sure. It's pretty disturbing that you never knew, and never censored your thoughts. Who knows what joys he's heard.'

Callum's expression turns queasy.

'Exactly!' Romy claps her hands. The echo, and her cry, are as deafeningly awkward to Kira as their plodding, crunching trudge. 'Now who's embarrassed about their brain?'

Kira huffs. 'Thanks.'

'You're welcome.'

For a moment, Kira's disquiet lifts; Callum's face is priceless. Every possible thought he's had around Jay seems to bob and grin through his mind.

'Women.' He scrubs a hand over his head, allowing a minute wince. 'Do you think you could be more impossible? I'm missing a kick in the balls.'

Romy sidles closer to him. 'Do you think'—she pretends to look thoughtful—'you could quote me some *Shrek*?'

Callum's hand shoots out to shove her. 'No.'

Laughing, she leaps aside, narrowly missing a drift. 'Oh, you big spoilsport. Tell me about brimstone. Or onions. Or…' She crunches back toward them, frowning. 'No, I'm out. It's a shame to waste that accent, though. You'd make such a good Scottish ogre.'

Callum shuts his eyes. 'Jesus Christ. Please never go to Scotland.' In the shadow of Karliquai, he stops. 'And I thought you two didn't get on? Can't we go back to that?'

'That was last year.' Kira pats him sweetly. 'You don't know anything, do you?' She nods at the old, chipping chalet. 'What's Karliquai, anyway?'

Finally, they've come to its foot, its shadow a tide at their feet. Sobered by its age, its bare-boned desertion, Kira lowers her voice. 'Is that how you say it? Karli-key?'

Callum's ego trickles back, as she thought it would. 'That's how I've always heard it said.' He points. 'It's on the front, up there.'

Above the dusted windows sits a weather-beaten plaque. As dark as the rest of the wood, it blends, the letters thick but blackened. They protrude from the plaque like they used to be proud, and poignant: *KARLIQUAI*.

Déjà vu comes swooping back. Had she dreamt that, too, or *known* it?

'As for what it is'—Callum squints through the moonlight—'that depends on who you ask. The most innocent is that it's a holiday home, but no one holidays here.'

Romy makes a noise in her throat. 'I don't blame them.'

'Me neither.' Callum rocks back on his heels. 'It's a relic, and that's being kind. We snuck around it as kids. There's skulls and everything.'

Kira eyes it. A rough balcony rings the middle. The bottom is piled with snow, and the top, with its shuttered, arrow-slit window, tapers sharply between the trees. 'What are the other ideas?'

Pushing off to investigate, she tramps up the slope. The chalet may be creepy, and the snow knee-deep, but she dreamt this. She painted it, and then it won a prize.

'Crack den.' Trailing her to the balcony, Callum pulls a face. Goat skulls hang on the warped wooden wall, ski tips nailed fondly to the boards above the plaque. 'Though that was what we thought as the kids sneaking round. When we got older, we realised drugs were way off Lally's Richter scale.'

'Pff.' Romy blows some kind of raspberry. 'Don't tell me no one does drugs up here.'

Callum smirks at her. 'I wouldn't know. There's a barn on the other side where kids go to smoke, but that's hardly a whistleblowing scandal.'

That included him, then. Stealing up the splintered steps, Kira glances back. The stirring feelings stir. 'Any other theories?'

Callum scratches his head. 'Um. Old skiing hut like the one at the top, haunted by a skier. Cult hangout that ended in murder. Hippie retreat, though really, that's synonymous with crack den.'

Romy elbows him. 'Brimstone.'

He ignores her warning, flicking her cheek. 'That'll do, donkey.'

'Yes!' Romy claps her hands.

Kira leaves them to it. Camouflaged in papery bumps, all the doors are locked. A candle stub leaks wax on a tree stump. The skulls may sing the song of a cult, but, as she creaks around the balcony, the carved wooden heads are worse. They're everywhere. *Everywhere.* Rough and eyeless in nooks and crannies, they lurk and grin, watch and leer, vacant, openmouthed. They're everywhere, and they *stare*.

Averting her eyes, she moves along. Across the field, the forest waits, and resting her forearms on the wood, she surveys her shady domain. Creepiness aside, it's the perfect place for sentries. It could be a guardianship, a protector; a watchtower, high and hidden, nesting with the crows. Time could slip, and be simpler—an old man sat here, watching from a rocker—and nothing would change but the seasons.

Caught in a vintage, wistful world, she turns. That's not why they're here.

'Spooked yourself enough?' Romy asks, as Kira wanders back. 'I never thought your painting would feel so…'

She waves a hand.

'Unsettling?' Callum offers. Retracing their bootsteps, he tramps down the rise, past a cracking bird's nest sheltered in the wall. Beneath the roof, a woodpile towers. 'Speaking of which, yeah. You painted all of this.'

Stumbling in the snow, Kira teeters. 'I did.'

Callum offers her a hand. 'So, if you're an oracle, I have a request. I'd like to know what the Chlause are—'

'Oh, god,' Romy interrupts. Her voice is strangled. 'Kira.'

She points through the night. Kira's breath slips away.

In the sky, a star is falling.

'If we're too late…' Carol threatens for the third time, manhandling the car to a stop. In the back, Talie cowers. All her character has gone. *Please, let them be in time.*

Please. Pinching her skin, she curls in on herself. She, who should have known so much better, who should have had so much more empathy…she condemned three people to her childhood scaretales. To the people her parents ran from, fleeing with an unborn child, only to be drawn to another entrance by the pull that never wanes. No wonder her father chose to die.

She pinches harder, bruising her hand. She wasn't thinking. Was she? With her mother's life on her shoulders, what else could she do but be cold?

The car door slams. Talie jumps from her head. Zipping up her puffy coat, Carol hurries off. The night is the coldest they've had this winter; the road was deadly, the air hot white—

'Come *on*!' Jay scrambles out of the car. Full of terror, full of dread, Talie tumbles after him. At Karliquai, the Chlause wait.

Dear God, if they're too late.

The star. *Her* star. At least, she always saw it as a star, a brushstroke nudged from the sky; in the frozen now, it's more of a light. Brighter than the constellations, fading at the edges. Mesmerized, Kira stares.

'How is this happening?' Romy whispers. The light pulses. A lonely speck, a lonely spark, it wanders toward them, radiating silence and stiller than the air. Kira's head starts to sway.

Dizzily, she grabs at Callum, tilting off the world. Her gut roils. Her vision ripples. Beside her, Romy totters, or maybe it's Callum, or maybe it's all of them, nauseous and drunk. She's black and sickly, zero gravity, stuck in dreaming free fall.

Kira.

The ripple lifts. Her vision clears. The night is back.

Back, and balanced, but no longer empty. Reeling, seasick, Kira plants her feet, washed with cold. A figure has fluttered from the shadows by the tree line.

Softly, Romy inhales. 'Is this what's meant to happen?'

Kira shakes her head. Her throat has closed. A stone's throw from Karliquai, the dark figure watches.

'This doesn't feel right,' Callum whispers. Reaching behind Kira's back, he tugs Romy toward them. 'Not at all.'

The figure steps out of the trees. It's larger than it should be, uneven and grotesque, a human shape in disguise. Its face is obscured by a white wooden mask.

'Jesus,' Callum breathes. Kira's mind is ice.

Kira, murmurs a voice in her head. It's a matte, dead sound, without echo, and she flinches. The mask has pursed, painted lips, wild tangles of black hair pouring around the edges. A burgundy dress toils stiffly down the body, made of nothing she'd think of as clothing, and two carved, disfigured hands sit crossed over the crotch.

'It knows our names.' Romy huddles into Kira.

Unblinking, Kira nods. A distinct foreboding sighs: this doesn't feel right. Not at all.

Kira, murmurs the voice again. The figure takes another step. It has the grace of a lady but the aura of a beast, something cool and ferocious. The air tastes close to metal. *Come.*

With another step, its approach is steady. *Callum,* it says. *Rosemarie. Kira.* Lifting a hand, it surrounds the fallen light, and snuffs it out. *Come.*

'Callum!' a voice yells, back across the field.

Callum starts. 'Jay?'

He turns. His forehead labours into a frown. Jay is pelting toward them, snow spraying up around his stumbling calves. His mother and Talie struggle behind.

Something is very, very wrong.

'Callum!' Jay trips, flinging out his arms. 'Come back!'

A gasp and Kira's clenching grip jerk him around again. The doll-faced figure has stopped in front of them, a tear glittering down its cheek. *Come,* it says.

Callum fades. His head is weighty, lolling and limp. He forces it back to Jay. Too much anaesthetic, far too much to drink. His brother staggers, panicked, yelling, but the dim words are lost. He's a dreamer, faintly there. Simply watching, unaware.

The night is bright. Metal in his mouth. Kira's hand, its low pressure, slips from his arm. Jay slams into his back.

The field grows empty. Carol screams. Ahead of her, Talie drops to her knees. The moonlight shines on nothing; no shadows. They've gone. They've all gone.

Carol's cries bleed into her ears. Gone. Talie stares at Karliquai in scalding disbelief. She didn't see the Chlause, but the stories say she wouldn't. Fuck.

Fuck. Her heart is a machine gun, blowing her to bits, oh, shit, oh, *fuck*. They've *gone*. She could have torn them away, if she'd been quicker. If she'd been quicker, the pull would have broken.

Her head droops, jarring on her breastbone. Carol staggers past, searching, searching. Calling. Crying. She knows the stories, too, the stories that aren't. Talie's body grows heavy. Her mind is lead. She could have told a safe, nondestructive lie. She could have stopped their ruin.

She could have done many things. She should have done more.

The night marches on. Ever the watcher for aching lands, Karliquai listens in silence. There's nothing in him, about him, around him; just monsters using his shell. Parasites on a host. Demons. Things that even Whiteland rejects. Gone.

'Callum!' Carol collapses. Her scream is ripped and raucous. *'Jay!'*

Talie can't face her. Her glasses fog. An endless time later, shuddering and icy, she stands and walks away.

41

Tales told by wanton liars

'I thought I'd slip into something more comfortable.' The man-being pats his jerkin. Having shrunk to more or less Mathew's height, he's gained a straw hat, a healthy grey beard, and boots over woollen trousers. The staff remains, gnarled and weathered, its handle shaped like a wolf. 'That was my frightening guise, as it were. Larger than life. In this form, I'm pleasant.' The man-being considers itself. 'I think, at least. Do you?'

Mathew considers it, too. Its green eyes glimmer with amusement. Its hands are more knotted twigs than fingers, and its face has kept an inhuman wilderness, but it's certainly grown less threatening.

'Thank you.' It nods. Mathew frowns. 'I try. Not with all folk, but most. Some, maybe, if we are being accurate. And you can call me Vasi.'

Mathew's frown deepens. He'd been about to ask.

'I know.' Vasi gives a slow, wrinkled wink. 'I'm one of the Leshy, by the way. My wolf is Grey; I can be many things, but inventive with names is not one of them. Once, he saved your daughters.'

Sense trickles even further away. Mathew's gaze flicks to Grey. 'What?'

'Last year,' Vasi says. 'He, and his pack.'

Proud, tall, but still a wolf, at least, Grey watches. 'What do you mean, he saved my daughters?' Mathew shakes his head. 'This is—how? And also'—he forces his aching limbs up. It feels like he ran seven leagues without the boots—'why do you keep saying a year? I've no idea what I was doing a year ago, but that doesn't mean I wasn't thinking. Existing.' He rubs a hand down his face. 'Christ. If I wasn't existing then, I shouldn't exist now.'

'Sadly, none of that follows.' Vasi taps the staff. Turning tail, the wolf trots away. 'Through no fault of your own, I might add. But we have enough talk to fill Ørenna, and a great deal of time. It can wait.'

He turns. Mathew's limbs tug. Fighting his brain for his memory, he lets the tug lead him, up the mountain and into the blue.

Kira opens her eyes. She'd been dreaming of Mathew: Mathew as he was, not the puppet he's been painted. Her affectionate, slightly clueless dad.

It helps. It helps her drowsy mind to separate the two, the man he is and the monster he's not. She's become a pro in separating the Romys, and she'll do the same now. She has to.

Her sister killed her dad. Her dad killed his parents. There's not much between them in terms of horror.

Horror. Blearily, she blinks, swimming toward awake. All of it's a horror: she fled the police, became a criminal, disguised herself, and now…now, she's running through the fringes of the worlds.

Running. The worlds. Like a stab of ice, she's awake. The Chlause.

They ran to the Chlause. They ran to Karliquai, found her painting, and the doll-faced figure sent everything strange. Carol, Talie, and Jay were running, running and shouting.

Where is she now?

Oh, god. Where *is* she?

Kira jerks up. Blood rushes to her head, and she wavers, her back ramming into a wall. 'Ow.' Her elbow smashes rock. '*Ow.*'

She's caught in a corner. Screwing up her face, she rubs her offended spine and slips up her guard. Last time she woke in a rocky hole, a dead coven tried to kill her.

Not only that, they tried to recruit her. She touches her delicate elbow with a wince. What's it to be this time? Burying her alive, so she sinks through the rock to the underworld? Sending her off in a Viking death boat and floating her up to the stars?

Shut up.

Scraping her fingers into fists on the rock, Kira draws her knees to her chest. It's not just a hole; it's a tunnel. The cold air is musty. The close, rust-red walls curl away around a corner, and although she's bunched in a dead end, a rabbit in a trap should danger come, what makes her tingle, what makes her crawl, what chills her head is the ceiling.

Is it a ceiling? A pull inside her hisses yes, but the sky flickers and sighs. Sniffing, Kira hugs her knees. Swathes of colour dance in the dark: curtains of green paling to blue, sighing to rose, moving with violet, so vibrant they could be alive. They travel with the tunnel walls, sweeping along the curve. With her view cut short by the corner, they could well travel forever, a rolling sea of colour, gentle, silent, sad. Breathtaking; heartbreaking. As much as dread sneaks through her skin, she can't deny it that.

She sniffs again. It has to be a ceiling. It can't be the aurora.

If it's not, though…what is this?

In the opposite corner, someone shifts. Kira starts, shot with shock again, flinching into the rock. She'd been too taken by the tunnel, by the speckling stars in the indigo sky; she hadn't seen the huddled lump. Tensing her limbs, she squints through the gloom.

'Ouch.' Groaning, Callum sits up. 'Where are we?'

Kira slumps. 'Oh, thank God it's you.'

'Mmm.' Callum rubs his head. 'Who else—agh.' His mouth pops open. 'I think I slept on a stone.'

Shifting her sore coccyx, Kira's eyes drift around them. 'I think you probably did.'

Slowly, Callum follows her gaze. Slowly, the sleep clears from his face, and slowly, he frowns. 'What happened?'

His attention floats up to the ceiling. 'I don't think it's real,' Kira says, as his contracting frown widens. 'There's no air.'

His disbelief slides down to her. 'Then how are we breathing?'

'No.' Kira shakes her head. 'I mean, it's the same as a cave, or an attic. Sniff and you'll see. We're not outside.' She twists her mouth. 'Don't the northern lights sound kind of electric?'

Callum shrugs.

Kira waits, but that's it. 'Either way,' she says, 'there should be something.' She rolls her head through the air toward him. 'We could be in the stillest place on Earth, and there'd still be a smell. A sound. Something.'

In the half-light, Callum's eyes seem deeper. 'You think it's an illusion?'

Oh, please, no. Kira peers down the tunnel. Is the rock reflected in the sky, glinting on the corner? 'No,' she says. 'I think it's a ceiling.'

Silence. To her surprise, Callum huffs. 'Of course.'

Kira blinks at him. 'What? What's funny?'

Dramatically, Callum exhales. 'It's always about glass ceilings.' He tuts. 'Women. Honestly.'

It takes a moment to click. 'Shut up.' Mock-serious, Kira punches his arm. He grasps it in mock distress. 'Is this really the time for your jokes? Or anyone's? It could be the end of the world.'

He lowers a figurative pair of glasses. 'When have I not made it time for my jokes? Without the banter last time, we would have gone mad.' He offers up his familiar smugness. 'And if Urnäsch is wedged between Whiteland and home, we are at the end of the world.'

Kira hits him again. 'Don't say "banter." It's become a vessel for lad-boys to pretend they've got some wit. That said'—she pats the spot she punched—'I'm glad that you're okay.'

'I did feel the same.' Callum clambers to his feet. 'Now, I'm peeved. Is that word better?'

Kira nods. 'Blame the glass ceiling. Wait.' Accepting his hand, she frowns at the tunnel. 'Where are our bags?'

Callum looks down. 'Ah,' he says. The rusty rock is bare. 'Well, shit.'

For a moment, they're quiet. Well, shit, indeed. 'Let's hope we don't get cold.' Kira sighs, morose. 'Or stuck in the dark.'

'Or in any kind of fix, really.' Callum pulls a face, more than peeved. 'I was so prepared this time, as well.'

Kira mirrors him. So was she; maybe the stress will play hormone havoc.

'We might as well go,' is what she says, sighing again at the rock. They'd packed all that *food*. 'We have to find Romy. Assuming she made it.'

'And assuming Talie's a wanton liar.' Callum takes her hand. 'Security,' he adds, catching her querulous look. This isn't like him. 'I'd rather not risk the separation trick they played in the woods. Or the boat.'

Quelling her hesitation, Kira laces her fingers with his. 'Okay.' She squeezes once, and they walk. His skin is cold. 'I guess they've already separated Romy.'

'Exactly.' Callum glances over his shoulder, as if expecting to see her there. 'Which brings us back to Talie. She must have told Mum and Jay the truth, however that bundle of joy turns out, and they came to try and stop us.'

Kira's apprehension bruises, growing and spreading to yellow, to brown. Her brief amusement has drowned. *However that bundle of joy turns out.* Wherever they are, it's markedly *other*, nowhere close to Whiteland-sharp but colder. Corpse-like. Stifled. Whatever Urnäsch is, it feels dead.

Like they've left the pan for the fire.

Kira tightens her fingers in Callum's. Edging around the corner, they leave the northern lights for a deeper, blacker night.

42

Time and fear and life and fire

She's probably hypothermic. Frostbitten, too, because she can't feel her toes and wouldn't dream of looking at her fingers.

With dawn hinting at the fringes of the sky, Carol stumbles toward her car. She hadn't even locked it; the key's in the ignition. Usually, she'd berate herself, but who cares? Her sons are gone.

If only she'd been faster. If only Jay hadn't run. She could have pulled them out of it, and it wouldn't have dragged him along. When they fell into Urnäsch, he fell, too.

A sob bubbles and bursts from her throat as she jerks the car uphill. Funny; she thought she'd run dry. The night died as she crouched in the snow, shivering, calling, crying until her throat was razed to the ground, and it felt like an age. An era. An eon. Layers of thermals or no, she's lucky to be alive.

The car vibrates. It's in the wrong gear, but her hands are too numb to change up. What she should be doing is slowing, but no. Manhandle the metal over the train line, up behind Les Sapins. Down, down, down the road, jerk to a stop at an angle. Others be damned if they want to pass.

The blue dawn is bitter, blurry. Carol blunders away from the car, through the gate, past the hutch. Her feet are bruising blocks of ice. She didn't know Hazal kept rabbits.

'Hazal!' Numbly, Carol bangs on the door. The chalet shudders. She can't feel her fists. Her throat needs lemon and ginger and rest. 'Hazal!' Bang. *'Hazal!'*

The door jolts open. 'What?' Hazal hisses.

Lost in her urgency, Carol trips. Her lips are thick and puffy. 'Hazal—'

'You wake up all the school.' Hazal's shrivelled olive face is war. 'What you—' She visibly double-takes. 'What's happened? Come in, but quiet.'

Hazal steps back. Carol stumbles forward. The house is a furnace.

'Thank you.'

'Sit.' Snicking the door shut, Hazal points to a grey, velvety sofa. Just as clumsily, Carol sits. 'I get you a blanket, you explain. Coffee? To warm you up?'

The coffee kicks like a sleep twitch. It's far too strong for the early morning, but that's Hazal. Excited: herbal brandy. Upset: herbal brandy. Potentially hypothermic: herbal brandy. Soon, Carol's shivers subside, and then, the story comes out.

'Did you know what Talie did?' Carol asks, her voice croaking. Her head is top-heavy; what's the last thing she ate? She's as bad as Kira. Carol pulls her gaze from her coffee to Hazal.

Carefully, Hazal shakes her head. 'I knew she did *something*.' Hazal folds her arms, rigid in her robe. Her tired, bony face is cut, webbed with a bluish bruise. 'But Talie refused to tell me. She did it to get me away from the woman.'

Dully, Carol rubs her eyes. 'The woman?'

Hazal puckers her mouth, as if she wants to spit. 'Not woman, sorry. Huldra. It come for me, made me sleep. Didn't leave until Talie did what it wanted.'

Carol grips her cup. Her fingers throb. 'To send the girls to Urnäsch.'

Hazal's Adam's apple bobs. 'Oh, oh, Carol.' She ducks her head, pressing her eyes. 'I'm sorry. So sorry. I should have gone around, ask if anyone saw Talie, know what she did. But I was so much shocked from what happened, and I didn't, and I never thought it hurt you. Your sons...' Hazal trails off, her voice hitching.

Callum's face fills Carol's mind, turning as she and Jay shouted. Jay, crashing into his brother, in time to disappear. The girls, who deserved none of this, but keep yanking Callum into danger. If she could get her hands on a witch, like the one helping the Kyo, she'd be tempted to have him enchanted. She'd be more than tempted, if it meant he'd forget he ever knew Kira McFadden.

'Carol?' Hazal says.

Blearily, Carol looks up.

'Did you hear me?'

Carol blinks.

'I repeat.' Hazal lifts her hands. 'We can't get into Urnäsch if the Chlause don't want.'

Grief swells so fast that it churns into nausea. Carol's mind becomes an echo: *we can't get into* Urnäsch *if the Chlause don't want*. She knew this already, but god, a reprieve, a shred of possibility, something. Anything. Saying it out loud makes it real.

'But…' Carol swallows the rock in her throat. 'But you got out. You and Yavuz.'

Hazal folds her hands together. 'Not by help from outside,' she says. 'There is nothing we can do ourselves.' She looks off, toward the makeshift run. Two piebald rabbits snuffle around. 'If they escape to here, they do it. It not easy. You have to keep running until they can't reach you.' Her hands start to twist. 'It eats your life, and your strength, and many cannot. They have to stop.'

'And those that don't?'

'They have to know how.' Intent, Hazal leans forward, but not toward Carol. Urnäsch is a magnet, drawing her in. 'Many, most, do not care, or cannot find out, but like Anneliese in Whiteland, there are some that do…'

Carol watches, waits. Her hope may gutter, but it will not die.

'They need time,' Hazal says, when Carol doesn't speak. Her careful words are slow. 'Time to learn how to get out. I do not think your boys and the girls will have it, before the fire.'

Carol's face flinches, and Hazal's eyes flit to her.

'I'm sorry.' Hazal presses her knees together, tightly coiled on the velvety couch. 'We had time because we were young, and the fire happens at an age we did not reach. They are strangers, and old enough, except Jay.' Hazal meets Carol's eyes. 'I think we have to ask in another place for help.'

Whatever the meaning in Hazal's gaze, Carol doesn't catch it. 'Why can't we do it?' Breaking the connection, Carol looks off into the fireplace. Towers of ash look ready to collapse. 'If we go back to Karliquai, the Chlause will come.'

Lifting her knotted fingers, Hazal drops them with a sigh. 'Carol.'

'The door will be open, and then—'

'Carol, *listen*.' Hazal's tone is a gunshot crack. 'You know more than that. They will know we're not innocent. They will recognise you, and maybe me. Even still, how would the children find where to go? It takes time *they do not have*.'

Hazal lets this hang before leaning forward, this time into Carol. 'We—you—talk to the Whispers. They might know something, or can do something. If the huldra sent the girls to the Chlause, there is a reason that involves Whiteland. Can you see it being different?'

The wall clock chimes. Eight a.m.: a jay. Staring through the ash, Carol swallows. 'No.'

Towers, glinting cities, monuments of stone. Shrugging off the blanket, Carol shuts her eyes. Breakfast time clatters through the walls from the dorms. Adults order. Children laugh. Baked beans mix with bacon, bread. The rabbits squeak and snuffle.

Carol sits up straighter. The walls of her mind are down.

The curtains start to rustle.

43

Magic, peril, power

'Wake up.' A pause. A huff. 'Wake *up*.'

The voice probes Romy's consciousness. It's a quiet, vaguely familiar bug; while drifting from a dreamless black, it's difficult to tell.

'Wake up, Romy.'

So it knows her. And it's young. Screwing up her face, Romy does as it says.

For all intents and purposes, she's lying in a church. Frowning at the ceiling, she rubs her gummy eyes, propping herself on her elbows. A normal church, too, not some otherworldly weirdness, the aura of which only tells her it's a church.

'I'll be beggared,' she murmurs. 'What fresh hell is this?'

It's a church; she already established that. Forcing her locked limbs to stir, she grimaces, grinds herself upright, and sags against a pew. Incense breezes toward her, the kind she burnt as a preteen hippie. She wrinkles her nose. It spirits her back to her dark, stuffy room, and she wafts it away. No flashbacks, please; the church is already scooping out memories. Something to do with Brownies, and singing Christmas carols, and the smell of orange, and falling on her face.

She wafts this away, too. Digging her knuckles into her eyes, Romy blinks around. Heavy wooden doors hulk. Stained glass windows stare and glow, reds and purples and greens depicting villages, sunsets, mountain scenes. A desolate lake in grey and blue. Above the altar—

Jesus Christ. Romy's eyes fly wide, and strain. It must be the *pièce de résistance*; three figures, in bulky costume, gather around a fire, in a chamber crawling with trees. The trees themselves crawl with vines, the roof a swirl of throbbing lights. In the flames, with her head thrown back, a burning girl screams.

'God.' Romy pulls a face. Even for her, it's distasteful.

The forgotten voice clears its throat. 'There's worse.'

Romy jumps. Her head snaps round. 'Oh, shit.'

Propped against the pew is Callum's little brother. 'I mean...' She flounders, grazed by guilt. Jay looks struck, and thoroughly afraid. 'I mean it's shit for you to be here, wherever here is.' Her eyes roam the church again. Cold stone, a soaring ceiling, tapering up to a spire. Wooden crosses hang from the walls, ever so slightly wrong.

Thick. Splintering. Bastardised. 'Urnäsch,' Jay says. 'With the Chlause.'

Romy looks back to him. 'Urnäsch,' she repeats. Another memory sifts like sand: a shout, and a collision. 'Oh, *shit*. You came after us.'

Miserably, Jay nods. Does he know what she'll say before she says it?

He shrugs a drooping shoulder. 'Yes.'

'You were running.' Romy continues regardless. A telepathic boy isn't something you accept; not at the drop of any old hat, no matter how witchy and wild. 'With your mother and that girl. Talie.'

Across the field, through the snow, running, chasing, yelling. Romy's insides clench. Okay, the packet had to go, but why did she let Kira have her hip flask? Screw cold turkey. She needs a drink.

'Why?' She lengthens the word, cautious. She doesn't want to know. 'Why did you all come after us?'

Jay studies his feet. He really is young; god, where is that *drink*? Even when she was younger, and desperate for money, she was never the babysitting type. She's never looked after a child in her life; whenever her odious cousins appeared, she'd slip down the rabbit hole, find the "drink me" and "eat me" concoctions, and scarper. Her trouble was a loner.

Now it has a twelve-year-old friend.

They're screwed. With a groan, Romy knocks the knob of her skull on the bench. They're so—

'Uh.' Staccato, the sound pops from her mouth. Her eyes grow huge.

'I told you.' Jay shakes his head at his feet. 'I told you there was worse.'

Above the opposite column of pews is a vivid, lurid window. Large, haunted, and rich in detail, it puts the *pièce de résistance* to shame.

'Do you know what it is?' Jay asks, flat.

It's not a question seeking knowledge; it's seeking affirmation. A dark cavern shimmers in purples and blues. The brittle women within are as pale as the candles cupped in their hands, thronging a girl with glasses and crow-dark curls. Wringing her wrists, she shivers in the centre.

Romy shivers, too. Each woman's head is cracked to the left, their black eyes and blacker mouths screaming silent screams. It may be her mind, but the more she watches, the more she swears the crowded girl is changing, growing taller, thinner, lowering her hands…

'The Kyo.' Romy hauls her eyes away. The glass above the altar was creepy; this one is malicious, and prescient. *Present.*

'Probably,' Jay mumbles, shifting beside her. 'If the Kyo's in Whiteland.'

Romy wrinkles her forehead.

'I've seen it in Mum's head,' he clarifies. 'Since you and Kira got here, I've seen it in Kira's.'

Romy's eyes dart to the flames above the altar, the trees, the northern lights. 'What about that one?'

Jay doesn't look up. 'Not in Mum's head,' he says. 'Or Kira's, or Callum's. They're the…' Breaking off crookedly, he seems to shrink. 'They're the people Talie was thinking about when she turned up at the house.'

Back, back, back. Romy's memory sifts. Her own memory, not planted by anyone else: wisps of women swirling at night, circling a fire. Entrancing her, taking her. The Kyo. She's never connected the words with a visual, never, but she knows.

'Why did you come after us?' she asks, skittering back. The Kyo were the start of everything, the terrifying, screaming beginning. Only one memory scars her deeper. 'What else did you get from Talie?'

Jay makes an indistinct noise, but says nothing. Five seconds. Ten.

'Jay.' Romy lays a hand on his shoulder. He doesn't react, and she removes it. 'You need to tell me, so we can work out where we are, and what we do. Right now, all I know is that the Chlause should be helping, but we've wound up in a church with our numbers cut.'

She cranes her neck around the echoing expanse. There's no one else here; of course there isn't. You can feel the presence of other people, the same way you know when you're alone.

'Yeah.' She sits back with a thump. 'Cut. So, we either have to find whatever help there is here, or whatever might be waiting to rip us to shreds. More importantly, we have to find Kira and Callum.'

Insufferable thing that he is.

Jay's lips quirk. Romy looks at him.

'Sorry,' he says. 'For listening. I try not to, unless it might be helpful, but I'm still learning how. Especially when I'm talking to someone.'

He flicks a glance up at her. Romy huffs. 'It's fine.' She pokes him. 'You can show your remorse by answering my question. Why'd you come after us?'

Jay's eyes flick down, to the bumpy stone slabs. Romy pictures a bee, makes her mind buzz, and shuts out everything else. No distractions for him to latch on to.

'Thanks.' Jay tugs on a lace of his snow boot. 'We came after you because…' He licks his lips. 'Talie lied.'

Romy stares at him. 'Talie what now?'

'Lied.' Jay shakes his head in a rush. 'She lied. About everything. She had to get you here.' He scratches his arm through his ski coat. Rapid-fire, one-two-three. 'She tried to make it right, but she tried too late. She must have been too late.' He scratches again, four-five-six. 'Because I'm here.'

Talie lied. The words won't settle. They feel like pollen, the day her hay fever starts to scratch. Talie lied?

'So there's no…' Romy fiddles with her ear-stretcher. 'They won't…'

The hay fever hits. It's a wallop, a rush of flu to the face. Talie *lied*.

Oh, no.

'When she told you the Chlause would help, she lied.' Jay's face contorts, as unhappy as Monday. 'It's confusing, because her thoughts were mad, but the Chlause aren't a good thing. This isn't a good place. She lied so the thing that tried to kill Callum wouldn't kill her mum, or something, and then she felt bad because a girl was nice. I think.' He shakes his head. 'She kept thinking about a girl.'

Somewhere in the church, a door shuts.

Jay jumps. Romy stiffens. It's not the click of subtlety; if not quite brash, it's bold.

They're not alone anymore.

'Why would the huldra kill Talie's mum?' Romy whispers. Taking Jay's hand, she holds it tight. The silence is far too loud.

'Because it needed you to come here.' Jay's eyes dart around. 'I don't know why, and Talie didn't know why, but the Chlause don't help anyone. They were chucked out of Whiteland for what they do.' He shrinks into Romy. 'Mum knew it, too.'

Footsteps start to click. Romy's chest chills, tremors sparking through her limbs. She shuffles as close to Jay as she can. She doesn't want to ask, but… 'And what do they do?'

Click, click, click.

'They make you one of them.' Jay squeezes her hand so the bones grind. 'They drive you mad, they torture you, and make you one of them.'

Click, click, click. The church rings with the steps. The sound is empty, coming closer, bringing with it cold. *They drive you mad, they torture you, and make you one of them.*

Even more chilling from the mouth of a child. Her mind is on a carousel, and Romy shuts her eyes. Jack be nimble, Jack be quick. Her heart skips through a candle flame, yearning for the dark. Focus. Breathe. Repeat. She has to find the little things that keep her in control; Kira isn't here to pull her out.

Oh, Christ. Romy opens her eyes. The footsteps click. She can't spiral, can't fall, can't let the rabbit hole drown her in tar. Alongside herself, she's got Jay.

Romy swallows, breathes, and grounds herself. Jay's crushing, sweaty grip. The ratty jeans drawn into his chest, his sideswept mop of hair. Her twinkling sickness, the hint of withdrawal. The love of a body that quickly adapts. The feeling of every church: heavy quiet, enigmas, Christmas.

Control. It's working. Fuck darkness. She breathes. The incense is strengthening; she used to know the name. Cold stone digs into her spine. The footsteps click and clack.

Those footsteps. Measured black shoes in an underground car park, shielded by a pillar in the sickly light. Awaiting discovery. Awaiting death.

That's what does it.

'Come on.' Gripping Jay tight, Romy scrapes up the pew, hauling them both upright. They can't just wait, like ducks on a pond. Not now she knows Talie lied.

What a bitch.

Jay stumbles. 'What are we doing?'

'Fuck knows.' Stiff and wooden-legged, Romy drags him down the aisle. The cold footsteps echo. They're everywhere, heading for a bodiless crescendo, but one of these doors must open. Dread stabs her full of needles. 'Check the doors.' She shoves him. 'Go!'

Needles, daggers, swords. Romy's feet slap stone. Blood fills her ears. She hurtles into a damp-mottled corner, shouldering the door. The monster is iron-studded, medieval. Where there should be a handle, there's a keyless keyhole, and slapping it, she moves on.

Nothing. The next has a bolt that doesn't slide, the next a useless knob. Jay shouts in frustration, kicking at wood, but nothing will open, nothing, *nothing*.

The footsteps slow.

Oh, shit.

The main door. Romy lurches over, wrenching the ring, but it only freezes her hands. 'Shit!'

'What about the others?' Jay gestures wildly. The doors span the whole of the church, wrapped within the echo.

Romy wrenches on the ring again. 'The footsteps came from over there.' She tosses a glance over her shoulder, her hair whipping her face. The church is empty.

Her fear swoons. The echo is a clamour, ringing, clattering, a hundred marching men.

'But a door shut at the back.'

'So?'

'So it means it must open.'

'It's not worth the risk.' Romy whips around to the locks, the bolts, scraping her hair from her face. She should have listened to Kira, and chopped the whole lot off. 'We're in here with something we can't see. I don't want to run straight—wait.' She spins so fast she staggers, bracing herself on the door. 'Can you hear it?'

Whey-faced, Jay shakes his head.

'Goddamn.' Romy's voice cracks. 'I thought you heard everything.'

Jay rocks back and forth on his heels. 'Not everything.' His moon-wide eyes meet hers. 'Everyone.'

The footsteps stop. The echo dies, as thought it was never alive.

Rosemarie.

Romy quails. Darkness yawns. The murmur in her head is flat, dull, sucking sound from the air. Tears spring to her eyes. No.

Standing in one of the pews is a figure. Romy grabs Jay's shoulder, pulling him toward her. The figure's hands rest quiet on its crotch, and it tilts its head. *You're afraid.*

Goddamn right they are.

Behave.

In a blink, the figure stands before them. Romy inhales. Jumping, Jay backs into her. Her spine hits the door, and she gasps. The figure is tall, taller than her, taller than the lanky boy she dated last year, whose shins hung off the bed. It's a phantom, a menace, a shadow.

But behave? Straightening, Romy grips Jay's shoulders, lifting her chin. Hell, no.

The air flickers. Romy blinks. The shadow becomes a mask.

Her resolve almost withers. Diagonal colours slash the mask, shifting and glowing like the rich, stained glass. The eyes gleam black. The mouth is a toothless, splintered gash.

Magic. Romy swallows. Magic, peril. Power.

Her teeth taste of metal. Her head starts to roar. The figure's shroud is a flutter of night. Clumps of black sheep's wool cramp the torso, snaking up the neck to a widow's veil. The long-fingered hands are chipped like china, cracked like porcelain, hard and cold. Whatever it is, it's not human.

Hugging Jay to her, Romy stares it down. She'd expected some kind of screwed-up preacher, and she won't be cowed by a priest.

The figure steps back. *I am not a priest.*

Romy doesn't relax. The way it speaks is weird, as if the words are in writing, shunted from mind to mind. It makes her feel over-caffeinated, or fuzzy after a binge.

This church is not for personal use. The preacher's glowing face shifts. *I am the Pretty-Ugly.*

Jay elbows her with a strangled grunt, but too late. 'You don't say.'

The words are out before she can stop them. Quicker than clockwork, the preacher's hand cinches Romy's neck. *Behave.*

As calm as ever, it lifts her up and slams her into the door. Her head cracks the wood. The air leaves her lungs. Her vision speckles, pain electric, a starburst shooting through her skull. The china fingers burn with cold.

Behave.

She's choking. The priest slams her back again, harder than before. The iron ring catches her tailbone.

'Agh!' She strangles a cry, hacking, coughing, her tiptoes trailing on the stone. One leg jerks.

Understand.

When her head turns hot and black, it drops her. She crumples, shins then knees then shoulder, her skull narrowly missing the ground. Her vision coalesces to the floor of the church. The stone slabs waver. Her breath billows hot. Deeply, she breathes, kneading her neck.

Somewhere above her, Jay cries out.

Woozily, Romy drags her head up. The priest has seized Jay's wrists, so hard the bones grate. 'No,' she mumbles. Her voice is thick, her tongue a weight. 'Leave him.'

Her limbs tremble. Her vision sways. The priest turns. *I will.*

Releasing Jay, it steeples its fingers. *There is worse than this. Up.*

Like the air itself has grabbed her, Romy flails to her feet. Her gorge rises. With a rush of black, her head swoons hot.

See. At a nod from the priest, her neck snaps round to a window beside the door. She staggers, but the air holds her, strung like a puppet. *See.*

Romy's eyes clear. She blinks at the window. Travellers trudge up a mountain face, a wide-faced man in a straw hat, a smaller man, and a wolf. The mountain's snow is flawless, the sky a matte blue.

Go.

The church churns around her. The window pulls her forward, filling up her mind: the muddy swamp of the straw man's tunic, the tartan of the small man's coat. The glinting snow, the pooling sky, kaleidoscopes from the other windows, purple-scarlet-fire-gold. Inside, outside, the colours surround her.

In a giddy swoop, the window pulls, and she falls through the glass.

44

Ghosts.

'here are we?'
'Purgatory.'
'Do you belong here?'
'Yes.'
'Do I?'

Talie drifts into waking. She didn't think she'd make it; in the calm, cold state of mind with which she entered the forest, she thought she'd lie down and turn to static.

She didn't plan to. She didn't plan anything; she simply assumed that, sooner or later, her legs would fail from fatigue and winter, and she wouldn't particularly care. She's been lacking life for years.

Across the snow and into the trees, she walked with blunted purpose. She could have been drunk, should have been drunk, or at least anaesthetised; staring ahead as she left the narrow wood-chipped path, she wandered like a ghost. The Chlause. Urnäsch. Gone.

There wasn't a goal. There wasn't a need. Eventually, caught between knowing and not, lucid and not, she knew what to do. Right here, right now, she needed to sleep.

Then, she dreamt of guilt. The huldra was there, damned and repentant, suffering by her side. It was simple: they sat cross-legged with their backs to trees. The hell-freezing cold turned them icy blue, and here, forever, they'd stay.

Except she woke up, and found it was a lie. She's not in the forest, where she must have gone to sleep, but nor is she with Freya, talking up sins; she's in a towering, soft-lit, candlelit cavern, and she's slumped against a wall.

A rocky wall. Woodenly, Talie rights herself. It may be comparably warm in here, but the woods have mothballed her bones.

'Little Chlause.'

The whisper snakes around her. The lights shift. Talie's eyes blur, and a little uneasy, she focuses, blinks. What she took for candles are cradled by women; not skulking on the walls, or fixed to the floor, but cupped in the palms of their hands.

'What?' Rubbed raw by the violent air, Talie's voice is a croak. '"Little Chlause?"'

She must still be dreaming. The words left her chapped lips, but the language leaves her lost. French? English? Turkish? Spanish?

She must be dreaming. She can't not know.

'Yes.' A statuesque rake in a trailing dress, the speaker steps from the crowd. Unease breathes its sour breaths; bar hair, skin, and facial foibles, these silent, ghosting figures are near enough the same. Talie digs her spine into the wall. They're wraiths fashioned from mirrors, and they watch with the night for eyes.

'I'm not...' She swallows, and shivers. A draft eddies around her ankles. 'I'm not Chlause.'

The speaker lets out a soft laugh. In the sputtering light, her eyes stretch. 'I think you are.' She smiles. 'Stand up.'

Hooked with talons, Talie's body jerks. 'Hey!' she cries, as the claws inside her scrape her up the wall. Through her clothes, her skin grazes. 'What the hell? I'm not a kid.' She folds her arms. Stupid harpies. One of them must be her ex; she wouldn't miss a dream like this. 'Who are you?'

Silence. 'Who,' Talie repeats, 'are you?' Louder, now, and slower, the way people talk when they think she just speaks "foreign." 'Hello?'

The speaker smiles. 'Hello.'

Talie's gut plunges. Punching through her flesh, it shreds muscle, crunches bone; the women's eyes are blackening, distending, yawning. Heads off-kilter, they start to scream.

The speaker's neck snaps with a crack like knuckles. 'Welcome to the Kyo.'

45

And so he sleeps

Fresh-cut grass. Romy lands on her kneecaps, crumples to her face, and the scent of it enfolds her.

Five seconds. Ten seconds. Fifteen. Grass tickles her cheek, her sore, burning neck. When the world is no longer spinning, she pushes back up to her knees.

A green square, a wicker chair, and four walls of mirrors. Romy blinks. 'Jesus.'

Her head swims as she takes it in. A line of kneeling Romys, a line of blinking Jays. Endless chairs. Suburban grass. She tips her head back as far as it will go, and there they are again: a tower of pale-faced, bruise-necked girls, of bewildered boys, of rickety chairs, sat in a square of grass.

'Je*sus*.' Romy drops her head back. Her neck spasms, and she rubs it. 'I feel like I'm Alice in Wonderland. Or a Gwen Stefani video.' She massages the slope of her shoulders. Too much too soon. 'Ow.'

Touching a blooming bruise on his temple, Jay winches himself upright. 'Who's Gwen Stefani?' He frowns, almost pouts. 'I fully agree with *ow*.'

Romy stares. '"Who's Gwen Stefani?"' She shakes her head. Her neck twinges. 'You make me feel old, and I'm only seventeen. Gwen Stefani'—she crosses her legs—'was my first celebrity obsession. She was weird, and she didn't give a damn, and I loved her.'

Jay shrugs. 'Okay.' Studying the mirrors, he worries at the grass. 'It'd make more sense if we were Alice in *Through the Looking-Glass*.'

Romy brushes the ground with her palm. It feels like that fake turf they had at school, a soft, plasticky tickle. 'Why?'

'Well.' Jay shrugs again, his eyes on his boots. 'We fell through a window, and wound up somewhere weird. It's more specific than *Alice in Wonderland*.'

Romy narrows her eyes. A barbed retort gears up in her head, but she fights to hold it in; he's twelve. The high road mocks her, and she wades toward it. He can throw her words to the dogs if he likes, if it helps him be less scared.

'Fair enough,' she says, wading with the best. She even attempts a smile. 'At least this place is nicer than the church. God's meant to welcome his children, right, but he seemed a bit pissed off.'

Jay huffs. 'He did.' He steals a look at her under his hair. 'And I don't know why you ended up with me.' A ghost of a smirk twitches his mouth. 'Do you really think Kira's lucky, though? You called Callum…'

He plucks at the grass. 'Insufferable,' Romy finishes. 'Yeah.' She shakes her head, gawping at him. It's *her mind*, goddammit; can no one stay out? 'And he is insufferable.'

'Then why's Kira lucky?'

Prodding him with her boot, Romy lumbers to her feet. Her body's as bungled as Frankenstein's monster. 'Because he's pretty,' she says through a groan. Stretching her spine is a bugger; that iron ring on the church door must have bled from the core of the Earth. 'If he stopped talking, he'd be stellar.'

Jay screws his nose up. 'Ew.'

Cleaning her thoughts, Romy shrugs. 'Keep out of my head, then. Fool.'

'Je*sus*.'

The words echo through the tunnel. Kira stops. 'Was that Romy?'

Callum lifts a hand: *listen*. They've been walking in tight-lipped, tight-gripped quiet for who knows how long, and only the sky has changed. The aurora's coloured curtains blackened to night, the black night became indigo, and now, the indigo fades into a premature dawn.

'Or a Gwen Stefani video.'

'It's up there somewhere.' Callum indicates the sky. A hushed heat whispers within her; the dawn is almost as rich as theirs, shared on the top of the mountain.

'How can it be coming from there?' she asks. He holds a finger to his lips, but a smile tugs around it. His thumb brushes hers. Perhaps he's noticed, too.

'Who's Gwen Stefani?'

Callum stills. His face unfurls, from amusement, through uncertainty, to grey. Kira's hope stutters. 'Is that…?'

'Jay!' Jerking into action, Callum kicks off the wall. His fingers brush the colour as he jumps, stretching, but if the sky is solid, he can't quite reach.

'Lift me,' Kira says hurriedly. Her chest is filling with nervous air; they brought Jay with them. 'Callum.'

She grabs for his arm, but in a puff of red dust, Callum grunts, and jumps again. A foreign look hangs crazed on his face. 'Jay!' he bellows. *'Jay!'*

'Callum.' Determined, Kira grabs him again.

He wrenches away from her. *'What?'*

'Lift me up.' She spreads her hands. That look on his face… 'If I'm not too heavy, I can sit on your shoulders. If it doesn't work, we carry on.' She glances down the rocky tunnel, soft with morning light. 'We'll get through somewhere.'

Squashing down her speeding pulse, she watches Callum consider. His dark eyes dart around. His hands flex. His face is harsh. One of them needs to be rational, and for once, it isn't him.

'Fine.' Sighing, he squats. 'Get on.'

As soon as she's settled on his shoulders, she's soaring. 'Callum!' she cries, ducking her head, leaving her gut on the floor. Bracing her back, she squeezes her eyes tight shut. 'For God's *sake.*'

Two seconds. Four. Callum steadies himself, gripping her legs. She and the sky don't collide, and slowly, Kira opens her eyes. 'Guess I'm not getting an apology then,' she mutters. Breathe: two, three, four. Breathe: six, seven, eight. The upward rush left her giddy and swooping, and inch by inch, she sits up. 'Okay.'

Tucking her hair behind her ears, she plants an unceremonious hand on his head, and stretches into the dawn.

'There's a hand!' Jay exclaims. Lowering his voice and clearing his throat, he amends, 'I mean, Romy. The grass has grown a hand.'

Romy had been knocking on mirrors when he shouted. Fizzing with the shock of the noise, she turns. 'You what now?'

Jay drops to a crouch beside it, as if the "it" hadn't scared him. 'Romy.' He looks up at her. The hand becomes a fist, bending at the wrist as if knocking on a see-through door.

The grass has grown a hand. The grass has grown a *hand*.

Slowly, Romy kneels beside it. 'Mary, mother of god.'

Jay sits back on his heels. 'I know.'

Shaking her head, Romy leans down. The hand has sprouted straight from the ground. 'How is that even possible?' Leaning closer, she peers at it. The pale hand extends its fingers, fluttering through the stalks.

In a rush, unreality hits. 'Holy shit.' She grabs the hand. 'It's Kira's.'

Jay blinks at her. 'It's *Kira's?*'

'Yes!' She pinches the little finger. Jesus, god, this is weird. 'See? The pinky nail is stupidly long. They're all wonky, and uneven, and there's two hairbands around the wrist because, you know, one is a lack of preparation. Kira?'

The hand retreats through the grass. 'No!'

'It just goes on and on,' Kira sighs, pulling her fingers back. Air and colour, nothing more. 'Can you hear anything?'

Callum lowers her down. 'No,' he says, as she slides from his shoulders. 'Maybe they've moved away.'

'Or maybe it wasn't coming from there.' Bleakly, Kira considers the tunnel. The red stone is still. 'Let's go.'

The words make Romy's insides plummet. 'Kira!' she hollers. No, no, *no*, they can't walk away. 'Kira! Come back!'

'They can't hear us.' Jay balls his fists, drumming on the earth. 'Callum! We're up here!'

'…Nothing else we can do,' Kira says, but faintly. '…Listen hard.'

'Callum!' Jay roars. Romy adds her fists to his. 'Come back! *We're up here!*'

Bang, bang, bang. Romy's hands complain. She wants to scream. She wants to cry. 'Kira!' she shrieks. 'Callum!'

In a field beneath a brilliant sky, another Callum sleeps.

46

Hollow and cold

'When are you likely to start explaining?'

Rubbing a glove around his face, Mathew battles the sweat. It isn't effective, or overly wise; the sweat remains, with added fluff. 'Now? In another mythic year? I'd like'—he pauses to rasp a breath—'at least to know where I am.'

Vasi doesn't turn. 'That needs no explanation.' The mountain rings with echoes, pure and tart and cold. They're in the shade of the final peak, one steep incline spined with rocks dividing them and the sky. 'Whiteland.'

Trudging shin-deep, Mathew scoffs. 'That's not a place.' He frowns, and doubts. 'It can't be.'

Can it? Christ, he's so confused.

The leshy looks back. 'Before you met me, you'd have said I can't be a creature.' His old face, his old eyes, glimmer at Mathew's word. 'Would you not?'

Mathew's frown is engraved. 'Well, yes. Of course.'

'Of course?' With a smile, Vasi carries on. 'Then of course Whiteland is where you are. Unless the Whispers fling you out, I imagine it's where you'll stay. The outside will have left you behind.' Pausing, he shakes his head. 'No, it is not so named for being white.'

Casting a crawlingly human look back, even Grey seems disapproving. Mathew's reality jolts. 'Did I say that out loud?'

A shadow passes over them. Mathew looks up. 'Of course not,' Vasi says, as the bird glides away, glinting metallic in the bright, bright land. 'And while this part is white, our destination is not. Many parts are not; that would be simplistic.'

In silence, Mathew watches the bird. Coloured like a magpie, it's shaped like a dove.

'No.' Vasi lodges his staff in the snow, heaving himself up the slope. 'You are not being kidnapped, and I am not mad.'

This time, when Grey looks back, he is definitely reproving.

'Sorry,' Mathew says, and stops. Reality bends even more; he's apologising to a *wolf*. 'All right. How is this possible?' He climbs a few feet, and stops again. 'Why am I here, alone, and not…?'

He waves a hand, sways off-balance, and focuses back on the mountain. The Christmas indulgence has taken its toll; he can barely think without tripping, or wheezing, and often a mixture of both.

Vasi bends to examine a hole in the snow. Outside is a frozen dropping. 'Where do you think you should be?' he asks.

Mathew scours his skull. A second passes. Another. Another. 'In bed…' he says slowly. Remembering feels like wringing water from clothes that have baked in the sun. 'In the hotel. I was…yes.' He clicks his finger and thumb. 'Before I went to sleep, I'd been looking for Anna. Romy's still in hospital, and Kira's been cavorting with the boy next door…' He trails off. 'Is this because of that brandy? I knew Hazal shouldn't have given me two.'

Vasi rumbles a laugh. 'I admire your hope, but this is not alcoholic. I do not profess to know details'—he plants his staff, on the far side of a powdered, jagged, rock—'but it would appear that you were brought here and relieved of your senses, not long after your last memory.' He heaves himself past the rock. 'A year ago.'

Exasperation sails out to sea. 'It was not a year ago,' Mathew gasps, using the rock as a prop. 'For the love of Christ, stop saying it was. Without a scientific reason, or psychological theory, it's impossible.'

Vasi tramps up the last of the slope before speaking. 'What I find impossible,' he says, 'is you.'

Creakily lowering himself to a rock, he looks down the mountain to Mathew. 'You, and all you're thinking of. You have a stone world you wish to return to. You live in blocks, and all you see are animals or men. You have no wonder. You have nothing extraordinary, or malleable. Your lives are uncompromising, and so is your land.'

He scratches Grey's neck. The wolf has perched on virgin snow, an erect Egyptian cat. 'The world is exactly what you see,' he continues, 'exactly the way you expect. Here, you expect the ice plains, and you find a mountain range. You try to weave toward Skarrig, and you come across three small deserts, a myling, and a troll who wants to be a fisherman. With you...'

He squints, as if fishing himself. 'You think of your home by the ocean, and it's always the same. You have a box that takes you down different paths, and that, too, is the same. The sun rises, the moon sets, and you know, all over the world, that it's going to be the same.' He sits back, laying one huge hand squarely on his knee. 'You keep animals as pets and think them less than you. To me, that's impossible.'

Wrapping both hands around his staff, he hauls himself to his feet. Mathew says nothing. He has no words. The way Vasi puts it, his life sounds fabricated, or, at the very least, bland.

'Precisely.' Vasi turns away, toward the peak. 'I know it to be real because I see you here, and happen to believe your mind. Unless, indeed, I am mad.' He chuckles. 'If it meant imagining human companions, I confess, I would find it enjoyable. Sadly, though, that is not the case.' He beckons Mathew. 'Come and look.'

Impossible. Mathew's legs won't move. He's been wrapped in the impossible since Romy wandered off, and now, he starts to drown. His stomach clamps. Romy, wandering off. Romy, found by the boy next door. Romy, breaking her own hand, and Romy, attacking Kira. That would have seemed impossible, until he had to believe it, when she writhed and raged like a demon, and kicked him in the chest.

The clamp in his stomach takes its metal to his heart, pinching his aorta, his arteries, his veins. Romy. Kira. Anna. He misses them. Christ, how he misses them.

A snout butts his hip. He claws his way back down to himself, to the glittering snow at his feet, and with the ever-reproachful Grey at his side, wearily crests the mountain.

The summit itself is a long, flat strip. Spanning the range like a ramble through the Dales, it leads to...

Mathew double-takes. It leads to more impossible, and astounded, he stares: the matte blue sky streaks over a forest. A lush, leafy trickle down the mountainside, the first lone trees sprout feet from their peak. The snow becomes pockmarked, wet like spring. In the furthest, farthest distance, the sky starts to rot, to a jaundiced, stormy grey. Beneath it, a blue-black, watery turmoil fills the edge of the world.

This part is, but our destination is not. Many parts are not; that would be simplistic.

You try to weave toward Skarrig, and you come across three small deserts, a myling, and a troll who wants to be a fisherman.

Mathew's mind is a hum. He can't stop staring. On the far right loiters a flat, white plain, similar to the valley they climbed from. Behind him, peaks upon peaks race away. So many climates; so many lands. To the far left, more gaping water. The blue is so unnatural that it cuts him with certainty: as much as he knows about marine biology, it'll prove no use at all.

'Impossible?' Vasi's face wrinkles, into crags, or a pecan. 'That, sir, is Whiteland. It looks small today, I admit; usually, it offers a grander display.' He lifts a humble shoulder. 'So be it. Last time this mountain accepted me, from here, there was only the Tomi desert. Above it flew the souls.' He pauses. 'If memory serves, I then met the troll. He was a fine fellow, but woefully misguided. He did not know how to fish.'

A noise escapes from Mathew's throat, part cry, part laugh, part *what?* He shakes his head. 'Excuse me, trolls? Souls above the desert?'

'Mmm.' Vasi's face crinkles further, from crags to cliffs and caves. 'That was when the souls received Anneliese, which may explain their verve. It's peculiar to see the lost so happy, and she's always caused quite the stir. Let us leave.'

Plunging his staff deep in the snow, he sets off toward the forest. Knee-deep and trepidatious, Mathew follows. The gradient is death-defying, and his mind is bawling *madness!*—but he can't remain alone in an unfamiliar land, at the top of an unfamiliar mountain. Even if he thought he could, Grey's keeping watch. Clearly, he's to do as he's told.

To a point.

'Who's Anneliese?' he asks, inching down the slope. If Vasi brought her up, he might deign to answer. It's more than past time for explanation. 'The desert souls received her? Is that a religious metaphor I'm failing to understand?'

Grey yips. It sounds like a laugh. 'No,' Vasi says. 'It is literal.'

In the first oak's shadow, he stops. Sprawling and odd in its ocean of white, it buds with acorns, bright green leaves, and a tatty, woven nest. Arms out, Mathew wades toward it. The land is growing flat, but the snow is growing damp. His limbs are tense enough to snap.

'How—' He staggers, and rights himself. His jeans are sopping. 'How is it literal?'

'Impossibility,' Vasi says. 'As I told you, there's a lot to talk about.' He looks round sharply. 'Ah.'

Oh, Christ. The valves of Mathew's heart pinch tight: loping along the edge of the woods are two large, yellow-eyed wolves.

Grey barks.

Vasi bows his head. 'Thank you.'

With a howl, the wolf takes off. The echo rings around the peaks. The others stop, lift their snouts, and howl in return. Every hair on Mathew's body stands up, electric.

'He led me to you,' Vasi explains. With their leader back in their midst, the wolves angle toward a bluff. 'He must have sensed your coming long before you arrived, for I was up a waterfall when he found me. They're faithful; very faithful.'

Shrinking to graceful specks, the wolves vanish into the rock. Vasi leaves the snow for the start of a dirt path. The staff's thud turns solid.

The sound fills Mathew with something he didn't know he needed, and can't grasp enough to define. 'Can you tell if Grey will come back?' he asks, turning away from the wolves. Their wild, impossible madness has somehow made him ache, striking, hollow, and cold.

'Perhaps.' The trees enfold them. Vasi's shoulders relax, and he breathes. 'Ah; warm forest air. Can you taste it?'

Never mind taste it; it's a wash of heat. Mathew coughs. The air swamps his throat, bathing him in greenish sunlight and turning him grossly, unbearably warm. Humidity wets his neck in seconds. Shrugging out of his smoky coat, he stashes the sweaty gloves and scarf and follows Vasi down.

The narrow trail twists and winds, bumped with sandy rocks. The woods block out the mountain range, the tallest of oaks, the thickest of bushes, the longest of vines. The loudest of birds, the softest of colours.

Vasi begins to explain.

47

Hell and fire

'You know what this walking reminds me of?' Callum angles a lacklustre kick at the wall. 'You'd think once a lifetime was enough.'

Kira nods, her stomach gurgling. 'It wouldn't be so bad if we'd kept that food.'

Squinting at the ceiling, she sighs in a puff. It's the last throes of a sunset, and although it's brilliant, blinding, rich, it's not the first they've seen. She resists the urge to give it the finger.

'I'd love some cheese on toast.' Heartily, Callum exhales, looping an arm around her neck. Kira blinks. Ever since they heard Romy and Jay, he's been uncommunicative. 'Wouldn't you? The Leerdammer melting. The smell of basil.'

Kira blinks again, and frowns. 'Um. This isn't helping my stomach.' She extricates her neck. 'Personally, though…' She thinks. 'I want cookie dough. The biggest lump of cookie dough that's ever walked the Earth.'

'So do I.' Callum groans. 'God, this tunnel never *ends*.'

'You're not wrong.' Taking Callum's hand, Kira looks around. Since they heard Romy and Jay, they've gotten nowhere. Red rock around them, twilight above, the faint smell of must; they're goalless, and lost. 'At least in Whiteland, we walked with purpose.'

'At least in Whiteland, we knew the rules.' Callum cranes his neck around a corner, and cautiously, they go on. 'Rule one: encounters were fairly straightforward. There was a fine line between "help" and "kill," but you knew it straightaway.' He cocks his head, and frowns. 'Was there actually anything else?'

Disquiet flutters in Kira's chest. The dusk is dwindling fast, leaving the tunnel in purpled gloom. Nothing's happened so far in the dark, but sometime, something has to. Sometime, somewhere, they'll meet the Chlause.

'You had to hold on to your mind,' she says, before this thought can root. Waking up separated, bagless, and solitary doesn't make meeting them sound so great. 'Whiteland played with us, but we knew it, and could guard against it.'

'Yeah.'

'Whoa.' Kira jerks them both to a stop. It wasn't there before; it can't have been. She only just looked around. 'Like that.'

In the belly of the upcoming bend is a hole. The size of a cockeyed manhole cover, it plunges into black, and torn between relief and unease, she stares. The tunnel is varying; they're getting somewhere.

Or, the tunnel is varying, and its demons are awake.

'As much as I'm sick of the aimless walking…' Callum looks across at her, one eye on the hole. 'Do we think this is good or bad?'

Relief. Unease. Relief. Unease.

If they don't chance the minotaur, they'll never leave the maze.

'Good.' With a wash of bravado, or maybe bravery, Kira squats beside the drop. At the bottom is a second, stony tunnel, close enough to count the bricks. 'Are you coming?'

Sweeping her chopped hair aside, she looks back at Callum. His face is more familiar than it's been since they got here: even before Whiteland, she often received *woman-what's-wrong-with-you?* looks.

It's comforting, but he's still being slow. She lifts her eyebrows. 'Callum?'

He bobs on the balls of his feet. He frowns. He eyes the dubious hole. 'Ah.' With a grumbling sigh, his shoulders slump. 'Ugh. I guess I'm coming.' Closing the gap between them, he lowers himself to the hole. 'Give me a minute, and I'll go first.'

Sliding her legs into empty space, Kira slips neatly down. Her feet slap and echo, but her knees hardly jar, and cautiously, she straightens. Behind her is a wall; before her is a tunnel. Damp, grey bricks emit an unsullied glow, like sun or moonlight through windows. 'It's fine,' she calls. 'No demons.'

Yet.

'A fact which you know now.' Callum echoes down beside her, sporting either a second or continued look of rebuke. 'What if it hadn't been?'

Kira glances up at the hole. A crooked space of violet light, the evening marches on. 'Let's go.'

Callum blows out his cheeks. 'Fine.' He rocks into a walk. 'You've made our bed now, anyway, even if it is the pits.'

Again, he's not wrong. Kira tenses, skin prickling, putting up all of her guards. The tunnel looks, feels, tastes, and smells like a journey from the dungeon to the gallows. The walls glisten. The ceiling drips. Their feet ring like bells. She pulls up her hood and burrows, shivering. How are the walls so damp? Every so often, the drops become trails, catching the shafts of light. She tugs Callum's sleeves down over her hands. The red-stone tunnel was an autumn evening; now, with their breath a mist in the air, they've returned to a winter's night.

Talking of beds, though…trudging through the shadowed stone, a weighty weariness creeps. No sky, bright or otherwise, holds her cold attention, and fatigue is a crucifix, damning on her back. Far too many sleepless nights, in far too short a time. Her legs have a dreamer's stubbornness. Her eyes feel every blink.

A yawn threatens to break her jaw. 'When we find anything remotely soft,' she says through another, 'I'm napping.'

The yawn slips into Callum. 'Same. There's never'—he dodges a puddle—'a snow hole when you need one.'

For a teasing moment, his eyes meet hers. Kira flares with heat. So he *has* been remembering. Does that make it better or worse?

Worse. Smiling, Callum looks away, and Kira sighs to herself. If they were in Middelburg, and none of this had happened, and he hadn't had to leave… they may be out in the cold still, but walking by the river, or on their way to eat, or at a rustic New Year's market.

Doubt expands like the pupil of an eye, and it feels like quicksand, a whirlpool, space. Would they really go to a market? Can she see them travelling, watching movies, drinking summer beer? If they could live without being set up, would they ever manage to be normal?

Down with the monarchy, up with the oppressed. The thoughts she's been suppressing since she got to Callum's house march forward with trumpets and flags. There's no time to send them packing; with bayonets, cannons, and the cavalry, they're in, and damn, they're here to stay.

She and Callum are based on adversity. On racing toward something, and away from something else. If it all stopped; if they weren't in a cave, a breath out of danger; if they hadn't collided on New Year's Eve, when they'd thought the other was dead; if they snatched more than moments, and an end to uncertainty; if they weren't currently all they had, and if other lands and memories became the past, and they sat back, and thought of the future…

Kira banishes the thoughts with a lockjaw heave. Breathe. Be present. The air is damp and tart. The stone is slick, and radiates cold. At this rate, they'll never have to deal with the future. Not in an outside sense.

Oh, god.

'What's wrong?' A pace or two ahead, Callum stops. The sound of her footsteps failing was loud. 'Did you see something?'

He scans the walls. Dripping and glinting and haughty, they watch. They listen. They plot. They pry.

'Not literally.' Crossing her arms, Kira rejoins him, but her brain has fluted elsewhere. Up, up, up through the stones, red and grey, through the galloping sky, to the world beyond the snow. The real world, of pinking sunsets, royal sunrises, and a future, or lack thereof.

'Not literally?' Callum presses. She doesn't look up; suddenly, her head is too heavy. The doubt expanded to the stars, and now, dilating and fusing to iron, it's a chain around her chest. 'Have you had another predictive dream? An epiphany?'

Link by hope, the band constricts. She can almost hear it clinking. 'Of sorts,' she murmurs. Her voice seems to come from far away. 'I know you were joking, but it only just hit me.' She drags her head up. 'This isn't like last time.'

Callum's eyes flick up and down her face, and he frowns. 'What do you mean?'

Link by hope by bubbling mass, she's magma, lava, a storm. 'I mean, I'm not some overzealous innocent, playing the hero.' Folding her arms, Kira swivels to face him. 'I had a place to go home to, if not a whole family, and the whole point was us getting back there. You had even more; you weren't a part of the freak show that made the village sing. You didn't have much at stake, if anything, other than staying alive, and that was only once you came with me. But now…'

She twists the ends of her shortened hair, a frantic, fevered motion. Callum's frown cuts deeper, and he works his mouth. 'Kira…'

'You know what it looks like back home.' The tunnel feels a world away. Her skin is growing hot. 'You nearly died. The police nearly found us. They'll come back to the house, and if we'd stayed on the outside, even if we ran somewhere else…' She ducks her head, fighting her lungs. She's starting to shake. 'We can't go back.'

She looks back up again, a rough wooden doll. 'Certainly not yet, and who knows if ever? Really, Callum, who knows?' Her voice pitches. She can't drag it down. 'However long we wait, we might still be found, and if we did escape, whoever sent the huldra and my dad, let's say, okay, it's the Kyo, would come after us again. Maybe they'd never *stop*. And what's worse is that wherever we are—' She dodges Callum's hands, trying to calm her, trying to speak, and steps clumsily back toward the wall. 'We don't even *know* where we are, only that it's probably definitely not the haven we wanted, and we have no clue about the future. We might not *have* a future. No.'

Jittery, she stumbles back again. Her arms whip out to block his. 'Kira,' he's saying, 'Kira, calm down,' but she ignores him. Everything blurs, far too hot. He doesn't know, doesn't see. Doesn't *care*?

'We killed a predictable future when we chose to listen to Talie.' She braces herself against him, speaking through her teeth. Her breath is a whistle. She's burning. Callum just stop just stop. 'Now everything's changed. People say it about love, or a job, but for us it's *real*. We have nowhere to go, and this whole time, we've been joking like everything's fine. Sauntering into different worlds, like it's nothing.' Her arm flies out. 'Like it's *nothing*, like we do it every day. We've thrown away everything, but we had to, right, if we didn't want a massive shitstorm, and now, who knows?' Her voice cracks. She's almost shouting, a cry like a bird in a cage. 'Maybe that would have been better than this, but we didn't stop to think. We just left. Three rocks and no hard places, because whatever we do, we're fucked.'

She flings a glance down the catacomb.

In that second, Callum has her. 'Right.' Seizing her arms, he pushes her back.

'Hey!' Kira cries, straining against him, but he shoves her into the wall. 'Callum, get off. This is stupid.' She struggles. The damp is freezing. *'Get off.'*

Raising her hands in his, Callum pins them beside her head. Déjà vu dizzies her, distant and strange, and she drifts out of herself. It's a mimicry of Callum, a replica, a clone, of things he's done before. It's not real.

'Sometimes,' Callum says, 'it's the only way you'll listen.'

He grips her wrists, and through her angst, she forces herself to focus. It isn't just strange; it's demeaning. They're past this. 'Callum, let me go.'

'No.' He grips her pincer-tight. The more she wriggles, the more he pinches. Frustration licks at her edges. 'Yes, we're between three rocks, and it's fucked. I'll give you that.' He lowers his face to hers. 'But a freak-out isn't going to help. I told you this before: if we don't joke, we'll go mad.' He gestures with his hand and hers. 'So we have no idea where we're going, or what we're going to do; dwelling on it every second will only make it worse. The way you're demonstrating is really quite stunning.'

Frustration boils. 'Don't patronise me.'

'For God's sake, then *listen*.'

Driving her wrists into the wall, Callum sets his jaw. Kira tips up her chin and does the same. She'd cry if she was alone, but she's not, and he's rapidly becoming a git. 'Fine,' she says through her teeth. 'Then talk.'

Callum loosens his grip a tad. 'Thank you.' He meets her eyes. She drops them. 'We are where we are,' he continues, more gently, 'and we've done the things we've done. All we can do is hang on to our heads. We keep going, and stay alive, and find Romy and Jay, and work out the rest when we need to. Did you know what you wanted to do after uni?'

Kira blinks at him. Her thoughts are limping. The tortoise overtaking the hare, her chest stilling its flutter. From the inside out, she's growing cold.

'Did you?' Callum asks.

Clutching her irritation like straws, she shakes her head.

'Neither did I.' Callum sighs in a gust, ducking his head. 'Not really.'

Kira shuts her eyes. All of a sudden, she's breathlessly tired. 'What's your point, Callum?'

He looks up. His face is shadowed, full of hollows and dips. 'When you were a kid,' he says, 'did you know where you'd be at nineteen? Did you think about being an adult at all?'

Kira shakes her head again.

'Exactly.' Callum releases her wrists. 'You couldn't, could you, when you didn't know what even teenage life was like.'

Kira's hands fall to her sides. Winded, exhausted, she lets them, and the straws drift away. As much as he's manhandled her, and wronged her, and put her firmly in her womanly place, at least she's calmer.

Still…

'Yes?' Callum steps back, turning his hands palms-up. 'Agreed? None of us know much until we're nearing it, full steam ahead. Often, not even then. Or ever. We've left our world behind, and that makes it seem worse, but we'll work it out just the same.' He lifts his hands to cup her face. 'Now let me fucking kiss you.'

Before she can think, or blink, he pulls her in, his stubble scratching her skin. Not soft, not earnest, like he's been before, but urgent. It feels like falling.

She falls, and it's winter, in the middle of the night, when your terrors are real in the dark. He moves his hands to her lower back, urging her closer. He's cold. Her eyes sink shut, but she wills them open. The fires from the sunrise kindle again, and she wills them to stop, for the tunnel to stay, for the catacomb not to get burned away, because this isn't right, it's greedy, and hungry, and crawling, and—

The wall behind her gives out.

'Ah!' Kira loses her breath and her balance, clutching Callum for support. He staggers, planting his legs on the stone, keeping them both upright. Her thoughts have been snuffed, pinched like a flame. She hugs him, hard.

For a moment, they're still. Cheek to jaw, hearts rebounding. There was something, though. Just now, there was something, a feeling. Something.

Yes, there was. A wall.

Kira twists around, her belly swooping. Where the tunnel should be, there's a wall, and where the wall should be, there's a church.

She stares. Against her spine, Callum tenses. 'Okay.' Twisting back, Kira licks her lips, oddly calm. 'So this is us.'

The tunnel's gone, and the church surrounds them. Behind Callum sits a set of wooden doors, embossed with iron and a corrugated ring. On one side skulks a stained glass window, of snowcapped mountains and two walkers and their dog approaching the top. On the other stands a rich, empty table, a window of a river and a yellow sky, and the beginnings of a wall of mismatched doors. Slowly, Kira turns back.

Callum cinches her waist. 'And so starts our trial.'

She thins her lips. 'Don't joke.'

'I'm not.'

He lets her go, stepping forward, trailing his fingers along her back. Pews extend around them, up to an altar and a pattern of burning. Nothing adorns the sides of the church, and the tapering spire is bare; were it not for the windows, and the ugly crosses, dumpy on the altar and warped on the walls, it would feel completely abandoned.

As soon as she thinks it, it's wrong. Indistinct incense wafts through the air, and the hairs on her arms stand up. They push against the hoodie, electric.

The faintest strains of music drift. A choral piece, it cranks like a gramophone. 'I feel…' She swallows. Her mouth has dried. 'Like I'm in the Triwizard Tournament.'

Callum doesn't smile. She'd hoped he would. 'Maybe.' He moves between the pews, tracing lines on the stone. 'But we don't know the rules. We must have to do more here, more than keep our minds.'

Sandy dust drifts up from his fingers. Kira watches it go. 'There's nothing to say it's a game,' she says. The chains are back, and burning. Edging down the aisle, she tries to dowse the flames. 'Whiteland wasn't, in the end.'

'We're not in Whiteland.'

'And don't we know it.'

Folding her arms protectively, Kira looks around. Stained glass in every wall, varied in menace, its colours falling bright on the age-old floor. The church should belong to a graveyard; it epitomises the Victorian Gothic, from its thin bones to its cheerful countenance, creeping like a bow-backed widow up a misty, forgotten path. Nothing good lies here. It's tangible, palpable, like a room's energy after a row. The stones are watchful. The church is alive.

Nothing tells her to stop at the altar. Nothing tells her to look up, at the same time as Callum, at the window of the crowded, burning girl. Like a puppet, she follows her instincts.

Her instincts skewer her whole. By the window hangs a crude wooden cross, and hanging from the cross is her sister.

All the blood she's ever had drains away through the floor. 'Romy!' Kira screams, blackened by terror, hit by horror in a deep black hole. Stumbling toward the steps, she sobs, swilling with sickness and blood. 'Romy!'

A second allegory swims from the shadows. Kira's head bays, and she staggers. Jay.

Jay, stretched out, crucified, a mirror on the right of the burning girl. Their chins on their chests, their arms horizontal, their legs limp and free. Callum barges past her with a bellow but she freezes, her mind growing dizzy as it yells, going numb. Romy's hair is streaked with blood. Her arms drip red, her wrists bound to the cross, and Jay.

Oh, hellfire, *Jay*. Carved in his chest, raw and sick, are five words.

Time to come home, girls.

Kira's knees and palms jarr hard on the stone at the base of the godless cross. She lifts her screaming, howling head. A yelling sob rips from her throat.

Romy's dead eyes look down.

48

Moulding gold

'We should try to find a way out.'

Jay may be stating the obvious, but she'd forgotten he was there. In a hopeless stupor of staring through the mirrored, dull-eyed girls, forgetting was easily done.

Romy blinks, and heaves herself back. She'd been balls-deep in the past, and, for some reason, at her high school prom. She'd gone for the after-party, the same as everyone else. She'd assumed a grown-up, fashionable boredom, the same as everyone else. The music was lame, the theme too young, every group uncool until you got drunk, remembered the lyrics, the wonders of Disney, and your friends from year four. Her dress was black and rockabilly, and people kept calling her Wednesday. The fallacy was plain—Wednesday Addams would never go rockabilly—but to them, being sullen was enough.

This led on to Kira's seventeenth birthday. She's so abominably lucky to have been born on Hallowe'en, but abominably, finds it annoying. She can't have a normal *party*, everyone just wants to dress up and get *drunk*, why would she want to spend her birthday losing herself, scaring people, and making out with strangers?

Why not? Romy always retorted. It was a pretty good life philosophy, although Kira sniffed at it like a snob…except on her seventeenth.

They were at a party. It was one of those thrown by sixth form guys still into high school girls, full of tacky drink and nineties music, and Peter was there. (Was he dressed as a Jedi? Or a druid? Whatever it was, it was him to a T—painfully overenthusiastic, but somehow winding up dull.) He'd been clinging to Kira all evening, like an anemone stuck on a rock: kissing her cheek, kissing her lips, kissing her mid-conversation, referring to her as "my girl, my girl." It was all he ever did, without seeing that it drove her mad, and at some point that night, she was done.

Maybe after his ceremony of presenting her with a ring. A glorious gift for his glorious girl, he'd slipped it on her finger and joked—or not, Romy thought upon seeing the rubies, with a vague attempt not to grimace—about marriage. Maybe after his seventh appearance, butting into her conversations and joking (or not) about guarding his girl. Every time Romy saw her, behind her Venetian angel mask, her skin was getting tighter, and her uneven nails were growing ragged. They weren't close, but she knew her sister. It signalled the furnace. The wrath.

The next time he interrupted her with a kiss, Kira exploded. Not long after that, he left. He was girl-less, chastised, and in possession of several lessons about respect, overattachment, and the meaning of personal space. The party clapped and cheered.

Later, Romy saw her in a corner with a guy. Later, she saw her with another.

Maybe she should have, but she didn't intervene. She was startled by the quick seduction, by the shameless flirting by the table with the booze, but all she really thought was damn, about time. Peter was pathetic, an overbearing drag, and Kira needed some birthday fun; not to mention the satisfaction of seeing her lose control. It was nice not to be the only one who falls.

Boys and anger, anger and boys. As a kid, she loved to toy with boys; her ten-year-old self would declare she loved them, cut out intricate paper hearts, deliver intricate paper hearts, and spread rumours when she got bored. Mathew found it funny. Anna found it obscene.

Her parents; that's where she'd ended up, when Jay decided to speak. Mathew making Anna her first mojito, astonished that she'd never tried. Anna finding it revolting, and spitting it over Kira, who didn't know whether to laugh or puke.

Mathew and Anna, here and then gone. Or, in the case of her dad…

'Okay.' Romy sits up, wincing at the jerk. Her stiff, aching neck is still sore, and probably blue. Hell *no* to thinking about her dad. If she drops the drawbridge to all of that—to feel the *click* that means acceptance—she'll tip into the pit and never climb out. 'Any ideas?'

Jay blinks at her, then away. A part of her twinges, annoyed. His telepathy is useful, but it really is intrusive.

Jay pulls a face. Drawing into himself, he mumbles, 'I know. Sorry.'

Romy twinges again. 'Don't be.' Stamping the irritation down, she struggles to her feet. 'It's a learning curve for both of us. How did Alice return through the looking glass?'

She sweeps her eyes around the mirrors. Since Kira's impossible hand, nothing's changed. Grass. Glass. The chair, which makes her feel somehow dirty.

'I haven't seen the film.' Glumly, Jay shrugs. 'Or read the book. Is there a book?' He plucks a stem of grass and adds it to a pile. It grows back at once, but after fifty repetitions, the novelty's worn off. 'We tried pushing already.' Discarding a final, moody blade, he stands. 'We tried shouting.'

They have. For a while, they yelled and pounded, with their fists and their feet, for all their caged-bird lives were worth. The glass didn't splinter, let alone crack.

So what's left?

'Right.' Swallowing her feeling of *dirty, dirty*, Romy seizes the wicker chair. 'We've tried everything except this. Which mirror?'

Jay's eyes fly wide. 'What are you doing?'

'Read my mind, Yoda.' Romy cuts her gaze around. 'Which—actually, never mind.' Cementing her grip on the arms, she braces. 'They're all the fucking same.'

Swinging around like a discus thrower, Romy rams the chair into glass.

With a throbbing bang, a sonic boom, the many mirrors shatter. The chair rebounds and ricochets back, ramming Romy's stomach. 'Fuck!'

She crashes down. Jay hits the floor, curling up tight. The room is crumbling, fracturing, falling. No longer solid, the ground starts to shake, less like grass and more a bouncy castle, and the booming, the booming, the *booming*. Dashed with splinters and jolted at the wrists, Romy slams her hands to her ears. Light spasms off the shards of mirror, blinding prisms in her vision, but Jesus, god, the *noise*; she's been to a hundred metal concerts, battling against being Barbie in the mosh pit, but they were never as loud as this. This is a cracking, a screeching, a thundering, clanging on her ribs and tugging at her goose bumps, rattling her teeth so they taste like blood.

The ground bucks. With a cry, Romy topples, squeezing her juddering eyes shut. It's going to make her vomit. It's going to knock her out.

With a cataclysmic bellow, it stops.

The aftershock throbs on. Five pulses, ten, twenty. Sprawled on her side, her vision sparkling, Romy slowly looks up.

Jay is uncoiling, watching the ground beneath them settle to stone. Half-dead and dull, the chair disappears. The glass glints away like rain.

Incense drifts toward them. Romy blinks, and in that second, the dust-lit church reforms.

'Oh, my—' She scrabbles to her feet. The stained glass is back, vivid and rich. Her breath retreats inside her, musty, freezing her blood. Lunging for Jay, she hauls him toward her. Is the priest here? Something else? Something worse? The pews hulk. The corners lurk. Those damn doors mock her. She smashed the mirror and shattered the illusion, literally. And now?

Jay gasps. Romy pivots.

A chill rain walks through her.

Her gasp joins Jay's, and she stiffens. It's autumn drizzle clinging to mist, but instead of her hurrying through it, it breezes through her body. A second of cold. Gone. Every inch of her tingles.

'Romy,' Jay says hoarsely. Floating somewhere outside herself, Romy turns.

For several seconds, her lungs don't work. Walking down the aisle are Kira and Callum.

'Kira.' Romy's voice hitches. She jolts forward. 'What are you doing?'

The crooked thought hits her then: they're the autumn mist. Callum and Kira are ghostly, unreal, faded, flickering holograms. Perfect pictures lacking dimension. Romy stares. From mirrors to mirrors to mirrors; it's going to drive them mad.

In front of the altar, the mirrors stop. Their faces tilt up. Romy frowns. They're carbon copies, beautifully synced. Is anything she's seeing real? The past? The future? Neither? Both?

She glances at Jay. His fists clench, his lip downtrodden. His eyes drill holes in Callum's head. Can he hear them, if they're ghosts?

'Romy!'

Romy spins back. Screaming again, torn and primal, the ghost-girl throws herself at the altar. Romy looks up, up, up.

Splashed like art on the cold church wall, the two of them hang from crosses.

Aghast. Sickened. Stricken. Repulsed. Jay snaps his face away with a gulp, a small, tortured noise. Digging her nails into her scalp, Romy scrapes her hands through her hair. Is this real? It can't be. The two of them are bleeding, replicas of Jesus, sawn to pieces by sacrilege. Lifeless. Darkness yawns, but she can't look away.

A tinny, Eastern tune winds up, like a gramophone lodged in her skull. With an indistinct shout, Callum barges past Kira, staggering up the steps. Screaming, staring up at the crosses, Kira cracks to her knees.

But they're not dead. They're not *dead*.

'We're here!' Romy shouts, as Jay whimpers beside her, as Kira screams and screams. She's never seen her sister so wild, distraught. Screaming, screaming, *screaming*. 'We're alive!'

'Jay!' Callum roars.

Jay flinches. Romy tenses. 'Fuck it.'

Throwing sense to meet the wind, flying into ghosts, she breaks into a run. Her feet smack the stone, and ring. The music is a sultry haunt, a resonant echo, the hiss of dancers, spirits, smoke. It stands her hair on end. 'Kira!'

In the stained-glass light, Kira shudders, fit to shatter. The wafting incense gusts, growing with the song.

'Kira!' Coughing, Romy tears up the altar steps. 'We're alive! Turn around, *please*, Kira, we're here, we're *all right*.'

She grabs Kira's shoulder, to shake her, turn her, but her fingers drop straight through. Instinctively, Romy jerks back. Her hand could have plunged into Arctic water.

Gritting her teeth, she tries again.

Again.

Again.

'Agh!' Romy yells, when Kira still doesn't feel her. Balling up her frozen fingers, she swaddles them in her sleeves. If she's not mistaken, they're purple. 'Ah!'

Her whole body chills.

'This is all your fault!' Stepping from her aura, Callum, ghost-Callum, heaves Kira to her feet. His unearthly knuckles pale on her shoulders, he shakes her. 'Look what you've done!'

Romy's eyes widen.

'*Look what you've done!*' Callum hauls her around, for a full-on view of the crosses. Kira's sobbing is appalled, her protests burbling, as stricken as if she's been struck. 'Jesus.' His mouth skews, an ugly twist. 'I should have listened to my mother. I should never have agreed to help Romy. I should never have talked to you on New Year's Eve.'

Kira wrenches herself from his grip. 'Get off.' She's red and swollen. 'What's wrong with you? This is not my fault.'

'The hell it isn't.'

'The hell—you *what*?' Viciously, Kira swipes at the air, at the sonorous, perfumed church. 'I didn't do this. Not any of this. I tried to stop you coming, and I tried to sneak away, so I'd stop hurting you and your family.' She jabs a finger at him. 'It was you who decided you had to be involved, and you who ended up here.'

Her face sets to bitter stone. Romy's own anger surges, beating back the horror. God, Callum's got some hell to pay. His fingers flex. His face is fire, his Adam's apple straining. His eyes dart between Kira and the crosses. Once, directly, *seeingly*, they seem to dart to her.

'Blaming me won't help,' Kira says, when all he does is fume. She's slapped a tremulous calm on her voice, like wallpaper worn thin. 'You said yourself that this isn't our fault, and that we need to keep going, together. We can't start fighting. We're in too much trouble.'

Boom.

'My brother is dead!' Callum roars. Storming forwards, he grabs her arm. 'Do you get that?'

Kira's calm explodes. 'You know what, yeah, I do,' she shouts, yanking herself away. 'God, I thought you were better than this. I thought you *knew* better than this. We've no idea if it's real or not, but they're screwing us over regardless. They're *winning*.' Her face contorts. 'This is just what they want. Do you *get* that, Callum? Are you ignorant, now, as well as a twat?'

'Stop.'

'No.' She shakes her head, folding her arms, hurt and thrown and lost. 'I can't—I can't believe you. I can't. I'm sorry about Jay—god, you don't know how much—and I'm sorry that any of you got involved, but *this is not my fault*.'

Callum's hand snaps out, and he slaps her.

'Hey!' The sound in the church is a gunshot. Romy lurches forward, smacked with white heat. With a cry, Kira reels back. Romy stops. 'Oh, my god, I'm *useless*!'

Clenching her fists, she swallows a storm, a locust plague of rage. Kira rights herself, glaring at Callum, holding her flushing cheek. Romy grinds her teeth. Talk about doling out a piece of her mind; when they find each other, she'll strip Callum's flesh and feed him to the Chlause in scraps.

'Romy.'

Fingers on her arm make her wheel around. 'What?' she snaps.

Jay hunches inwards, away from the scene by the altar. Romy's anger is touched, but not dowsed. 'Remember what Talie said,' he says, his voice as pale as his skin. 'About Urnäsch, and the Chlause.'

'Talie's a cheapskate, two-faced liar.' Romy swivels back. 'Whatever she said, I can't think about it.'

Not when Callum continues to shout. Not when he's hit her sister once, and could well do it again. If there's any kind of god here, make him stop. She'll repent. She'll convert. She'll—

Grasping Kira's shoulder, Callum shoves her backwards. She hits the stone with a yell.

'No!' Romy's lungs implode, and she doubles over. This isn't happening. How is this happening?

'Romy.' Jay's breaking voice wobbles. 'Listen to me. It's important.'

Romy's heart could literally be in her mouth. 'Important?' she manages, caught and strangled. The music swells and resonates, that smoky, sinister, god-awful dance, at its spirit-summoning peak. '*This* is important. My sister, your brother.'

'They drive you mad, they torture you, and make you one of them.' Jay rushes the words, and grabs her sleeve. '*Listen*. It might not be real.'

The smoky, sinister, god-awful dance crescendos, peaks, and dies.

Suddenly, her breath is too loud. Her temple beats a fearsome drum, and Romy turns to the altar.

The church is an empty, echoing husk. No bleeding crosses. No violent ghosts. 'Mary, mother of god,' she murmurs. The silence winds her, spins her around, and drags her through a hedge. 'How do we tell what's real?'

Jay shrugs, glancing back at the altar. No one but the burning girl is there to meet his eye. 'At least we know that some of it can't be. If that was real, they saw us dead, and believed it. And if it wasn't…' He kinks his knotty fingers up into his sleeves. 'Don't know. They could be okay.'

Or not. Slowly, Romy nods. 'If it *was* real, it was to get to them.' She lowers herself to the altar steps. 'And their fight was to get to us. That's what we're thinking?'

Jay says nothing. She looks up. 'Jay.' His eyes are closed, and he's started to shake. 'Oh, Jay.' She pushes up again, awkwardly taking his arm. He'll hear her mind before she speaks, and she's fairly rubbish at comfort, but her specialty is destructive thoughts and the way they nibble and gnaw. 'Jay, that's not going to happen to us. We're not going to die on the cross, like some psycho's Satanist joke.' She pulls him into a stilted hug. 'We're not going to die at all. Okay?'

Although he stands stiffer than boards, Jay's head wilts to her shoulder. 'Mmm.'

'No "mmm."' Romy rests her chin on his shaggy Callum hair. '"Okay."'

It's not okay, but he echoes her. Sighing, Romy hugs him close. How did everything get so screwed so atrociously, monstrously fast? A week ago, she was planning with Harvey, getting hyped for New Year. She was cursing coursework, and dreaming up gifts. If there's one thing she's worse at than kids, it's Christmas.

'You smell of Callum,' Jay mumbles. A pause. Turning his head, he mashes his face in her coat. 'Romy?'

'Yeah?'

He sniffs. 'I really want to go home.'

The words are bleary, masking tears. Romy's discipline ruptures. The pit is inviting, dull and destroying, obliterating, a void. Home.

They never should have left.

'You will.' She sets her mind to a buzz. 'We'll find Kira and Callum, I'll find out whether I need to kill him, and then you'll both go home. With me and Kira here, we're untraceable, so the police have to leave him alone.' Gingerly, she rubs Jay's back. 'He has alibis for everything. You'll go back to normal.'

Wetly, Jay huffs.

'You *will*.' Romy shuts her eyes. 'You will. Whatever happens'—she squeezes him tight—'I promise we'll get you out.'

And her? The thought draws blood. And Kira? What happens to them, the blamed, the indicted, here, stuck on the run? Hiding in other worlds?

Shut up. She snaps this off and stamps it out. Gone. Compartmentalised. Squashed in a cabinet, squished in a box, and given a meaty kick. Not today.

At least therapy taught her something. Without her boxes, and without her cabinets, her personal hell would explode.

'Ghost-Kira was right, though.' She pulls away from Jay. He's not as bleary, not as drained, and his attention is unashamed. 'We need to keep going, together. We need to hang on to our hats, and our shit, and *not*'—she stabs a finger at the altar—'end up doing *that*.'

Jay sketches a withered smile. 'Yeah. If it was actually real.'

It feels like moulding gold, but Romy returns the effort. 'If it was actually real,' she agrees. 'You're too short to be a match for me, but either way, let's avoid it. And now…' She spins, desolated. 'We have a new game to play.'

She lets the thought ring: *what's the time, Mr. Wolf?*

Jay looks around. 'So we don't wake the priest.'

'I knew it.' Romy winks. 'You're the clever one. Now hush.'

49

And so she dreams

The man at her feet had been dead for a while.

It's dark, and she's dreaming. On the outside looking in, she's a metre away from her better, less feeble self. This is how things were. This is how, mercifully, they'll never be again.

The man. She was about to leave him and head to the edge when his pretty little wife came home, and in the heat of seduction, of beautiful violence, it was oh-so-tempting to take her, too. She was such a droning *bore*.

For outside-Freya, it's crystallised: her exasperation at this endless wail, baying to the woods like a hunting horn. Garbled questions from a bawling mouth, too shocked to be scared of the infamous huldra. She scored some points for that.

'Why?' The girl clung to her husband's sleeve like the wool would bring him back. Her round, wet face was puffing up. 'Why'd you kill him?'

Freya almost walked off. She always walked off, but this was different. She'd been *seen*. She'd never been seen before, but neither had she taken a man in the forest, outside the walls of his home. It was luck, he was dozy, and she craved her own escape.

So, out of interest, or fun, she stayed. 'Why?' Freya cocked her head. Even in grief, the girl was cherubic, to a horrible degree. 'I think you mean, my love, why not?'

Crouching, she pouted. Outside-Freya smiles: she'd aimed for condescension, and my, did she succeed.

'Have you never heard of the big, bad wolf?' Past-Freya reached over the body, curling a lock of his young wife's hair. The girl flinched, so violently that she toppled from knees to rump. Freya stood. 'In here, that's us.'

Oh, what drama. Oh, such delight. Freya cocked her head again; beneath the shawls and the wool and the furs, she'd swear the girl was pregnant. The sense, the scent, was faint enough that the mother herself might not yet know.

She'd better teach the boy not to linger in the shadows.

'Your husband'—Freya flicked a nod at the open-trousered corpse—'should have watched where he was going. It's what we do. It's who we are.'

'No.' The girl shook her head, to Freya's great amusement.

'Really.' She crossed her arms. 'I'd love for you to tell.'

The girl gulped and burbled. 'Not all of you are murderers.' Another sob hiccupped from her, splintering her bones. 'I've heard'—she sniffed grotesquely—'stories. Some of you try to fight it off.'

She was manic. Pathetic. Freya shrugged. 'You're not wrong.' She scanned the pines, skimming over her silent dreaming self. 'Sadly, I've got things to do, or we could chat. You're a plucky cub.'

She took a step. The girl wailed.

'Oh, come on.' Freya laughed, holding out a hand. 'I won't hurt you. The killing's done.'

Seduction simmered behind her eyes, but the pretty wife wasn't looking. Sobbing, coughing, crying, crying, she dropped her head to her husband's chest. Freya smiled. Never mind. One was enough, and soon she should—

Outside-Freya sees herself shriek and hit the snow.

She slits her eyes at the recollection. It wasn't pain so much as a rush of burning ice, a wave from her toes to her head. It stripped her, cored her, and left her breathless, slumping to her knees. She spasmed. She shivered. She nearly blacked out.

And then she started to shimmer. Outside-Freya lifts her eyebrows. She missed it when it was happening to her, caught up in its throes: Her hair, clothes, and form shimmer, shifting through a glittering grey. Her dress pales to skin, and then away.

She was so glad to be rid of it. Heavy and dull, its exit, stage-right signalled many weights gone.

She was ready. Ready to run, ready to live. Past-Freya gets to her feet, and dream-Freya lifts up.

50

In the flames

'I'm sorry that any of you got involved, but *this is not my fault.*'

Kira lets the words ring. Her fury is a Molotov cocktail, quick to light and quick to burn, but oh, did he deserve it. Callum's attacking her; he's honestly attacking her. It's unbelievable. Yes, everyone ending up here is an iron maiden, spiked with guilt, but Callum's change of heart and mind stings like fifty bees. Although it made her realise this is *not* her fault, his words amount to one thing: he wishes he never met her.

'They've gone,' he says suddenly. He'd been looking away, his fists clenched, his face screwed up with a foreign blackness, but now, he slumps. 'They've *gone.*'

At first, it doesn't click. Kira stares at him, livid, horrified, hurt. But then…

'How can they have gone?' She gapes, snapping around like whiplash. The sides of the centre window have emptied; kaleidoscopic colours pour, but there's nothing to illuminate. No Romy, no Jay. The shadows creep alone. 'How?'

A crash rocks the hideous quiet. Already teetering over an edge, she jumps from her skin to the sky.

The fat cross from the altar lies sprawled at Callum's feet. 'It wasn't real,' he mutters, ground through his teeth. 'They're not dead. It was as much an illusion as the ceiling sky, and the tunnel wall that…' He flounders angrily. 'Melted. I hate this *fucking* place.'

He slams his fist on the altar. Starting, Kira recoils. 'Callum?'

'What?' His rage is carved and wild. He throws up his hands. 'Don't you? Don't you hate it? I'm so sick of everything happening to us, like we're nothing and probably worse. Nothing's been real since we saw that doll. We were just too shocked by the crosses to realise that killing Jay and Romy, and sticking them on a wall, gains them nothing.'

Swelling in the air, the choir sings dissonance, a discordant haunt that chills. 'What does it gain them not to?' Kira asks, harsher than she intended. Really, though, she doesn't much care; a thousand emotions ricochet through her, and he's blossomed into a beast. A brute. He's spiteful, and he means it.

'Don't be stupid.' Dismissing her, Callum looks away.

Sting. A beast. A brute.

'I'm not.' Kira reins her temper in, thread by thread. 'We weren't sent here for tea parties, or, or caviar. We thought we were, and there, we *were* stupid. There's clearly something sick going on, so why not kill us off?' She spreads her hands and steps toward him. The threads start to burn. 'Who knows why Talie lied to us, but it's all going to be linked. You can see that, right? You're not too blind? Someone wants revenge on me and Romy, so why not split us up, drive us mad with horror-film stills, divide us more, and kill us? It'd make a great spectator sport. Kind of like in *Saw*.'

The choir ebbs, and rises. A shrill soprano flutes the descant. Kira shivers.

'It wasn't *real*.' With an aggravated sigh, Callum pushes off the altar. 'Christ, Kira. Just stop. Sure, it could be a spectator sport, but they wouldn't get tired of this quickly. Something else is going to happen, and we need to get out before it does.'

Ebbing again, the music is changing. Floating in snatches through the air, it deepens, less unearthly, speeding up.

'We don't know that.' Her voice is a battle. 'We don't know Romy and Jay aren't…'

Dead.

She swallows, breathes, and lifts her chin. 'When Dad died,' she says, the words catching, 'it was real.'

Callum scoffs. 'Yeah, and how's that going?' He shakes his head at her. 'He's achieved quite a lot, for a dead man. Framing. Murdering. Even with harpies in his head, it's impressive.'

'Mum—'

'Don't.' He lifts a scornful finger. 'Don't bring up your mother. According to you, all she did was vanish. She's probably out there somewhere.'

Sting. Sting. Kira's breath feels trapped. 'Stop it, Callum.'

'Stop *what*?'

'Stop assuming you know what I'm going to say.' She quashes the angry urge to cry. He'd only get more condescending. 'What happened to the you in the tunnel, saying we'd figure everything out? You're being cruel. Irrational, and cruel.' Her throat closes up. 'Why?'

Callum smiles. It's not his smirk, or his smug smile, or the grin that crinkles his eyes. It's small, and sly, and it makes her feel ill. 'Because Callum was never in the tunnel.'

Her first thought is *why third person?*

Her second is *oh, my god.*

Callum clasps his hands over his jeans. 'Oh, my god, indeed.'

Kira's head swoons into a black, black hole. His dark expressions, his off-kilter actions, even the danger she felt in the kiss. She passed it off. It slipped away. All of it slipped away.

Oh, god. The realisation gusts through her, like she's facing into the wind. That's exactly what they wanted; they wanted her fooled. They wanted her trusting. They wanted to nip at her mind, to bend it, to toy with her senses and watch her dance.

A spectator sport; a game. It makes Whiteland seem tame.

'Who are you?' Kira whispers. Her voice feels very far away. 'If you're not Callum…'

She falters. The words physically won't come out.

Callum steps toward her, a saunter, a spring. Something ticks. Something whirs. 'Are you sure you want to know?' The smile becomes a smirk, and it makes him cold. 'You were very…alluring.'

In a blink, he's in front of her. Pinching her chin between finger and thumb, he tilts it up. He's far too close, moving like a flicker. Kira can hardly breathe. 'Get off.'

Softly, he laughs. 'That's not what you want.' Bending down, he strokes her waist. 'Pity that Callum's not here.'

His voice tickles her neck. Kira shudders, tensing to dread, disgust. 'Where's Callum?' She clenches her fists by her sides. 'What have you done with him?'

Behind her eyes, the northern lights flicker, a ripple of purple and gold. Kira blinks. The distorted music settles around them. It's a rumbling, blooming blanket, and it's almost making sense.

'Mmm.' Callum kisses her neck. Cringing, Kira shuts her eyes. God, if she could faint, or scream and never stop. 'He's having fun.'

Kira swallows. The sound is too loud, her mouth too dry. 'What does that mean?'

'It means'—his lips brush her neck again—'that he's with another of us.' His fingers dig into her waist. She represses a flinching, frightened whimper. 'Maybe another you. One'—he smiles against her skin—'who's even more alluring.'

The jibe doesn't bite. She just needs to get out. Kira angles her head away, her neck away, her waist away. This isn't Callum. He's not in there. He'd be strong enough to fight, and strong enough to win.

Kira grits her teeth. Breathe. Focus. 'Who are you?' she forces out. 'What—'

The music shatters. As though it had been muffled by glass, as though she'd been muffled, too, it shatters, and like a kick in the teeth, she knows. The bassline, the thrashing drums. Enraged guitars and men.

Let's become a carnival now Ragnarok is visceral.

Kira's fortress crumbles.

'Funny how we know you,' Callum whispers.

Unable to stop it, Kira whimpers. The song blazes, and she's back in Holland, back in her house, inching upstairs. Her bedroom is the image at the end of a telescope, close but far, and beyond the door lies carnage.

Other memories scuttle in, ones that aren't her own: an open-plan, white-panelled room, moonlight sighing in the dark. The song plays a burning ballet. On a bed sit bodies, lined up neatly, a sketchy tree etched into their wrists. *Funny how we know you.*

Kira blinks, and blinks again, but the afterglow remains. 'What do you want?' she manages. It's stilted, barely more than a breath, but the effort stops her falling. Breathe, focus, *think*. Get out.

A pause. Callum chuckles, slinking and snaking, cold on her neck. When he pulls back, with a slow relish, the man's face has gone.

In its place is a mask of fire. Amber slits make snakelike eyes. A hooked beak masks the nose, scarlet, yellow, orange feathers melding to leathery skin. Around the feathers' edges the scorched face puckers, furious at being so foully defiled. The slashing mouth is a Chelsea smile.

The horror steps back, and links its hands. Its body burns. 'I am the Pretty.'

Darkness swallows Kira whole. With a bloody, brutal scream, she runs.

It's sacrilege. All of it. Tripping down the steps, she bolts down the aisle to the door that took the tunnel. Her feet pound with pain. The stone jars her knees.

Hunting wolves in curtained skies.

The church is growing longer. It must be. She's gasping, dizzy, weakened, hot, slowing to a stagger. She should have reached the door by now.

Are we dead when we have died?

The music roars louder. A gale in her ears, a tolling bell, heavy in her chest. Her calves shake. Her feet throb. She breathes through her teeth, tears in her eyes.

Oh, how the world lusts after nothing.

Suddenly, the door is there. Kira slams into it. 'Ah!'

Rebounding, she teeters. The song screams, a hundred screams, women and children on fire, in agony. One by one by one they burn, beneath the northern lights. A chamber with a grove of trees, shadow-figures gathering around a crooked bonfire. She's one of them, becoming them, it's *her* in the flames, slashed and spliced, her very being tearing, shredding, torn—

It's *not*. At a spark of pain, real pain, physical pain, she wrenches back. She's here, scrabbling at the door. Smacking with her palms, scraping with her nails, her fingers bitten by splinters.

I am the Pretty.

Kira's knees buckle. Something wrestles with her mind, ripping and fleshy.

Funny how we know you.

No, you don't. She shakes her head, again, again, picturing the words, *feeling* them. *Not as well as you think.*

Consciousness wavers, just for a second. Kira focuses on the now, the wood, her frenetic fingers fumbling. The air is laced with blood and smoke. Where's the—

There. No flamed arms restrain her as her hands hit the handle. She yanks the iron ring around, letting out a sob, and to her half-feral shock, it grates open.

She flies out into white sunlight, and for a moment thinks she's free.

51

Lies of lives

She grew up hearing of this, and now, she's bearing witness.

In all honesty, she'd happily have lived her life without it. For her benefit, Carol is speaking aloud; at the start, she was appreciative, but now, it needs to stop. Watching someone talk to the air is so much worse than silence.

Hazal crosses her legs, adjusting her robe. The room rustles, humming with static, as if the Whispers are charged. Their voices hiss and trickle. They feed her unrest, her tension around any world but this. She needs the human; she needs the mundane. The what-you-see-is-what-you-get. Out here, the Whispers are stretching thin, but she can't shake the sense that their skeletal words are nothing but a skeletal smoke screen.

We have no access to Urnäsch, they say, as Carol looks more and more desperate. *Exile goes both ways. If we wanted to keep the ability, we would not have pushed them out.*

Would that we made that choice with certain others we let remain.

An invisible smile ripples, but Hazal stays cold. Over and above all of this, where's Talie? Where did she go after leaving Carol? She's an adult, but she's never been overly balanced. If oily guilt soaked her, and something struck a match…

'So there's nothing?' Carol sinks to a red knit pouf. Hazal makes herself listen; this was her idea. She'll call Talie again as soon as they've gone. 'You'll do nothing? Someone has linked the Kyo and the Chlause, and you won't so much as *try?*'

Careful. The Whisper surges, the cool, calm amusement of the unamused. *We do not exist to please you.*

We do not exist to please anyone. A second Whisper brushes past Hazal. The skin of her neck prickles; if she were an animal, she'd raise her hackles. *But there may be something we can do. Although we cannot access* Urnäsch, *if we find how the Kyo are communicating, perhaps we can intervene.*

Carol screws up her mouth. 'Maybe you need to take your cue from the Kyo, and find a witch.'

Hazal's face flinches. Despairing or not, Carol should know better. The Whispers are Whiteland's phoenix. How far would they go in a lesson on respect?

Maybe we do, one murmurs, flitting past Hazal's ear. She sags against the couch cushions. Oh, for all of this to end. *We did not think it was possible to break through the worlds. We made it so; we threw them out. A witch shut the door.*

A new one, another croons, *must have torn it down.*

We missed the breach, a third breathes. *With all she's done, whoever she is, we need to find her.*

She's formidable. Several swell, a murmuration, like spiders on the ceiling. *She can't be allowed to carry on. She could break the world apart.*

Hazal recrosses her legs. If a witch has got to the Chlause, the world is already broken.

Exactly. A Whisper is upon her at once. Brush around her ankles, up to her face. Its presence is cool and inquisitive. *She endangers everything. If we find her, and her link to* Urnäsch, *perhaps we can make her stop. And you?*

The Whisper slithers around her skull, fluttering close to her ear. Her pulse lurches, but she doesn't move.

Ah, we cause you discomfort. The Whisper flits away.

Carol's face drops. 'Leave her alone.'

Why, Carol? the voice sighs, kissing Hazal's lips. She flinches back, away from the chill. *Because you said she shouldn't be involved? Enlighten us, Hazal: do you wish you'd stayed in* Urnäsch, *and embraced it?*

'No.' The word is flat and final, and Hazal sits up straight. 'I could not be how they are. If I were throwing them from Whiteland, I would do more. You give them their ways, their meadowlands. But they are barbaric; you said it. They should not be left to live.'

Is that what you think? The voice slithers, through her twisting fingers. In spite of her poise, her memories roar. *Once you metamorphose, you are gone. You are nothing; you are mindless. Or,* it purrs, close to a chuckle, *your mind is not what it was. You care nothing for the self you've lost. Is it then a crime?*

The fire.

Hazal shuts her eyes, but the image takes root, worming its maggoty way through her gut. The fire, and the northern lights, hung like a rippling sail. The trees that tower, that grow in the chamber, and the masks, the personas, the *things* that tear your head apart. That put it back together like a patchwork doll, a mess made by someone who's forgotten being human. All the while you're in the fire, and all the while you scream.

So you don't regret it. Several voices curl around her arms. *It's worth making sure. In one way or another, everyone's a traitor.*

All but one drift down her fingers. *You could have been helping them,* it hisses. *It's good to know you're not.*

Carol exclaims, but the words slip away. The memories are everywhere, snaking around her, tying her up in their web: sensing the atmospheric shift that meant an entrance was open, which *oh*, took so long for them to learn; staring at each other in the sunlit grove, and breaking into a run. Past the children they were leading from the village, through the trees, along the hedgerows, down the innocent track. Past the church, and the endless field, along another, little-used lane, pushing, sensing, *willing*, and down the tunnel of earth.

Into the red-stone Schönengrund labyrinth, praying not to be stopped. Running, running, praying, running, up the edgeless stairs in the beautiful circular library—up, up, up to the top—and, if you know where to go, the glass turns into air.

Jostling each other through to the dusty autumn forest. They ran, and ran, and ran, until the trees stopped, and the sea appeared, dark in the distance, and they were so close and couldn't breathe and cried at the thought they might fail. The phoenix was there. Of course it was him. He was taking a group of reckless men, and with as wide a manic berth as possible, before he could stop the process and them, they ran and hit the world.

The air burned; the real air. It was full of taste, full of life. They hurtled down the rocky hill toward the blinking town, the night hot and the trails steep, and then, only then, did they realise the utter lies of their lives.

Stale air. Stale views. A cramped illusion based on truth. It wasn't real; they'd been nothing, nowhere, trapped in shimmering spaces no better than the dark, but this—as they fell to the tarmac on the edge of town, a thousand lights in their eyes and all the smells, the sounds—fried food, rubbish bins, pounding music, the sea on the humid air—this was real. It meant a *life*.

They could hardly bear it.

Fascinating.

Hazal tows herself through time, spiked by the voice's amusement.

Touching, even, another sighs. *It does not help us now, but if we have to act against them…*

It flutters away, and a rustling swells. A hush, a rise, and the Whispers drop.

Kira brought us Freya.

Carol's hair lifts. Hazal shudders, but Carol doesn't react. 'Freya?' She frowns. 'The huldra?'

Yes. There's a way we can stop the chaos.

Carol looks at Hazal. 'I thought she was here.'

She was. The rustle returns to life, a breeze in the corners of the room. *But Kira, belying her idiocy, decided to give her back. Her father,* they hum, *is also here. We should probably not let him stay.*

Hazal couldn't care less about Mathew damn McFadden.

'The children were told the Chlause would help,' Carol says. Apparently, neither can she. 'When they're still so clueless, and the victims of a witch hunt, can you blame them for jumping on a haven?'

Her eyes flick to Hazal. Ashamed, Hazal looks away.

It's not important. The Whispers surge. Distant waves, or leaves through wind, the voices almost drown within. *We'll attempt to disentangle the worlds, and if that can involve returning your sons, it will. Now, however…* They crackle, electric. *The witch-hunters are here.*

The doorbell chimes. The Whispers lift. By Hazal's ear, they pause and hiss. *The Kyo have your daughter.*

52

Tricks and games

Someone barrels into her and knocks her to the ground. The air leaves her lungs with a whump. 'Ah!'

The bright day reels. Everything is pain, sharp in her shoulder blades, shocking her pelvis, her ribs. The man on top of her raises a rock.

'No!' Kira wheezes, rolling her head away. The rock smashes into the earth. 'I'm real! Callum, I'm real!'

She stops. Her hair is trapped. Time expands. Callum wouldn't fly at someone unprovoked, no matter how threatened he felt. He suffered enough when he knocked out the huldra, and she'd come to the house to kill.

It's not him. It's his smell, his hair, his frenzied face, acknowledging her, recognising her, but no, it's a trick, another damn *game*. Beneath him, she stills. Her heart is painful. It's no more Callum than the fire man was, and she has to run.

'Are you okay?' The not-Callum stares. The sunlight blinds her. She could trust him, let him help her up, recover in the country air for a while before finding Romy and Jay.

No. Kira seizes her paling mind. That's not her, and this isn't Callum. Wrenching herself to the side, she thrusts him off her, scrambles up, stamps on his ankle, kicks his gut, grabs his rock, and runs.

Halfway down the lane, Kira dares a glance back. The earth in front of the church is empty.

Gripping the rock, Kira judders to a halt, her legs a tangle that could carry on for life. At least she was right, and it wasn't Callum she assaulted…but how many more are there? Do they regenerate? Rasping, sweating, she clutches her chest. How will she know the right one?

That's not a bridge to cross right now. Ignoring her battered body's groans, Kira staggers back into a run. All that matters is putting space between her, the Callum, the fire man, and that sickly, sickening church.

The church which, when she looked back, had shrunk to a quaint parish innocence. It sat alone, ringed by bluebells, its steeple on a level with the woods behind. Kira runs, and gasps, and gawps. She could be on an English country lane: tractor trails through clipped hedgerows, drystone walls, a field of sheep. Hills in waves, bushy trees, yellow-orange grasses.

Quaint. Innocent. Fields. Fells. A pond, a brook, rushes and reeds. After all of this, she's in Cumbria.

No. A breathless laugh puffs from her chest. No, don't be stupid; the sun never shines in Cumbria.

Another laugh erupts, more than slightly manic, as Kira fights her brain for control. She's not in Cumbria, but that's not why. The sheep are bigger than they should be; the church is smaller than it's possible to be, from the cavernous space inside; and not-Callum tore from nowhere with a rock. If they were on the outside, he wouldn't have stayed by the door, hanging around to attack. He'd have fled, just like her. He'd have run for his goddamn life.

And if it was that easy to leave Urnäsch, nobody would stay.

Which means she's still there. Which means she needs to move. Amassing her scattered, fractious wits, Kira runs, for her goddamn life.

The countryside ambles by. On the outside, she'd hit a portly, rambling village, with a pub named the Cheshire Cheese. Tearooms, musty bookstores, whitewashed cottages. Sweetshops that don't exist anywhere else, full of sherbet and fudge and rock. Bags of mint humbugs, that she and Romy peered at, on a fusty, forgotten trip. Mathew rolled his eyes, and sighed. *Kids today. These girls of ours.*

He bought a bag of everything, and Anna only smiled.

No wonder. Does Whiteland have sweets? Chocolate branches? Liquorice death? Curling through the rustic, cloudless day, Kira laughs. It's a tad less manic than before, but still; liquorice death? She's slowly going insane.

Her body is, at least. Hitting a stile, she stops to climb it, and, shaking, aching, gasping, her legs and lungs collapse.

Okay. Sliding to the grass by the low, mossy wall, Kira leans back and gives in. It's uneven, and uncomfortable, but you know what? Who cares. Her heart whoops. Sweat lifts off her. She needs a sleep. She needs to pee.

She needs three years of food. A howl in her stomach declares it succinctly. How long have they been here? God, she's *starving*. Shading her eyes, Kira squints against the sun. What did the first not-Callum say? *I hate this fucking place. I'm so sick of everything happening to us, like we're nothing.* He wasn't real, but he also wasn't wrong.

It's time to make things happen.

Having found a convenient bush, the first port of call is food. Flopping back down with a healthy dose of pessimism, Kira rummages in her coat. Her pessimism rings true: everything was put in the bags, and the bags are dead to the world. Why did she not fill the coat up, too?

Because it weighs a ton as it is. No; three tons. The whole of Scotland. Frowning, she shifts, hot against the wall. The sun and the run have put her in a kiln, but exhaustion is a juggernaut, and frankly, she can't be bothered to take it off. Not to mention that, last time she did, everything sailed off without her. Her shoes, her phone, Erik's water, Erik's coat…

Erik. The thought of him sparks in her chest, through her growing fug. She should have left Fiona with a message for him.

Yes, because they had such a good conversation, and left on amazing terms. Kira shifts against the mossy wall, her eyes slowly sinking. There's a bump on her skull, and a hundred bruises clamouring on her back. She never even spoke to the huldra.

No. Fiona, though…the memory swims through a woolly doze. She said to enjoy the Chlause.

Softening into sleep, the jumbled thoughts drift.

Kira jolts awake with a hot shock of horror. She slept. She *slept*?

She slept a long time. Kira's eyes adjust to dusk with a twinge of disbelief. The sun, and the light, and the day have gone. How could she have been so daft?

You've got a thing for suddenly falling asleep.

Kira's chest pangs again, and aches. Callum; the real Callum, wry and dry. The real Jay, the real Romy. Her real dad.

She'll find them. She'll stay on fifteen separate guards, and find them. Time to make things happen.

Using the rugged wall as a prop, Kira stands. Her bruised back grinds. Her jabbed ribs gripe. Her cramped thighs groan, and, as arthritic as a puppet, she leans against the stone. She's still alone; nothing befell her while she dozed, nothing crept up to leer. Rubbing the clogs of sleep from her eyes, she surveys her odd domain. Lavender twilight, fields of sheep, the overlarge sheep themselves asleep. The country road she pelted down curves to the left, and rolls away through the hedgerows.

Thank God she can't see the church from here. Letting out a small breath, she turns. Beyond the stile is a ploughed field, and above it…Kira blinks. Above it rise two slivers of moon.

A low laugh splits from her lips, a bewildering-news kind of laugh; *Mayday, Mayday, two moons in the sky tonight.* It sounds like a song.

It's mesmerising. Kira watches them, suddenly soothed, trickled through with peace. Curled like cats in the purple evening, the silver slivers conjure something magical. Even here, even now, there's light.

Like a singing husky, her stomach cries. The howl snaps her back, and reluctantly, she turns. She can't risk keeping her back to the lane. Playing murderous Statues with her would only increase the Chlause's fun.

And she really, really, *really* needs to eat. Kira blinks through a giddy, black-spotted head rush, holding as still as if she were the statue, gripping the warm stone wall. What was the last thing she ate? Pretzels?

Trees. Hope leaps inside her: beside the stile grows a thick, gnarled tree, short and stumpy with oceans of leaves. Throwing caution to the moons, she ducks beneath its branches. Right now, she'll eat whatever. It's not like she can get any more screwed.

The smell beneath the leaves is heady. Gripping a bendy, weedy branch, Kira peers through the shade. There must be something here. There must be something here. There must be something.

There is. As her eyes adjust to the unlit canopy, Kira wilts. Big, fat olives, as hefty as the sheep.

Typical. Normally, she'd bite her cheek and graciously decline, but beggars can't choose when their bellies are pits. Touching an olive to her lips, Kira waits. No tingle, sting, or burn. When her tongue is also safe, she devours like she's drowning.

They may not be poisonous, but god, they're repugnant. Dropping stone after stone to the scrubby grass, Kira sets her face in a pucker. Do they have to taste so much like dust?

This is crazy. Almost choking, Kira laughs, and again, and again, and again. She's alone in the shade of an olive tree, under a two-moon purple sky, on the run across three different worlds…and, at the end of it all, she's feasting on stale fruit. What has life become?

'Kira?'

Her throat dries. The laughter dies. She whips around to see the voice pushing through the leaves, and in one strange motion, she tenses and relaxes. It's Callum. Is it Callum?

Kira lifts her fifteen guards and more. His planetary coat drapes over his arm, bemusement stained like ink on his face, and he doesn't seem to have a rock…but does that mean anything?

'Are you real?' she blurts.

Callum frowns at her. 'What?'

'I've met two of you that weren't real.' Folding her arms, Kira looks him up and down. What happened to *her* rock? Did she drop it by the stile? 'I was with one for ages before he went weird.' She hunches into herself. 'Creepy. Lecherous. He turned into a fire man. Are you him?' She steps forward carefully, searching for deceit. 'Did you follow me from the church?'

'Whoa.' Callum lifts his hands. His widening eyes are brown, not dark or full of something off-kilter. Kira's guards start to droop. He looks so *Callum*. 'You've got some horses that need holding. What happened while I was asleep?'

Asleep?

'You…' Kira blinks at him. This, she wasn't expecting. 'What do you mean, while you were asleep?'

Warily, Callum shrugs. 'I mean I was asleep? I woke up in the field with a bunch of sheep, and thought I saw you by the wall.' A peculiar expression crosses his face. 'Aren't they the biggest bloody sheep you've ever seen?'

Kira laughs, a single peal of surprise. 'You…' She peers between the low branches, the simple, waxy leaves. 'You haven't been—seen—I mean, you've been sleeping this whole time?' She casts her eyes across the field. Asleep. With sheep. 'Nothing's happened to you?'

Callum lifts his shoulders. 'Not since Karliquai.' He searches her face. 'What's happened to you?'

He steps forward, as if to reach for her. On instinct, Kira steps back. The guards are not done yet.

'Okay.' Frowning, Callum stops. 'Okay.' Toying with an olive nestled by his head, he flashes his furrowed eyebrows. 'Big olives, too.'

Kira twists her fingers together. Guilt blends with awkward blends with *funny how we know you*. It still might not be him.

'Okay.' Callum flicks the olive. 'Okay. I know what to say.' He plucks it free, tosses it up, and catches it with a slap. 'You only started trusting me once we'd seen the mist.'

Kira stares. 'What?'

Oh.

'I'm getting you to trust me.' Callum spreads his hands. 'I remembered how you changed when it happened before. It was obvious.' His lips twitch to the side.

Another guard drops. It's his usual smile, uncertain but there. Kira balls her hands in her sleeves. 'It was?'

'Yeah.' Callum dumps his coat on the ground. 'The way you acted, more than how you talked. You were less self-conscious. I guess you stopped doubting what I was doing so much. I remember, because it was weird, how careful and reckless you could be, somehow both at once.'

Now, he smirks. Kira's face feels strange, like her features are in disarray. It's probably funny, but he's far from wrong: pressing together in the dark, having trapped themselves in the community hut…it changed things. The fear, the incredulity, at what they'd just outrun, at the escalating web that was tying them in knots. His argument with Lena about it, when, hours before, he'd denied all belief.

And then, when he patched her up, and she took off her shirt without thinking about it…she hadn't noticed, but things were different. He'd soared past the accidental acquaintance, the stranger she'd tangled with; he was involved. They both were. Was that the trust?

'Callum.' Closing the gap between them, she throws her arms around his neck. It's not that other-Callum couldn't be this *right*, but rather this unwrong. 'Please don't hit me with a really big rock, or blame me for the Russian Revolution…'

'I have no idea what you just said.' Callum taps the small of her back. 'My shoulder might know.' His voice lifts, as if halfway through a sentence. Kira pulls back to find him squinting around, at leaves and sunset fields. 'Now can you tell me what's going on? I'd like to know why we've returned to my homeland.'

Kira tilts her head, looking at the hedgerows, bushy and bristled in the dusk. 'I thought it seemed more like Cumbria.'

'Bah.' Callum scratches his head. 'Same difference. It's a big-sheeped version of the motherland.'

Kira snorts, and instantly covers her nose. 'You sound like a Nazi farmer.'

'Well, you should know that about me by now.' Callum shrugs. 'Unless, you know, you're not real.'

Batting him, Kira rolls her eyes. 'Oh, now aren't you funny.'

'I try.'

'Mm-hmm.' Kira plucks an olive. 'You won't be poking fun when you've heard everything.' She holds out her prize. 'Have an olive. They're delicious.'

It's her turn for smugness. His revulsion goes to town. 'Don't you like them?' She sits against the knobbled tree, a sweet, innocent picture.

The look he shoots her is shrivelled outrage. 'Don't you—no, I bloody don't. They taste like gone-off beer.'

Kira swallows her lips. 'Yeah, but once you've had eighteen, they're fine.' She pats the stubbled, rooty ground. 'Sit down. Storytime.'

Watching him pick his scowling meal, Kira's tension starts to drain. Kira shakes her head at herself. Already, the horror is fading; the false crucifixion, the false friend, the real attack with a rock. Now that there are two of them, nothing seems as bad.

Kira stretches out her weary legs. Either that, or everything's too unreal to really feel real at all. Or maybe, beneath a dappled tree on a balmy country night, it feels as though nothing can touch them. It's an island in an impossible river, to be seized with grasping hands.

'You're an evil pixie.' With his olives cradled in his hands, Callum lowers himself to the bumpy roots. 'Go on, pixie. Bewitch my mind. Fill it with lies. I can resist your fairy stories far better than food.'

'I'm sure.' Kira slips out of her sticky coat, chucking it onto Callum's. Now they could be picnicking.

Callum prods her cheek with an olive. 'Hey.'

She frowns. 'Callum.'

'Hey.' He prods her. 'Hey. Hey.'

Exasperated, she turns. *'Callum.'*

Pushing the olive past her lips, he pops it into her mouth.

'Nngh!'

'Have an olive.' He grins as her face rucks in, squawking like a wound-up cat. 'They're delicious.'

53

Things she never meant to say

Now, the jokes are as silent as the night.

'Jesus.' Callum rolls his head along the tree to look at her. 'Is that why what you said earlier was something to do with a rock?'

Kira blows out heavily. 'Yep. I've had such a lot of fun.'

'Mmm.' Callum taps her knee. 'If we ever get back to some kind of normal, you should write a novel. Call it *Whiteland*—he unfurls a banner in the air—'and expose all the mind-screwing heathens. It'll sell.'

'It might, but they'd come for us.' Kira yawns. With the sultry night roosting around them, and their hideout so prettily, safely framed by crowded leaves, sleep is starry velvet. 'All of this would have been pointless.' She shuffles her back down the tree, resting on Callum's shoulder. 'Do you think it was an illusion? What I saw in the church?'

The question is ginger, and hangs in the air. Somewhere, a sheep bleats. A warm breeze murmurs, sifting the scent of a barn.

'Like the fake me who made out with you?' Callum twines one of her hands into his.

Kira pokes him in the ribs. 'Oi.'

He snorts. 'Sorry. Ish.' He lifts their fingers before them. The twinned moonlight makes them soft. 'Yes, I do.' He smiles into her hair, and huffs. 'Can't say I'd have thought that straightaway, if I'd seen what you did, but from here, now, yes. I don't think they'll kill us.'

'That's what the other you said.' Kira shifts around to peek up at him. Shadowed and thoughtful, he watches the dark. 'Why?'

Callum's eyes narrow, a quick tic. The corners of his mouth flatten. 'Because…' he says, slow and sighing. His lips part, and close again, turning slightly down. 'Because where's the fun for the Kyo in that?'

The Kyo. Dead, cracking, screaming. Kira shivers, and drops her eyes. 'You think they did this?'

'I think…' Callum lifts a finger. 'I think all of this is planned. Did you hear something?'

Another sheep bleats.

'Oh.' He slumps back. 'Never mind. Yeah.' He rubs his eyes. 'Yeah, I mean, the plan never seems to have involved killing us. Or you and Romy, at least.'

Kira twists her mouth against his T-shirt. 'Callum.'

'No, it's true.' He works an arm around her, kissing the top of her head. 'If it did, you'd have kicked the bucket five times over. I think there's a lot laid out for us, and that it involves the Kyo. They're a bunch of crazy exes.'

A small smile twitches. 'Really.'

'Sure.' He drums his fingers on her shoulder. 'In the end, they'll always want to be the ones to stab you with revenge. And I know, when you've seen so many crazy things that were kind of real and kind of not, it's hard to be objective, but seeing as I was asleep—' He stops, and stills. 'Okay, that time I heard something. I definitely heard something.'

Voices. Kira chills from her scalp to her gut. Voices?

Jerkier than a marionette, she scrambles to her feet. Callum is beside her at once, and she waits, peering through the branches, barely breathing, listening to the dark.

The argument drifts around the corner, shielded by flourishing hedgerows.

'…Telling you,' one entreats, 'it was way, *way* too simple. Last time we tried, we were cornered by a priest and pushed through a stained glass window. Walking out the front was too easy.'

'Maybe.' The second voice is more offhand. Kira's heartbeat slows, as if doctored by a drug. 'If it was, we'll find out, and if it wasn't, well, there's not a lot we can do. At least we're somewhere normal.'

Quietly, Kira pushes the branches aside. Her stomach is tying in sickly knots, greyish, fleshy lumps. Romy.

'Is it them?' Callum whispers, emerging behind her. 'By which I mean, are they real?'

Kira lifts a finger.

'You call this *normal?*' the first voice exclaims. 'There are two moons, and that fox we saw was the size of a Saint Bernard.'

'Stop whinging.'

'It's not whinging if it's important.'

'Nothing's important when you've said it twelve times.' The second voice is snide. 'I heard you the—'

'Callum.' The first voice wobbles up into falsetto. 'Kira. They're here.'

The footsteps erupt. An *augenblick* later, Jay hurtles round the bend.

'Callum!' he yells, colliding with his brother.

Slammed in the stomach, Callum doubles over. 'Oof.' He staggers back.

'Kira?' Romy rounds the corner, wild-eyed and almost running. 'Oh, my god.'

They hug in the lane like the world is burning. Kira's thoughts fragment: Romy's not dead. She's not dead, she's not dead, she's warm, and smells of incense, and sweat, and her earrings scrape Kira's neck, and her tangled hair is everywhere, and both Callums were right: it's all just one big game.

'This is so messed up,' Kira mumbles.

Ferociously, Romy nods. 'Jesus Christ in a bucket, I know. We've seen so many crackpot things, and sadistic things, and…that reminds me.'

A dagger stabs her voice. Untangling herself, she walks away, and boots Callum in the shin.

Kira's eyes stretch so wide they strain.

'Ow!' Callum yelps. His knee folds, and he drops to the grass, a grimace spreading like blood. 'What the hell?'

Romy glowers at him. 'You know full well.'

Kira cuts her eyes between them. 'What—'

'No, I don't. Bloody hell.' Groaning, Callum drags his leg to his chest. 'Jesus, Romy.'

Romy's face turns red. 'Well, you shouldn't have hit her.'

Silence. Kira stares. 'Hit me?' She glances at Callum. 'He didn't—he didn't hit me.'

Accepting Jay's hand, Callum struggles to his feet, shooting Romy blue murder. 'No.' Testing his leg, he winces. 'I only'—he grits his teeth—'hit women who try to kill me.'

'With a poker,' Jay adds.

'True.' Releasing Jay's shoulder, Callum reassumes his glare. 'Nice to see you're alive and kicking, Romy, but really. *What the hell?*'

Kira's mind starts to tick. False friends. False grief. Real, righteous anger.

She's not the only one being tricked. 'Romy.'

'You had a fight in the church.' Distinctly less satisfied, but no less stubborn, Romy sticks a hand on her hip. 'You and Kira. You were shouting at her, and then you thought, hey, let's macho it up.'

'Romy.'

'I trusted you, when you said you—'

'Romy!' Kira throws out her arms. 'Shut up for a second! Just…' She lifts her hands, palms-out. 'Just wait. Let me talk to you.'

Romy glares at Callum. 'Ten seconds, and then I kick him again.'

Tipping her head back, Kira sighs. The moons hang high, silvered and bright, in the flat, midnight blue. 'We did have a fight, but one, he didn't hit me, and two, it wasn't him. He was sleeping in a field.'

Darkly, Callum huffs to himself. 'Honey, I blew up the sheep,' he mutters, as Jay ducks into the tree. 'Great.'

Kira shoots him a look of exasperation. 'Not helping, Callum.' She turns to Romy. 'How did you see us fighting, anyway? We never saw you.'

'That's not the point.' Romy jabs an accusing finger at her. 'Do you mean to say that you're letting him off because he thought his brother was dead?' She spreads her hands. 'And sheep? What's the deal with Urnäsch and *sheep*?'

'Wait.' Callum pivots. 'The fire man hit you?'

'Stop!' Jay hurries from the bowing tree, one hand chock-full of olives. 'Before you kill each other. You'—he points at Kira and Callum—'need to know what the Chlause do, and then we need to find out from everyone else what's *happened* to everyone else.' He looks between them, a teacher at a rowdy playground fight, before wriggling back through the branches. 'The olives are nice, by the way.'

Water babbles. A night bird flutes. Kira watches Callum watch Jay. His face is a painting with too much colour: confusion. Sadness. Red-gold pride. She feels the same about Romy.

'Where are these explanations, then?' Romy drops cross-legged to the ground. Ripping out a handful of greyscale grass, she shreds it. 'Jay's right.' Her eyes flick up to Kira, and instantly away. 'The Chlause are…' She tears another handful. 'Jay?'

With cheeks like a hamster, Jay reemerges. 'Basically, we need to get out.'

Lying beneath the olive tree, Kira's mind spins far from sleep.

I'll watch for a while, she'd insisted, and the others didn't much protest. She was wide awake then, and is wide awake now; something here is wrong.

They're not being toyed with. They've been left alone, and it's less like false security than the calm before a storm. They've been allowed to find each other, which can only mean that whatever's next, it'll be more of a joyous cataclysm with all of them together.

They drive you mad, they torture you, and make you one of them. Kira stares through the moonlit canopy, digging her nails in the dirt by the roots. The words flash like afterglow. They've been treated to a warm-up, the pre-match show, and the main act is ready to start.

Locked rooms with constant screaming. A blackness where you hear everything you've ever feared. The feeling of a lifetime stuck in a nightmare, only to wake and you're here, still here, launched into trials of agony under the mocking northern lights. Beneath the beauty your mind is burned.

Burned, and rent, and lacerated, your body staying still. Your bones are shifted, adjusted, bent, and then, and then, and *then…*

Unless Callum's right, and the Kyo are waiting. God knows she'd rather be in Whiteland than here.

Kira's throat swells, and she lets it, awake and alone as Jay's snores drone, as Romy tosses and turns. In Whiteland, she had hope. Here, they're momentously open, vulnerable, helpless, and ignorant, blithering fools. No parents will swoop to pick up the pieces, to buy them creme eggs and make it okay. Her mum. Her dad. Her life. Her world. However much the longing yawns, they're gone.

It descends like a night terror: the four of them are fucked.

'Kira.'

Callum's whisper sends shocks through her skin. She looks down to see him watching her, his coat draped over his legs. How long has he been awake?

With a sigh, Kira shuts her eyes. 'Go back to sleep, Callum.' It's a struggle to handle silence, let alone a conversation.

'I will if you're okay.' Callum shifts, dislodging a clump of earth. It trickles past a root, crumbling and cold on Kira's skin. He pauses. 'Are you?'

No. Yes. Kira bites her cheek, tensing her bones. The truth, or a conscientious lie? Don't cry, don't cry, don't cry.

In the end, she settles for silence. Rustling over the grass, the breeze sighs through her hair. She bites her cheek harder.

Callum clears his throat. 'You do know'—he taps her forearm—'that I don't blame you for this. No matter what the fire pervert said.'

This triggers a tiny, ironic smile, and a tiny, ironic huff. 'Yeah,' Kira manages, choked and wet. Swallowing, she drags up her tearstained voice. 'Believe it or not, I wasn't thinking of that. I hoped you didn't, but…'

She trails off. After a moment, Callum lifts his coat.

Kira sniffs, sniffs again, and smiles. 'That barely covers you on your own.'

Watching her, he doesn't move. 'That's not really the point.'

Kira meets his eyes, and looks away. Sitting up away from the tree, careful not to knock Romy, she takes the coat edge and lies down. The night is summer-mild, but this is warm.

'Hey,' Callum whispers.

'Mm?'

'Look at me.'

Kira tries not to. Their faces are close, too close to hide, and all she can do is unfocus.

'This,' he says, 'is not your fault.'

Kira fixes her eyes on a freckle on his neck. 'That's what I told the fake you.'

Callum lifts her chin. 'The fake me was a dick.'

'Maybe.' Moving away, Kira hooks her toe in her jacket. 'Either way, he wouldn't listen. For a while I was really fired up, enough to believe he was wrong, but then the anger went away, and after what Jay said…' She drags the coat through the dirt, arranging it over their legs. 'All of this did start with me.'

Awkward and grudging, she settles back. She's spent the last year feeling guilty, and now the guilt is out.

Callum regards her sardonically. 'I'm not sure you've ever been more wrong.'

Kira pushes out her mouth.

'No, listen to me.' He puts a finger to her lips. She frowns. 'This part of everything started with Romy getting wasted, lost, and possessed. Originally, it started with your mother. I've told you before, and I'll tell you again. Stop feeling guilty for the world and his dog.'

'I don't—'

'You do, and you know you do.' Callum crooks his mouth to the side. 'Do you know why?'

Slotting her hands beneath her head, Kira wriggles on the crumbly ground, and sighs. 'I feel like you're going to tell me.'

'I am.' Callum's crooked smile remains. 'It's because blaming yourself is easier than believing others have flaws. Personally, I rant and rave and curse the world and his dog, but you…'

He shakes his head against the grass. Kira waits, an odd feeling squirming in her stomach, but that's it. In their dusky, dusty cocoon, he's quiet.

Rolling over, Romy harrumphs in sleep. Her butt bumps Kira's as she gets herself comfy. Jay's snores tickle on, and still, in their dusky, dusty cocoon, Callum is quiet. Her eyes slide to his freckle again. Nothing wants to come out of her mouth. He knows her. He *sees* her.

'How do you do that?' she asks eventually, in a murmur lower than the ground. 'I mean…I don't want to say "know me," because that sounds cheesy, but…'

'No, I know what you mean.' Callum rests a hand on her hip bone. It's warm on the skin where her vest rides up. 'I see through people's crap. That sounds fairly naff as well, but it's true.'

Kira keeps her eyes on his freckle. There's another just below it, close to his jaw. 'You make it sound easy.'

Callum smiles. The twinned freckles lift. 'It is for me, I guess. I'm like the non-psychic Jay: I see the obvious things, that most people miss, about their own personalities or others. You, though,' he says, tapping her hip. 'I can read you better than most.'

Kira's eyes slide unbidden to his face. 'Really.' She shifts, looking away. 'That makes me want to hide.'

'Too bad.' Callum watches as she shifts again. 'You've taken it to heart, even more than before, what that fire pervert said. You think your name is ruin and you've savaged everyone's lives.'

The stark truth of this is black, a sense like déjà vu. It's a chasm, an abyss, a sinkhole, peat. Kira curls her legs as far as they'll go before knocking Callum's knees.

'Ah.' Callum shakes his head, again, again. Suddenly, he's no longer smiling. 'Kira, listen to me. When I got home and realised I had no way to find you, or to know if you were *alive*, it was…'

A relief? Kira thinks, as her heart flutes and flurries, as her thoughts stain like rot. Ruin. 'If it's like it was for me,' she murmurs into the grass, 'it wasn't so fun.'

Callum makes a noise between a laugh, a grunt, and an effort not to choke. 'It was about as fun as the Russian Revolution,' he says. 'Remember that? You asked me not to blame you for it. Turns out'—he smiles dryly—'I don't. In fact, and bear with me here.' He widens his eyes, leaning in close. 'I don't blame you for any revolutions.'

The hazy weight of her mind says no, but Kira's lips turn up. 'None of them?'

'None of them. Well'—Callum pulls a David Tennant-style face—'maybe just the Glorious one. But that's your fault for being English.'

The smile breaks through her haze. 'Hey.'

'Maybe the US Revolution, too, but that's your fault for being English.'

'Hey!' Kira bites her lip to keep from laughing.

'Basically'—Callum puts a finger on her cheek—'what I'm trying to say is this.' Shifting closer, he kisses her forehead, and murmurs, 'You didn't ruin my life. Beyond the mortal peril part, you might have even improved it.'

Kira's breath catches.

A long time later, she pulls away. 'That's the nicest thing you've ever said.'

She taps his cheek in soft amusement. Narrowing his eyes, he removes her finger, and she smiles.

'Don't get used to it.' Callum joins his hands in the thin gap between them. 'The philosophical and the literary, man and woman. Coming together in metaphor and truth.' He adopts an airy Oxford accent. 'Even if the universe can't choose whether to link us or tear us apart.'

Kira laughs. 'I think that's how love works.'

Oh, god. The words are out before she can stop them. Kira's vision glazes over. Oh, *shit*.

Squeezing her eyes tight shut, she rolls over. Her chest boils. Her stomach roils. Lord, let the ground rip open and swallow her, or let her morph into a worm and squirm through the mud and the dirt and away. She curls her knees into her chest, and braces. Her heart thuds. God, it's hot. She shifts her head off a stone. Is it hot?

Maybe he didn't hear her. Maybe it can be one of those times when someone speaks, no one responds, and the someone is left wondering if they ever spoke at all. Maybe he missed the accidental inference.

Maybe, had she not had a silent freak-out. Kira opens her eyes, straining in horror, staring through Romy's pale, snarled hair. Her lungs are on strike. Why, why, why? Why did it come out? She didn't even know it existed as an embryo, let alone wanted to be born. She should become mute, run for the hills, and live out her days in a cave full of—

'Kira,' Callum says. 'Turn around.'

Thud. Thud. Thud. Thud. Inside, Kira thrashes and writhes. She's home to an acrobat, wringing its hands and repeatedly tripping off the tightrope. Biting her cheek, she shakes her head.

'Yes.' He puts a hand on her shoulder. The acrobat pirouettes through her memories, none as heinously awkward as this. She shakes her head again. 'Kira, come on.'

'Tell me again I've got horses to hold.' Kira rushes the words in barely a breath. 'And then forget it. Please?' The acrobat flips and falls in her stomach. It feels very much like vertigo, or the dreams where you drop from a cliff. 'I'm sorry. It was stupid, and I didn't mean to say it. I didn't mean to think it. I didn't know—'

'Right.' As determined as she is to get what he wants, Callum rolls her over to face him. Rocking like a boat unexpectedly adrift, Kira opens her eyes. 'That's better.'

He kisses her. 'It's not stupid,' he says, and smiles.

54

Dimming, swimming, grainy, grey

I'll say one more nice thing.

Kira loops the words, over and over, through the endless morning field. Clouds scud at the sky's edges; the lazy sheep ignore them. Right now, if she had stage directions, they'd read *most satisfied.*

Or, *as satisfied as can be given present circumstances.*

'Left?' At a gap in a hedge, Romy turns to walk backwards. Ahead pootles a rugged lane, lined with ordinary bluebells.

Left. The sun throbs at Kira's temples, beating on her back. Lifting her hair, she fans her forehead; the olives, gathered by the vulgar pocketful, are probably already wilting. It's a glorious, fully fledged summer.

Low, distant hills smear the horizon. Crickets buzz in the bushes. The wildflowers, nameless but flying with colour, bob the size of corn on verges, scenting the air with a perfumed, heat-drenched bounce. Kira lets her hair fall. It reminds her of Duke of Edinburgh walks, except for the lack of tent, back-numbing pack, and nagging to hurry up. If it wasn't for the constant monkey, whispering about threat, and the elephant denoting the lack of a plan, it would be pleasant. It would be summer.

A butterfly flits above a clear brook, rocky in the shade of a rowan. Kira stops. Her chapped lips tingle. Her throat is lumpy. Water. Water, water, water. They must be dehydrated for days.

Crouching, dipping her hands, she breathes. She hadn't noticed how much she'd needed a drink until it was there.

'Oh, my giddy aunt, this is good.' Squatting beside her, Romy tips forward, plunging her face in the water. 'Nngh.'

Kira laughs. The brook is fresh, and cool, and divine, and she splashes her face and neck. 'Hey, Romy?'

Romy emerges, dripping. 'Yeah?'

Kira glances upstream. Jay is drinking, Callum watching, smirking like he wants to push his brother in. 'Can you shield me?' She gestures to the rest of her body. 'I want to freshen up a bit.'

Romy follows her gesturing path. 'I mean, sure.' She cocks her head. 'Have you not had sex?'

Kira's eyes fly wide. 'Romy!' she hisses. The water could evaporate off her skin. 'That's not—I don't—I just want to wash!'

Romy grins the grin of the devil. 'I know. But it's funny to watch you cringe.' She scrubs at her face. 'I'll watch the men, if you help me get rid of my makeup.'

'Deal.' Kira ducks her red-hot head. 'You're the worst.'

They're buffalo around a watering hole when a voice thuds up behind them. 'Run.'

Inhaling, Kira wheels around, clean and waiting to leave. In the sloping lane, there's a girl.

'Run.' She staggers forward, haggard and breathless, a berry-red scarf tied tight in her hair. Kira chills. 'Escape into Whiteland. There's someone waiting to meet you by the—ah!'

Her head snaps back. Kira swells with alarm.

'Go!' The girl claws at her neck. 'Go! They're coming!' Gasping, heaving, she starts to choke. 'The Whispers want—'

She drops. Her skull rebounds off the bumpy lane.

Openmouthed, Jay reaches for Romy. 'I can't…'

He glances at Kira, at Callum. 'Can't what?' Kira hears herself ask.

'I can't…' Jay blinks, and frowns at the girl. 'Hear her. She's not…'

The girl coughs, a hacking wheeze, forcing herself to her knees. 'The Whispers.' She topples forward. Her dark skin sheens with sweat. 'The house that…' Her eyes pop white and hysterical. 'That looks like—'

'This is mad.' Romy starts toward her.

'No!' She waves her stubby hands. In her rough, sack-like dungarees, she gasps and cries. 'I don't need help. They're coming. Ah!'

Her head snaps back again. 'Kira!'

It's another voice, shrieking in the morning. Kira's breath shrivels.

'Girls.' The girl's gaze blackens, glassy. Her head wobbles on her neck. 'Listen to me. Run.'

Kira's stomach bottoms out. The voice she hasn't heard since last December, since the argument in the hall. 'Mum?'

'Run!' The braided girl wobbles upright. Her voice doesn't fit her mouth. 'All of you! Kira, please.' She staggers, vacant. 'Kira, *please*, take Romy and go. I can't stay here. They're pushing me out.'

Splashing brook. Scorching sun. A weirdly heady scent of garlic. Kira works her heavy lips. 'Wh—'

'They're coming.' The girl lurches forwards. 'They're coming for you.'

She crumples to the lane.

Scorching sun. Splashing brook. Kira stares at Romy. 'Mum,' she manages. 'That's not—'

'No.' Romy shakes her head, her eyes too wide. 'It's not.'

'Run.' The girl's eyes pop. Spit webs across her lips, and she heaves a breath. 'For God's sake, *Kira-Romy-run!*'

Time staggers. Kira's eyes flick to Romy, openmouthed and clammy. To Callum, poised by the brook, off guard. To Jay, mouthing *run*.

Time slams back to Earth. Grabbing Romy, Kira runs.

The lane is silent bar their boots, bar her gasping, bar her heart. It's more unnerving than any pursuit; if something's coming, it's quiet, out of sight, in her mind. Kira's head roars as she pelts uphill. Romy's weight is a drag. Everything blurs.

Escape into Whiteland.

How? *How?* Kira's vision tunnels. Hot, bright, sticky, clutching Romy's sweaty hand. The clumps of trees give way to hills. Fat grey walls trundle through fields, as sleepy as old-time ploughs. She trips in a rut, rushes hot, staggers on. Fields upon flowers upon gates upon sheep. This lane, this dipping, swerving, crotchety farmer's lane, crawls on, and on. A sob bubbles up, and she crushes it. The house that looks like something. The house that looks like what?

Escape into Whiteland. There's someone waiting. Kira pushes her searing body faster. Legs like pylons, lungs like dust. Her mind is a room with encroaching walls. She slews around a bend and—

Three figures step out.

Pebbles fly. Kira skids to a stop. Romy slams into her shoulder. Overshooting, Callum staggers. The figures don't move.

Jay grips Callum's arm. 'I can't hear them, either.'

The encroaching walls thud down to her chest, trapping her breath in the gap. Kira's head roars louder, to a white-noise gale. The Chlause have found them.

She steps back, into Romy. One is the doll that lured them. Its patient, painted face is worn in the daylight, as lurid as a pantomime dame. Two are bulky, bulging, more like crude golems than the fire man's danger, sly and sleazy and sleek. Kira bumps Romy back again. The walls start to squeeze. One is hewn from stone and ivy, one shaped from moss. The moss man is masked, a rough, screaming skull, its paper eyes punctured and its painted jaw askew; the other looks lifeless, dulled. The walls squeeze her messy heart. A square straw hat is jammed on its head. Wicker weaves its face and beard, pierced by three sharp holes. It could be close to friendly, but…

The walls slam. Her heart explodes. Its empty gaze is on her, and behind it, something burns.

Go.

Wheeling around, clumsy, blurring, Kira lunges for the edge of the lane. Low wall. Shaking arms. Slapping the stone, she hoists herself up, and scrabbles into the field.

She hits the long grass with a thump. Teetering over the shallow ditch, she throws out her arms, rocks herself forward—

As though the Chlause cut her windpipe, suddenly, she can't breathe. Kira stops. Her eyes strain. The air isn't there. Her chest moves, up-down-up, her nose working, but *the air isn't there*. There's a block. She's floating in dead, dead space. Jay gasps beside her, falling on her shoulder. Kira gulps, and heaves, so hard she feels sick, spinning around in a dream. Romy and Callum, red and frantic, are halfway over the wall. Jay drops. Her head flutters. The blood beats in her neck, screaming *why won't you let me breathe?*

Dizzy. Hot. Floating. Wrong. She's dimming, swimming, grainy, grey.

Kira.

The air returns in a sweet explosion. Kira rasps like a dying man, walloped in the chest. Her watery legs give way, and she spills onto her hands, sucking in the stale taste of wildflowers, summer.

Good.

Kira's chin jerks up, unwitting, unwilling. The doll steps in front of her: the rough dress, the folded hands, the made-up, porcelain face. Unfocused and light-headed, Kira thrills with fear.

'What…' she tries, and heaves a breath. Her lungs weren't ready, still too shallow. She digs her fingers into the dirt. 'What do you want?' she manages hoarsely. Pushing back weakly to sit on her heels, she coughs. 'Why have you—'

We are the Pretty. The doll inclines her head. *And the Ugly.*

Kira's eyes swivel against her will. The fear thrills and thrums. The moss man lists at an angle over Romy, the stone and ivy standing stock-still beside Callum as he breathes like a beast by the wall. Prone on the grass, Jay has passed out.

Fear becomes venom. 'Meaning what?' Kira snaps. Blinking fiercely, she drags her shuddering eyes back to the doll. Her body prickles, a little loose, as if it longs to disobey. 'Meaning you can play with us? Half kill us? Make us think other people are dead?'

Propelled by an anger that licks like flames, she breathlessly shoves to her feet. 'The *Pretty.*' She screws up her mouth. 'Do you not see anyone else as people? I guess you can't, when you make your own monsters. Why can't you just let live, *god!* Why can't anyone just let live?'

Her voice is soaring. She doesn't try to stop it. The Ugly are moving toward her, leaving everyone turned away from Jay. Jay, who…

'Kira,' Callum says, soft and cautionary. 'I don't think now is the time.'

'Oh, it is.' Kira jerks her head around. 'We're already in hell, so to hell with them, too.'

You came to us. The words slice into her, innocent, naive. Serenely, the doll steps forward. *We did not force you. We did not trick you.* It shifts its hands. *Far be it from us to say what brought you here, but we did not.*

Kira could explode. 'And that justifies the rest?'

'Jesus, Kira,' Callum mutters, pushing off the wall. 'Just stop.'

'No!' She flings her arms out, spinning round to face him. Meeting his eyes, she cuts a fevered glance at Jay, and spins back to face the Chlause. 'Even if there wasn't some deal with the Kyo, how is your screwed-up tradition not wrong? It's disgusting. It's sadistic. You steal your kids' lives, and they don't have a choice?'

From the grass, Romy mouths something, cutting her throat with a finger. Kira's chest pangs, but she won't stop. She can't. Not when Jay is inching away, and all empty eyes are on her.

'What are you going to do to us?' She flips an angry hand. The moss man's mask flickers. The stone and ivy turns its head. Its gaze aches with melancholy, burning deep behind her ribs. 'How far are your mistresses going to let you go before taking over?'

The burning ache yawns, spreading tendrils of black. Kira buries her nails in her palms. Good; she's pissing them off. If they come even closer, maybe Jay can get away.

'It's a bit like "jump, how high,"' Callum says, abruptly stepping up beside her. Gratitude sparks and booms. 'You've got a license to play, so you bring out your toys, but you've got no more control than us.'

His eyes flick to her. Kira keeps her own still. They ache from not skittering over to Jay; inching along on his belly, he's nearly at the wall.

'You do realise you're being manipulated?' Kira narrows her eyes to a glare. 'All of this, it's stupid.'

'It's gone beyond stupid.' Planting his feet, Callum tightens his jaw. 'Beyond unreasonable, and beyond your crazy, warped, *hellish* system of belief. What, are you hanging around until someone crazier takes us away?' He lifts his shoulders, palms-out. 'Why don't you do something? Make your whole little fake world worth it?'

'Oh, my god,' Romy moans.

Reckless. Ridiculous. Kira keeps up a glare, but her anger is retreating, burrowing into its den. It's nonsense, literal monster-baiting. She swallows, hard, twisting her fingers, scrunching her toes in her boots. It's not even *convincing* monster-baiting. Kids could do better.

And why are they calm?

The thought settles like froth in her stomach, a filmy, acidic wash. Kira flits her gaze between the figures, flick by sickly flick. The doll hasn't moved, and the Ugly have stopped, ignoring Callum's gauntlet. The yearning, burning ache is cooling.

Dread slithers from the froth, snaking up her throat. Why are they not reacting? Have they unwound and died, like clockwork? Are they the grotesque advance guard, and something worse is coming?

No. The dread turns to horror, filling up her mouth. The Chlause speak inside their minds. They speak inside their minds, which means they *get* inside their minds. Romy said the priest always knew what she was thinking.

Edging onto the wall, Jay stills.

Kira's horror bursts out like bile. 'Run, Jay!'

On the ground, Romy flinches. Callum whips around. 'What the hell are you doing?' His voice soars. Scrambling over the wall, Jay runs. 'We could have…we were…'

'Callum, they know.' Kira jerks a jittery hand at the Chlause, quiet, watching, calm. 'They know what we're doing, they're in our heads.'

She sucks in a teary, despairing breath. Fixed on hers, Callum's eyes still, then widen. 'Oh, my—Jay!'

He spins, staggering in the grass.

Slowly, the doll turns. *Jay,* it echoes dully, a throb in Kira's skull. *Fall.*

Up the lane, without a sound, Jay crumples to the ground.

'Jay!' Callum bellows, cracking like ice. Flinging himself toward the wall, he blunders after his brother.

Tricks. The doll turns its painted eyes on Kira. *You're as clever as you are stupid.*

It's as cool as it is calm. Kira stumbles back. Her body is water, her mind is space. Run. Run?

You can't. The doll tilts its head. The Ugly start to move. *You'll go to where the youth find life.*

The stone and ivy shuffles toward her. The melancholy longing burns, deep and black and cold. Kira shakes her head. 'No.' She crouches, keeping her eyes on the Chlause, fumbling for Romy. 'No.'

You'll see. Behind the mask, the doll smiles. *We don't steal life; we alter it.* The smile bruises her brain. *Who wants to feel this hurt of yours?*

It turns like a windup toy on a stand, toward the lane and Callum… and stops.

Hauling Romy up, Kira tenses. The doll isn't moving. Callum's still running. The Ugly have stopped where they stand.

'Go,' a voice slurs behind them.

Kira wheels around. The girl.

Hobbling along, she shuffles down the lane, her wobbling ankles kinked. Her head lolls strangely. 'Go,' she mumbles, as slurred as a drunk. 'Karliquai. Go.'

She lifts a sloppy hand. The air shifts and glitters. 'Run.' A pause. The lidded eyes scream open. 'Run, Kira, run, Kira, *run, Kira, run!*'

The voice plunges, ripped from her throat. Not Anna's, not even a woman, it's a man, a roar, a primal storm, and so like Romy before she killed Mathew that Kira's mind goes black.

'*Go!*' the girl roars. 'Karliquai! Go!'

An invisible palm slams into Kira's back, and she goes. Locked and tilted, the Chlause don't move. Red tears streak their masks. Barging past, Kira's stomach sours. Blood. Their eyes are bleeding.

Good.

'What was that?' Callum shouts, as they hurtle toward him. Wild-eyed, he grabs Jay's hand and turns tail. Jay's face is as pale as the moon. 'What happened?'

Gasping, Kira shakes her head. 'The girl.' She swings around the bend, towing Romy behind her. The grass is overgrown, the crackled road buckling. God, don't let them fall. 'She made them stop working.'

'She made them *bleed*.' Romy's voice is shrill. Skidding through a creek, her arms fly wide. 'There was something inside her, but it wasn't Mum, and she was creepy as the Chlause them—'

'There!' Callum yells.

Hope is a starburst, hot and white: halfway up a field sits a dark, tatty chalet. With her arms pinwheeling, Kira skids to a stop, scrabbling over the wall after Jay. Beside a patch of olive trees, as shrivelled as Karliquai; surely there can't be another.

Can they trust it?

Barrelling up in a burst, Kira sobs. They can't trust anything. Is this another trap, a game inside a game? Is this how the Kyo gets hold of them? Teasing their terror, making them run, and giving them hope for release?

Maybe. Pelting through the long grass, she's hectic, bedlam, every bone in her body baying for rest. The sun sears. Karliquai looms, bitter against the sky. Kira trips, flails, and flounders on. The field is made of tuffets, of bumpy, hidden hillocks. Her breath and blood are deafening. They have to get out.

They have to get out. They have to get out. Rasping, gasping, Kira speeds up, hopeful and hopeless and starting to cry. If the Kyo are the frying pan, the Chlause are the fire. They have to get out.

Dark wood. Burning limbs. Lungs that scream, a head that blurs. Her temples pound. Nearly there.

The air shifts and glitters. *Kira.*

Kira's mind muddies. No. No, no, no, no—

Fall.

55

Trees and wind and ending worlds

It's not so much waking up as having a heart attack. A bluster of powder blows into the snow hole, gusting her into the pale morning before she can protest.

Charming. Woozy in a haze of sleep, Freya skids across the icy crust, comes to rest at the base of an aspen, and tugs her clothes down over her stomach, already sprayed with snow. Just as she was warming up to Luke; typical. Having spent the night creating a nest in the back of the hole, a crevice within a crevice, to be torn out invisibly is a cold, undignified, *rude* shock to the system.

Help, and you can leave.

Great. Freya laughs, and doesn't temper it. 'Not beating about any bushes, are we?'

Quiet, Freya.

She snorts. 'No.' What's left to lose? She's already facing a river of wrath. 'What great acts of mine'—she gestures to the snow hole—'brought the kings themselves to my boudoir? Should I bow? Or curtsy?' She pushes to her frozen feet. 'I'm afraid, my lords, I now wear trousers.'

She looks around, but the forest is empty. Her nose wrinkles. The smell of pine; what a treat. Her senses may be human-dim, but it's the scent of a life of shadows. The tart taste of winter air, her childhood. Stupid half-girl.

Freya's lips curl round in an ugly-feeling sneer. Good to know she can still be pissed off, and rightly so. Kira would be, too, if she wound up here again. Trapped in the white, grey, green of the forest, all you can do is be pissed off, or pissed.

If you help us end the disorder, we will forget you helped cause it.

The Whispers sigh around her. Snowflakes drift at the brushing of the air, delicate in their dance. Freya huffs sourly. Wonderful; it's even started to snow.

You should listen, a single Whisper murmurs. *This is not a judgment.*

Freya eyes the grooves her body made, from the snow hole to the tree. 'Oh, really?'

It is not. A second voice ghosts past her cheek, into the collar of her coat. *We wish to sever the Kyo and the Chlause, and remove the outsiders completely.*

We will give your freedom back. Three, four eddy around her knees. *But first, you need to help.*

Freya laughs again. 'Do mine ears deceive me?' She flings her arms out wide. 'You want to associate with me? *Me*, Freya, a lowly huldra? Oh, how the prouder among you must swoon!'

Feigning a faint, she falls to the snow.

Be quiet, a Whisper hisses in her ear, and despite herself, she jumps. Glowering, she swats at it. *You wish to attract the Kyo even less than we do; when they hear you were captured by outsiders…*

'I know.' Irritably, Freya stands. 'He hit me with a metal stick.'

Beneath her snowy hair, she touches her cheek. Hot and stiff and sore, its reminder is galling.

They knew you were coming. The Whisper flutters across the burn, like a breath.

'Well, I gathered that.'

The son of the watcher. The voice lifts her icy tangles. *Are you going to insist on speaking aloud?*

Spindly fingers scuttle around her throat. Freya risks a roll of her eyes. *Come on. If you need me so badly, you won't get rid of me. Kill me, or disintegrate me, or whatever you did to Anneliese.*

Anneliese. Freya frowns, opens her mouth, and shuts it. *Why haven't you done the same as before? Made some deal with the Kyo?*

At once, the Whispers surge. *It made them think they were more than they are,* they hiss, on a gust of wind. Hard-edged, they pinch at her jeans, swarming past her face.

Pray tell. Freya plants her boots, fighting for balance. The throb of air is dizzying, and unsettlingly warm. *If you're in my head regardless, why did you drag me from my woman cave?* She blinks against the pine needles whipping in the wind. *To assert your manly authority? It was you who put me there in the first place.*

The wind drops to nothing. *We do not need to explain ourselves,* a single Whisper sighs.

Freya snorts. *That's exactly what you're doing.*

The Kyo must be contained. The Whispers speak as if she didn't. *They like to forget they are simply the dead, no more and no less.*

Freya snorts. *And you don't?*

A slap cracks her head to the side. It heats her neck with a twinging spasm, clacking her teeth so they taste of metal. Grimacing, Freya swallows the anger boiling dark inside her. *Thanks. Now both my cheekbones hurt.*

Consider the chance you are getting, Freya. The sole purr is silky, sweetly stroking the spot where it slapped. *And watch what you say.*

We could always send you to Urnäsch. Another laughs, soft and low. *When the Chlause lose their current toys, they'll be ever so dismayed.*

Freya's pulse swoops, and she chills. *You don't know how.* She straightens her spine. *That's why you're hoping I'll help you.*

The Whisper winds around her neck. *Do you really want to risk it?*

No. The hairs on her arms and legs stand up, buzzed with prickling cold. No, she certainly doesn't. She was bold in Whiteland, brave and brash, but she gave it up for freedom; now, she lacks the spirit to stick to her guns.

Freya stares through the grove of trees, slowly pulling taut. No guns are worth the Chlause. No one alive has ever seen them, but they've all grown up with the stories. The human shades beneath the costume, flickers of the folk they were. Their spirits, rendered less than real, as the being is torn from their faces, and scorched away by the fire.

Freya blinks herself back, and the scaretales fade. She may be Huldra, and a killer, but destroying kids is horrific. Kids who start off human, and end up shredded, frayed. Nothing.

This is why we cannot have a door between the worlds. The voices come together in a breeze, the rustle of deep-forest leaves. *This is why we shut them out.*

And locked them in a gash. Freya flashes with an image of the masked, hidden monsters, a mass in the distance as they slit the gash apart. Bringing the souls from the Tomi desert, and spilling like blood on the ice.

Be careful, don't wander, watch your head; if the Chlause catch you, you're worse than dead.

Be careful at night when the stars may fall; if you're dragged through the fire, you're dead to us all.

Freya slaps the rhymes away before she starts to feel vulnerable, alone in Atikur, talking to ghosts. They're stupid tales. Glorified.

But more or less true. The sweet Whisper caresses her scalp. *They don't eat their children if they catch them escaping, but the rest...* It drifts away through her hair. *When you see the outsiders, you can ask.*

'I'll help.'

The words march out before their cue. Repulsion writhes like sickness, and Freya takes control. Hatred. Horror. Humanity. She won't be ripped to strips of meat, trailing bits of soul.

She won't, and neither will anyone else.

Our little hero, a solitary murmur says, a wisp of a smile. *Humanity becomes you.*

Wind flurries through the pines, dusting the air with white. Snowflakes roost on her head. Freya shivers. *What do you want me to do?*

Creating a hush of a breeze of their own, the Whispers start to rise. *This.*

Freya shivers again. It never used to be this cold, and the lifting Whispers make it worse. Around her legs, they rustle round her torso, sidling up to her neck. The frozen draught in the Kyo's cave, they snake around her throat—

They're a noose. Airy fingers pinch her breath, and Freya's eyes pop. Her hands fly to her neck, but they flap like waterless fish, as she coughs, and gasps, and the fingers squeeze, and her head sways with a rush.

A nauseous rush. A smothering rush. It's blacker than nightmare water, than the gullies in the heart of the forest. Her stomach plunges with it, down, down, down, hot and dark and dizzy. She's falling through a crack in the earth, melting through the snow, losing her mind to the Chlause, and—

This is what we want you to do.

Freya goes rigid. *What?*

Sobering up, the world swims back. The Whisper has settled in her skull, like she's talking to herself, and a cry billows up her throat. Her mind feels like it's recoiling.

I'm not, the Whisper murmurs, *going to hurt you.*

Recoil. Freya staggers back, but her mind stays put. Recoil, reject the interloper, sound the hunting horns, claw with bloody nails at her skull. It's an ambush, a panic attack. She can't breathe.

You can. The Whisper nestles in. *If you fight, this will be difficult.*

Freya clenches her fists. *You don't say.*

Shutting her eyes, she flares her nostrils, and breathes the pine she despises. It's fine; she's fine. She's upright, she's alive, and she's no longer cold, which however it works, is great. The strangest thing is that the voice is male. All she's ever heard is that the Whispers are genderless, stripped of masculinity and made cerebral by death. She thought they were things, not men.

We are neither. The Whisper roots deeper, colonising flesh. Freya twinges. It's so present, now, so prescient, so solidly *male*, and to have it in her mind is uncanny. Unpleasant.

She swallows her heart. *So what are we doing?* She sweeps her arms around, at the green-and-white day, the sheltered grove, the forest, silent and watching. *Now that we're nicely acquainted.*

The Whispers rustle around her, in their sighing, dying breeze. *You're going to the witch,* her intruder murmurs. *When you get there, I will take over.*

Freya nods, and starts walking. The sooner this is over, the better…and yet, she's already adjusting. She peers through the trees, acquiring her bearings. The Whisper is a neighbour, just moved in, who you grow to feel has been there forever.

Won't the Kyo pick up on the fact you're here? She waves a hand, veering toward a snowy, shrunken pine. *As in, in my head?*

No. The Whisper pauses. At the ends of her hair, the others curl. *They take over other minds, but cannot see inside.*

Freya's thoughts wrinkle, like she's frowning. Following the smaller, thicker pines, beneath the open sky, she does. She may be adjusting, but this is *strange*.

Imagine, the Whisper continues, *that you are disciplining a child. You come along, and give it instructions, but you don't know what it was doing before you arrived.*

Freya's mouth twitches. The Whisper is smiling. *You also can't make it tell you what it wants to do now. The difference between us and the Kyo is that they can then control this child, while we rely on persuasion.*

He smiles again. Freya grins, too, but it's rictus puppetry, as false as a loveless kiss. *Persuasion.* She trails the tracks of a lonely wolf, into denser scrub. *Let's just say, it works.*

Another thought scratches her, arrows on ice.

The Kyo will not have picked up on your return. The Whisper responds before she asks. *For one thing, we were watching the exits, and concealed you at once.*

A frown replaces the rictus grin. All this mind reading is enough to drive you mad. *And for another?*

Their focus is Urnäsch. The Whisper shifts. The others eddy, cool and thin. *We've seen many unexpected souls drift away.*

He jerks. Freya's bones spasm.

She stops in alarm. *Don't do that.*

The Whisper says nothing. With a sighing, ghostly moan, the others lift up, and Freya's anger gutters. The sound is haunting, haunted, of things more than men. Snow drops from branches, landing with a whump. Her hair snaps her face. Her baggy coat ripples. Squinting, she watches the treetops sway.

In a gale, the Whispers whip into the sky. With a throb of the air, they're gone.

The forest stills. *What was that?* Freya asks, eyeing the trees. The Whisper's thinking scrapes like sandpaper, but her own can't break through. It feels like a skulking memory, or a word on the tip of her tongue. *Where've they gone?*

For a moment, the Whisper is silent. *To get Anneliese.*

Another rush. A dizzy shock, liquid through her chest. *What?* Freya asks. Even in her head, it's skeletal. *She's alive?*

She's reachable. Impatient, the Whisper wills her to move. *We need the outsiders to come to us, and Anneliese will help. She'll want to get her daughters away, from the Chlause and from here.*

Slowly, Freya starts to walk. *You're actually planning on saving them?* She ducks beneath a bowing branch, left of sodden ferns. *That doesn't sound like you.*

We need them out. The Whisper wills her faster. Freya ignores it. *Once the door to* Urnäsch *is shut, we can deal with the Kyo, restore order, and assure any who doubt that we are still the ones to look to.*

Freya lifts her eyebrows. Is it her, or is the lofty man verging on spite?

No, he says, but his voice is a spear, tipped with yew seed. *Not spite. Necessity. Imagine a world with the Kyo untied, and the threat of the Chlause returning. Whatever the Kyo are trying to do, they can't achieve it.*

Squeezing through two conjoined trees, Freya joins a thorny track. *You don't know?* She bats the snow from her legs. *I thought you'd have taken it from me by now.*

Her head shakes of its own accord. *We can't,* the Whisper says. *We see your thoughts as they come.*

Ahead of her, a tall tree shakes. Freya's hands twitch, instinctively craving a knife, a bow. Whatever's in there would taste enchanting in her stomach. *Okay,* she says, and fills her mind.

Anxiety washes over her, so deep she could drown. Tears block her throat.

That's what they want? the Whisper asks, as brittle as winter. The wave slips back from the shore, but the grooves in the sand are deep. *How?*

As close as she's come to crying in years, Freya swallows. Really, she can't trust anyone, but the Whispers are fair, if brutal. The Kyo do what they wish.

Everything relies on the witch, she says carefully, then, *she thinks she can make them forget.*

Reaching a snowy, thicket-rife rise, she wearily starts to climb. If Taika hasn't moved, she'll be close. Atikur's secrets aren't secret when you've hidden, and lived, and hidden some more, for nearly twenty-five years.

Taika?

Freya stops. The Whisper is quiet, unobtrusive, and she sinks with relief. Unexpected relief, but relief nonetheless; she didn't mindfully give Taika up.

Still. Uncomfortably, Freya shifts in her skin, pushing on up the rise. Taika gave her safety. She wove a web through which no one could break, and wrapped Freya up inside.

How human, the Whisper comments. He's dry now, wry.

I could say the same for you. Scanning the trees, Freya taps a gnarled trunk. Smoke coils up some way away, where the ground slopes to the right. Salo; the village she preyed on first.

She banishes this before humanity bites. Turning left, she heads for a knot of warped roots, a spider with tangled legs.

Where did Taika come from? the Whisper asks, as Freya nudges an especially obnoxious root.

An image of the Zaino swims through her mind. She sighs, and huffs, and almost smiles; now that she's started, she can't stop revealing. *She's a river girl.*

At a shift in her vision, she turns. The smoke and slope have given way to a close, sheer drop. *Or she was.* Freya crunches over the snow toward it. *She's a healer's daughter.*

The Whisper lifts her eyebrows. *A healer.*

I know. Freya picks her way along the edge. This is never her favourite part. *It didn't go down too well when she went for more than healing.* A clump of snow breaks away, and she slows. *When she ran off, no one but her father really cared. She watches them sometimes.*

She stops, both inside and out. The forest has fallen down a bluff, continuing across a rocky valley in a dim haze of cloud. An extremely steep, extremely narrow, and extremely windy path descends, and counting her stars, a canary in a mine, Freya extends a foot.

Ørenna. When the path doesn't crumble, she sighs and starts to walk.

And the Kyo? the Whisper murmurs.

They took her. Alert to every slip and slide, Freya keeps her eyes on her feet. The path is barely wider than she is. *She didn't want to help. The Kyo scared her, as much as they scare anyone, but they showed her how fast people forgot.* Her mouth contorts. *If she'd gone back, the village would have burned her.*

Steeply, the track tilts down. A breeze blows powder into her face, and Freya spreads her arms. The threadlike river in the valley's vein will help nothing if she falls. To the skies with Taika's choice of shelter; it's canny, but she's never felt closer to death.

There were other choices, the Whisper says.

Freya huffs, but it's hollow. *She's seventeen. Being an outcast hurts.* She whets her words to a point. *We bonded.*

The Whisper ignores this the same way she would. *How has she broken through to* Urnäsch? he asks, as the breeze sends ice shards into the valley. She's a tree in the wind on the edge of the world.

I don't know. Inching along, she trails the track around a spiny ridge. Out here, it's even colder; if she leaned toward the clouds, they'd be close enough to touch. *I know where she's done it, but I've never been involved.* Bodily, she shivers. *What are you going to do?*

Ask me no questions, and you'll feel no guilt. The Whisper is sly amusement. Deep in her rib cage, something twinges; something very much like guilt. *But ask yourself this: would you rather she was dealt with by us, or that you were dealt with by the Kyo?*

The guilt wavers.

Or the Chlause?

Slipping back whence it came, the guilt shuts its door.

Precisely. The Whisper smiles.

Edging along the ridge, Freya shakes her numbing head. *Persuasion,* she mutters. Lowering herself to her rear, she shuffles uneasily forward, firming her hands in the glinting snow. *Are you sure I'm concealed?*

Her jeans are wet already, and cold. With a grimace, she inches her feet, her calves, her knees, over the lip of the rock. The frozen air buffets her boots. She's a tree in the wind on the edge of the world.

Yes, the Whisper replies. *Why?*

Pushing off the bluff, Freya lets herself fall.

56

People seeking missing girls

'Do you think they'll do it?' Carol asks. She's broken the record five times over, but it's all she can fix on. Callum and Jay are trapped between worlds; cops seeking missing girls in this one don't compare.

Damn this village, though. Hazal's doorbell rang—*bonjour, Mesdames*—and there were the police. Someone came forward, claiming to have seen Callum with Kira and Romy; one busybody or another, eager to stick their long nose in other people's pies. Her shock was genuine: who would *do* that?

Hazily, she hoped it would come across as horror. How could someone be so wrong about Callum? She was righteous, hurt. Not guilty. Baffled.

The officers were baffled, too. They didn't have to say it; their bedside manner was ruffled, disgruntled. They'd been sent to the early-morning mountains to question a woman in a blanket, on the basis of a note in England, a past connection to fugitives, and a nosy, gloating neighbour. Anyone would be peeved.

Yes, of course, she said, when their baffled queries petered out. Should she hear from him, she said, she'd call them at once.

She shut the door in tears. Will she hear from him? Ever?

'I don't know.' Hazal sighs, balanced on a blade. 'I never know a link between Whiteland and Urnäsch, but the Whispers say they try, so they try.' She rubs her forehead. Her other hand grips a coffee cup to death.

Death. The Kyo. Talie.

Carol doesn't know. If only she would leave. Hazal's lungs hang heavy, sagging to the table. If it wasn't for Carol; if it wasn't for Callum; if it wasn't for his obsession with Kira… Hazal clicks her ridged nails on the cup. Callum's a nice boy, and Kira's a nice girl, but nice people still cause chaos. They caused chaos before, and now, they're affecting everyone.

The police came to Lally. The neighbours are watching. Lena's twins have been sent away. Jay's in Urnäsch, and Talie is dead.

Talie, dead. Lena, dead.

The bird clock chimes with a jay. 'Carol.' Hazal shuts her eyes. 'Please. You need to go.'

The jay keeps squawking. Every cry is a kick.

Across the scratched wood, Carol blinks. She'd probably been speaking, but Hazal's mind is scraping: if the Kyo have Talie, then she died in Whiteland.

Get out. Get out, get out, get out.

'Sorry?' Carol says. Her brown hair is ratty, her under-eyes wrinkled. Her eyes themselves are milky, glazed.

'I like,' Hazal pushes out, 'you to go.' Calm. Numb. Her sagging lungs have shrivelled, whistling with emptiness, tumbleweed, slipstreams, long-dead air. 'All of today is too much for me. I think you understand?'

She has to understand. She has to leave. Everything suddenly points to Talie: the tub of madeleines by the microwave, that she claimed not to like then devoured. The velvet-cloaked wizard grinning on a hook, who she claimed to like, and later said was a galling error in judgment. The fish-shaped chalkboard beside the fridge: *days passed without hating kids*.

The tally chart is empty. They've only just arrived.

'Really?' Carol's face is a masterpiece, da Vinci, Munch. *The Scream*. 'With everything that's happened?'

'Yes.' Palms splayed, Hazal stands. She's heavy, so heavy. Too cold with the chimney's winter draught. Too hot in her clothes. It's all too much. 'I like you to leave. Please.'

Over the table, their eyes meet. Carol's laughter lines pull in. 'Fine.'

Yes, this is selfish. Carol's distressed, it's more than clear, but Callum and Jay are alive. Probably together, with the hope of rescue. They may not be okay, but they're more than madness, and madness, for Talie, is all that remains.

Talie. As Carol's car snarls to life, Hazal's legs stop working. Sliding down the wall, her head meets her knees. Her insides wrench. Her chest feels bloody.

Through her teeth, she screams.

57

Masquerading

Fall.

For now, it's a whisper. Kira's legs cramp. The pain clamps her jaw shut, sobbing as she runs. Her jeans chafe her thighs raw. Her vest rides up. Her chest is a slit of shallow air, but Karliquai is close.

Stop.

The long grass whittles her sides. Hair sticks to her neck, her lips. The field's uphill slant is pitted, and she can't lose focus, can't look round, but Romy, Callum, Jay, god. God, let them be there.

God. Hurtling, stumbling, new tears ache. She's never been religious, but God let them down. What do they do when they reach the chalet? Knowing it's linked to Whiteland doesn't—

Stop. The whisper becomes a giddy hiss, tipping her off-balance. *You are not finished. We are not finished.*

Terror lodges itself in her throat. It's a breath, it can't control her, but the Chlause are coming.

Run. Breathing in manic, spit-sprayed spurts, Kira narrows her mind to a tunnel. The voice grows stronger as it splinters and seeks, but she clings to the *here* with sticky, sweaty hands. The Karliquai masquerade is coming into focus: a thin-pillared balcony, an out-of-place chimney pot, hewn from a chipped, toothy stone. The narrow watching window. It's a dream replica, or a replica of something that should stay in a dream, but with *KAR* carved in the front, it's a dream that's close enough.

Ragged breathing heaves behind her. Romy, Callum, Jay, close. Smacking sweat from her eyes, she presses on her legs. Burning feet. Straining eyes. Thumping head, insistent whisper, *God, you let us down.*

Run.

58

Made of knives

The snow cushions Freya's landing. She knew it would, but it didn't ease the drop. Fifty feet up, with the valley crashing down? Nothing makes that feel fun.

Stretching her jarred legs, she swipes them free of snow. *We're here.* She turns to the cliff wall, nodding at the ice. Baffling the Whisper would be beautiful. *See?*

Above the river, the wind whines. *I assume you'll explain,* the Whisper says, *why we're facing nothing.*

Freya lifts her chin. Somewhere, boulders crack and crash.

The Whisper shifts, and Freya's eyes widen. *Not nothing.* It shifts again, shaking her head. *Taika's protected this?*

Freya rubs her arms. She acquired the heartiest coat she could, but humans get so *cold*. Blown about on this thin, snowy spine, she's nastily exposed. *She took the idea from the Kyo,* she says. *Only three of us get in. Me, her, and Mathew. It's...* She tenses. *Unpleasant.*

Folding her fingers into her sleeves, she steps forward. When her front is flush with the glassy wall, riddled with frozen rivulets, Freya shuts her eyes, holds her breath, clamps her lips, and pushes.

Ice. Fires of ice. Flooding her body like a water-skin, it crystallizes her mouth, her nose, so even if she was trying to breathe, she wouldn't be able to. The first time she came, she tried.

Swallowing, Freya pushes with her shoulders, thinking of something, anything else. Sun. A fruitful, tailless life. The *skydd* she left behind.

Closing at her back, the snow compacts.

This is what it's like to be buried alive. Freya fights her eyelids, aching to open, her nose, aching to breathe. Her mind, aching to panic. Taika explained it once: if someone new ever wound up here, the pulse, the tingle, and charged enchantment would sense the intrusion, crackle to life, and trap the poor intruder. She tested it on a faun.

Roughly, the fires of ice subside. Freya tenses every muscle. The pulse of the enchantment throbs in her ears, tingling over her skin. Hung in Taika's magic, in the dark, forever, severed from your senses but not allowed to die…what a hideous thing. A violent thing. Taika was a girl, fairly nice, fairly not, but she's grown to be cruel, as cool, as ruthless, as the Kyo and Whiteland have made her.

The tingle flares and fades, dripping from her fingers. Freya's lungs expand with the lapping panic. What if her immunity no longer exists? She left Whiteland; she's a different creature. Could the Whisper get her out if she was trapped?

I imagine not. He nestles closer to her sense of self. Their suffocation is iron. *If Taika has something strong enough to blind us, I doubt we would manage to break it.*

Wonderful. The panic mounts to a tidal wave, no matter how much she curses. Why is she not pushing through? Did it take this long last time? Any time? She should have thought of this risk *before*.

She can breathe. Her body warms from front to back. Her eyes flick open, and there's Taika, young and bright, surprised. 'Freya?'

Freya's wrist becomes a fist and clouts her in the face.

Pain bursts up her arm. 'What?' Freya grabs her fist, her knuckles hot and jilted. Slumping to the floor, Taika's head cracks stone. 'I thought I was making her trust me?'

Excellent trust. The best trust. The punch-to-the-face-for-your-shelter trust.

How do you think the Kyo work, Freya? The Whisper is urgent, impatient, now, more human than she could have imagined.

But then again, so is she. 'Not like this.' Made of knives, she cups her knuckles. 'This will make us conspicuous.'

True. Freya feels her eyes tugged to Taika. Her lips wince. *But without her, they're helpless. Without others, they're always helpless.*

They're not.

They are. The Whisper scratches at her skull, like a cat in a cage. *They take the women who are near them, or the souls that fit. The abused, the murdered.*

Whatever they say. They could try to reach you, but either our protection or Taika's would stop them.

Freya says nothing. At least Taika's breathing. Sprawled on the stone, with that scarf in her braids, she looks even younger than she is.

That scarf. That gaudy, lurid scarf, and those stupid dungarees. She never shrugged the river people off.

Okay. Freya drags her eyes away. *Look around.*

Fundamentally, it's a cave. A small one, by any standards, and while it hangs low and uneven, enough candles glow in hollows to almost make it homely. Freya scans it for the hundredth time. Two piles of furs line one wall, blue flames licking up another. Log-less and baseless, they make no sense, but they're skinny, warm, and always there. That's all the magic she needs.

It's not what we expected, the Whisper remarks.

Freya shrugs. *She spent her time with the Huldra. This place was for Mathew and magic.*

And the door?

Freya flips a hand at the last wall, by the blank rock of their entrance. It's as innocent as virgin snow. *There.* She cuts her eyes away. *She wakes it up, and gets to work. Helping me, controlling Mathew, channelling the Kyo. She saw everything she needed to.*

The Whisper moves her eyes around. *The outside?*

Freya pauses. Taika never whinged, but for a time, she was bony. It drained the Huldra to return her to herself. *Yes, but it was hard,* she says. *Urnäsch was nearly impossible.* Tilting her head, she frowns. *What happened to Mathew?*

The Whisper flutters like feathers. *Vasi collected him.*

The feathers bloom, and start to flap. They're wings, beating faster, a hectic murmuration, snow-white swans in a dance through her mind. Freya blinks, but they're spreading. Filling her vision, they flap and fly, clogging her throat with down. She blinks again, trying to breathe.

Ørenna, not again. Her breath sticks behind her teeth. Her mouth tastes of animal. The swan wings beat themselves into a gale, and she staggers, images swarming in front of her eyes. Anneliese, surrounded by white, backed by distant polar bears. A fossegrim on its knees, beautiful, begging, and briny. Flitting shadows above a desert, a mountaintop and a pack of wolves. Snickers-whispers-laughter-spitting, the cavern underground—

Pain blisters her temple. Freya's head snaps back, and she screams. It's boring a scorching spike through her skull, searing a hole through the flesh of her brain. Red and black explodes in her mind. Her knees give out, and she screams again, buckling to the stone. The wings are on fire. Fuelled by the gale, they're *wild*fire, billowing, roaring, taking her over, the cave cracking like ice in her eyes. Ørenna, no, why won't it *end*?

The spike punches through the opposite temple. Red-hot, Freya howls, bucking forward to retch. Her eyelids flutter beyond her control. The gale is all around her, burning her alive, and there's nothing she can do, trapped and tortured, oh, let her faint, let all of this leave, before she vomits her organs and screams herself bloody and her eyes erupt from their sockets.

Anneliese.

With one word, everything drops. Freya's head coalesces. The agony lifts, and she gasps, gutted, like a scooped-out, jittery shell. All around, the Whispers sigh.

'What,' she spits, on her hands and knees, clammy and heaving, 'was that?'

The Whisper inside her settles again, and her urge to vomit thumps. Had she thought he was human? He's not. Not at all. Shocking and sparking, jagged and sick, she shudders and quakes like frostbite. If the Whispers had bodies, she'd eviscerate them.

The one inside her lifts her eyes. *You didn't take much convincing.*

Anger surges like acid bile. 'It's not like you gave me a choice,' she rasps, pushing up to her heels.

Not you. The Whisper turns her rag doll head.

Freya stills. Frissons of childhood strike her senses, a match lighting tinder and running dry riot. The smell of the pool they went to, where it's rumoured you lose your heart. The sound of creaking branches, every time Freya got scared at night and climbed down from her *skydd*. The sight of those blue eyes, the last time they killed, remorseless while the mouth said sorry.

Anneliese. In front of the furs, a ghost of a woman, in outside clothes a lot like her own. Staring, Freya struggled to her feet. Long hair, thin and blonde. High cheekbones. Pale eyes. Anneliese, the woman she saw as a sister. Anneliese, who left. Anneliese, the pariah. Anneliese, surprised and stilted, who's meant to be worse than dead.

Shaking her head, Freya folds her arms. If there's one good thing about humans, it's their language. 'Holy shit.'

59

Carnivals and hides

Callum risks a fast look back. His body thickens, as gloopy as sludge, like he's sprinting through fog in a dream. The Chlause's hissing anger mounts. It's there in his mind, nipping at his neurons, trying to snatch control. Are they coming?

Don't know. Can't see. Callum whips around again, dragging Jay in a death grip. He's never run this hard, or sweated this much, even when he cared about competitive skiing. Kira's ahead of them, racing like a drunk. Romy?

Don't know. Can't see. The sun glares, far too bright.

'Callum,' Jay pants, at the end of their arms. 'I can't go this fast.'

'You can.' Callum jerks him on. The chalet's getting closer, so close the letters on the wood are clear: *KAR*. One more dip. One more hillock. He has to get his brother out. He has to follow Kira.

Run.

By a fallen oak, Vasi looks up sharply. 'Something,' he says, 'has happened.'

Mathew takes the opportunity to stare through the greenery, sinking into his mind. After all Vasi's told him, aliens could land, and unless they brought his daughters, he wouldn't much care.

'Something…' Vasi angles his head like a listening bird. A woodpecker whistles. A tall fern bristles. His knotted eyebrows mesh. 'Oh, dear.'

Mathew sighs, and rolls his neck. None of this is the leshy's fault. 'What?' He leans against the oak, its girth as high as his chest. 'What's happened?'

Even in the sunny green, Vasi's old face is hacked from stone. 'The worlds are splitting open.'

Ready? the Whisper asks.

Not really. Making sure he knows she's still pissed off, Freya nods. It's the strangest situation she never thought she'd be in: a live huldra, a dead huldra, and a score of invisible wisps of wind crowding a passed-out witch.

The Whisper spreads its wings. Freya flashes with remembered pain: white swans, the fossegrim, the tunnel through her skull. When she's finally free, no one's going near her head again.

It was necessary, the Whisper murmurs. *Thank you, Freya.*

Freya slits her eyes, bracing herself, but one leaving is nothing when you've been a gate for them all. In a blink, the Whisper lifts and leaves, like anxiety resolved.

A strange feeling twists her gut. It feels like a shadow of twenty years ago, when Anneliese left her behind.

Freya, the Whispers say, in their breathless, flighty draught. The blue flames crackle.

Yes, yes. Freya crouches. *I know.*

Shaking Taika's shoulder, she rolls her tired eyes. By all accounts, it's a terrible plan, steeped in magic and supposition and spearheaded by ghosts. Great. Digging her nails into Taika's skin, she huffs. This, now, is rock bottom.

Freya.

The Whispers lace their way through her fingers. Waving them off, Freya squeezes Taika hard enough to bruise.

Taika groans in her throat, but her eyes stay closed. Four seconds. Five.

'Well, Taika, I tried.' Standing, Freya pulls a face, and kicks her in the side.

Anneliese winces. Taika jolts. Her braids slap the stone, and her eyes unstick. A slurred, bleary *nngh* vibrates in her throat.

The Whispers hiss like snow on sparks. Fluttering Freya's coat zip, their draught swirls down. Taika's eyes widen, and glaze.

I can't keep her. The Whisper is a murmur, already faint. *She's fighting. Lift her up.*

Freya does.

Hold her fingers to the wall.

Freya does this too. Taika weighs nothing, dark skin and bone, and hoisting her up, spine to chest, Freya presses her hand to the wall.

Move right, the Whisper instructs. Freya obeys. *Down.*

Lines of blue fire spark where Taika touches stone. They sizzle in a vicious burst, and spread in webs of ice: four branches, a slash for the ground. A spiny tree. Whiteland.

Freya's scalp prickles. It's magic, true magic. Taika talked about it, but practised on her own, and Freya never asked why. Even the Huldra avoid magic, for the feeling that scuttles from its energy. It's life growing where life shouldn't be, roses blooming in rot. It skulks from the blue fire, circling the cave, and as it crawls, as it mocks, it leaves her cold. Bone-shatteringly, achingly cold.

Let go, the Whisper breathes. Freya drops Taika like a corpse. This is bad. Sickening. Wrong. Her spirit is draining, becoming less *her*, as though it's pushing against her skin. No wonder witches cause open mouths, hushing tongues, and scandal. Can she call it wicked?

The blue lines flare, and Freya's thoughts scatter. The symbol is changing.

She steps back. The fire snakes out, branching new lines, touching the old and branching again until the web engulfs the wall. She moves back again, away, away. Anneliese's ice is an aura, but the cold barely registers. The web is becoming a picture.

In the back of beyond, it's a beautiful day. A lane winds up through fields and trees, sunned by the clearest of skies. The sun shines in a vivid haze, and distant enough to be small and blurry, four people walk. Two girls, two boys, oblivious to danger.

Anneliese's breath catches. 'Is this the door?'

So this is Urnäsch. Freya stares. It looks so…nice. 'Yes.'

No, the Whisper breathes, frailer than an autumn leaf. Around Taika, the others surge. *The door is somewhere else.*

Freya starts with shock. 'What?' she exclaims. She's high-pitched, young, like a whickering child, but right now, it doesn't matter. 'This is the only place I've ever…' She works her mouth, staring at the wall. Fields, bright colours, a beck. 'What is it, if it's not the door?'

A spyglass. The Whisper is dying, the brittle leaf crumbling. *Clever, splitting her magic like that. You were right.* His voice rattles in a dying throat. *It's a base. The door can be opened from here, but…*

Anneliese meets Freya's eyes, and holds them. 'But what?'

The Whisper's reply is almost regretful. *But it sits above the Kyo.* The others swell around them. *Freya, I suggest you run.*

What are you planning on doing? Anna asks, once Freya has pushed through the thin blue flames. Her loosened shackles are ill-fitting, complex; words present a tongue twister, even in her mind.

Taika holds a lot of magic. Strained and fading, grasping at life, the Whisper mirrors how it feels to be nothing but a soul. *She can…project.* It drifts out. *Here. When I…* It crackles, a wartime radio. The signal starts to die. *Now.*

Anna looks between Taika and the day on the wall. Fear can't hold her like it did when she was human, but it whittles her grip on her half-body, worse than when she gave herself up. The trade on the ice was meant to be the end.

End, the Whisper echoes in a gasp. *Touch her…now.* The others swirl around Taika, rippling over her dungarees. *When I say, you have to speak.*

Suddenly, Anna understands. Hope curls through her like smoke as she crouches, touching Taika's temple. She'll be banished back to the desert after this, but if Kira and Romy are finally safe, as they should have been last year… She swallows, easing down to her knees. Taika's skin is hot beneath her blurry fingers. She's heard of this magic. It'll work.

Once upon a time, she was interested, but now, it leaves her cold. Cold, and as sick as Freya looked. This is the darkness that led to the Chlause. Taika's too young to have meddled.

Focus. The Whispers wind through her, colder than she is. Anna shivers.

The Chlause… the one inside Taika manages. It's becoming hard to hear. *Sense. Come for us and them, too… Tell them. Have…*

A long, long pause. Longer, longer, longer. Anna focuses on Taika, willing herself not to look at the wall, to break whatever the Whisper is doing to try and make this work.

RUN.

Anna's mind throbs with the shout, the vicious, dying growl. Does the Whisper know it's dying? Can it stop? Smoky hope bleeds into fear. Kira. She shuts her eyes. Romy.

Anneliese, the Whisper sighs, fainter than ever. *Talk to…Chlause… Push us.*

Behind Anna's eyes, Urnäsch unfolds. Taika starts to tremble. Anna holds tight. 'Run. Escape into Whiteland.'

She's never moved so fast. Driving her bones through the blue-fire warmth, Freya bursts from a tree in a close-knit grove, kicks through bushes, branches, roots, and blunders into a run. If she isn't there when they all fall through, they'll keep on going to the Kyo.

What a plan; what a game. What a gleeful range of faces, on tenterhooks to kill.

Not kill. There's that at least; if she's not quick enough, no one will die, unless the Kyo want to play with Callum and Jay. They rarely meet men, and despise them when they do.

If she helps them now, is she saved?

Just run.

She hadn't thought the door would be close to a village. Haavö, no less, with the crazy witch-sniffer. Speeding up past it, she battles through the snow, ignoring the grizzled man by the slope, his startled skis askew. Her nails sting in her palms. Every vein in her body throbs. She'll make it.

The human in her is screaming.

They're being pushed out. Both the Chlause and Taika herself, rising to blurry consciousness, are fighting.

Anna had to leave. The Whisper wasn't strong enough to keep her there, not with the phoenix creeping in, so now, she watches and tries not to crumple.

The Chlause take Kira. Kira, then Romy, then Callum, as the boy creeps away. Kira shouts something, and he drops.

Anna inhales, colder and colder. With her children verging on ruin, she's never felt so useless, and when the magic surges through again, she could cry.

An image of Taika solidifies, cumbersome, staggering forward, speaking. Anna could holler, howl, beat her fists against the wall. The Whisper's talking to Kira and Romy, and all she can do is watch. It's vile, viler than the desert. Without scuppering everyone's chances, she can't even try to help.

Callum's hauling the boy to his feet. Kira and Romy are standing still. Anxiety slaps her, again and again. Why are they standing still? They should be running. Freya should be there by now.

A flare of energy flames around her. Anna bites back a cry. The cave shakes. The image might break. Dizzied by the throbbing, Anna sways on her knees.

In Urnäsch, the Chlause stop.

The door is open. More a thought than ever, the Whisper quavers.

Kira and Romy start to run.

Kira's chest clamps shut like heartburn. Karliquai clouds with black, but she falls to its feet in the grass. What do they do? Did anyone say?

No. Shaking her head free of clouds, she swallows a breathless, desperate panic. Nothing moves. Nothing changes. What do they *do*? There's nothing here. She grasps a corner of the splintering wood, dragging herself to her knees.

Her head plunges. Everything's cold, and she tumbles down, nauseous, weightless, Alice in the dark. Rushing in her ears. Fire in her blood.

Before she can scream, it's over.

'Kira!' Someone tugs on her arm. 'Get up. Get up, Kira.'

The darkness doesn't lift. The fall wiped her mind. She left her tongue by Karliquai.

'Move!' The someone heaves her up.

'I'll take her.' Someone else is here, an animal smell. The air is colder than bones. 'Trust me, Kira.' He lifts her away. A whimper burbles up inside her. 'It's all right, Kira. You're okay. You're okay.'

The lights sputter and die. The fire, the candles, the image and its underlying web; in a blink, they whine to black.

Taika's body exhales, and stills.

Anna shuts her eyes. A scream is building, a rumble within her: *no, no, no, no, no.* They were so close, so goddamn close. There must have been enough time.

The darkness settles, sour and dead. Please, Anna begs, to no one and everyone. The rumble is a river, bursting its banks. Let them all have been quick enough. Please.

The Whispers rise through the rock in silence. Anna is blown away.

Beside the fallen oak, Vasi turns to Mathew. His rock-hewn expression has lost its shine. 'Your daughter is back.'

The woodpecker whoops. Mathew stares. 'Here?' A chill pools within him, sliding through his body; after everything, one of them's *here*? 'Where?'

Ahead of her, Kira disappears.

'Kira!' Romy shrieks, but the sound is barely there. Kira touched the chalet, and vanished. Romy cuts her eyes to Callum, but his face is out of view. They're almost there, all of them. Ten metres. Five.

None.

Jay reaches it first. He slaps the balcony, but nothing happens. 'Crap!' he yells. 'How do we do it?'

Romy hits the steps with the force of a juggernaut. The wood is warm on her shaking skin, but she doesn't disappear, scraping down the steps to the grass.

'What the hell did Kira do?' Callum spins in a circle, yanking his sweat-slick hair.

Lapping the chalet, Jay punches the wood. 'She's not *here*.'

Romy drags herself up with mounting anguish. This is not how it ends. This is not *where* it ends, in a field with a whole lot of fuck all, by a hut that was meant to save them.

Romy.

Mary, mother of god. Romy's bowels shift. Her legs lose their bones. Halfway down the hill are the Chlause.

The priest, the Ugly, some she doesn't know. A man bedecked with fire.

The doll smiles, just a twitch. *Too late.*

Romy grabs Callum's arm. 'What do we do?'

Callum shakes his head, pinning Jay to his side, his face tuned to terror. 'I don't know. Shit. I don't know.'

Animals in stolen hides.

Unbidden, the song that started it all slams back into her brain. It's a physical roar, a deafening force. Romy crashes and burns.

Dig the grave and watch them cry.

The phoenix steps forward.

Singing her way into black, she sways. *I hope the wilderness will call. Let's become a carnival now Ragnarok is visceral.*

60

No.

Gradually, Kira comes back to herself. The scent of pine, of wilderness. Her heart thudding through her body. Her bare arms, throbbing with cold. Her breathing fills her ears.

A rustle shivers through the air. It's a low, familiar wind, an electric current, if this place had such a thing.

This place. The rustle. Kira opens her eyes.

Towering, Grimm-esque trees greet her. The snow is blinding, as white as the sky.

Her breath stutters. Whiteland. She's back.

'Kira.'

Gloved hands hold her bare arms. A body props her up.

'No.' Jerking away, she spins unsteadily. Her mind isn't working, her senses a whirl. She's not safe. Is she safe? 'Who are you? Where are—oh.'

She stops. His hair and beard are shaggier, but everything else… He's tall and broad, widened by layers, alone with a pair of skis. A thick hat grips his head. 'Erik.'

Regarding her with gruff concern, he nods. 'I have to say'—he unhooks his coat—'I'd hoped I wouldn't see you here again.'

He shoots a glance of displeasure at the Whispers, rippling the clothes of a pale-haired woman. Manic in her mayhem, Kira looks around. The woman. Erik. The Whispers. Other than that, the forest is empty.

No.

Her chest constricts. Slowly, her gaze swivels, landing on the woman. Her brain chugs. The woman. The huldra. Fiona. Recognition is dull. Fiona was the one waiting.

And no one else got through.

Kira sways. The huldra pulled her out, when she touched Karliquai…and no one else got through.

'No.' The word barely leaves her lips. She covers her mouth, her cheeks, her throat, scraping up to her hair. 'No. Take me back. I have—I have to *get* them.'

She staggers around in place, as if a door will split the air. Glancing at the gathering crowd, Erik steps toward her. 'Kira.' He shrugs off his coat. 'Take this. You don't want to get—'

'No.' Dully, Kira shakes her head, holding up her hands. 'Keep it. I don't need it. I have—I have to go back.'

'You can't.' Moving away from the wind of the Whispers, Fiona's face is white. 'The door shut. They couldn't keep it open.' She glances back, at the rippling air. 'The Whisper that opened it died with Taika.'

Kira presses her hands to her eyes. 'I don't know what that *means*.' She presses until her eyes heat, and X-ray colours swarm. 'I have to go back. My sister is there, and Callum, and Jay.'

She drops her damp, shaking hands. One by curious one, the crowd murmurs, points, expands. Preparing the torches? Whetting the pitchforks? Two escapees are too good to miss.

'No.' Kira shakes her head consistently, forcing back the tears. Erik holds his coat out. The huldra looks away. 'They can't be stuck. Not for the Chlause to—to—'

The door is shut. A Whisper skitters past her neck, down her naked arms. Kira flinches away, strangling a cry. *The witch is in no state to open it again, assuming it could be reopened. If one of our own perished…*

Its words become a ring in her ears. Staring through the pines, Kira sinks toward the snow. After everything they've seen. After coming so close. For her to…to…

Falling forward over her knees, Kira starts to shake. She should have looked back. She should have made sure they were with her. She didn't know the wood would bring her here, and she was only trying to stand, but still. If she'd waited, maybe they'd be here.

If she'd waited, they wouldn't be trapped with the Chlause.

Clenching her jaw, she screams in silence, piercing her arms with her nails. Mum. Dad. Romy. Callum. Jay. Her chest hurts the way nothing ever has. They're gone. They're all gone.

As Kira starts to heave and cry, Freya shuts her eyes. *Is there no way to get them out?* she asks. *No backup plan? No loophole?*

No. Dead leaves. The Whispers whisper, crackling, surging, whirling snow and laces. *See Kira to the edge, and go.*

Lifting into the crowded branches, the Whispers sigh away. Freya watches the trees until they still. Kira's wracking fills the air. The villagers murmur. Just like that, it's over.

In the snowbound cave, lit with blue, Taika opens her eyes.

RAGNARÖK

Lyrics by Rosie Cranie-Higgs
Written for *Karliquai*

Papillon of winter light
Are we dead when we have died
Did you ever think we'd be lost among this

Animals in stolen hides
Dig the grave and watch them cry
Oh, Hell, they care enough to lie

You're living in a dream now
Can't you taste it
You live what you believe now
Don't you hate it
I hope the wilderness will call
Let's become a carnival now Ragnarok is visceral

Hunting wolves in curtained skies
Are we dead when we have died
Oh, how the world lusts after nothing

Dig me up and watch me dance
Poke my bones and watch me prance
A pound of flesh means nothing

You're living in a dream now
Can't you taste it
You live what you believe now
Don't you hate it
I hope the wilderness will call for us

Your vanity is waiting
Don't you want it
You know the game you're playing
Won't you flaunt it
Your vanity is waiting
I know you want it
Let's become a carnival now Ragnarok is visceral

You're living in a dream now
Can't you taste it
You live what you believe now
Don't you hate it
I hope the wilderness will call for us
Your vanity is waiting
Don't you want it
You know the game you're playing
Won't you flaunt it
I hope the wilderness will call
Let's become a carnival now Ragnarok is visceral

Let's become a carnival now Ragnarok is visceral
Let's become a carnival now Ragnarok is visceral

ABOUT THE AUTHOR

Rosie Cranie-Higgs is the author of the Whiteland series. She enjoys writing about darkness and ghosts.

Rosie grew up across Europe, and now lives in Malta with her family where she is currently working on her next novel.

Lightning Source UK Ltd.
Milton Keynes UK
UKHW011949221121
394396UK00003B/921